ST. MARTIN'S PAPERBACKS TITLES BY LORI HANDELAND

THE PHOENIX CHRONICLES

Any Given Doomsday

Doomsday Can Wait

THE NIGHTCREATURE SERIES

Blue Moon

Hunter's Moon

Dark Moon

Crescent Moon

Midnight Moon

Rising Moon

Hidden Moon

Thunder Moon

DOOMSDAY CAN WAIT

Lori Handeland

St. Martin's Paperbacks

This is a work of fiction. All of the characters, organizations, and events portrayed in this novel are either products of the author's imagination or are used fictitiously.

DOOMSDAY CAN WAIT

Copyright © 2009 by Lori Handeland.
Excerpt from *Apocalypse Happens* copyright © 2009 by Lori Handeland.

For information address St. Martin's Press, 175 Fifth Avenue, New York, NY 10010.

ISBN: 0-312-94716-X
EAN: 978-0-312-94716-3

Printed in the United States of America

St. Martin's Paperbacks edition / May 2009

St. Martin's Paperbacks are published by St. Martin's Press, 175 Fifth Avenue, New York, NY 10010.

10 9 8 7 6 5 4 3 2 1

ACKNOWLEDGMENTS

Grateful thanks to:

The usual suspects, my editor, Jen Enderlin, and my agent, Irene Goodman.

Anne Marie Tallberg at St. Martin's Press for loving books and helping to promote mine.

My media specialist, Shannon Aviles—she of the great ideas, boundless energy, and never-ending enthusiasm to get my books out there and noticed by everyone.

Claudia Dain, Pam Johnson, Linda Jones, Peggy Hendricks, Isabel Sharpe—thanks for always being at the other end of the computer whenever I need a cyber hug and or just an ear to listen. I appreciate that more than I can ever express.

CHAPTER 1

A month ago I put a stake through the heart of the only man I've ever loved. Luckily, or not, depending on the day and my mood, that wasn't enough to kill him.

I found myself the leader of a band of seers and demon killers at the dawn of the Apocalypse. Turns out a lot of that biblical prophesy crap is true.

I consider it both strange and frightening that I was chosen to lead the final battle between the forces of good and evil. Until last month I'd been nothing more than a former cop turned bartender.

Oh, and I was psychic. Always had been.

Not that being psychic had done anything for me except lose me the only job I wanted—being a cop—and the only man, too: the aforementioned extremely hard-to-kill Jimmy Sanducci. It had also gotten my partner killed, something I had yet to get over despite his wife's insistence that it hadn't been my fault.

In an attempt to pay a debt I could never truly pay, I'd taken a job as the first-shift bartender in a tavern owned by my partner's widow. I also found myself best friends with the woman. I'm not quite sure how.

After last month's free-for-all of death and destruction, I'd come home to Milwaukee to try and figure out what to do next. The army of darkness was winning. Their former leader had taken me prisoner, turned Jimmy evil, then nearly wiped out my whole troop before I managed to kill the creep and escape with Jimmy in tow.

Now three-quarters of my Doomsday soldiers were dead and the rest were in hiding. I had no way of finding them, no way of even knowing who in hell they were. Unless I found Jimmy. That was proving more difficult than I'd thought.

So while I hung out and waited for the psychic flash that would make all things clear, I went back to work at Murphy's. A girl had to eat and pay the mortgage. Amazingly, being the leader of the supernatural forces of sunshine—I'm kidding, we're actually called the federation—didn't pay jack shit.

On the night all hell broke loose—again—I was working a double shift. The evening bartender had come down with a case of the "I'd rather be at Summerfest" blues, and I couldn't walk out at the end of my scheduled hours and leave Megan alone to deal with the dinner rush.

Not that there was much of one. Summerfest, Milwaukee's famous music festival on the lake, drew most of the party crowd. A few off-duty cops drifted in now and then—they were the mainstay of Megan's business—but in truth, Murphy's was the deadest I'd ever seen it. Hell, the place was empty. Which made it easy for the woman who appeared at dusk to draw my attention.

Tall and slim and dark, she strolled in on dangerously high heels. Her hair was up in a fancy twist I never could have managed, even if my own hair were longer than the nape of my neck. Her white suit made her bronze skin and the copper pendant revealed by the plunging neckline of her jacket gleam in the half-light.

Megan took one look, rolled her eyes and retreated to the kitchen. She had no patience for lawyers. Did anyone? This woman's clothes, heels, carriage screamed bloodsucker. In my world, there was always great concern that the term was literal. I nearly laughed out loud when she ordered cabernet.

"With that suit?" I asked.

Her lips curved; her perfectly plucked eyebrows lifted past the rims of her self-regulating sunglasses, which had yet to lighten even though she'd stepped indoors. I could see only the shadow of her eyes beyond the lenses. Brown, perhaps black. Definitely not blue like mine.

The cheekbones and nose hinted at Indian blood somewhere in her past, as did the dusky shade of her skin. Mine was the same hue. I'd been told I was mixed race, but I had no idea what that mix was. Who I'd been before I'd become Elizabeth Phoenix was as much a mystery to me as the identity of my parents.

"You think I'd spill a single drop?" she murmured in a smoky voice.

How could something sound like smoke? I'd never understood that term. But as soon as she spoke, it suddenly became clear to me. She sounded like a gray, hot mist that could kill you.

"You from around here?" I asked.

Murphy's, located in the middle of a residential area, wasn't exactly a tourist attraction. The place was as old as the city and had been a tavern all of its life. Back in the day, fathers would finish their shifts at the factories, then stop by for a brew before heading home. They'd come in after dinner and watch the game, or retreat here if they'd fought with the wife or had enough of the screaming kids.

Such establishments could be found all over Milwaukee, hell, all over Wisconsin. Bar, house, bar, house, house, house, another bar. In Friedenberg, where I lived, about twenty miles north of the city, there were five bars in the one-mile-square village. Walking more than a block for a beer? It just wasn't done.

"I'm from everywhere," the stranger said, then sipped the wine.

A small drop clung to her lip. Gravity pulled it downward, the remaining moisture pooling into a droplet the shade of blood. Her tongue snaked out and captured the bead before it fell on the pristine white lapel of her suit. I had a bizarre flash of Snow White.

"Or maybe it's nowhere." She tilted her head. "You decide."

I was starting to get uneasy. She might be beautiful, but she was weird. Not that we didn't get weirdos in the bar every day. But there was usually a cop or ten around.

Sure, I'd once been a cop, but I wasn't anymore. And pretty much everyone, even Megan, frowned on bartenders pulling a gun on the clientele. Of course, if she wasn't human—

My fingers stroked the solid silver knife I hid beneath my ugly green uniform vest as I waited for some kind of sign.

The woman reached again for her wine. Contrary to her earlier assertion, she knocked it over. The ruby-red liquid sloshed across the bar, pooling at the edge before dripping onto the floor.

I should have been diving for a towel; instead I found myself fascinated by the shimmering puddle, which reflected the dim lights and the face of the woman.

The shiny dark surface leached the color from everything, not that there'd been all that much color to her in the first place. Black hair, white suit, light brown skin.

Slowly I lifted my gaze to hers. The glasses had cleared. I could see her eyes. I'd seen them before.

In the face of a woman of smoke who'd been conjured from a bonfire in the New Mexico desert. No wonder she hid them behind dark lenses. Those eyes would scare the pants off anyone who stared directly into them. I was surprised I hadn't been turned to stone. They held eons of hate, centuries of evil, millenniums of joy in the act of murder, with a dash of madness on the side.

I drew my knife, threw it—I ought to have been able to hit her in such close quarters—but she snatched the weapon out of the air with freakishly fast fingers.

"Shit," I said.

Smirking, she returned the knife—straight at my head. I ducked, and the thing struck the wall behind me with a thunk and a *boing* worthy of any cartoon sound-track.

I straightened, meaning to grab the weapon and leap across the bar. I had supernatural speed and strength of my own. But the instant my head cleared wood, she grabbed me by the neck and hauled me over, breaking bottles, knocking glasses everywhere.

"Liz?" Megan called.

I opened my mouth to shout "Run!" and choked instead as the woman squeezed.

She lifted her gaze to where Megan must surely be. I wanted to say "Don't look at her," but speech was as beyond me as breathing.

I heard a whoosh and then a thud. Like a body sliding down a wall to collapse on the floor. Had the woman of smoke killed Megan with a single glance? I wouldn't put it past her.

I pulled at her hands, tugged on her fingers, managed to loosen her hold enough by breaking a few to gulp several quick breaths.

What in hell had happened? The woman of smoke was obviously a minion of evil out to kill me. Being the leader of the light, in a battle with the demon horde, seemed to have put a great big, invisible target on my back.

However, the other times I'd always had a warning— what I called a ghost whisper. The voice of the woman who'd raised me, Ruthie Kane—whose death had set this whole mess in motion—would tell me what kind of creature I was facing. Even if I didn't know how to kill it—and considering that I'd been dropped into this job with no training, that was usually the case—I still preferred advance notice of impending bloody death rather than having bloody death sprung upon me.

I tried to think. It was amazingly hard without oxygen, but I managed.

The woman of smoke had grabbed my silver knife and her fingers hadn't broken out in a rash. Not a shapeshifter, or at least not a common one such as a werewolf. When you mix silver and werewolves, you usually wind up with ashes.

Her strength hinted at vampire, though most of those would just tear out my throat and have a nice, relaxing bath in my blood. Still—

I let go of her arm and tore open my uniform so that Ruthie's silver crucifix spilled free. Vampires tended to flip when they saw the icon, not because of the shape, or the silver, but the blessing upon it. She didn't even blink.

I pressed it to her wrist anyway. Nothing. So, not a vampire.

Suddenly she stilled. The pressure on my throat

eased; the black spots cleared from in front of my eyes. She stared at my chest and not with the fascinated expression I often got after opening my shirt. If I did say so myself, my breasts weren't bad. However, I'd never had a woman this interested in them. I didn't like it any more than I liked her.

"Where did you get that?" Her eyes sparked; I could have sworn I saw flames leap in the center of all that black.

"Th-the crucifix is—"

"A crucifix can't stop me." She sneered and yanked it from my neck, tossing the treasured memento aside.

"Hey!" I tore her amulet off the same way.

The very air seemed to still, yet my hair stirred in an impossible wind.

Dreadful One, Ruthie whispered at last, *Naye'i.*

A *Naye'i* was a Navajo spirit. I'd heard of them before. Several puzzle pieces suddenly fit together with a nearly audible click.

The woman of smoke backed away, staring at the stone I had recently strung on its own chain rather than continuing to let it share Ruthie's.

"You don't like my turquoise." I sat up.

Her gaze lifted from the necklace to my face. All I could see between the narrowed lids was a blaze of orange flame. "That isn't yours."

"I know someone who'd say differently." My hand inched toward the blue-green gem. "The someone who gave it to me. I think you call him . . . your son."

As soon as my fingers closed around it, the turquoise went white-hot, and the *Naye'i* snarled like the demon she was, then turned to smoke and disappeared.

CHAPTER 2

A movement near the bar had me crouching and swiveling in that direction, even though I was fresh out of weapons except for the turquoise. I doubted the stone would do me much good against the shotgun in Megan's hands.

Though short, Megan was strong, probably from hauling three kids around—first in her belly and then on her hip—not to mention being a single mom with a thriving business. She didn't get much sleep; she frequently forgot to eat; yet her pale skin, which fried like bacon in the sun, glowed as healthy as her thick, curly red hair and dark blue eyes.

She was cute as a button—and several other similes for cuteness, such as puppies and kittens, all of which drove Megan crazy. She wanted to be elegant and classy, but you get what you get. I, myself, was tall, dark, and different when all I'd ever wanted to be was normal.

Nevertheless, Megan's adorability, her girl-next-doorness, would have been adequate grounds to put her on my "too annoying to live" list except she also had a dry, sarcastic wit that matched my own and a genuine lack of interest in how she looked or who she impressed.

All Megan cared about were her kids, her bar, and me. Crazy woman.

She lowered the shotgun, cast me a quick, unreadable glance, then poured herself a shot of Jameson's and slammed it back like water.

I let out a sigh of relief that she was alive and standing, with all her faculties still intact. Obviously the woman of smoke had the power to knock someone unconscious with a single glance, but she couldn't kill anyone that way. The first good news I'd had in weeks. I wondered why she hadn't tried it on me.

Without raising her voice, Megan said, "You're gonna sit right down and tell me what the fuck that was."

I hesitated. Panic was just around the corner if the world at large discovered Doomsday was at hand. But I didn't know how I could avoid telling Megan something. Unless I just left and never came back. Probably a good choice considering my presence here had nearly gotten her killed.

"Uh-uh," Megan said. "You're not going anywhere."

Damn, she was good. Raising three kids had no doubt given her mom's ESP. One tiny flicker in my eyes, a slight twitch of my shoulder, and Megan had known exactly what I was planning,

"And don't think you can disappear like your pal did." Megan paused, frowned. "*Can* you disappear like your pal did?"

I opened my mouth, shut it again. Gave up. "No. I can't."

Her eyebrows lifted. She was as surprised as I was that I'd admitted the woman of smoke had gone poof.

"What *can* you do?" she asked. "Besides figure out where people are, or what they've done, or where they've hidden someone or something just by touching them."

"I don't always have to touch them," I muttered. Sometimes I only had to touch something they owned. That was how I'd found Jimmy the last time. Unfortunately, Sanducci hadn't left anything behind for me to fondle.

"I . . . uh . . . hell." I went to the door, flipped the open sign to closed and locked it. "Pour me one of those." I flicked a finger at the whiskey bottle, then scooped up both the crucifix and the amulet from the floor and stuffed them into my pocket.

After brushing glass off a stool, I sat. Megan yanked my knife out of the wall. She handed the sparkling silver weapon across the bar without comment. I tucked the thing back where it belonged, then did my best to straighten my clothes. I'd lost too many buttons, so I gave up and sipped at the whiskey. I didn't know where to start, so I just kept sipping.

"Ruthie died," Megan suggested.

I guessed that was as good a place as any to begin.

The public believed Ruthie Kane had been murdered, and she had been—just not by human hands or conventional weapons. The local police department had been stumped. Couldn't blame them. It wasn't every day little old ladies died on their sunny kitchen floors from the bite wounds of wild animals.

In the end, Jimmy had framed a dead demon killer—mostly to get himself off the hook—and the police had accepted the ruse. They'd had to explain things somehow.

"Liz?" Megan murmured, bringing me back to the here and now.

"Ruthie touched me and gave me her power," I said.

"Power," Megan repeated.

"To see, to know—" I moved my hands helplessly, uncertain how to explain.

When a supernatural entity came near, seers heard a

voice—for me, it was Ruthie's voice—telling us what type of demon lay behind the benign human face. Or, if we were lucky, we received advance warning through a vision. Then it was our duty to send out a demon killer to end the problem.

Before Ruthie had died she'd passed her sight to me, and given me a helluva coma—but I'd survived. It had taken some time to learn how to control the power; sometimes I still wasn't sure how in control I was, but I thought I was getting the hang of it.

"There are monsters in the world," I continued. "Always have been."

"I'm aware of that."

"I'm not using a euphemism. When I say *monster* I mean tooth and claw—magical, ancient, legendary beings that plan to destroy us."

"I'm Irish," Megan said. "I know."

"What does being Irish have to do with anything?"

"I was raised to believe in magical, legendary creatures—both good and evil." When I continued to frown, Megan fluttered her fingers in a "get on with it" gesture. "Just tell me."

"Ruthie was killed by the Nephilim."

"Offspring of the fallen angels and the daughters of men."

I blinked. "How do you know that?"

"It's in the Bible, Liz."

I waggled my hand back and forth. "Eh."

Oh, here and there a line about fallen angels, Satan, giants, and monsters could be found. In truth, the Bible was a scary, scary book, and that was before you even got to Revelation. But the whole story of the Nephilim—that had been left out.

"You've read the Book of Enoch?" I asked.

"Yeah." She shrugged. "I was curious."

Over the centuries, several sections had been removed from the Bible. Enoch had originally been beloved by Jews and Christians alike until it was pronounced heresy and banned. They did that a lot back then.

"In the interest of saving time," I said, "why don't you let me in on what you already know?" I had places to go, people to question, demons to kill. The brand-new story of my life.

"Certain angels were given the task of watching over the humans," Megan began. "They were called the Watchers. But they lusted after them instead and were banished by God. Their offspring were known as the Nephilim."

"Some say they were giants," I continued when she didn't. "They devoured man and beast; they drank the blood of their enemies. Their strength was legion. They could fly. They could shape-shift."

Megan's eyes widened, and her mouth made an O of surprise. "You're saying—"

"Vampires. Werewolves. Evil, dark, creepy things. The legends of monsters in every culture down through the ages."

"Are all true?"

"Pretty much."

"The sons and daughters of the Watchers are still on earth," Megan murmured. "That explains a lot."

"It does?"

"Didn't you ever wonder how some people could be so purely evil? How they could do what they do to others and still be human?" Megan tilted her head. "It's simple. They're not."

She was handling this a lot better than I had. But then, she was Irish.

"Ruthie could see what these things are, even when they look human?" I nodded. "And now you can?" Another nod. That about summed it up.

"So what is she?" Megan jerked her head toward the center of the room, where we'd last seen the woman of smoke.

"Trouble," I murmured. But then what evil half-demon wasn't? I got to my feet. "I'm gonna have to go."

"Without telling me what she was?"

"You're better off not knowing."

Too much information could get Megan killed. As it was, I wasn't going to be able to come back here anytime soon—if ever.

"You're headed after her?"

"Eventually." First I needed to have a little chat with Sawyer—the man who'd given me the turquoise that had kept his mother from killing me.

Coincidence? I didn't believe in them anymore.

"So you're what?" Megan asked. "Superpsychic hero girl? Leader of some cult of antidemonites?"

"Close enough," I answered, then hesitated. Should I hug her, or shouldn't I? I was never quite sure about things like that. "Listen, Meg, if you need anything, call my cell."

She stared at me for several seconds. "You're not coming back this time."

"It's not safe for you if I'm around."

"I can take care of myself," Megan said.

"Thanks to me, you have to."

She let out an impatient sigh. "Let it go, Liz. I've told you before that Max's death wasn't your fault."

But I knew differently. If Megan died because of me, I didn't think I'd be able to go on. And I had to.

The fate of the world was in my hands.

* * *

I headed home to pack a bag and get myself on a flight to Albuquerque. Since Sawyer lived at the edge of the Navajo reservation, which was hell and gone from the airport, I'd also have to rent a car.

It would certainly be easier to give him a call. Unfortunately, the man didn't have a phone. Sawyer was—

Hard to explain.

I pointed my Jetta north on Highway 43, hopped off when I got to the suburbs, drove west until I hit Friedenberg. What had begun as a tiny hamlet on the Milwaukee River had become the commerce center of a wealthy subdivision. I lived in the original tiny hamlet, where the buildings were old and the taxes reflected that.

The town was quiet and dark. The single stoplight flashed. Nothing ever happened in Friedenberg. At least until I had moved in.

I parked behind the combination business and residential two-story I'd purchased after leaving the force. A knickknack shop, understandably empty at this time of night, rented the ground floor.

After opening the outside door, then closing and relocking it, I hurried upstairs to my apartment. A quick glance into the two rooms—one for living/sleeping/dining and another for bathing—revealed I was alone. For now.

Quickly I changed out of my jeans, torn shirt, ugly vest and sandals into another pair of jeans, a navy blue tank top—July in Wisconsin was still July and the temps hovered in the high seventies long after the sun went down—then tennis shoes. Running in sandals never worked out very well, and lately, I ran a lot.

I threaded Ruthie's crucifix onto the chain with Sawyer's turquoise, then pulled the amulet from my pocket to take a better look. In the center of the circlet a five-pointed star had been etched. Carved into the opposite side were several words in a language I didn't know. Since my repertoire consisted of English, English, and then a little more English, it could be anything.

I shoved the amulet into my jeans. Since I'd yanked it off his mother's skinny neck, maybe Sawyer would have a clue as to what it was.

And speaking of Sawyer's mother—

I opened the dresser drawer next to my bed and removed the photo I kept there. When I'd first seen this picture in the lair of the leader of the darkness—a quaint term for the other side's big boy—I'd nearly had a heart attack. I'd recognized her face from the night Sawyer had conjured her in the desert.

Until today, I hadn't known the woman of smoke was also a *Naye'i*. I hadn't known she was Sawyer's mother.

I *had* known she was evil, and I hadn't liked at all finding her likeness next to the place where Satan's henchman slept. So I'd snatched it.

Now I was wondering if that hadn't been a less than brilliant idea. Before I could think about it too much, I tore the photo into itty-bitty pieces, then ground it up in the garbage disposal. Maybe that would keep her from finding me again. But I doubted it.

I kept a duffel under my bed, always packed and ready—clothes, cash, my laptop. I'd had no call to use the bag in the past month. My visions of supernatural baddies had dried up as thoroughly as the small plot of grass in my backyard.

I hadn't been sure if that was because I was a little short on demon killers, having only two in my arsenal after last month's massacre. Jimmy, who was in the middle of a mini-meltdown and no help at all, and Summer Bartholomew, who I just plain didn't like and wouldn't call unless I had to.

When push came to shove—and it would, it always did—I had myself. I was the first demon-killing seer in history. Let no one say that I am not an overachiever.

However, I found it hard to believe that the head honchos upstairs—my name for whoever sent me information via Ruthie's voice or an old-fashioned vision— would have given me a break in my duties just because I was shorthanded.

The other option was that I'd lost my power, and it hadn't felt that way, even before Ruthie had whispered *Naye'i*.

But now I had a third option in the amulet I'd yanked off the woman of smoke. She'd been able to get close to me because I hadn't received the usual advance warning of impending doom. Until I'd gotten my hands on the medallion, Ruthie's ghostly voice had been silenced.

I really needed to find out what that thing was.

I stowed my knife in the duffel, then cast a glance at the safe under my sink where I kept my gun when I wasn't at home. I could bring the knife on the plane as long as I checked the bag, but there were rules about transporting firearms by air—particular cases required, certain ways the ammunition had to be packed—and I didn't know them all.

That sense of urgency that had been riding me since I left Murphy's won, and I decided to make do with the knife. Guns weren't all that useful against Nephilim anyway, unless you knew where to hit them, how many times, and with what.

Looping the luggage strap onto my shoulder, I turned. Someone stood in the doorway.

CHAPTER 3

Ruthie's voice remained silent. But after the incident with the *Naye'i*, the lack of that whisper wasn't as dependable as it used to be.

Whoever this was, they were short. Really short. But if they were a demon, short didn't mean squat. Ha-ha.

I hoisted my duffel at the person's head, then rolled across the floor in the direction of the safe. I'd been a state champion in high school gymnastics, which was coming in a lot more handy than I'd ever dreamed.

I doubted I'd get the safe open in time to shoot, had no idea if the silver bullets I now habitually loaded into my Glock would work, but I had to do something.

The duffel connected with the intruder's chest. I heard a soft "Oof," then "Hey!" just as my fingers touched the keypads. I lowered my hand; I recognized that voice, should have known from the tiny stature who was here even before the lights went on without either one of us touching them.

Tiny and blond, the woman in the doorway resembled a pixie with a country-western fetish. Her tight jeans, fringed halter top, cowboy boots, and white Stetson were slightly out of place in a land where people wore cheese on their heads.

"What the hell do you want?" I climbed to my feet.

She lifted her eyebrows and pursed her perfect mouth. I wanted to slug her. I usually did, but I refrained. Summer Bartholomew was the only one of my demon killers, or DKs, still alive and available. She was also a fairy.

Really.

To fight supernatural evil, more than just plain folks were required, so most of the DKs were breeds—descendants of Nephilim and humans. The added influx of humanity with each successive generation diluted the demon enough so that breeds could make a choice about which side they fought for.

The ones who weren't breeds were angels who hadn't succumbed to temptation but were caught on the other side of the golden gates when God slammed them shut on the fallen. Not good enough to go to heaven, but not bad enough to go to hell, they became fairies.

"There's a problem," Summer began.

"I know. I was on my way to New Mexico."

"He's gone."

"Gone? That's impossible."

"No," Summer said. "It isn't."

"How long?"

She shrugged. "I hadn't seen him for weeks. Then I stopped by and . . ." She spread her hands.

"Weren't you supposed to be his keeper?"

"He goes missing every year. He always comes back."

I suddenly remembered—once a year Sawyer went hunting.

For his mother.

That she'd showed up at my place was becoming more and more interesting.

"If he always goes off, why run across the country to tell me about it?"

"I'm not here because of Sawyer," she said. "I'm here because of Jimmy."

I forced my fingers to uncurl from the fists they'd automatically made at her words. Stupid to be angry and jealous over his leaving me and choosing her. We'd been eighteen. Grade A idiots, both of us. But mostly Jimmy, since he had to have known the next time I touched him I'd see her.

I'd been born psychometric. Basically when I touched people, I saw things. I'd seen way more than I ever wanted to of Jimmy and Summer.

Imagine—your first love, your first time, all rolled into one. Alone and lonely, a street kid who'd found a home, found him. Thinking he loved you, believing you'd be together forever, then "seeing" him in the arms of someone else. I'd reacted badly—for the past seven years.

"What about Jimmy?" I asked.

Something in my voice must have tipped Summer off to my mood because she inched back.

"What are you afraid of?" I moved forward. "You're a fairy. You've got powers, too."

"You know damn well I can't use them on you."

I smiled and Summer stepped back again. If she kept it up she'd fall down the stairs. Not that it would hurt her any.

"I do love the fairy rules," I continued. "Can't use your magic against anyone on an errand of mercy. And since my whole life is one long errand of mercy . . ." My smile widened. "Sucks to be you."

"You have no idea," she murmured. Before I could ask what that meant, she went on. "Getting back to Jimmy."

My smile faded. "I don't know where he is."

She glanced down, the brim of her hat shading her too beautiful face. Fairies could practice glamour, a type of shape-shifting that made them more attractive than the average human. However, since fairy magic didn't work on seers, I had to think that Summer was truly gorgeous. So how much *could* it suck to be her?

"I do," she said reluctantly.

"You do?" For a second I forgot the question. Then I stiffened. "You know where he is? He called you? Came to you?"

"I saw him." She waggled her fingers—manicured and painted pale pink—toward her head.

"I thought you could only see the future."

"Right."

"What good does that do me today?"

Summer's gaze lifted. "There was a Fourth of July parade, right down the center of town."

"The Fourth is in two days."

"Which makes it the future."

"What town?"

"Barnaby's Gap, Arkansas."

"And you think Jimmy's there why?"

"I saw him watching the parade." Her lips, the same shade as her fingernails—who does that?—tightened. "He didn't look good."

My heart took a sharp leap, then fell with a heavy thud. Jimmy hadn't exactly been himself the last time I'd seen him.

"You could have just gone and gotten him. Why come to me?"

"You two have a connection."

"Seems to me that you two have the same connection."

"No." She took a deep breath, let it out slowly, the

movement perking up her already too perky breasts. "What we had—" She broke off at my glare. "He loves you."

I had a hard time believing Jimmy Sanducci had ever loved anyone—except for Ruthie. She'd taken him off the streets same as me, but Ruthie was dead.

"Even if he did love me once, what difference does that make in dragging him back from Arizona?"

"Arkansas."

"Whatever."

"There's going to be trouble."

The hair on the back of my neck tingled. "You've said that before."

The day after I'd killed the leader of the darkness—a.k.a. Jimmy's father.

"It's here."

"Here?" I moved toward my duffel and the knife inside it.

"Not right this second here, but soon. It's coming."

"What's coming?" I asked, though I had a pretty good idea. The woman of smoke was going to be the next big pain in my ass.

"I'm not sure," Summer said.

"Then what good are you?"

"I found Jimmy." She lifted her just-pointed-enough-to-be-cute chin. "You didn't."

"Fine, you give me a ring when you've got him in hand."

"No."

"No?" I raised my eyebrows. "You seem to have forgotten who's the boss of you."

"You have to come with me. You're—" She paused and bit her lip.

I narrowed my eyes. "I'm what?"

I was a lot of things—some of them good, some of them kind of creepy. I still wasn't used to it myself.

"The leader of the light. You're stronger than any of us."

I wasn't sure about that, though I knew that I could be. Unfortunately, what I had to do to increase my powers was slightly more than I was willing to, unless absolutely necessary.

"Jimmy's going to need help," Summer finished.

Panic flared. Had the woman of smoke gone after him?

"How do we kill her?" I blurted.

"Her who?"

"You aren't talking about the *Naye'i*?"

"*Naye'i*," she murmured. "Dreadful One. The only time I ever heard that was—" Her eyes widened. "Sawyer's mother?"

"Yeah."

"That bitch has been a nightmare since she was born," Summer said.

Hearing the word *bitch* come out of Summer's sweet mouth gave me a nearly irrepressible urge to giggle. The only way I was able to stop it was by remembering that I did *not* giggle. Ever.

"Haven't all the Nephilim been a nightmare?" I asked. "I think it's part of the definition."

"She's different."

"Why?"

"She's more than a Navajo evil spirit, she's a witch, too."

"I know. She gained her power by killing Sawyer's father." Who'd been a powerful medicine man in his own right.

I'd said Sawyer was hard to explain. That was one of the reasons. Being raised by a murdering-evil spirit-witch-demon would give anyone issues. We were lucky the guy hadn't been gibbering in a corner for the last few centuries.

"She's the reason I was headed to New Mexico to talk to Sawyer," I continued. "She showed up tonight and tried to kill me."

"You'd better get used to it," Summer muttered.

"Ruthie didn't have to deal with constant assassination attempts."

"None of the Nephilim knew Ruthie's identity."

"True." Everyone and Satan's sister knew who I was.

" 'Leader of the darkness kills leader of the light and sets in motion Doomsday,' " Summer recited. "But when you reverse that, you reverse everything. Or at least that's the rumor."

"Say what?"

"Haven't you noticed there hasn't been a whole lot of chaos going on?"

"Well, yeah."

"The scuttlebutt on the streets is that by having the head good guy—you—kill the head bad guy, we get a rewind. At least until—"

"Some other bozo with a god complex kills me."

Summer shrugged. I guess I knew now why the woman of smoke wanted me dead.

"Are you sure this is good intel?"

She nodded. "As soon as I heard the whispers, I nabbed a few Nephilim, beat the truth out of them."

When she said things like that I was never quite certain whether she was serious or not.

"They all spilled the same story." She twirled her finger. "We get a do-over."

"Why didn't we know this?" I asked. "Why didn't Jimmy or Ruthie or even Sawyer tell me?"

"I'm not sure *they* knew. The prophesies about the

end times are confusing to say the least. Everyone inter-
prets them differently."

"You'd think that Ruthie, having died and gone to her
version of heaven, would have a pretty good handle on
the truth."

"You'd think," Summer agreed. "But what is truth?"

I groaned. I hated existential questions. Give me black
or white, good or evil, truth or lies. Please.

"We have free will," Summer continued. "So, we
choose one path instead of another and the whole prophesy shifts."

"Swell."

"Ruthie's the first leader of the light to be killed by a
leader of the darkness. They've tried, but they've never
succeeded. Doomsday hasn't been set in motion before,
though many believed that it was."

By definition Doomsday is the period of chaos that
leads up to the Apocalypse. I'd really been hoping to
avoid that ticking clock. Sure, it was going to happen
eventually. The end of days was inevitable. But why
couldn't it happen on someone else's watch?

"What do you mean, people believed that it was?"

"Every generation thinks it's living in the end times.
The events of Revelation—Doomsday, chaos, tribulation, the beast, 666—could have played out at any point
in history. But we've always stopped them."

"We. The federation?"

"Yes. The list of historical figures that could have
turned out to be the Antichrist without us around is
pretty long. Nero, Caligula, Stalin, Hitler, Mussolini, to
name just a few."

"Those guys were Nephilim?"

"Did you seriously think they were human?"

Not really.

"You're saying that any demonic nut bag can become the Antichrist?" I asked.

"If he manages to fulfill all the requirements before one of us kills him."

"Requirements. Like killing me?"

"For starters, then killing all the DKs and seers."

The last nut bag had made pretty good headway on that.

"Then?"

"Charismatic leader of the world, rebuilding the temple, abolition of paper money, rising from the dead."

"Whoa. What was the last one?"

"Eventually, one of them is going to heal a head shot and then . . . what's that expression?" She tapped her pink nail against her pink lips. "All hell will break loose. Literally."

"Healing a head shot isn't much of a chore for most Nephilim."

"I know."

"Then we move forward on the assumption that we've been granted a reprieve."

"We move forward as we always do," Summer said. "Kill them, kill them, kill them."

"At this rate," I said, rubbing my forehead, "the cycle might never end. Kill the leader of the light—Doomsday; kill the leader of the darkness—not. Doomsday, not, Doomsday, not." I was getting dizzy.

I lowered my hand as something occurred to me. "Ruthie told me the final battle is now."

"Maybe." Summer's deceptively innocent blue eyes met mine. "There's never been anyone like you before."

"So according to the rumor"—which should be a legend by next week—"by killing the leader of the darkness, I thwarted Doomsday. To start up another, they'd have to kill me. But I'm not going to be as easy to take out as Ruthie."

"Then there's nothing to worry about."

"Except psycho evil spirit bitch—"

"Witch," Summer corrected.

"No, I had it right." We shared a smile, then realized what we were doing and stopped. "She's—uh—after me," I finished. "And I don't know how to kill her."

"First things first," Summer said. "We get Jimmy, then we find Sawyer."

"Does it have to be 'we'?" I asked.

Me and Summer on a road trip. Hunting down Jimmy Sanducci and confronting him together.

Talk about a nightmare.

CHAPTER 4

A '57 Chevy Impala was parked in front of my building, light blue and so gorgeous it brought tears to my eyes. Summer walked to the driver's side and got in.

"This is yours?"

She shot me a *duh* look.

Summer the fairy couldn't fly—at least on a plane. She messed up the controls, and when dealing with several tons of airborne metal and fuel . . . extremely bad idea. She could hit the skies without wings, a trick I'd yet to see, but cloud-dancing people tend to get noticed. So, unless there was a dire emergency that required her immediate presence—and there were quite a few—Summer stuck to cars.

"I meant, what happened to your pickup?"

"That's for New Mexico. This"—she smoothed her hand over the dash—"is for the road."

Yes, it was.

I wasn't a classic car nut. I drove a Jetta, for crying out loud. But I'd always admired old automobiles, the ones that really sucked the gas. Those cars had balls, guts, chutzpah—real staying power. It had always made perfect sense to me that Christine, Stephen King's car that never died, had been a 1958 Plymouth Fury.

Summer pulled away from the curb and pointed the Impala southwest. "What's in your pocket?" she asked.

My hand stilled in the act of rubbing the amulet. I hesitated, then realized that two heads were better than one, even when one of them was Summer's. She'd been around as long as the woman of smoke. That had to be good for something.

I drew out the necklace. "I tore this off the *Naye'i*."

Summer glanced at the copper circlet and frowned. "That's a pentacle."

"Never heard of it."

Which wasn't surprising. Ask me how to clean a gun or mix a martini and I was a damn genius, but ask me about secret Satanic things and you could color me worthless.

"Pentacles are amulets used in magical rites," Summer said. "The star is a pentagram—five points. If the symbol is drawn with one point up, we're talking good magic."

"And if there are two points up and one point down, like this?"

"Black magic."

I wasn't surprised. "Until I tore the amulet off the *Naye'i*, I didn't know what she was. I think it blocked my sight."

"Fantastic," Summer muttered. "What if there are more of them out there?"

I hadn't thought of that. I'd just been concerned that there was one.

"How do you know all this stuff?" I asked.

Since I'd been thrust into my role as leader of the federation, along with my destiny as a seer, with virtually no preparation, I didn't know all I was supposed to about the Nephilim. In truth, I didn't know anything.

DKs were trained in killing tactics. Seers were just supposed to see, but I was both. However, I hadn't had the time to study the ancient texts, the legends of every country and people. The way things were going, I doubted I ever would.

Thus far I'd made do with consulting any available DK and that friend to seekers of knowledge everywhere, the Internet.

"I've been doing this a while," Summer answered. "There's also a Web site where DKs and seers have begun to enter into a database what they know about a particular Nephilim or breed. Cuts down on research time."

"Why don't I know about this?"

"Just went live in the past few weeks." She rattled off an address, then told me how to access the files with a code. "It's not comprehensive since DKs are better at killing than typing, and a lot of knowledge was lost when three-quarters of the federation was wiped out."

I cursed.

"Live with it," Summer said. "And move on."

I didn't have much choice.

"Have you ever seen anything similar to this?" I held up the amulet.

Summer took it, and I tensed, half afraid she might go up in flames when she touched it. Who knew what that thing could do? But she didn't.

"The woman of smoke probably made it," Summer said. "Cast a spell. Sacrificed a goat."

I stilled. "Why would you say that?"

"There's always a sacrificial goat." She glanced sideways, then back at the dark road. "You do know that a goat isn't always a goat?"

"Huh?"

"The goat without horns. It means human sacrifice." I must have made an involuntary movement because she lifted her brow. "Don't tell me you're surprised? We're talking pure evil. For demons, humans are prey. Cattle. Meat. Goats, if you will."

I'd known that, had seen it practiced by the leader of the darkness, who'd kept a harem of women snacks. I was so glad that guy was dead.

Summer laid the amulet on the seat between us. "Something else is bothering you besides this."

Her intuitiveness was nearly as annoying as her manicure.

"I've seen the *Naye'i* before," I admitted.

"And you didn't kill her?"

"I was a kid." I'd had no idea what I was seeing. One glance into the demon's eyes, and I'd hidden under the covers for the rest of the night.

"What happened?"

"Sawyer. He—" I searched for the words to explain what I'd observed. "He . . . conjured her. By killing a goat."

The car swerved as Summer's hands jerked on the wheel. "A goat, goat or—"

"A goat." It had still been quite a shock.

"And then?" Summer asked.

I closed my eyes and saw again what had happened so many years ago.

Ruthie had sent me to Sawyer the summer I was fifteen to discover all that I could about the psychometric talent I'd been born with. I'd needed to learn how to live with it, and Sawyer had helped.

Sure, it was weird to send a fifteen-year-old girl to an isolated part of New Mexico to stay with what appeared to be a thirty-year-old man.

However, Sawyer wasn't thirty. Hell, he wasn't even a man. And I was no ordinary fifteen-year-old girl.

I don't think Ruthie had been wild about the idea of sending me there, but I also don't think she'd had much choice. I was special in a way she'd never dealt with before, just as Sawyer was special in ways no one else could understand. As much as he'd scared me—as much as he still did—he'd also thrilled me, tempted me, and taught me.

On that long-ago night, I'd woken in the dark, heard a voice, peeked out the window just in time to witness the death of the goat and a whole lot more.

The blood had poured over Sawyer's hands and into the ground. Smoke had risen wherever the blood struck as he'd chanted in another language—Navajo, no doubt—and lifted his gory palms in supplication to the night. The smoke had twined with the bonfire at the edge of the yard before racing around and around as if trying to break free. Sawyer had snapped an order, and the dancing flame paused, lengthened, and became the woman of smoke.

When she'd stared at me with her bottomless black eyes, I'd tried to hide, but it was too late. She'd seen me, and I knew deep down in my trembling soul that she would come for me one day. How right I had been.

"Why would he do that?" Summer murmured when I finished my tale.

"I never asked him."

"Why not?"

"He scared the everloving crap out of me back then."

Summer nodded in agreement. Sawyer scared her, too. Which meant she was smarter than she looked. She just had to be.

"He probably wouldn't have told you the truth," she said.

"Does he ever?"

Sawyer had a lot in the way of power and very little in the way of conscience. The last time I'd seen him he'd drugged me and fucked me—and that wasn't a euphemism, either.

Sawyer did a lot of training for the federation—both DKs and seers—for a price. Regardless of his lack of ethics and his annoying habit of doing whatever and whoever the hell he wanted, the fact remained that he knew things. When you lived for centuries upon centuries you couldn't help but know.

"What are the powers of a *Naye'i*?" I asked.

"Traveling on the wind. Turning to smoke."

"She dropped my friend Megan unconscious with a glance."

Summer nodded slowly. "Add it to the list. Although that could be a power she learned through witchcraft. Hard to say."

"Why didn't she drop me?"

"She likes to get her hands bloody? Who knows? Maybe that talent only works on humans."

"I'm human."

Summer snorted. "Sure you are."

"What the hell does that mean?" She'd once told me that I'd meet my mother someday and that I wouldn't like it.

"Relax. I was just . . ." Her voice trailed off.

"Messing with me?"

"Yeah. You do ask for it on occasion."

I asked for it constantly.

"My parents," I began.

"Are unknown to us. For now. That's a worry for another time. Don't you have enough to deal with?"

"Yeah." I sat back in my seat and watched the road roll by.

Since I'd discovered that the world was inhabited by demons with human faces, I'd begun to wonder what had lurked beneath the faces of my parents. No one seemed to know, or if they did they weren't telling, but for me to have the talents I had, I figured either one or both of them had possessed special talents, too.

"I still wonder why Sawyer had to conjure his mother," Summer mused a few minutes later.

"Considering that he goes on an annual 'Kill my mother' hunt, I don't think they bonded well."

"He never did get over her murdering his father."

"Yeah, he's funny that way," I said.

Summer cast me an exasperated glance. "What I'm getting at is, why conjure her? She's flesh and blood, not a spirit."

"Was she always? Flesh and blood, I mean? A *Naye'i* is an evil spirit."

"The Nephilim were called evil spirits down through the ages, but it doesn't mean 'spirit,' like a ghost. Just . . ." Summer lifted one hand from the steering wheel and turned it palm up. "Spirit of evil."

"And we're right back to why he conjured her."

I guessed I'd just have to break down and ask him.

We traveled all night. Fairies didn't appear to need any sleep. Since I did, I conked out well before St. Louis.

Dawn over the Ozark Mountains is a beautiful thing. The mist hangs heavy on the hills, causing the streaks of sunlight creeping across the peaks to turn every shade of crimson and gold.

The sight made me want to save the world all over again. After viewing a sunrise like that, who wouldn't want to go out and kick some half-demon ass?

Except we were here to find Jimmy, learn the names of the remaining seers, do whatever it was that needed doing to get him back on the job. I wasn't certain I was up to that. I'd never been much of a psychologist. And Jimmy definitely needed his head shrunk, or a nice padded cell.

Or a hug. I wasn't sure which.

We reached Barnaby's Gap in the afternoon, much later than I'd planned. Despite Summer's fairytude, we'd gotten lost, floundered around, backtracked, wasted time.

The town was old, had probably been there since long before the Civil War. In the past, the Ozarks had been a hotbed for mining, but as is the case with most mines, the ore ran out. The towns that had sprung up to meet the needs of the industry either died or found a new livelihood.

Most of the Ozark settlements had recently begun to court the boom of tourism brought about by the success of Branson. Barnaby's Gap had not. Couldn't say that I blamed them. Why mar the spectacular view with a bevy of condos, complete with swimming pools, tennis courts, workout facilities, and spa? Why commercialize the main street with shops full of candles, holiday decorations, antiques, crafts, and candy?

They'd no doubt survived without catering to the masses because of the impressive sawmill we'd passed on the way in. I was certain the majority of the citizenry worked there while the minority made their living on the sidewalk-lined streets where family-owned businesses catered to kith and kin. We rolled past a grocer, doctor, pharmacy, and—yippee and yahoo!—a coffee shop.

"Coffee," I croaked, pointing.

My croak must have tipped Summer off to the necessity of said coffee because the Impala coasted to a stop at the curb, and she followed me inside without argument.

The place was nearly empty this late in the day. We didn't have to contend with tourists sipping their four-dollar brews and reading the most recent *New York Times* bestseller or the romance novel they wouldn't be caught dead opening back home.

I ordered a large Mountain Roast from an overly pale young woman who seemed extremely jumpy. She started when I ordered, as if I'd spoken too loud, then dropped my change, flinching when the coins pinged against the countertop. She'd had way too much Breakfast Blend.

I slugged several sips in quick succession before I turned away from the register.

Summer eyed me with interest. "Do you have asbestos mouth?"

"Excuse me?"

"Most humans would burn their mouths."

I wasn't most humans, wasn't even sure just how human I was. But I'd been able to drink really hot coffee without burning my mouth even before I'd become superpsychic hero girl.

I shrugged. "I'm used to it."

Summer strolled to an empty table. Her outfit seemed less conspicuous here, or maybe I was just getting used to that, too.

"Now what?" I asked. "We wait around until Jimmy shows up for the parade?"

"I don't think so." Her gaze was fixed on the wide front window that overlooked the main drag of Barnaby's Gap.

The street was deserted. I started to get uneasy. Sure, this place wasn't a tourist trap, but there should be someone moving around.

"Come on," she said.

We walked along the sidewalk, peeking into each storefront. All the places were open, the employees doing their jobs, but everyone was twitchy. When we appeared in the window, they'd start, glance up with wide eyes, then just as quickly look away. I didn't like it one bit.

Up ahead an elderly man shuffled toward us—tall and thin, with snow-white hair. He was dressed well, not a street person, though the way he hunched his shoulders and mumbled to himself reminded me of many I'd seen. As he neared, his words drifted to us on the sultry afternoon breeze.

"Red eyes," he intoned. "Teeth and blood. Demon in the hills. Demon in the caves."

I guess that explained the overcaffeinated conduct of the populace.

I immediately crossed in front of Summer and set my hand on the man's shoulder.

For the most part, strong emotions—fear, love, hate—transmitted, giving me a view of the situations surrounding them. Since the guy was nearly scared witless, I got smacked with so many images I staggered.

Night. Dark. Trees. Water. The acrid scent of terror, the heated brush of danger. Running. Falling. Pain. Blood. Then merciful, blessed oblivion.

Hell. There was definitely something out there.

The poor guy stared at me as if he expected me to turn into a monster. I couldn't blame him. Regular people aren't programmed to accept the arrival of a horror movie in their hometown. Usually the Nephilim didn't leave anyone alive, so we didn't have to deal with the zombielike behavior of a survivor. Which only made me wonder all the more about what kind of beastie we were dealing with.

The old man wasn't as old as I'd first believed. The way he walked, the mumbling, the white hair hinted at seven or eight decades on this earth. But his face appeared more like forty-five, and I realized that what he'd seen had aged him, perhaps overnight.

"Anything?" Summer asked.

I nodded, then jerked my head at the guy, and she flicked her fingers, shooting fairy dust from the tips.

I'd wished on several occasions that I possessed the talent to dispense magical sparkles and make people obey my every unvoiced command, but I couldn't.

As soon as the twinkling particles—invisible to anyone but us—hit the guy's face, his eyes cleared, his back straightened, and he walked off with the gait of a much younger man.

"He won't remember?" I asked.

Summer's answer was a withering stare. Of course he wouldn't remember.

"What are we dealing with?" Summer pressed.

"I don't know."

She frowned. "No whispers? Not a flash?"

"No."

"Huh," she said.

"Yeah." I thought of the amulet still sitting on the seat of the car.

Did whatever was stalking this town have an amulet of its own? Otherwise why hadn't I seen the monster in a vision, or heard Ruthie's whisper as soon as we rolled past the city limits?

Loud voices drew our attention to the other end of the street where several people carried on a heated conversation. Lots of hand gestures in the direction of the distant mountains, the pantomime of picking up a rifle, sighting and shooting. It appeared that more than one citizen had met up with the thing in the hills.

Another man, and a woman wearing a bright green, sleeveless sundress, joined the crowd. I admired the high neckline, and the interesting heart-shaped cutout that revealed her chest and just a hint of cleavage. The man continued the argument with more gesticulating and extensive miming of weaponry. The woman remained silent; she looked a little drugged.

"What do you think?" Summer asked.

"I think you'd better zap them, too." If they went into the mountains with conventional weapons, they were going to get killed.

"I don't understand this," I muttered as we headed for the crowd. "I haven't heard anything; I haven't seen anything. And if Jimmy's in town, the demon in the caves should be dead by now."

Before he'd had his mini-breakdown, Jimmy had been the best hunter in the federation. He wouldn't have needed me to tell him that something wicked had come to Barnaby's Gap.

"You're sure he's here?" I asked.

Summer flicked a huge cloud of fairy dust over the assembled throng. Instead of walking away with a very bad case of short-term memory loss, the group stilled as if they were the best cadre of freeze-tag players in the country.

"Am I sure Jimmy's here?" Summer repeated, and approached the woman in the green dress. She tugged down the mock turtleneck to reveal familiar puncture wounds before her gaze met mine.

"I'm sure," she said.

CHAPTER 5

Summer clapped her hands, and the people wandered off without ever looking in our direction.

I felt as frozen as the townsfolk had been. Jimmy was the demon in the mountains. Now what was I going to do?

Kill him, most likely.

"We need to get the names of the seers out of him before—" I paused at Summer's gasp.

"You can't kill him!"

"Oh, yeah, I can."

"You love him."

"What's love got to do with it?"

Maybe I did still love Jimmy. Probably. But I hated him, too. He'd hurt me so many times in so many ways. Not more than a month ago, he'd kept me as his sex slave; he'd nearly killed me. That he'd been possessed by a medieval vampire witch—a strega—who just happened to be his dear old dad was beside the point.

Jimmy was a dhampir—part vampire, part human—a breed. He had many vampire characteristics—blinding speed, incredible strength, and the ability to heal just about anything—combined with a dhampir's talent at identifying creatures of the night. However, once he'd shared blood with Daddy, his vampire nature had been aroused. He'd gone off to try and put it back. From the appearance of Barnaby's Gap, he hadn't had much luck.

I turned, headed for my duffel, where I'd not only stowed the silver knife, but also, since we were traveling by car, the gun I'd retrieved from the safe.

I knew how to kill a dhampir. Strike twice in the same way. Last time, I'd only managed to stake the bastard once. I wouldn't make that mistake again.

"He hasn't killed anyone." Summer hurried along at my side.

"We don't know that."

She stopped dead, and I did, too, though I have no idea why. Her fairy dust didn't work on me.

"He wouldn't," Summer said, "and I'll prove it." She spun on her boot heels and clippety-clopped back down the sidewalk.

Pausing a few storefronts away, she glanced at the sign. BARNABY'S GAP MEDICAL CLINIC.

Ah, hell. What was she up to?

Before I could ask, she yanked a wallet out of the back pocket of her jeans—how she could have squeezed a wallet in there along with her ass, I wasn't quite sure, had to be magic—and opened the door.

I joined her as she flipped the thing open and snapped, "FBI. Have there been any unexplained deaths?"

I probably gaped as badly as the young man at the reception desk. Except he was gaping at her face, I was gaping at the ID. It seemed pretty real to me.

"I—uh, well. Hmm. I don't rightly know. You'd better talk to the doctor, Agent—" He leaned over, squinting at the ID. "Tink." He disappeared into the back.

"Agent Tink?" I asked. "You think that's funny?"

"Hilarious," Summer said, though her lips were tight and her eyes weren't laughing, either.

I lowered my voice to just above a whisper. "Where did you get that ID?"

"Where do you think?"

I opened my mouth to demand an answer, then shut it again. What did it matter where she'd gotten it—if it was real or if it was magic?

"You think DKs can just wander around killing people?" she continued.

I hadn't really thought about it at all. And I didn't think Nephilim were people. Not anymore.

Except they looked human, led human lives in order to blend in, cause the most havoc. When they disappeared, questions would be asked, even though, for the most part, Nephilim disintegrated into ashes if you killed them the right way. No body solved a lot of problems, but not all of the problems, and in a lot of cases, no body probably only served to create a different set of problems.

"Sometimes, even with the seers' visions to guide us," Summer continued, "we have to hunt these things down. It helps to have a free pass." She wiggled her wallet.

"Why don't you just hit everyone with glitter dust and make them spill everything in their heads?"

"Compelling people to tell me information gets me just the information."

"And that's bad why?"

"I don't get impressions, thoughts, feelings, which, when dealing with the supernatural, are important. For instance, if someone saw something bizarre and rationalized it away as most people do, they wouldn't tell me about it if I hit them with the truth dust."

"But they'll tell the FBI about the demon in the mountains?"

"You'd be surprised what people will tell the FBI."

Somehow, I doubted that.

"What happens if a person checks with the bureau about the unbelievably pretty agent who was asking some very strange questions?"

Summer cast me another withering glance and I understood.

"You hit them with a dose of 'forget me now' as soon as you're done."

She winked and turned to greet the doctor.

Dr. Gray personified the Hollywood version of a small-mountain-town physician. Tall and thin, his hair matched his name. His eyes, also gray, were bright and avid behind round wire-rimmed glasses.

"Never had the FBI knock on my door before," he said with the slight accent common to the border states.

"We won't take much of your time," Summer said. "Have there been any unexplained deaths in the area over the past month?"

"None."

Summer cast me a triumphant glance.

"Is there a hospital nearby?" I asked. Seemed to me that a hospital would be the place to ask questions about unexplained deaths, not the local physician.

"Not for a good sixty miles."

"So," Summer continued, "any death certificates would be signed by . . . ?"

"Me," Dr. Gray answered. "I'm the only game in town, doctorwise, so I act as the medical examiner. Bodies go right from here to the funeral home."

"No morgue?"

"No need." The doctor contemplated Summer for several seconds. "Though I doubt this would concern you, we have had a strange rash of animal attacks. People are so traumatized they can't remember anything but red eyes. Descriptions sound like a bear. Which has started people whispering about the Ozark Black Howler."

"What's that?" I asked.

"Legendary creature that wanders the hills."

I glanced at Summer; she no longer looked so cheery. In our world, legendary being meant "Nephilim," and they were real. We'd have to be on the lookout for a howler, too. Just in case.

"They're bear-sized," the doctor continued, "with black shaggy hair and horns. Cry is somewhere between a wolf's howl and an elk's call. But I've never heard of the howler biting anyone."

"People have been bitten?" My question was nothing but a lead; I'd already seen the evidence.

"Yes. Which is strange since howlers usually drop people dead in their tracks just by glancing at them."

"The wounds, Doctor?" I prompted.

"Oh, yes. The wounds are like nothing I've ever seen. Animals rip and tear. People . . . well, people would leave a recognizable upper and lower demarcation in the flesh. What we have are puncture wounds. Like someone's trying to make us think there's a vampire on the loose."

I laughed, so did Summer. Dr. Gray did not.

"What's the FBI's interest in Barnaby's Gap?" he asked. "No one's been killed, so we aren't talking psycho or serial."

Summer's fingers twitched. She wanted to blast him, but she needed more information first. "Can you tell us where this creature has been sighted?"

"The caves." He walked to the window, pointed at the nearest, tree-covered peak. "West side of the ridge.

Folks have been talking about going up, shooting anything that moves. I don't think that's a good idea."

I didn't, either, since shooting would probably just piss him off.

Jimmy could heal any wound, unless someone just happened to hit him with two bullets in the exact same place—and that place had to be a kill shot.

The only way for that to happen would be to get close enough to put a gun to his head or his chest and pop him twice. Jimmy might not be himself, but that didn't mean he would let anyone with a gun come near him, even me.

"Legends say that to kill a howler you have to remove the head while it's still alive." The doctor let out a short, sharp laugh. "I've been trying to figure out how—"

Jazzy floating sparkles shot past my face and rained down on Dr. Gray, stopping him mid-conjecture. He continued to stare at the distant mountains as if we were no longer there. To him, we probably weren't.

The inner door opened, and Summer flipped a hand over her shoulder, catching the assistant full in the face as he came into the room.

We slipped out without saying good-bye. I didn't think we'd be considered rude since they'd both already forgotten who we were or that they'd ever spoken to us in the first place. We made our way back to the Impala.

"You drive," Summer said.

She didn't have to tell me twice. I leaped behind the wheel, fired her up, and drove away. Summer lifted her hands over her head. Fairy dust streamed down the center of town, swirling into doorways, dancing down the chimneys and through the open windows.

"That power is very handy," I murmured.

"Forget it." Summer placed her hands in her lap,

kneading her fingers as if they ached. "I don't swing that way."

For a second I didn't know what she meant. When it became clear, my face heated.

Not only was I psychometric with latent channeling abilities—I saw dead people, or at least Ruthie—I was also an empath. The common-variety empath feels what another person feels; they empathize. Of course I was not the common-variety anything. Instead I absorbed supernatural abilities through sex.

Yeah, I hadn't been too happy about it, either.

"If you want the power so badly," Summer continued, "and I can see why you might, I know someone who could help you."

"Someone . . ." I began.

"Male."

"A male fairy?"

"You think fairies are only female?" Summer reached for her cell phone. "I'll call him. He wouldn't mind."

"I would." I stayed her hand. She peered at me, confused. "Just because I *can* absorb powers doesn't mean I should."

"Then why have the talent?"

"It's the only way we can win."

I was going to need to be stronger than what I was to keep the Nephilim from overpowering the earth. Just being psychic wasn't good enough. It certainly hadn't been for Ruthie.

Nevertheless, I balked at blatantly screwing every breed I could find. And I'd been warned never to have sex with a Nephilim. I might absorb their evil as well as their strength. No one really knew how my empathy worked, and I wasn't willing to take the chance and wind up batting for the other side.

I'd made a vow to myself that I'd only absorb powers that were absolutely necessary. I'd kind of hoped I wouldn't need any more. Sure, that hope was far-fetched, but what hope wasn't?

The highway curved upward, and we began the ascent to the top of the ridge where I assumed there'd be a sign: THIS WAY TO THE CREEPY CAVERNS.

"I imagine everyone in Barnaby's Gap is going to forget we ever rolled through?"

Summer nodded, still kneading her hands. "Along with anything spooky in the hills."

"What if someone was out of town for the day? On vacation? Just couldn't take Hicksville one more second?"

"If no one else remembers, they'll forget eventually, too. It's the nature of the human mind to rationalize."

"What happens in the places you don't go?" I wondered. "Jimmy doesn't have forget-me talents."

Because if he did, I'd have them, too.

"Like I said, people rationalize. Once the threat is gone, the memories fade, especially when those memories are so hard to believe in the first place. They'll start to think they had a nightmare, a fever."

"An entire town will rationalize away mass murder by monster?"

"Mass murder doesn't happen." I flinched, and she corrected herself. "Much."

I'd seen mass murder, been too late to prevent it, and was still haunted by the images nearly every time I closed my eyes.

"DKs are sent at the first hint of a problem," Summer continued, "if not earlier. The federation's goal is to stop the Nephilim before they cause death and destruction. Why else would all our seers be psychics?"

"Then what happened in Barnaby's Gap?"

"Jimmy's one of us."

"So we weren't warned that he's snacking on the little people? Sounds like a breakdown in communication to me."

"I saw him," Summer said quietly.

My eyes narrowed, and my mouth tightened. I didn't need reminding. "Why was that?" I asked. "You aren't a seer."

"And Jimmy's not a Nephilim."

"I'm not following."

"If the powers that be had sent a flash of Jimmy to any of the seers, a DK would have been dispatched and he'd be dead. Obviously they don't want him dead, hence the message to me."

"Conveniently minus the intel that he's gone off the deep end and started sucking on townspeople like a hungry six-month-old."

"That was left out for a reason. We're supposed to find him; we're supposed to help him. We are *not* supposed to kill him."

"The jury's still out on that," I said.

"Seems a little unfair since you're the judge, the jury, and—" She broke off, biting her lip.

"The executioner?" I finished. "Got that right."

"You want to punish him for something you don't know all the facts on."

"I know the facts, Summer. Jimmy shared blood with the strega; he became just like him. He started to kill people in that chrome tower in Manhattan. I know this because I was there. He kept me captive. He drank from me until I was too weak to fight back."

And the only reason I'd survived was because Jimmy hadn't known I had the power of empathy. He'd made me his sex slave in an attempt to take away first my will and then my life.

But the joke was on him, because in trying to hurt me, debase me, subjugate me, he'd actually made me stronger. When he'd taken my body, he'd given me his supernatural abilities. Those powers had allowed me to destroy the leader of the darkness.

"That wasn't him," she whispered.

"Walked like him, talked like him, looked like him." I didn't mention that it had fucked like him, too.

I'd been so confused. I'd believed that Jimmy was still inside the thing that wore his skin, that if I could get him to remember what we'd had, I might save him. I'd been a fool.

"When I said you didn't know all the facts I wasn't talking about Manhattan," Summer said.

"Then what—" My fingers clenched on the steering wheel. I did *not* want to have this conversation.

"Didn't you ever wonder why he'd be so stupid as to sleep with me when he knew damn well you'd see it the next time you touched him?"

"I figured he was a man." I let my gaze sweep from the tip of her stupid white hat to the toes of her just-scuffed-enough boots. "He couldn't keep it in his pants any more than the next guy if you paid him."

"You don't have a very high opinion of men."

"Should I?" Every man I'd ever trusted had betrayed me.

She sighed. "You should think a little longer about Jimmy. He isn't as big of an idiot as he seems."

"That would be impossible," I muttered. If he *were* that big of an idiot, he wouldn't be able to walk and talk at the same time.

I continued to drive up the mountain, but I started to think, and I didn't like where my thoughts took me.

Summer was right—how I hated to admit that—

Jimmy had known what I could do, so it followed that he knew I would see him with Summer.

"You're saying he wanted to end things?" I asked. "But he was too big of a weenie to face me, so he . . ." I made a vague gesture in the direction of Summer's breasts.

"For someone with a standing reservation on the moron train, you throw the word around pretty easily at others."

I gaped. That was something I would say.

"If you think about it with your head instead of your childish heart," Summer said, "you'll see the truth." Her eyes lifted. "We're here."

I followed her gaze. Above us on the next curve of the highway, the large, black half circle of a cave loomed. Dotting the incline around it were no less than a dozen others. I didn't have time to worry about what Jimmy had done so many years ago. I had to deal with what he'd done lately.

I wheeled the car around the final bend, pulling it off the road and onto a gravel area carved out for breakdowns. We stepped out, glanced up, sighed.

"You take the ones on that side." I pointed with my left hand. "I'll take the ones on this side. Whoever finds him first—" I stopped, uncertain where to go with that.

"Wins?" Summer murmured, and floated upward without benefit of wings.

CHAPTER 6

I had to ascend the old-fashioned way—shuffling across the rock-strewn dirt, yanking myself over steep areas using exposed tree roots, sliding downward several feet here and there, then cursing Jimmy Sanducci, Summer, the Nephilim, and anything and anyone else I could think of.

Luckily I had superior strength and speed, thanks to Jimmy, and the cuts and scrapes I received healed almost immediately, thanks to him, too. Still, I would have preferred to fly. That had looked liked fun.

But I was sticking to my guns at least figuratively and making do with the powers I already possessed for as long as I could. I was certain that sooner rather than later, I was going to need more magic than I had to fight the Nephilim.

I'd left my Glock in the car and brought only the knife. Ricochets, rock chips, not to mention lack of adequate lighting, made shooting a firearm in a cave a tad ill-advised.

Hauling myself over a dirt embankment, I contemplated a dark, nasty cave. If I hadn't known better I'd think dusk was falling, but it was still too early.

I glanced to the west and cursed some more—just what I needed to make this day complete. Huge, indigo clouds of thunder rolled across the horizon. My luck, the storm would turn into a tornado.

Inside the cave I pulled out the trusty flashlight that had also been in my duffel, and scouted every creepy corner. No sign of Jimmy. It would have been too simple for him to be lurking in the first place I searched.

I continued upward, listening with one ear for Summer and with the other for a swish of wind. I remembered reading somewhere about storms in the mountains making the roads impassable. Wouldn't it just be special to get stuck up here all night with Jimmy the vampire on a rampage?

I talked big, thought big about killing him, but when push came to shove, it wasn't going to be easy—neither emotionally nor physically. Jimmy was dangerous. He had been even before he'd gone vamp.

Jimmy's real job—or perhaps it was his cover and the demon killing was his real job, hard to say—was portrait photographer to the stars. He traveled the world; he was in high demand. He'd always had the best eye for color, light, people, and it had taken him places.

But once he'd been a street kid like me, handy with a knife—I stroked the hilt of the silver blade—and he'd had a hair trigger of a temper. No one had crossed Sanducci back then; if they had, they'd been very, very sorry.

At the fourth cave, I hit pay dirt. At first I thought it was another empty, damp hole. But this one kept going; it was slightly bigger than all the others.

The air became cooler; I could smell water, hear a trickle somewhere in the distance. The narrow, rock walls widened until they opened into a cavern.

Something squeaked. Bats or mice. Either one didn't work for me. I swished the flashlight around and was turning to leave when my brain registered what I'd revealed in the far corner.

Feet clad in shoes, legs covered by blue jeans. Could be anyone, but it wasn't. I'd know the scent of Jimmy Sanducci anywhere.

Even when his scent was shrouded by dirt, water, moss, and other less pleasant odors, I could smell the last hint of cinnamon and soap.

Slowly I turned, casting the round yellow light upward. He was a mess.

The T-shirt had once been white but was now brownish gray and hung in tatters. His skin, always tan, even in the longest, coldest of winters, glistened; the ripples of his belly and the supple curves of his biceps and pecs shone lusciously in the light.

His dark eyes were closed; he muttered in a tense and uneasy sleep. Dark hair, tangled with sweat and dirt, fell across his just short of pretty face.

If I'd needed any more evidence that Jimmy was not himself, the dirt would have done it. From the moment he'd arrived at Ruthie's, he'd taken two or three showers a day. He always smelled better than anyone I knew. I figured his obsession with soap stemmed from so many years on the streets without it.

There were worse compulsions. Sucking blood, for instance.

I inched my knife from the scabbard at my waist, clutching the hilt so tightly my fingers ached. I crept forward, uncertain what I meant to do. I couldn't kill him while he slept, although if I needed to kill him that was probably my best bet. I just wasn't sure . . .

It would be so much easier if he opened those eyes to reveal a spark of red in their dark depths, then smiled with a mouthful of fangs and tried to kill me.

"Jimmy." I could barely hear myself speak, my voice drowned out by my own thundering heart.

Or maybe that was just thunder. The ground seemed to rumble with it.

"Jimmy," I tried again. This time I managed some volume to the word. Again it was drowned out but not by thunder.

The wind I'd expected rolled through the cave, stirring my hair as Ruthie's voice murmured, *Black Howler*.

I faced the entrance, far away and very small. Something moved into the gray fading light, making it flicker down the tunnel like a strobe.

From the tone and the volume of Ruthie's whisper I deduced the howler was a Nephilim and not a breed. Usually I could tell just by the number of bodies lying around. Nephilim like to kill.

However, certain breeds did, too. Some fought for us, some for them, and still others had yet to be swayed to either side. Same goes for the fairies.

I glanced at Jimmy. He continued to twitch and mutter, but he didn't wake up. I caught a few words. "No . . . Can't . . . Won't . . . Thirsty." And then, "Sorry, Lizzy."

Hell.

He was the only one who called me that, and when he did, I knew it was Jimmy. When he'd been controlled by his freak show of a father, he'd called me "Elizabeth." I'd hated it almost as much as when he sometimes called me "baby."

The thing in the doorway moved forward. I clutched my knife tighter and went to meet it.

Big and shaggy, with a huge rack branching out from its bearlike head, this was quite possibly the ugliest Nephilim I'd yet to see. I wondered idly where the human part of it lay hidden, until I got close enough and saw that the long black hair shrouded a nose that would have been at home in the middle of anyone's face.

I kept my gaze averted, flicking glances at it out of the corner of my eye. I couldn't risk dropping dead, though I was starting to wonder if that power was a myth. If this beast had been long in the mountains, corpses would have been strewn all over the place.

Nevertheless, I couldn't take the chance that I'd be downed; I wouldn't let the howler walk over my inert body and make his way to Jimmy. I might have to kill Sanducci later, but there was no way I was going to let a Nephilim do it.

According to Dr. Gray, the way to kill a howler was to separate the head from the body. Too bad I'd forgotten my samurai sword as well as my axe. I wasn't sure how I was going to kill this thing, but I had to try.

The beast made me nervous the way it kept arching its neck, trying to peer around me and making a noise that sounded suspiciously like *mmmm*. Perhaps dhampir was a howler delicacy. What did I know?

Suddenly the thing threw back its head, spread out its arms, and released a horrific, inhuman howl. The sound bounced off the cave walls, pounding at my eardrums until I wanted to cover them with my hands. I was paralyzed by it, so when the howler stepped forward and tried to bitch-slap me, I barely managed to duck.

Off balance, I fell to my knees. My ears rang from the lasting echo of the call, but I dipped my shoulder and rolled, even as it swiped at my head with razorlike claws. A whiff of air skated past my cheek.

I gained my feet, spun away from another swipe, then back-flipped to avoid the bear hug, and clipped it on the chin with my heel. I held on to my knife, but I lost the flashlight. It didn't really matter since we were now close enough to the entrance to be illuminated by the fading daylight and the flashes of lightning from the approaching storm.

Where the hell was Summer? She had to have checked her half of the caves by now. She'd no doubt flitted back to the Impala to wait for me. The way things were going she'd be waiting into eternity.

How long before she came looking for me? Would she be in time? Would she be of any use if she was?

I couldn't depend on her, couldn't depend on anyone but myself. What else was new?

The howler lumbered after me, took a ponderous swing. I ducked, and when I came up, I stuck him with my silver knife.

He roared that horrific combination of howl and bugle—wolf and elk—that made my ears ache, but he didn't burst into ash. I hadn't figured he would. He wasn't a shape-shifter, so silver wouldn't kill him. I was just buying time.

I tried to yank my knife out, maybe stick him again if I could, but it was buried to the hilt. My fingers, slick with blood, slipped, and I ended up leaving the weapon in the howler's chest.

I was down to my speed, my strength, and my wits.

"This oughta go well," I murmured.

My voice infuriated the Nephilim. He brayed that dreadful sound again, and the slight paralyzation that followed the near-bursting of my eardrums allowed him to step in close.

This time when he bitch-slapped me, I flew. As my back hit the rock face, I caught a flash of movement from the rear of the cave.

I slid to the ground, blinked hard to clear away the stars in time to see Jimmy shove the howler in the chest. The beast fell back several paces. Jimmy's eyes blazed—just as I'd imagined they might—red at the center. Fangs flashed. He snarled like a rabid animal, and I tensed, expecting him to spring forward and sink those sparkly whites into the Nephilim's neck.

Instead, he placed one hand on the howler's head, the other on its shoulder, and yanked the beast in two like the wishbone on a chicken.

CHAPTER 7

Blood sprayed everywhere, turning the dirt floor black, my white shoes red, speckling my shirt and my face.

Jimmy dropped the howler's head, and it landed on the ground with a sickening thud, bouncing a few feet before stopping with the human nose pointing skyward through the overgrown, bestial dark hair. The body stayed upright for several seconds, still pumping blood toward the ceiling in a bright crimson stream.

Why hadn't I thought of that? I'd been stuck on weapons—knives, swords, saws. I hadn't learned yet to think outside the box when it came to killing.

Would my superior dhampir strength have been enough to tear a Nephilim in two? I doubted it. Most likely the superhuman powers of a vampire were necessary.

Covered in blood, Jimmy stared at the howler. Fists clenching and unclenching, he licked his lips.

All that blood. How could he resist?

My chest began to burn as I held my breath, waiting for him to lean over and put his mouth beneath the slowly dying stream like a child with the garden hose on a hot summer day.

I drew in a lungful of air, wincing at the pain in my ribs. They'd heal, probably in the next few minutes, but right now—

"Ouch."

I should have kept my mouth shut. Jimmy's head jerked in my direction. The red light at the center of his eyes had faded, his fangs retracted. He would have looked exactly like the boy I'd loved, if not for the blood all over his face.

His mouth formed the word *Lizzy*, then he held out his red-slicked hands and cringed. Before I could say or do anything, he ran, straight past me and into the depths of the cave in a blur of speed that my eyes could barely track.

I forced myself to stand, retrieve the flashlight, and follow him. In the distance something large hit a water surface. I followed the scent of rain to another, smaller cavern, which contained a pond.

In the distance, thunder rumbled. Water trickled down the rock face, making gentle, peaceful music, in direct contrast to the sight of Jimmy bobbing in the center, scrubbing frantically at the blood on his face, his neck, and his hands.

I really wanted to jump in, too, but with Jimmy channeling Lady Macbeth, I figured I'd better wait, so I took a seat on the edge.

Jimmy went under, then he stayed there so long I nearly went in and hauled him out. At last he burst above the surface, flinging droplets every which way.

"What are you doing here?" He faced the rock wall, rubbing at his skin, even though I didn't see any more blood.

"What do you think?" I asked. "We're in a war, San-ducci, and I'm a little short on soldiers."

"I won't be any good to you."

"You looked pretty good a few minutes ago. I'd say you've still got it."

He shook his head, and his shoulders slumped. "I've been trying to beat the monster back. I thought I had it under control, then I saw that thing hit you and—"

"You saved me. What's so wrong about that?"

"I wanted to drink its blood, Lizzy."

"I know," I said softly.

"I can never leave here while I want that, and I'm starting to think that I'll never be able to *stop* wanting it."

"Maybe Sawyer—" I began.

Jimmy spun around. "No."

They never had gotten along. I'd never been sure why, though I had my theories.

"He knows things," I said.

"If I let him mess with my head, I'll end up crazier than I already am."

"I don't think he'd—"

"No, Lizzy."

Since I didn't know where Sawyer was anyway, I let it go.

Jimmy studied my face, then as if someone had cued the sound effects, one loud, earthshaking burst of thunder rattled the earth. "You came here to kill me."

I hesitated, then told him the truth. "Maybe. I don't know."

"I've been feeding on people."

"No one's dead." I couldn't believe I was using Summer's argument.

And speaking of Summer, where was she? I didn't have time to go on a fairy hunt right now. I had a very strong feeling that if I turned my back on Jimmy, he'd be gone.

"Yet," he said, taking my side of the argument.

"You said you'd been trying to control the—" I paused, uncertain what to call the part of him the strega had awoken.

"Monster. Beast. Vampire. Thing. Say it!" His voice bounced off the walls of the cavern, full of both anger and pain.

"Fine," I said. "How do you control your inner bloodsucker?"

"I don't know. Being near people . . ." He shrugged, his wet shirt clinging to his wet body. "It's too hard. I can hear your pulse, the blood streaming through your veins." He put his hands over his ears, then let them slowly fall back into the water. "It's deafening."

"So you came here because it's isolated?"

"Not isolated enough," he muttered. "But yeah. I'd been here before, searched these caves."

"For what?"

"The howler. Always bugged me that I never found him."

"He found you this time." Probably figured Jimmy was after him again and decided to end things once and for all.

Jimmy seemed calmer, so I emptied my pockets—cell phone, money, et cetera—then jumped into the pool, shoes and all. They were pretty much ruined anyway.

He tensed. "What are you doing?"

I didn't answer, just ducked beneath the water and began to scrub at my face, neck, hair, as he had.

When I came up, Jimmy sat on the edge of the pool. "You shouldn't have come after me," he said. "I didn't want you to see me like this."

"I already have."

He closed his eyes; his lips tightened. "How could

you stand to be near me after what I did? How could you have—"

"Touched you?" I swam closer. "Made love to you?"

"Why did you?" he whispered.

I'd needed to drown out the bad memories with good ones. I'd hoped that he could get past all that had happened, all that he'd done, if I pretended that I'd gotten past it. But when I'd woken the morning after, Jimmy had been gone. One of the things Jimmy was very good at—besides sex—was leaving.

I didn't want to bring up the time I'd spent as Jimmy's captive in the strega's lair. Those recollections would do neither one of us any good.

Instead, I set my hands on his knees. His eyes sprang open. As always, whenever we got near each other, we had a hard time thinking with our heads and ignoring other more interesting parts of our anatomy.

My palms slid over his thighs, the clenching muscles like stone against my fingertips. He smelled like rain, different yet still the same. I stepped between his legs, looked into his face. He tried to scoot back. Maybe get to his feet and run away again, I don't know. Off balance, he tipped forward, and all it took was a tiny tug for him to join me.

His body bumped mine, here and there, then here again as the water brought us together and apart.

He gained his feet; I did, too, so close my breasts slid across his chest. I lost my footing, nearly went under, and he grabbed me. We froze, but only for an instant. Then we were kissing as if we'd been separated for a decade.

I don't know what got into me. I hadn't planned to kiss him, to touch him. I hadn't had any sort of plan at all.

But once I did, it seemed right to show him that some things hadn't changed. That *this* hadn't changed. We only had to be near each other to want, only had to brush against each other to need.

Familiar yet forever exciting, his mouth met mine. Tongues touched, hands wandered. I shoved mine under what was left of his shirt, warmed my chilled fingers against him, learning again the contours of his skin.

His erection pressed into my stomach, warm where I was cold. The kiss melted toward more; his mouth traced my jaw, my neck; he mouthed first one nipple, then the other, through the gauze of my soaked shirt.

I couldn't help it, I lifted my feet, wrapped my thighs around his hips, and pressed us together through several layers of soaked clothing. The fit was close, but not quite there.

As if knowing what I wanted, needed, probably because he wanted it, too, he swung me around until my back was against the side of the pool, then ground us together, even as his mouth opened, taking more of me, his tongue pressing, laving, teasing.

I arched, gasping, begging. Against me he pulsed, the rhythmic beat calling my own. The cave echoed with the rasp of our breathing and the lap of the water upon the rock face, the two sounds syncopated, nearly as arousing as the heat of his body and the pulse of his heart.

He pressed his face to the curve of my neck. Inhaling deeply, as if he wanted to memorize my scent. Right now I probably smelled like—

Blood.

I stiffened, even as he licked my skin, grazed the damp flesh with his teeth, took a fold into his mouth and suckled.

Images flickered—other women in his arms, other

men. The taste of the blood, the sexual pull of it. The desire to feed, to devour, to possess, the struggle not to kill.

I felt everything as if those feelings were mine. I tasted the blood; I wanted it, too. I wanted him to feed on me while he took me, hard against the wall, the orgasm made stronger by the draining of my life into his mouth.

I shuddered and pushed at his shoulders. Without any hesitation, he let me go.

"You saw?" he murmured.

My eyes narrowed. He'd done that on purpose.

"Did you think I'd be disgusted?" I asked. "That I wouldn't understand? That isn't you, Jimmy."

His lips curved into a humorless smile. "The strega's dead. Who else could it be?"

"I felt your struggle. You didn't—" I paused. "Did you?"

"Didn't what?" He looked at me, one quick glance and then away. "Force them? I never have to force anyone. Once I drink from them a few times, they'll do anything I want."

"Excuse me?"

He hauled himself out of the pool; his clothes dripped enough water onto the dirt floor of the cave to create a puddle of mud. "Remember the strega's harem?"

How could I forget? The women had behaved like something out of a sci-fi movie—robots on parade.

"The more a vampire feeds on someone, the more they're tied to him."

I sloshed to the side of the pool as my mind mulled over Jimmy's words. Was that why I couldn't seem to let him go? How many times had he fed on me in Manhattan? I couldn't remember.

Except I'd staked him in that glass tower, had planned

to stake him again, until, at the death of the strega, Jimmy had snapped out of his evil twin persona. I wouldn't have been able to hurt him if he were capable of controlling me.

And the undeniable attraction I had for him dated from way back. Even when he'd broken my heart, walked out of my life, I'd never been able to forget him. That I couldn't now was just more of the same, not some new mind control brought about by his sinking his fangs into me one too many times.

I hoisted myself out of the water as a sudden thought drove out the others. "If vampires can control humans by feeding on them, that means they could take over the earth."

"I think that's what Daddy had planned."

"Why hasn't it happened already?" I asked. "I'm sure there are plenty of bloodsuckers out there; they're feeding at will, so how is it that the whole world isn't one big vampire harem?"

"Because most vampires kill. Once they start feeding, they can't stop. They don't want to."

"So what was wrong with the strega?"

"He was powerful enough to control himself."

I tilted my head. "So can you."

He threw up his hands; droplets of water smacked me in the face. "If that were true, Lizzy, I wouldn't be here."

"You aren't killing people, that's control. If you've managed to do that much in a month, eventually you'll be able to stop the vampire urges altogether."

"Maybe," he murmured. "But I can't take that chance. For all I know, the more I feed, the less human I'll get."

He could be right.

"These things take time," I said.

"We don't have time. You need me now."

"It appears we've been granted a reprieve."

He frowned. "What?"

"Did you ever hear the rumor that by killing the leader of the darkness we could end Doomsday?"

"You can't end it. Doomsday is inevitable."

"Fine," I said. "Then postpone it."

Jimmy shook his head, but he was thinking. "Reverse the prophecy, reverse the results. It makes sense." He smacked his hands together in frustration. "I should have thought of that."

"Wouldn't have mattered, I'd have killed the strega anyway."

He remained silent for several seconds, then, "What's it like out there?" He jerked his head toward the mouth of the cave.

"Calmer than it should be if chaos were reigning."

"All this means is that they'll have to kill you to start Doomsday all over again."

I shrugged. "They were trying to kill me anyway. They're trying to kill all of us."

Jimmy pressed his palms to his eyes. "I've got to get rid of this thing inside of me. You need help."

"What I need is you healthy, sane, at the top of your game."

"What if I never get there?"

I didn't answer. I couldn't leave him in this cave indefinitely; I probably shouldn't leave him here at all. But what was I going to do with him?

"Jimmy, I have to have the seers' contact information that you got from Ruthie."

"You mean the ones I stole out of her mind while she was sleeping?"

Besides being a dhampir, Jimmy was also a dream walker. He could slip into a person's dreams, steal their memories, their knowledge, their secrets, and leave no trace that he'd ever been there. That he'd been compelled to dream walk, along with everything else, didn't seem much comfort to him at all.

"If you hadn't," I said, "we'd be in trouble. I need that information."

Luckily he'd begun to remember things the strega had made him forget soon after the miserable bastard had died.

"You couldn't just ask her when you 'see' her?" He made quotation marks in the air around the word *see*.

"I haven't had a visit from Ruthie since I got home."

I left out the woman of smoke and the amulet. He had enough problems without mine.

Jimmy frowned. "How did you find me?"

"Summer saw you in Barnaby's Gap and here we are."

"Jesus." He rubbed his forehead. "You came together?"

"Yes."

He lowered his hand. "Where is she?"

"In the car, I think."

"Please tell me you haven't been comparing notes."

I wrinkled my nose. "We have better things to talk about than your sexual prowess, Sanducci. She is, after all, a DK. I'm a seer, and even though I killed the last leader of the darkness, that just means there's a new one on the way. We need to replenish the federation and quick."

"How?"

"I have no idea."

"Some of the kids Ruthie had at her place were probably future federation members. She always took on the problem kids, the ones with too much imagination, the ones who lied, the ones who had problems staying with families because weird things always happened around them. That kind of stuff usually translates to special powers."

"Those kids are too young for this," I said.

"We may have no choice."

I shook my head. There was no way I was sending teenagers after demons. Unless I had to.

God, I hoped I didn't have to.

"The names, Jimmy."

He strode out of the cavern. I hurried after. All I needed was for him to take off again.

But I saw him turn and disappear down another stone hallway in the opposite direction of the exit. A few hundred yards away I found him in a cavern along with his duffel, a brand-new sleeping bag, a fire pit, canteen, and other evidence that he'd been living here. He'd already begun to strip.

"What are you doing?"

"Putting on dry clothes. You want some?"

I shook my head, unable to make my mouth move as he peeled off his tattered shirt and then his pants. He was the same beautiful, sun-bronzed shade all over. The sight of all that skin made me want to lick him like an ice-cream cone.

Hell. I turned around.

"You should get out of those wet things," he called.

"That's what they all say."

He laughed. The sound gave me hope. I hadn't heard Jimmy laugh with true humor since long before Manhattan.

A sheet of paper appeared next to my face. On it were names, addresses—both snail and e-mail—along with phone numbers.

"Thanks." I took it.

Because each seer worked independently with his or her own psychic connection and personal contingent of

DKs, there'd rarely been any need for the leader of the federation to contact them. According to Ruthie, when a new leader appeared, the seers would come to him or her once it was safe, to pledge their allegiance.

"They aren't going to be there," Jimmy said. "Everyone's in hiding. I blabbed their identities to the enemy."

"*Blabbing* isn't exactly the term I'd use."

"They're all dead because of me."

"Not all."

He cast me a look.

"Are you going to give up?" I asked. "Just lie down and die?"

He glanced away, and I got a very bad feeling. "Why did you write this down?"

Jimmy shrugged.

"You didn't think I'd get here in time."

"In time for what?" he asked, but I knew.

"In time for you to tell me the names before you killed yourself."

"You always were a smart girl."

Jimmy had been taking the blame for Ruthie's death, and everyone else's, since he'd snapped out of his evil twin phase. Certainly he'd been the one who'd compromised their identities, but he hadn't meant to. Jimmy had adored Ruthie as much as I did. He never would have revealed her identity to the bad guys if he'd been able to stop himself.

However, she was still dead—something he'd pointed out to me often enough—and all the regret in the world wasn't going to bring Ruthie back. Neither would Jimmy killing himself.

"Don't do it, Jimmy."

"I can't." He sounded disgusted. "And not because I'm gutless, but because of what I am, how I have to be killed."

"Twice in the same way," I murmured.

"Every time I manage the first death, I lose consciousness; I die, and then I can't kill myself again. I wake up completely healed." His eyes met mine. "Someone's going to have to do it for me."

"Not me," I blurted.

He shrugged. "I know someone who will."

I opened my mouth to tell him that I needed him. That I couldn't win this fight without him. That he couldn't die and leave me alone with the monsters.

Before I could, the room spun, lights that weren't there flashed. My stomach rolled.

Not now, I thought.

But as soon as I closed my eyes, I had a vision.

CHAPTER 8

A small room full of people holding hands and chanting. Candles flickered; the faces did, too.

Woman, wolf, woman. Man, wolf, man. Over and over the human guise gave way to that of a beast.

I stared so hard my head began to ache, trying to remember the appearance of each and every one, but there were so many.

"Kill them all," they whispered as one. "The earth will be *ooouurrss*."

The last word became a howl, and this time when their faces went wolf, they stayed that way. Their bodies contorted. Hands and feet became paws, spines crackled and shifted, fur covered every inch of skin.

I'd seen werewolves before, killed them, too. Silver bullets worked as well as the legends said.

However, werewolves were bigger than their animal counterparts, with glowing yellow eyes and creepily human shadows. These wolves looked just like wolves, except I'd seen them shape-shift and knew better.

Luceres.

The word whispered through my head. I'd never

heard it before, didn't know what it meant beyond a name for the Nephilim I was seeing.

The beasts began to mill around the room, agitated, revealing as they paced what made them different.

They didn't have tails. That oughta make them easy to spot.

Suddenly, the largest of the group leaped through the window, and glass rained down. The others followed, springing gracefully through the now wide-open portal.

Beneath a moon-drenched sky, the luceres ran as a pack. I'd hoped for a nice open field, no sign of a house or a town. Maybe even a sign that read: NOWHERE, WYOMING—POPULATION 3. But nothing was ever that easy.

Instead, the wolves raced through suburban streets. The houses had been recently built; bicycles, tricycles, and Flintstones cars cluttered the driveways.

"Where are you?" I muttered.

As I watched, fireworks exploded in the distance, illuminating a familiar skyline, the resulting thunder rattling the earth.

Then I was falling out of the vision, waking up on the floor of the cave nauseous, sore, and dizzy. My clothes were still soaked, cool against my flushed skin. My shoes squelched when I wiggled my toes. The earth beneath me shook with thunder, the sound reminiscent of the fireworks I'd viewed hundreds of miles away near the—

"Sears Tower," I muttered.

"Chicago."

Summer leaned in the doorway. I stayed right where I was, too out of it to sit up. From prior experience I knew the dizzy nausea would pass; I just had to keep my head still for a few minutes.

I received information in one of three ways. Ruthie

spoke if a Nephilim came near; she told me what they were in visions like the one I'd just had; and she also came to me in dreams to answer what questions she could. There were rules about ghost whispering, and some information she couldn't reveal—usually what I really needed to know.

Visions always left me weak and loopy, but they also imparted the most useful information.

"Ever heard of a lucere?" I asked.

Summer came closer, then sat on the ground and drew up her legs so she could rest her chin on her knees. I wondered if she'd practiced that adorable pose in front of a mirror.

Rain trickled into the pool, pinging against the surface with a quick rat-a-tat-tat. Outside it was pouring, yet Summer was as dry as the desert in July.

"A lucere is a type of lycanthrope," she answered.

"I got that when they changed from people into wolves."

Her blue eyes narrowed. "You want the information or you want to be a smart guy?"

I didn't answer because obviously I wanted both, and after a few seconds, she went on.

"Luceres roved near Rome. Some call them 'lucumones,' derived from *loco*."

"So they're crazier than the average werewolf?"

"Yes. In ancient times luceres would form tribes or packs and wipe out entire villages."

Kill them all.

"I think they're still following that plan," I murmured.

"Luceres shift following a ceremony." Which coincided with what I'd seen in my vision. "Once they decimated an area, the land, the homes, the businesses became theirs. They'd send a part of the tribe on to the next town they coveted, forming a new pack, blanketing entire areas with their kind."

"An ancient Roman version of a hostile takeover."

"So to speak," Summer agreed. "Some scholars believe the first lucere was King Lycaeon, a Greek king—"

"How could the first lucere be Greek," I interrupted, "then wind up in Rome?"

"Didn't all roads lead to Rome back then?"

"You tell me."

"Are you insinuating I'm old?" she asked.

"I'm *saying* you're prehistoric."

"Sticks and stones," Summer murmured. "I don't age, and you will."

She had me there.

Fairies didn't grow old; neither did Nephilim. Breeds were born and therefore died. They aged, but because they rarely got sick and healed all wounds, they didn't age as badly or as quickly as humans. I had no idea what I was, but definitely not ageless.

"Getting back to Lycaeon," I prompted.

"The myth was brought to Rome by Greek colonists. When they were confronted with lycanthropes, they called them by the name they knew. Lucere."

"And the legend?"

"King Lycaeon was visited by passing gods, but he didn't quite believe they were who they said, so he devised a test. He served them dishes laced with human flesh, a major insult. Being gods, they discovered the deception and changed Lycaeon into a werewolf, a more proper form for devouring people. From his name, we get lycanthrope."

Legends of supernatural beings came about as people tried to make sense of what didn't. The Nephilim had been hunting the earth since time began, which meant the luceres had been here since the angels fell and mated with humans. They just hadn't been given their name until the story of Lycaeon began to circulate.

"You didn't tell me the most important fact." I sat up, thrilled when my head didn't pound, and my stomach didn't roll. "How do I kill them?"

"Pierce their hearts with fire. I'd suggest a burning arrow."

"Do I look like Robin Hood to you?"

Summer didn't reply. What could she say? I'd asked the question; it wasn't her fault I didn't like the answer.

My archery skills were as adequate as the next woman's, which meant pretty damn inadequate. The last time I'd touched a bow it had been to shoot at a target in high school. I hadn't been terrible, but I doubted I was capable of nailing a werewolf's heart from twenty yards, let alone a dozen of them.

"There's no other way?" I asked.

Summer spread her hands and shrugged.

"Swell."

Regardless of my lack of skill with the necessary weapons, I needed to get to Chicago right away. I'd seen fireworks, which could mean two nights away, but could just as easily mean one. A lot of big cities shoot off their rockets on the third. I contemplated Summer; maybe I should send her.

She stared right back, biting her lip. "There's a pile of ashes out there," she began.

I was so glad to hear that the howler's body had disintegrated that I nearly forgot to tell Summer what it was.

"Hey!" she shouted.

"Oh. Sorry. Remains of the howler."

"There was one?" She let out a relieved breath. "For a second I thought—"

"Shit!" I glanced around. "Where's Jimmy?"

"You found him?"

"Shit, shit, shit!" I jumped to my feet. Everything that had been in the cave before was gone.

"What happened?" Summer asked. "What did you say?" She grabbed me by the arm. "What did you do?"

I yanked out of her grasp. "I have the information. That's why we came."

"And now you just forget about him and go on your merry way?"

"Did I say that?" We had to find Jimmy. He was a danger to himself and others.

"Was he . . . himself?" she asked.

"Yes." I took a breath. "And no. He talked about suicide."

Summer's brow furrowed. "But he's a dhampir. He—"

"I wish I had something he touched," I interrupted. "I might be able to see where he is."

Summer held out her arm. At my curious expression, her eyes widened with false naïveté. "Something he touched."

"Do you *want* me to slug you?" I asked.

"You can try."

I turned away. I didn't have time for a catfight right now. Maybe later.

My gaze wandered the cave. He'd left nothing behind. No map, no notes—

I paused, practically laughed out loud, then reached into my pocket for the list. As soon as I touched it, I got a flash of a face and stilled. "He's gone to Sawyer."

Summer cursed.

"Luckily, he won't find him." Because if Jimmy wanted to die, Sawyer would be happy to oblige.

"What if Sawyer came back?" Summer asked.

Now I cursed, resisting the urge to run from the cave,

jump in the car, and head for the nearest plane to New Mexico. I had to think, then act. I had to decide what was best for the world before I did anything.

Though I desperately wanted to follow Jimmy, to find some way to convince him that he needed to live, if not for me, then for the human beings he'd sworn to protect, there was still the problem of luceres in Chicago.

I sighed. I didn't have much choice. We all had our strengths, and in this case, Summer's strengths outweighed my emotions.

"You go after Jimmy," I said. "I'll head to Chicago."

"Keys are in the car." Her voice was matter-of-fact. She'd known my decision before I had. "Put a scratch on it and we *will* have words."

I had no doubt we'd have more than words, but that was a concern for another day.

With Summer's gift of flight, she'd be able to beat Jimmy to New Mexico. Even though he had the superior speed of a dhampir, a commercial airplane was still faster with the added incentive of not having to use his feet. Summer could meet Jimmy at the airport, or on the road, or wherever the hell she wanted to, as long as she caught up to him before he reached Sawyer.

"Do whatever you have to do," I said.

Her gaze flicked to mine. "Anything?"

"Anything," I repeated. "Just keep him alive."

CHAPTER 9

Time in that cave had moved a lot faster than I'd thought. By the time I retrieved my cell phone and the other items I'd left by the pool, then made my way outside, dawn had broken. The air smelled of rain; the pavement was soaked, strewn with torn leaves, and a lot of tree limbs were down. I guessed the thunder and the lightning hadn't just been for show.

"How long was I in there?" I demanded.

Summer shrugged, her expression sheepish. "I fell asleep. Figured you'd wake me when you got back."

Huh. I guess fairies did need to sleep.

"Lucky I wasn't depending on you to save my ass."

"Lucky," she agreed, her voice perfectly level so I just knew she was being sarcastic.

I left by car, she left by air; and ten hours later, I-94 spilled me into Chicago. I'd managed to discover, through judicious use of my cell phone, that Chicago's fireworks were held on the third of July and shot off at Navy Pier. Which was both good news and bad news.

Good news in that I should have time to stop the luceres from running free if I could find the appropriate suburb in—

I glanced at my watch. "Three hours."

Bad news—I still wasn't sure where they were and my knowledge of the Chicago area was mighty slim despite having lived less than a hundred miles north of the city for most of my life.

While a lot of Milwaukeeans made the trip to Chicago regularly to shop, to eat, to go to concerts and plays, I'd been content with my own city on the lake. I'd never traveled much until lately. In the past month I'd visited more states than I'd visited before in my life.

Now that I was here, and I knew I wasn't too late, some of the panicky edge faded. I'd arrived too late in Hardeyville, and I still relived what had happened there in the darkest part of the night.

I found it hard to accept that some things were meant to happen, some people were meant to die, and there was nothing I, or anyone else in the federation, could do about it.

That I'd been able to stop the werewolves in Hardeyville from moving on to the next town on their hit parade of horrors was small consolation to the dead who still danced through my dreams.

I'd run through every phone number on Jimmy's list. No one answered. I hadn't expected them to. The seers were in hiding, which meant they weren't going to pick up at any of their numbers or hang around their known locations. If they did, they were just asking for it.

So I'd also stopped at a wireless-ready Starbucks and sent a blanket e-mail informing the remaining seers of all the latest Doomsday developments and ordering them to check in via the Internet until further notice.

I wasn't sure how many of them were going to be able to access their accounts "underground," but I had to try. In truth, Jimmy's list was probably as useless to me right now as Jimmy was.

I assumed that each seer was still in touch somehow with all their DKs, continuing to give them assignments and thwarting the Nephilim's plans as best they could with their decimated forces. Just because we'd put chaos on hold didn't mean the demons weren't still out there doing their demon dance.

My phone rang as I stopped to get a map. I snatched it up, hoping that one of the seers had decided to take a chance and return my call. No such luck.

"Sawyer's not here," Summer said, not bothering with hello any more than I had.

The weight on my chest lightened. "Jimmy?"

"Not here, either."

For an instant, I believed one of my problems was solved, until I thought about it for more than a second. The weight dropped back with a thud that left me gasping.

"What's wrong?" Summer asked. "I'll just wait for Jimmy to show and then—"

"They might have gone into the mountains." Silence followed my statement. "Summer?"

"I'm here." Her voice was faint. She understood what going into the mountains with Sawyer meant. The last time I had, I'd definitely been sorry.

The mountains were sacred. They were considered magic. Sawyer practiced a lot of magic, most of it black.

Though the mountains were part of the Dinetah, the ancient land of the Navajo, in truth they belonged to Sawyer, and he pretty much did whatever the hell he wanted to in them. He'd certainly done me. No telling what he might take it into his head to do to Jimmy—especially if Jimmy asked him to.

"Find him," I ordered. I wasn't sure which man I was talking about. Right now, either one would do.

"I will."

It felt strange to be working with Summer. Stranger still to realize that she was the one I trusted most in this world to do what needed to be done.

Summer was Jimmy's best bet for survival, because no matter how I felt about him, I had other responsibilities, and if those responsibilities would be better served by killing him, I'd do it. I had before.

"Come across anything out of the ordinary?" she asked.

"Not yet."

"If you see a wolf, you should probably shoot it."

"You think?"

"With a flaming arrow," she reminded me.

Where was I going to get flaming arrows so close to a holiday?

"I have supplies in my trunk," Summer said.

Sometimes I swore she could read minds, though she denied it.

"What kind of supplies?"

"You haven't looked?"

"I've been a little busy."

"Make sure no one else is around when you open it. You could get arrested."

"Terrific." If I'd gotten stopped for speeding, which had been a distinct possibility since I'd hauled ass all night, I cringed to think what the cop would have seen if he or she had decided to pop the trunk.

I'd have wound up in jail since I didn't have the ability to shoot magic "forget me" dust from my fingertips like Summer did. That lack was becoming more and more annoying as time passed, but I still wasn't willing to sleep with Summer's fairy friend to get it. Not yet anyway. Who knows what I'd have to do eventually.

"Do the luceres change back into humans when the sun comes up?" I asked. Regular werewolves did.

"They don't have to," she said. "Luceres are ruled by a spell and not the moon. They can stay in wolf form as long as they want."

Which meant I could keep hunting once dawn broke, if they cooperated and remained wolves. However, I doubted the luceres would continue to run around with ears and no tail once they knew I was in town and capable of killing them.

Sure, I could probably identify most of the luceres since I'd seen their human faces in my vision, but shooting people—even if they weren't people—with burning arrows tended to make *me* seem like the psychotic murderer. Go figure. Better to finish this business tonight.

After filling the tank, I pulled the Impala around the back of the station to a grassy area, which I assumed was used to give any pets a chance to relieve themselves. Right now it was deserted, so I opened the trunk and found all sorts of goodies.

Rifles, shotguns, pistols, and ammunition for each one. Swords and knives in a vast array of metallic shades—silver, gold, bronze, and copper. But the best find of all was a crossbow.

I lifted it gently, almost reverently. A crossbow was more accurate than a compound bow, which was why, in Wisconsin anyway, only disabled hunters or those over sixty-five years old could get a permit to hunt with them. Combine a crossbow with a fit young man and deer didn't have a sporting chance. I didn't think they had much of a chance anyway, but no one had asked me.

I wasn't sure what the rules were on crossbows in Illinois, but it didn't matter. Owning a crossbow wasn't illegal, only hunting without a permit for one was. And since I was hunting people who'd turned into wolves . . . well, if anyone caught me, I'd have more problems than my lack of a license.

Next to the crossbow lay a quiver of strangely made arrows—they appeared wrapped in white linen—and several bottles filled with clear liquid.

I took a whiff and nearly choked. "Gasoline."

Sheesh. I was lucky no one had rear-ended me.

Considering Jimmy drove a Hummer with a similar cache of weaponry, I had to think all DKs were similarly decked out.

I shut the trunk, then climbed inside the car and made a wide turn until the skyline of Chicago became visible. Closing my eyes, I recalled my vision. To have seen the Sears Tower and the fireworks at Navy Pier in the way that I'd seen them, the luceres had to have been—

"Right around here." I tapped the map.

Many Chicago suburbs were upper middle class and similar to the place I'd seen in my vision. I had little choice but to drive around and hope something struck a familiar chord. In a tiny hamlet called Lake Vista something did.

The sun was falling fast, darkness only an hour away at most. The panic had returned, pulsing behind my eyes like the low drone of flies on a hot summer day.

Lake Vista wasn't truly a suburb, more of a development—a huge one—situated outside all the other city limits. I had a feeling they'd applied, or would apply soon, for a charter to create the village of Lake Vista.

If they lived long enough.

I toured the streets—up, down, crosswise—and at last I saw the building where the luceres had "become."

Not wanting to be too obvious, to scare them off, if that were possible, I parked a block away and strolled in that direction. From the side of the building, I could see the city skyline in the distance. When I turned and glanced back toward Lake Vista, the array of houses, driveways, bikes, and trikes made me shiver.

This was the place.

A quick glance inside revealed an empty building. A small sign named it LAKE VISTA COMMUNITY CENTER.

Since I needed to move on before someone became suspicious, I headed for the Impala. The suburb seemed nearly deserted, many of the families no doubt headed for the lakefront and the spectacular fireworks display.

Those who'd decided to forgo the crowds, whether from exhaustion, too many children, or a genuine dislike of fireworks, had either gone to bed or were watching television in the darkened houses where blue-white lights flickered against the windows.

I saw the luceres' plan. Wipe out the ones who'd stayed home, then lie in wait for those who'd gone away. It was a good plan—if you were a pack of evil half-demons bent on murder.

Sliding behind the wheel of the Impala, I scanned the area for a place I could lie in wait myself. Lake Vista had a view of the lake on one side, hence the name. But on the backside lay an anomaly, a great towering grove of trees—as out of place here as the wolves would be.

We didn't call people from Illinois flatlanders for fun. Well, actually it was fun, but Illinois was also really, really flat. Until you got to the Mississippi.

We weren't anywhere near the Mississippi.

Illinois had once been prairie; in a lot of areas it still was. Farms surrounded by cornfields, silos, and massive electrical poles were the only structures with any height for miles once you left Chicago behind.

In Chicago there were plenty of skyscrapers, and even some bluffs near the lake, but there weren't too many trees. I wondered where in hell these had come from.

Suddenly I understood why the luceres had picked Lake Vista for their massacre. They could run into those woods as wolves if they needed to, then pop out the other side as human beings.

I made my way around to a dirt track that led into the tree cover. The Impala rocked on the rough terrain, and the carriage scraped against dirt, even as dry grass whispered against the bumpers.

I made it to the trees, slid the Impala between two of them, and the shadows closed around us with a near audible sigh. The dying sun flickered through the lush, swaying leaves and light danced across the windshield.

Behind me civilization loomed—suburb, city, freeway upon freeway—but in front of me lay a seemingly endless forest. Sure, if I kept going I'd hit another suburb or a highway that led to one. But right now I could see nothing but trees, not a flash of a car, not the faint grayish-white wash of cement. There could be anything out there.

"Even the big bad wolf." I laughed, but the sound was forced. I'd seen the big bad wolf. He did not wear Gramma's nightdress, nightcap, or glasses. He wore nothing but fur, and then he killed you.

I reconnoitered the area, searching for the best place to stand so that my shots would not be sent wide by low-hanging branches, but I could still remain far enough in the shadows so no one would see me if they happened to glance out of their windows. Once I found such a location, I doused the arrows with gasoline and built a pile so they'd be easy to reload.

All I had left to do was wait. I listened for the wind, thrilled to discover it had died, almost as if it were waiting, too.

I had no warning—not a shuffle of feet against the earth, not a whisper of a breath, but suddenly that invisible target on my back burned. Slowly, I turned.

In the depths of the trees, where the light had faded and the shadows ruled, a single pair of eyes flared. Too short to be human, too soon to be a lucere, nevertheless, I knew a wolf when I saw one.

Only that single set of eyes; was this a scout? Did the luceres plan to enter Lake Vista through the woods as I'd feared? I didn't want to shoot what appeared to be people with burning arrows, but I would if I had to.

However, my arrows were on the ground and so was the unloaded crossbow. I could make a grab for them, but I doubted I'd be able to get off a shot before the wolf was on me.

My Glock was in the car, useless against the luceres, but my knife rested in a sheath at my waist. I put my palm on the hilt. The weapon might at least slow the beast down.

The wolf snorted—not anger, more like amusement—and I stilled.

"Come into the light," I murmured, and when it did, I lowered my hand. "Sawyer."

I should have known.

CHAPTER 10

"What are you doing here?" I demanded.

The black wolf stepped completely out of the shadows. He looked just like a wolf—huge head, long legs, teeth and tail. I could never mistake him for a werewolf—he wasn't large enough and his shadow, when there was one, reflected only his animal form.

Sawyer was a skinwalker—both witch and shapeshifter—a powerful medicine man who walked a fine line between good and evil. He'd been cast out by the Navajo, who were very wiggy about the supernatural.

Sometimes one of his people tried to kill him. They never succeeded—it was damn near impossible to kill a skinwalker—which only added to his spooky-ass legend.

Long ago Sawyer's mother, the woman of smoke, had put a curse upon him. He could not leave the Dinetah as a man, which made it damn difficult for him to do anything but drool anywhere else.

The wolf was his spirit animal, but he could change into just about anything, as long as he wore a robe that reflected its likeness. For Sawyer, his skin was his robe. Upon it he'd tattooed the images of every animal he wished to become.

He strolled to my pile of arrows, sniffed, sneezed, and rolled his eyes in my direction. Then he sat and waited.

I opened my mouth again to demand answers, then snapped it shut. Despite his many powers, Sawyer wasn't a talking wolf. So far, I hadn't met anyone who was—one of the few disadvantages of shape-shifting, along with that annoying lack of opposable thumbs. I headed for the Impala.

In my duffel I carried a silk robe in all the shades of midnight: blue, purple, black with sparkles of silver. A gift from Sawyer, or perhaps my own personal curse, I hadn't yet tried it out. Guess now was the time.

The thing was bunched into a corner of the bag, beneath my clothes, gun, and toiletries. I held it up and the luscious material tumbled downward, revealing the shimmering image of a wolf—there, gone, and then there again.

I glanced at Sawyer, who still sat patiently, panting a little as he stared at me.

"Turn around," I ordered.

He snorted again. His repertoire of commentary was a tad limited in this form. Nevertheless, I could practically hear his thoughts. *Nothing I haven't seen, and touched, and tasted before.*

Which was how I'd gotten into this predicament in the first place. Sex with Sawyer had given me the ability to shape-shift, too.

He needed only to brush his clever fingers across one of the inked images that graced his body, and he would become that animal. Since I'd gotten my power from him, I could shape-shift the same way. Touch a tattoo, become a beast. It was slightly more complicated than that, but not by much.

However, since Sawyer's tattoos appeared on his

human skin, this avenue wasn't open to me now. Luckily—I clenched my fingers more tightly around the purple silk—there was another way.

I glanced at the western horizon. No time for modesty; I had maybe half an hour of daylight left. I needed to talk to Sawyer, and then fight the invasion of the luceres.

Quickly I lost my jewelry and clothes—I didn't have enough with me to just burst through them—then I spun the robe across my shoulders. As the material settled against my skin, I changed.

A burst of light made me close my eyes. My skin went cold then hot, and I was falling. By the time my hands met the ground they were paws.

In this form, I could think like a human. I could reason; I could plan. I could also kill.

Shape-shifters are stronger, faster, better than their bestial counterparts. We were stronger, faster, and better than humans in a lot of ways, too.

For instance, as a wolf I could see into the damp darkness of the forest much farther than I'd been able to seconds before. I could smell everything, hear so much. In the distance, cars swooshed down a highway. Beneath that tree, a deer had slept.

I shook my head, felt the breeze brush my fur, fought the urge to run until I found that deer and brought it down with ease. My mouth watered. I hadn't eaten since yesterday.

Phoenix.

The word whispered through my head in Sawyer's voice—so deep, so luscious, yet treacherous, it made me shiver.

Sawyer had always called me "Phoenix"; I couldn't ever once remember him calling me "Liz" or "Elizabeth." He'd definitely never called me "baby."

I winced at the memory of Jimmy, then immediately brightened. If Sawyer were here, he wasn't helping Jimmy to die.

He slid along my body, rubbed his snout against mine. As much as I wanted to stick a knife in him most days, in this form we were pack, a connection that sang to me like a siren. I couldn't resist it, even when I knew that following him might get me smashed to death on sharp and dangerous rocks.

How did you find me? I thought.

"Speaking" as animals was a form of telepathy. Words were thoughts; feelings were scents. It's hard to explain.

I will always find you.

Not only did the stone apparently protect me from the *Naye'i,* it was also a homing device. Sawyer sensed where I was whenever I wore it.

I had a visit from your mother. She didn't much care for the turquoise.

His snout opened in a doggy grin, the most amusement I'd seen from Sawyer in any form. I caught the scent of something sweet; he was definitely laughing.

You thought she'd come after me?

Eventually.

Why?

I knew you'd become someone special, Phoenix. Which only meant killing you would be at the top of every Nephilim's to-do list.

Killing me appears to be the new favorite pastime of the next up-and-coming Antichrist wannabe.

His laughter died. *I don't understand.*

Quickly I filled him in on Summer's theory.

Have you ever heard that before?

No, but the fairy's right. Prophecies are guidelines and they can be interpreted many ways. Regardless of if

Doomsday is still in motion or on hiatus, the Nephilim will try to kill you, and the Naye'i *needs to be stopped. We continue on the same way we have been.*

Why did you come looking for me? I asked.

I had a feeling you might need help.

I stared at him for several seconds, suspicious, but who was I to argue with a premonition.

I had a vision, I said. *This place will be wiped out by luceres if we don't do something.*

What do you suggest?

In wolf form, Sawyer wouldn't be able to help me shoot luceres, even if I'd had an extra bow. However . . .

One of the ways to kill a shifter is a fight to the death with another shifter. Healing is accelerated by the shift itself, and if you're dead you can't shift, which means healing a mortal wound . . . ain't gonna happen.

Technically, I could have gone that route myself, shifting then fighting. However, I wasn't the killer Sawyer was. I hadn't been a wolf often enough or long enough to be much more than bad at it.

I'd been concerned that I wouldn't be able to shoot with sufficient speed or accuracy to kill all the luceres. But now that Sawyer was here . . .

I'll blast them as they come out of the window. Any that I miss . . .

Sawyer's gaze swung toward the nearby community center, his strangely light gray eyes assessing the layout. *I won't.*

I had no worries that he wouldn't be able to handle himself. I'd seen Sawyer fight a pack of coyotes once, with a little help from me. He knew exactly what to do when he was outnumbered. The luceres wouldn't stand a chance.

Nearby, a dog began to bark frantically. Several others joined in, and the ruff on the back of my neck stood up. Domestic animals go ballistic in the presence of shape-shifters. They sense our otherness.

They can smell us, I thought.

Sawyer appeared at my side; he lifted his snout, and his fur ruffled. *The breeze is blowing in our direction.*

Which meant the dogs had caught wind of something arriving from the opposite end of Lake Vista.

I caught a whiff of something myself—human with just a dash of beast, the scent of skin with a touch of ozone.

Though I should have shifted back, get dressed, move my ass, I wanted to see them. I needed to know.

With the superior eyesight of my wolf form, I detected a hint of movement. A line of people walked right down the center of the suburban street. Shoulder to shoulder they came, looking like gunslingers in an old Western. Tombstone by way of the Land of Lincoln.

They obviously had no fear of being seen, of being asked what they were doing, why they were here. They believed they would own this town, and even if someone saw them, questioned them, tried to stop them, it wouldn't matter. They'd be killing every living soul soon enough.

I hadn't realized I'd moved toward the Impala, that I'd reached for my human form and become me again until the breeze brushed across skin instead of fur and made me shiver.

Quickly I dressed and moved into position. Sawyer glided past me as the luceres disappeared into the community center. I lifted the first arrow and fitted it into the crossbow. Sawyer sank onto his belly and wiggled through the long grass until he lurked right next to the building.

Darkness fell; candles flickered on the other side of the window. I swore I could hear the low-voiced chants from within. Maybe it was just a sliver of memory from my vision, probably it was the increase in my senses from the absorption of either Jimmy's or Sawyer's powers.

A sudden flare of light and color to the east was followed by the soft pop of the gunpowder, and the first lucere burst through the window in a shower of glass.

Though I was now in human form, and my eyesight was not as good as it had been when I was a wolf, it was still better than most. I could see the dark shadow of the lucere arching toward the ground.

I lit the arrow, let it fly, enjoyed the trail of orange cutting through the night, followed by a soft thunk and then a burst of gray-black ash sprinkling over the grass as the lucere disappeared from this world forever.

Another came through the window, hitting the ground and loping off toward the houses before I could grab a second arrow. Sawyer sprang out of the tall grass, a low blurry shape that moved so quickly he seemed to vanish from one place and reappear in another.

He landed on the back of the lucere and knocked it to the ground. I couldn't see what he was doing, I could only hear the snarling, the growling, then the yelping. Since Sawyer would never yelp, I murmured, "Two down," and fit another arrow into my bow. I lifted the weapon to fire and nearly dropped everything.

Between me and the community center, a column of smoke swirled, faster and faster, until I could no longer follow the morph from wisp to woman.

Suddenly she was there, solid and deadly. Her smile said she'd won even before the battle had begun. It didn't take me long to realize why.

The turquoise was no longer around my neck. Instead, it hung over the rearview mirror of the Impala, where I'd placed it before I'd shape-shifted, then left it forgotten in my hurry to shift back.

No wonder she was smiling. The woman of smoke had been waiting for this.

I loosed the burning arrow. Couldn't hurt. Maybe I'd actually have my first piece of incredible luck, and she'd burst into flames, dying in agony as I roasted marshmallows over her corpse.

I should have known better. Any luck I had was usually bad.

With the speed she'd shown when she'd snatched my knife at Murphy's, the woman of smoke plucked the arrow out of the air and tossed it to the side. The long, dry summer grass began to smolder.

"Uh-oh."

Luceres tumbled out of the window, ran toward the houses. As far as I could tell, Sawyer was still messing with the first one.

"Sawyer!" I shouted, but the woman of smoke lifted her hand like a crossing guard stopping traffic, and the word was flung back down my throat, the sound never reaching the air.

As she stalked toward me, an ice-cold wind that smelled of brimstone singed my nostrils, making my eyes water. I'd never smelled brimstone, but what else could it have been? The scent was hell unleashed, fire, ashes, death, all that was evil, the end of the world come upon us.

I coughed, choked; tears streamed down my face. Then I reached for my knife—at least I'd remembered to lace that back around my waist—but before I could pull it from the sheath her hand closed about my wrist.

Wherever her fingers touched my skin it sizzled, but not with heat, with cold. The sensation reminded me of the pain that followed near frostbite, the aching, the burning, the tingling that occurred when frozen flesh began to warm.

She snapped my wrist, the dry click made by the bone breaking exactly the sound of a twig being crushed beneath a boot in the depths of a winter wood.

As I opened my mouth to scream, she yanked my knife from its sheath and killed me.

CHAPTER 11

One strike straight to my heart, then another in exactly the same place. The woman of smoke knew what I was. Did I have no secrets left?

A horrible, dying gurgle bubbled from my lips, and she laughed, a bizarre sound of both joy and malevolence. Nearby, something howled—a mournful wail of pain and fury.

The *Naye'i* glanced over her shoulder, lips pulling away from her gleaming white teeth into a snarl. She spun, becoming smoke again, before whirling upward and disappearing into the night.

I tumbled to the ground with the knife still embedded in my chest. As my vision faded, more snarls erupted in the distance, and the earth seemed to rattle beneath the heavy thuds of an epic battle.

The air around me went dark, and the world went out like the snuff of a candle's flame beneath the rain.

I woke at Ruthie's place. I wasn't surprised. Not only did I go there when I needed help, but Ruthie often welcomed those who'd died too soon to her own little purgatory. This meant that Ruthie's house was usually filled with children, just as it had been on earth.

Ruthie had run a group home on the south side of Milwaukee. When she'd first opened her doors to stray kids and the occasional dog, Ruthie had been the only African American within thirty miles. She hadn't cared. Amazingly, no one else had, either.

I went through the gate in the white picket fence, strolled up the pristine sidewalk to the green-trimmed white house, and knocked. The music of children's laughter, the trill of their happy voices, rang from inside. The door opened, and there she was—the only mother I'd ever known.

She looked exactly the same as the day she'd died—minus the blood splatter, torn throat, and various bite marks.

"Lizbeth," Ruthie said, and gathered me into her arms.

Despite the knobbiness of her elbows and knees, the boniness of her entire body, Ruthie gave the very best hugs.

She'd taken me in when I was twelve, fresh from another foster home that didn't want me. She'd seemed ancient even then—her lined face the shade of rich coffee, her dark eyes so sharp she saw everything about you, even things you'd spent a lifetime learning to hide.

None of that mattered to Ruthie—where you'd been, what you'd done, who you were. Once she took you in, she never let you go. For throwaway kids, that promise was worth more than money, it was worth our very souls. To be accepted, to know that no matter what happened, Ruthie would love you . . .

We'd have done anything for her.

I was still having a bit of a problem accepting that Ruthie had purposely gone searching for kids who were "special," taking them in and preparing them to become part of the federation. I knew she hadn't had any choice—we were talking about the end of the world—

still, it would have been nice to be chosen for myself and not my psychic abilities.

However, since my psychic abilities were what had, more often than not, gotten me tossed from every foster home I'd been in, being chosen *for* them instead of despite them wasn't the worst thing.

I drew back, and Ruthie let me go. She touched my cheek and worry shadowed her eyes.

"I'm dead, aren't I?"

She sighed and turned away, leaving the door open as an invitation to follow. I trailed after her, down the hall and into the sunshine-bright kitchen, where the large back windows allowed her to watch over the children in the yard.

I counted four. The small number, and lack of a baby carriage, lightened my spirits. The last time I'd been here the place had been bursting with kids I'd failed to save, as well as a tiny bundle that wouldn't stop crying.

That was a memory I'd do just about anything to erase from my brain.

"Sit," Ruthie ordered. "We've got a situation here."

"Me being dead is going to throw a bit of a crimp in our plans. This is gonna start the Doomsday clock ticking all over again."

"You aren't dead," she said.

"The woman of smoke—" I paused, then sat. "You know about her?"

Ruthie gave me one of her patented stares. Ruthie knew about everything, even before she'd become . . .

I wasn't certain what she'd become, but she was definitely more powerful dead than alive. Having her killed had been the strega's first mistake.

"She stabbed me with my own knife." I made a sound of disgust. How lame was that? "Twice in the chest."

I glanced down, thrilled to discover that the weapon

wasn't sticking out of me so that I resembled a shish kebab. My broken wrist appeared to work just fine, as well. I flapped it a few times just to be sure.

Of course no one came here with the wounds they'd died from; that would be too upsetting to the kids, not to mention gross.

"You aren't dead," Ruthie repeated.

"But—"

"Twice in the same way kills a dhampir."

"Right. I—" I stopped, not wanting to say out loud what I'd done to get that talent.

But Ruthie knew. Not talking about my strange gifts didn't make those strange gifts cease to exist.

"We do what we have to do to survive, to fight, to win," she said. "You wouldn't have the power of empathy if you weren't meant to use it, child."

Same thing Summer had said. *Huh.*

"It's because of that empathy you're still alive." At my blank expression, she continued, "You're more than a dhampir, Lizbeth. You're a skinwalker, too."

I lifted a brow. "How do you kill those?"

She lifted her own brow in return. "I'll just keep that to myself."

"But—"

"I know 'bout your temper when it comes to Sawyer. If you'd known how to kill him, you'd have done it already—ten times."

True. No one annoyed me more than Sawyer; no one frightened me more than him, either—unless it was his mother.

"We need him," Ruthie said. "You need him."

As much as I hated to admit it, she was right. Still—

"How can I avoid getting my skinwalker nature snuffed out if I don't know how that can happen?"

"It won't. Skinwalkers are some of the hardest beings

to kill on God's earth. You think Sawyer would still be breathin' otherwise?"

I wasn't the only one who wanted him dead. Sometimes I wondered if there was anyone who actually wanted him alive. Except for Ruthie.

"I still don't like it," I muttered.

"I still don't care."

"Is it true what Summer told me?" I asked. "Doomsday's on hold?"

"Appears to be. The demons are still killing, but—" She spread her gnarled hands. "Not like they used to."

"So we've got some time to regroup."

"I don't know," Ruthie murmured. "I can still feel the evil on the air like an approaching tornado. That buzzing stillness, which always comes right before the skies turn green and the whirlwind starts."

Hell. That sounded exactly like what I'd felt in Barnaby's Gap.

"It's strange," she continued. "Almost like nothing's changed. Like Doomsday's still brewin'." She shook her head as if she were shaking off the thoughts. "I'm just an old woman who's seen too much. Can't stop smelling trouble even when it isn't here."

"Oh, trouble's here. It's called a *Naye'i.*"

"They'll have to go back to square one." Ruthie put her hand over mine where it lay on the table. "They have to kill you."

"The woman of smoke thinks she did. She'll believe she's the new leader. What will happen when she finds out she isn't?"

"Hopefully she'll die from the disappointment," Ruthie muttered, "but I wouldn't count on it."

"You have no idea how to end that—" I broke off before I said something I shouldn't. "Thing," I finished.

"'Fraid not. She's much more than she started as.

Evil spirit became witch became Satan only knows what."

"Terrific." I glanced out the window, absently counted children, came up with five this time. They must be playing hide-and-seek.

"Where have you been?" I asked. "Not a word from you since I left Manhattan. I was starting to think I'd lost the magic."

"The amulet," Ruthie said. "It blocked me. From seein' them, from talkin' to you. Messed with my radar." She tapped her head. "I still feel fuzzy. Might have a hard time now and again gettin' through."

"That can't be good."

"You'll be all right. Sawyer's here. He'll help."

"You're sure about that? Sawyer's always seemed to be on the 'help himself and screw the world' plan."

Ruthie's lips curved. "Sawyer likes the world as is. He'll help." She sobered. "You're gonna have to destroy that amulet."

"How about I toss it off a cliff?"

Ruthie was shaking her head before I finished the sentence. "She'll find it. You must go to the benandanti. She lives in Detroit, on Trulia Street. A gray house, red shutters, you—"

"Hold on," I interrupted. "A what-who?"

"*Benandanti* means good walker in Italian."

"All right. So a benandanti is a good walking . . . what?"

"Witch."

"A good witch," I repeated. "Like Sabrina? Samantha? Tabitha?"

Ruthie gave me the look. I shut up.

"The benandanti has the power to heal the bewitched."

"And this will help me with the amulet, why?"

"Jewelry doesn't possess powers. It's the bewitchment that gives it the magic."

I thought of the turquoise and crucifix, still in the car along with the amulet. The strength of the crucifix lay in the blessing upon it. The magic of the turquoise lay in Sawyer's talents as a medicine man. So it followed that the power of the amulet had come from a spell—curse, blessing—it didn't matter.

"You're saying that a benandanti can 'heal' the amulet?"

"Not a benandanti, *the* benandanti. There's only one at a time. And yes, she'll take care of that amulet just fine."

"A benandanti is a good Italian witch; the strega was a bad witch." I frowned. "Was there only one of him, too?"

"Until there's another."

Good news, bad news. The strega was gone, but knowing the Nephilim, another would appear soon enough.

"Is there a good and a bad of everything?" I asked.

"Life craves balance," Ruthie answered. "We wouldn't have devils if we hadn't had angels first."

"Then it follows that we should have enough seers and DKs to fight the Nephilim. Otherwise things are out of balance."

"Lack of balance is what the Nephilim crave. It creates chaos. We need to find more soldiers, and we need to train them. Which isn't gonna be easy when we're also fightin' Nephilim with the few we have left."

"So what do we do? What do I do?"

"Lead them."

"That is *so* not helpful."

Ruthie's lips curved. "You're on the right track. Get Jimmy back; he's the best soldier you've got. Summer ain't bad, either. Have Sawyer search out new federation members, those who don't know yet what to do with their powers, and have him show them."

"Sawyer?"

"He's always been very good at finding new seers. DKs, too. Though usually seers draw their own DKs to them."

"Unless they inherit them." As I had.

"Unless," Ruthie agreed. "You need to gather the ones in hiding, keep fightin' at their side. It's all you can do."

"It would be nice if Sawyer could walk on two legs and use his words anywhere but on Navajo land," I murmured.

His going *to* the new recruits and training them ASAP would be more practical than his having to find them by osmosis, draw them to New Mexico, and then deal with them there.

"Take Sawyer with you to Detroit," Ruthie ordered. "It's dangerous."

I wondered if she meant dangerous because it was Detroit or dangerous because of the benandanti and other assorted supernatural beings, then decided it didn't matter. Dangerous was dangerous, and Sawyer was the best bodyguard, even if I couldn't get him on a plane without a wire cage and a muzzle.

Luckily I had the Impala, and Detroit was a short, but extremely annoying, trip around the tip of Lake Michigan from Chicago. We'd be there by morning.

The laughter of the children drew my attention to the window once more. Seven kids now. Where had they been hiding?

I got up and moved closer, peering through the glass. Between one blink and the next, there were eight kids.

"Son of a—" I murmured, as understanding dawned.

The children hadn't been playing hide-and-seek; they'd been appearing—bing, bing, bing—as they died one by one in Lake Vista.

CHAPTER 12

"People are being killed." I spun away from the window to face Ruthie. "And we're chatting in a sunny kitchen?"

Ruthie's eyes were moist. "You think I want them to die? You think I like having a full house?"

I threw up my hands. "I don't know what you want or what I think. I only know that people, *children,* are dying by lucere attack. An attack I was sent to stop."

"But you went down in the field."

"According to you, I'm not dead yet."

"You needed time to heal." Ruthie's gaze became unfocused as she stared past me. "Sawyer's done all he can."

"Did you put a hex on me, make me forget what was going on back there?" I couldn't believe I hadn't remembered until I'd seen that child appear out of nowhere.

"You were here for a reason—to listen, to learn, to heal. Until those things were done, you couldn't leave. No use worryin' about it."

"I need to go back."

"Go." Ruthie flipped her hand, dismissing me.

I fell, fast and hard, slamming into my body, choking, coughing, tasting blood. My face was wet, hell, all of me was wet and my chest hurt. I reached for the pain, expecting to encounter the knife, but it wasn't there. I came upright with a curse, and my eyes snapped open.

It was raining, had been raining for quite a while considering the soaked state of my clothes and hair. One side of my body was warm, the other slightly chilled despite the remaining heat of the summer night.

Sawyer was pressed the length of me. He lifted his head; his snout and paws were covered in blood.

Nearby lay my knife, as pristine as if it had never been buried to the hilt in my chest. Considering the sharp, shiny agony that pulsed between my ribs, I had to think the rain had washed away the blood.

Had Sawyer yanked it out with his teeth? Had I done it myself in the throes of death? Or had it magically disappeared from here and appeared over there? Did it matter as long as the weapon was no longer sticking out of me?

In the distance someone shouted, and I glanced at Lake Vista, then immediately hit the ground again. The suburb was lit up like Christmas, and there were cops all over the place.

I wanted to ask Sawyer what had happened, besides the obvious—death, death, and more death. However, I didn't have time to shape-shift and play twenty questions. We needed to get out of here, and I wasn't going to be able to drive a car with paws.

"Come on," I whispered, inching back to where the Impala was parked in the shadow of the trees.

It wouldn't be long before the police widened their search. If they found a woman and a wolf near that massacre . . . Well, it would make their job a whole lot easier. They'd blame us and close the case.

Even if we were able to get out of jail by some combination of shape-shifting and magic, we'd be marked from then on. I wouldn't be able to travel with the freedom I needed. More people would die. I had enough of them on my conscience already.

The memory of the children popping up one at a time in Ruthie's backyard made me want to punch something. I considered putting a dent in the Impala, but knew from past experience that I'd hurt, maybe break, my hand. Sure, I'd heal, but the kids would still be dead. Those kids were forever dead.

I rubbed my palm over my face, brushing away all the raindrops.

We reached the car and I opened the driver's door as quietly as possible. Sawyer hopped in. I put it in neutral and pushed the vehicle through a slight track in the trees until we emerged in another subdivision, just as I'd expected. Superior strength was so damn useful.

Only when we were far enough away that no one would hear the rumbling of the engine, did I turn the key and leave Lake Vista behind.

Sawyer sat in the passenger seat and hung his head out the window like a dog, mouth open, tongue lolling. If no one saw his long, spindly legs and huge paws, or peered too deeply into his too intelligent yet just short of feral eyes, he could pass for a dog.

We both needed a shower in the worst way. If anyone got a look at my gory wet clothes and my blood-covered . . . I glanced at Sawyer—I'd been about to say *pet*.

"Companion," I murmured, and he huffed. Sometimes I could swear he read my mind. At least he could understand me even if he couldn't talk.

"We'll stop at a hotel, get cleaned up." And while there, I could shape-shift and find out what in hell had happened in Lake Vista. Then, depending on the tale, we'd either chase luceres or continue on to Detroit.

I drove southeast for an hour. I needed to put enough distance between us and the massacre so that we wouldn't attract immediate suspicion.

On Interstate 94, I found a nondescript motel used by truckers. A place where I could check in—after I'd covered the bloody hacked and slashed tank top with a jacket despite the heat—then drive around the back to my room, park directly in front, slip the wolf in through the door.

Once inside, Sawyer headed for the bed.

"Shower first," I ordered. "We don't need bloodstains on the sheets. I had to give them my license plate number."

Sawyer bared his teeth, but he went into the bathroom, then sat on the tile and stared at the bathtub until I turned on the water.

The blood had dried on his snout and paws. The hot water loosened it somewhat, but soap would work faster. I sighed and went to my knees. I was going to have to bathe him like a dog, then, I was going to have to dry him like one, too. From the expression in his eyes, Sawyer thought this was hilarious.

"Don't get used to it," I muttered as I tore the paper wrapping off the tiny bar of soap.

He might not get used to it, but he certainly enjoyed it, moaning a little as I worked the soap through his dark, coarse fur. He ducked his head beneath the stream, then shook droplets all over me.

"Hey!" I protested, but the tickle of the water made me smile until I realized what I was doing and stopped. Smiling after so many had died was a lightness I couldn't afford.

I shut off the water, grabbed several towels, and backed up so Sawyer could leap out of the tub. Then I rubbed him down as quickly and efficiently as I could.

As I scrubbed the brilliant white cloth over his ebony fur, he hung his big head over my shoulder, and his face brushed mine. He smelled like wolf and man—like a desert breeze across the mountains, like the smoke of a fire in the night.

I pulled away. No matter what he'd done to help the federation, the fact remained that he was the son of the *Naye'i,* the woman he'd conjured from smoke, and we needed to have a chat.

"Go." I pointed to the bedroom.

He lifted his upper lip, but he went. I guess I couldn't blame him for being annoyed when I talked to him like a dog, but honestly, when the paws fit, what did he expect?

I shut the door, then locked it, though I have no idea why. Sawyer couldn't open it as a wolf, and he was stuck in that form as long as he was away from Navajo land.

However, I'd seen Sawyer do unexplainable things. Who knew, maybe he could walk through walls. I didn't want to find out while I was naked and vulnerable.

I dropped my clothes. The wound on my chest wasn't gaping, but it wasn't gone, either. An ugly red slash remained that still hurt if I moved too fast or too far. Since I'd never been killed before, I wasn't sure how long it would last or how well it would heal. As long as I was alive, I guess I didn't care.

Before I got into the shower, I removed my gun from my duffel and set it on the toilet tank. Most things that might come through that door wouldn't be bothered by a gun, but better safe than sorry.

A half hour later, I dried off, then, after wrapping myself in a towel, picked up the gun, the duffel, and went into the room.

Sawyer lay on the bed watching TV, the remote next to his paw. On the screen, a hunting show played; his gray eyes followed a huge deer as it gamboled back and forth across an autumn field. When a shot rang out, he started forward, ruff rising, a growl rumbling from his throat, eyes fixed avidly on the buck as it leaped, ran a few yards, then slowly crumpled to the ground.

I guess a wolf was a wolf, even when it wasn't.

I stepped in front of the television. Sawyer leaned to the side, trying to see around me. I dropped the towel. He slowly leaned back, his interest in the deer lost.

I guess a man was a man, even when it wasn't.

Quickly I laid the gun on the nightstand, removed the wolf robe from the duffel, swirled it around my shoulders and shifted.

It was always the same. That burst of light, the chill followed by the scalding heat. The fall from a great height as my bones crackled and changed, as I became something else.

My attention was immediately drawn to the flickering television screen. Another deer pranced across, and I found myself fascinated. When the shot rang out, my heart jolted; adrenaline flared. When it jumped, I wanted to chase it. I knew it would go down; it was vulnerable; it was mine.

The screen went black with a muted thunk.

Phoenix.

I swung toward the bed, where Sawyer stood with his paw on the control. I shook my head to clear it of the bestial hunger, that burning need to kill—it always freaked me out.

Your wound will fade more quickly in this form.

I lifted my neck, stretching the skin of my chest. He was right. Already, it didn't ache or pull quite as much.

What happened? I asked.

I saw you fall, then she disappeared.

And then?

I kept fighting.

I should be glad that he'd stayed on task. There'd been nothing Sawyer could do to help me anyway.

Except I wasn't glad. I was just a tad pissed.

With me lying dead on the ground, you just kept fighting?

I knew you weren't dead.

Would have been nice if I'd known it, I muttered.

You need to wear the turquoise. Always.

He wouldn't get any argument from me.

Speaking of that, you never explained why the sight of it made her go poof.

The stone marks you as mine.

A low growl rumbled from my throat. I wasn't anyone's, especially Sawyer's.

His nostrils flared, no doubt from the scent of fiery fury that must be rolling off me like a flame. *Relax, Phoenix, it was the only way to keep you alive.*

Let me get this straight—if I wear the turquoise, she can't kill me?

Exactly.

So I'm invincible.

He tossed his head disdainfully. *Just because she can't kill you doesn't mean the rest of them can't.*

Damn. Invincible had sounded so good right now.

I returned to my original question. *What happened in Lake Vista?*

Sawyer lay down, rested his nose on his paws and sighed. *What you might expect.*

What good is knowing they're coming if we can't stop them?

We would have stopped them if not for her.

I stilled. *She planned it?*

Either she followed the luceres or she sent them.

Sent them?

Controlling Nephilim was a power of the leader of the darkness, and the woman of smoke couldn't be that unless she killed me. Which she hadn't done until *after* the luceres arrived. Even so—

The hair on the back of my neck lifted. *She killed me. Does that make her the new leader of the darkness?*

She didn't really kill you.

Then how could she control the luceres?

She couldn't. Not in the true sense of control. But she's persuasive. Especially when what she's suggesting is what you want to do anyway.

His tone and choice of pronoun made me glance up sharply. Was he remembering his father—the medicine man who'd embraced his bear spirit, who'd lived as an animal all of the time and come to crave human flesh because of her?

Or was he speaking about himself? Sawyer had told me once that she could make anyone do anything that she wished.

Despite my fur, I shivered. What had she made him do? What might she still?

If the Naye'i *is that powerful, she doesn't need to kill me. She can rule all the forces of darkness just by wanting to.*

It doesn't work that way.

Seems like the way things were supposed to work aren't the way they're actually working.

Certain things will happen. The leader of the darkness will kill the leader of the light, resulting in Doomsday. Doomsday will lead to Armageddon.

Some people say Apocalypse, some Armageddon. Is that like potato, po-ta-toe?

What does a potato have to do with anything?

I wanted to rub my forehead, but I had no hands. He was so damn literal all the time.

What is the difference between Apocalypse and Armageddon?

The final battle between God and Satan is called Armageddon. Apocalypse is a general term for the end of the world.

I guess that made as much sense as anything else.

We need to go after the luceres.

I killed most of them.

Sawyer wasn't a seer or a DK, he was something else, something I'd never been quite sure of. I wondered if Ruthie was. She trusted him. I didn't. He was a killer. But then weren't we all?

We should round up the few you missed.

No point. They'll return to their hidden lives until they're called again. Luceres spread out, blend in. They could be anywhere.

I growled and scraped my claws across the carpet, reveling in the ripping and tearing shriek, wishing it were a lucere beneath my paws, or the woman of smoke.

How do we kill her?

If I could, I'd have done it already. We'll just have to keep searching, keep trying.

A little random, wouldn't you say?

What isn't?

I lifted my head, sniffed the air, caught again the distant drift of flames and ashes. *Why do you smell of smoke?*

I've told you before; she's part of me.

The Navajo are matriarchal. They believe the mother's side is strongest. No matter what I said, Sawyer wouldn't stop believing it, too. Sometimes I worried that she would bring him to the dark side. The thought scared

me almost as much as Sawyer did. If he ever joined the
Nephilim, we were finished.

The power that poured off him—morning, noon, and
even in the dead of night—reminded me of the tornado
Ruthie had spoken of. Inside Sawyer lay a storm of destruction just waiting to get out.

*Is that why you conjured her all those years ago?
Because she's part of you? Because, like all neglected
children, you long for her approval?*

His eyes flared. I'd never asked him about that night;
I hadn't wanted him to know I'd been spying. But he
must have known; otherwise why had he given me the
magic turquoise that would keep her from killing me?

You think I'm secretly working for my mother?

Had I? Not really. But I couldn't be sure. Not with
him.

I'd touched Sawyer, in the most intimate way a
woman could touch a man, and I'd seen a lot, but I hadn't
seen everything. Sawyer was capable of blocking me in
a way that no one else could. I knew he was hiding
something, but I didn't think he was hiding that.

Why did you call her that night? I pressed.

He rose to his feet, shaking his fur as if he'd just
climbed out of a mountain lake. I half expected cool
water to sprinkle over me like rain.

We had things to discuss.

Call her now, I ordered, *I'd like to discuss a few
things.*

You've always had more guts than sense, he muttered. *Did you learn nothing from getting your ass
kicked the last time? You aren't ready to meet her
again.*

Make me ready.

His amusement fled, and he glanced away. *I can't.*

Who can?

He didn't answer.

So you aren't going to conjure her?

There was a time when I could bring her to me with fire and blood and magic, but that time is gone.

Why?

She's stronger. She resists the spell. Maybe she always could, but now she knows there's no point in trying to seduce me.

Seduce you? I swallowed, tasting something rotten, something green and slimy and just plain wrong, at the back of my throat.

His eyes met mine. *If it meant getting me on her side, she'd do anything.*

You're her son.

She's an evil spirit, Phoenix. The only thing being her son means is that I've got magic, and she wants it.

Can she absorb power like . . . I paused. *Well, like I can?*

No one absorbs power like you can.

I wasn't sure if I should be happy about that or even more freaked out.

She can't take on the talents of others. To get stronger, she either seduces them to her side—like she seduced my father—or she kills her enemies and removes their powers from this earth.

If you aren't with me, you're against me.

It's a philosophy that's kept her alive a long, long time.

Sooner or later she's going to get tired of waiting and just kill you.

You're probably right.

Another shiver passed over me, making my skin ripple beneath all the fur. The only thing more frightening than Sawyer being on the side of evil was Sawyer not being on any side at all. My feelings about him were complicated to say the least.

Can she kill you?

He gave a little sneeze—amusement and derision rode on the sound—then pawed at his snout as if that had tickled.

I might be very hard to kill, Phoenix, but that doesn't mean I'm immortal.

You could wear a turquoise, I suggested.

That wouldn't work for me.

Why not?

Magic. He took a deep breath. *It's difficult to explain.*

I'd have to take his word for it. Though I'd dealt with my share of magic lately—spells and witches and fairies, oh, my—I still didn't know much about it.

So what do we do?

Sawyer lifted his large, shaggy head, and his gray eyes, which were both bizarrely human and savagely wolf, peered into mine. *We find a way to kill her first.*

CHAPTER 13

Considering no one, including Sawyer, had a clue how to kill a *Naye'i* his words weren't as comforting as they should have been.

Let's get some sleep, Sawyer continued. *By morning you'll be healed, and we can get back on the road. In order to kill her, we've got to find her.*

We have to make a detour. He tilted his head. *First Ruthie wants us to go to Detroit and meet with the benandanti who can remove the spell from the amulet.*

What amulet? he asked.

I guess I hadn't explained everything, so I did. Then, considering the turquoise, I had to ask.

Did you make it?

You think I'd give her something that allowed her to murder at will unseen?

When he put it like that . . .

Did you?

No. I'm not capable of that powerful a spell.

I snorted. I thought he was capable of a lot more than he ever let on. Still, I didn't think he'd do his mother any favors.

Could she have made it herself?

Perhaps, but I have to think that if she could have, she would have, long ago.

We live and learn, I pointed out, and he dipped his head.

How she got the amulet is irrelevant, Sawyer continued. *We have it now; it's useless to her.*

She'll keep coming after it.

Isn't that what we want? She comes after the necklace and we . . . He paused, a frustrated sound escaping his throat. If he'd been in human form, he'd have thrown up his strong-fingered, magical hands. *Do whatever it is we have to do to end her.*

In theory, I agreed. *In practice, we don't know how to end her, so she probably ends us. Ruthie was very adamant about meeting with the good witch of Detroit. And she wanted you to go with me.*

What Ruthie wants, Ruthie gets.

I'd thought he would argue or outright refuse to go along, then disappear into the night on his own witch hunt, leaving me to travel alone. He was full of surprises lately.

Come to bed.

My head went up as he leaped to the floor, crowding me until my flanks hit the spindly, scarred excuse for a table and it rattled. His eyes flared, but I refused to look away. Alphas stared down betas. Problem was—Sawyer and I were both alphas.

I growled and bumped his chest with mine. He snarled and bumped me back. This could get ugly.

He ran his open mouth across my shoulder, teeth just brushing my skin, and I shuddered.

Or it might get something else.

Images flickered—of us together in the desert. The best sex I'd ever had.

No. I dropped to the ground, crouching, tail tucked beneath, a position of submission—until I rolled away.

He followed, stalking me like the predator he was. *Come on, Phoenix, you know you want to.*

The frightening thing . . . he was right. I wanted to. I would probably always want to. Except—

You're a wolf.

So are you.

He kept coming; I needed to stop retreating. I'd never be the alpha if I let him push me around.

But—

His mouth opened in an expression that was pure wolf, in any form, and I understood.

The first time I'd touched him after Ruthie had died, I'd seen the eons of his life rushing past me, people he'd killed, women he'd loved, the many ways he'd lived. Sawyer had spent time as a wolf. He'd mated as one, too.

Gack! I don't think so.

Try it, Phoenix. I know you'll like it.

He moved with the blinding speed that was his in animal form, the speed I had in both forms, thanks to him and Jimmy. Nevertheless, I couldn't get away. In this small room, there wasn't anywhere to go.

His body slid along mine, and I saw what he meant; I felt it, too. The animal lust, the uncontrollable urge to be taken, to forget everything with a few minutes of sex, the joining of bodies without the complications of human thoughts, of emotions, an orgasm that would make me howl.

I cringed at the thought and leaped onto the bed, standing stiff-legged at the edge and letting the fury rumble from my throat. His muscles bunched as if he meant to join me, and I bared my teeth, lifting my lips far enough to reveal the red flare of my gums.

This was my place—higher ground. He could stay down there, where his very lack of height made him the submissive—even if it was in name only. If need be, I'd fight him. I'd probably lose, but there could only be one alpha, and it had to be me.

As if nothing had happened, Sawyer jumped onto the other bed, circled three times, and plopped down, tucking his nose beneath his tail before closing his eyes.

My heart, which had accelerated at the confrontation, slowed. He hadn't meant what he'd said. He'd just been messing with me—Sawyer's specialty. He messed with everyone. Still . . .

The images that had exploded in my head at his touch were primal—maddening, exhilarating, both frightening and exciting. My body responded in a predictable manner, throbbing in places that hadn't throbbed in over a month. Places that had never throbbed that way with anyone but him.

I tried to resist the urge to circle as Sawyer had, to make a nest and burrow in, but I couldn't. I might be woman and wolf, but in this form, wolf was hard to ignore.

Surprisingly, or maybe not so much, I fell immediately to sleep. Sure, the adrenaline from all the confrontations—the luceres, the woman of smoke, Sawyer, not to mention dying, if in name only—should have kept me wide awake. However, the letdown after so much excitement was exhausting, as was the shapeshifting, and no doubt the healing my body had done already and still had left to do.

In my dreams, the things I'd seen in Sawyer's head, the memories of what had happened between us in New Mexico, were impossible to forget.

Sawyer and I beneath the moon and the stars. My hands sliding over his body, my fingers tracing his tattoos, absorbing the essence of his beasts, of him. The lightning that seemed to flash when we came together, the rumbling of the earth, the heat and flare of the power he'd released within me.

I dreamed of that night, and then I dreamed of this one. Of coming together as wolves, the pure bestial lust of it, the sex for sex alone, no future or past, an exchange of nothing but bodies. We had only now, only us, and the near-violent pace of his body within mine.

In my mind, in my dream, I was woman and wolf. My form flickered from one to the next as his did. The bed dipped as he leaped between them, the arc of his body in one form, the slide of his skin when he shifted to the other.

His flesh was marked with the images of his beasts—a wolf on his bicep, a mountain lion across his chest, an eagle taking flight from his neck. I'd always found it both amusing and disturbing that Sawyer had made the adage "drain the snake" literal by having a rattler tattooed onto his penis.

I'd asked him once why the markings didn't heal when he shifted.

They weren't made by a human wielding a needle, but by a sorcerer who wielded the lightning.

In other words, magic tattoos. Hey, ask a foolish question . . .

Regardless of how they'd come about, the fact remained that Sawyer's tattoos never disappeared.

In the night, in the dark, in my dreams, I explored the spirits of those beasts as I explored him. I brushed the eagle at his neck, the hawk at the small of his back, and for just an instant I could fly.

My palm cupped his shoulder, his chest, his thigh, and I was a wolf, a cougar, a tiger. I could smell prey on the wind; the urge to chase and kill was irresistible, almost evil in its gleeful intensity.

There were nuances to Sawyer I didn't understand,

might never understand, probably didn't want to. He flirted with both sides, and I was never certain which side he was on. I wasn't certain he knew.

"Are you evil?" I whispered.

"Perhaps."

My other hand brushed his other shoulder, and I could smell blood in the water; I relished the chill lap of the ocean around my cold-blooded body. As a shark I ruled the sea; all creatures fled from me, and they should.

He rose above me, hip to hip, pressing us together intimately and lights flashed behind my closed eyelids. I grasped his forearms, and I was a tarantula, scampering along the desert floor, the canyons rising above me, yet there in the sand I was king.

Another image flickered, something new. Something that hadn't been there the last time I'd touched him. I reached for it and became for a single flickering instant a crocodile. The strength of my jaws was legendary; if I captured something in my mouth, it was lost.

The idea enticed me, and I slid downward, capturing something else in my mouth. A long lick up his length, I wrapped my palm around him and heard the distant whisper of a rattler; cool fury washed over me, and I moved my body in a slinking, boneless motion that felt delicious against the sheets.

He pulled away; I let him go, enjoying the glide of his skin along mine. I tasted salt even as fur brushed my belly, my thighs, and in between. I arched, an offering to the beasts, to the man, begging him to take me in every way and in every form.

I wanted to run my hands over him again, to stare down at him as moonlight filtered in through the window, to watch his face as he came, as I did.

While Sawyer wasn't conventionally handsome—how could he be?—he had the best body of anyone I'd ever seen, both in person and in any underwear ad in America. I suspect the centuries of his life had allowed him to hone his pecs and abs more thoroughly than anyone around.

He was perhaps only a hair taller than my own five ten, a height that would have been impressive in any previous age but was merely average in this one. As if Sawyer could ever be average.

His face was all angles and planes; sharp, high cheek-bones and annoyingly thick black eyelashes framed his spooky gray eyes. In human form his hair was long and straight and black, as soft as his body was hard. As a wolf it was just as dark, but coarse with an underlayer of silver that made him shimmer beneath the moon.

Around us the room kept changing. One minute we were in his hogan in New Mexico, the next we were in a motel room in Indiana, then we whirled through places I'd never been, or perhaps had yet to be—on a bed, the ground, atop a blanket, in the sand. The passing of time and place became dizzying.

Words flared on the walls, in the sky, there and then gone, some I could read and some I could not.

Stars sparked against the black of the night. I thought they said: *Never surrender.*

Across the dingy white motel ceiling, words appeared in paint as red as fresh blood. *Toss evil to the four winds.*

Then, the sand of the desert swirled, an invisible hand casting the phrase: *The birth of faith approaches.*

Dreams are so damn weird.

Sawyer skimmed his palms down my waist, my hips, then over my belly and back up to cup my breasts. He laved the nipples, suckled and bit gently until I thought I'd go mad if he didn't take me.

Instead, he turned me over, made love to my shoul-

ders and back with his mouth, urged me onto my knees
and draped his body over mine. His hair sifted past my
cheek, shrouding us both in shadow. His breath puffed
against me, first across skin and then across fur as he
plunged.

The act was both virile and violent, his mouth on my
cheek, his teeth at my neck. Me on all fours, hands, paws,
fur, skin. Was I woman or was I wolf? I didn't know.
When Sawyer was inside of me, I didn't care.

I clenched around him, cried out, the sound his name,
a curse, a howl. He pulsed, hot and heavy and deep, and
I awoke in the still quiet of the dark all tangled up in
him.

Snout across my neck, his warm breath stirred the
fur on my face. My body ached, from sleep, from sex, or
both, I couldn't recall. Once before I'd believed a dream
just a dream only to find out that my dreams were too
often reality.

I smelled like him—smoke and fire, human and wolf.
Because we'd slept curled together, or because we'd
done it doggy-style?

I jerked, my legs flailing as if I chased a rabbit through
my dreams, but I was no longer asleep, and from the increased tempo of his breathing, neither was Sawyer.

He lapped a lazy lick down my cheek, and my body
leaped in response. I wanted him again.

Again? Hell. I was going to kill him.

I shot from the bed, landed on the ground. My chest
no longer hurt. I had no doubt that when I shifted back
the scar would be minimal to gone, but that wasn't my
main concern now.

*What the hell were you doing in my bed? You've got
your own.*

You cried out in the night.

I narrowed my eyes. There was crying out and then there was crying out—fear or passion, memories or reality?

Did we—

He lay on the bed, paws extended, snout resting between, at home amid the tangled sheets, warm, languid, and comfortable with himself and all the worlds he lived in.

Did we what?

You know what! I told you no.

Then the answer must be no.

I sniffed. Sawyer's powers were based on sex. He reeked of it in any form. Seers and DKs were often sent to him to be unblocked, to get past any "issues" they might have and embrace what they were. Sawyer accomplished that by embracing them.

He lifted his head; his gray eyes flared. *Did you dream of me, Phoenix? Did you dream of us?*

You know I did. You made me.

I don't have the power to walk in dreams. You do.

I'd inherited that power from Jimmy. When necessary, I could stroll through a person's mind and discover the answer to my most desperate question. Only problem was, I needed to be half dead to do it. It was quite possible that yesterday's fiasco with the woman of smoke had been just enough to warrant such a walk. But if I'd walked through Sawyer's mind that meant the dreams had been his and not my own.

I lifted one side of my mouth in a soundless snarl. Though I'd enjoyed sex with Sawyer, both in reality and in my head, that he was dreaming of me nightly was kind of creepy. But then so was he.

What information had he imparted during the dream? What desperate question had I needed an answer to?

I had no idea. But I'd learned over the last month that sooner or later, the truth would come to me.

At least I hadn't really done him. The images I recalled—wolf, man, woman, wolf, and several in between—gave me the willies. Shape-shifting was for beating the bad guys. It wasn't a new and innovative sex toy.

Someday you'll mate with me, Phoenix. He laid his head back between his paws. *It's only a matter of time.*

I took a step forward as my hackles rose. Those dreams, which had felt far too much like memories, *had* been seductive. I wanted to touch him in both forms, to shift as we mated, to come screaming as he took me, to clench around him, to make him spurt, the heat both scalding and comforting, the scent of him my own.

*You're being—*I broke off. I'd been about to say *an asshole,* but instead I finished with a murmured *you,* before I disappeared into the bathroom.

I nosed the door too hard and it slammed. I heard his laughter in my mind. I wanted to shut out his voice; I wanted to forget everything I'd remembered. The first was easy, the second impossible.

Closing my eyes, I imagined myself human. I welcomed the brush of air past my face as I lengthened from quadrapedal to bipedal, my skin prickling with gooseflesh as the air went from hot to cool.

I stood in front of the mirror. My dark hair stuck up every which way, my usually tan cheeks appeared pale, the skin beneath my eyes bruised.

"Rough night?" I asked the woman. She didn't answer.

At least the wound was gone. Completely, as if it had never been. Sawyer was right again. What else was new?

In an attempt to get rid of the scent of him that clung

to me like perfume, I took another shower. The hot spike of the water hitting my still vulnerable flesh made me bite my lip to keep from moaning.

Instead of feeling satiated, as I would have if I'd actually done him, I was instead so on edge a slight buzz thrummed at the corners of my consciousness. That stinging sense of thwarted lust. The hum that signaled sexual deprivation. If Sawyer were a man, I'd jump him just to make it all go away.

I tried to think of something else. What I thought of was Jimmy. Not a good way to make the needy hum disappear. If anything it got worse.

I had to call Summer, see how she was doing with the Jimmy hunt. Maybe I should have touched her as she'd suggested. Maybe I would have gotten a clearer flash of where he'd gone.

"Touch something he did." I gave a halfhearted laugh and let the water pound on my face. If that worked, I might as well touch myself.

I stilled, then lifted my head out of the water, tilting it as if I'd just heard something very far away and very interesting.

I laughed again, this time putting more heart into it. "Why the hell not?"

Slowly, I laid my palm across my stomach and thought of Jimmy.

"Squat," I muttered, but I didn't give up easily.

I smoothed my fingers across my ribs, then upward, cupping the heavy weight of my own breasts. Jimmy's face flickered behind my closed eyelids. I might just be on to something here.

Perhaps, in order to "see" someone who'd touched me, I had to touch myself in the same way they had. Or at least in the way most likely to invoke some kind of response.

I rolled my own nipples between my fingers, lifting my breasts until I could take the rosy tips into my mouth and suckle, first one and then the other. The sensation shot through me like a dying star across the sky. My skin tingled; my toes curled. I was so close to eruption, thanks to the dreams I'd had, that a single stroke between my legs brought me home, and in the seconds that followed, I saw everything that I needed to.

CHAPTER 14

Jimmy *was* in New Mexico, staying in a virtual clone of the motel we now occupied. Two signs were visible through the open window at his back—THE SLEEP CHEAP—a name like that really made you want to curl up on the sheets, didn't it?—and INTERSTATE 25.

It was daytime, and Jimmy was reading the *Red Rock Sentinel*. He appeared awfully interested in what was inside.

"Friday," he whispered, and then he smiled. His damn fangs were out, and the sun sparked red off the glare at the center of his eyes. I could say he didn't look himself, but I'd be lying. The new and not so improved Jimmy Sanducci was beginning to look just like this.

He placed the paper face up on the table, and my gaze flicked over every advertisement, every article. The only one that said anything about Friday spoke of a traveling show.

The Gypsy Fortune-telling Circus Extravaganza.

Wow. Something for everyone.

What did they have for Jimmy? The question gave me a bad, bad feeling.

Wrapping a towel around myself since I'd left my

duffel in the other room, I barreled through the door and grabbed my phone.

Sawyer was watching the hunt, fish, kill channel again and barely spared me a glance. He probably knew I'd bean him with the nearest heavy object if he messed with me right now. The man might be annoying, but the wolf learned fast.

Summer picked up on the other end sounding wide awake and far too chirpy—when didn't she?—for what had to be long before dawn in the west. "I'm glad you called."

"You found him?"

It would be too much to ask that she'd already corralled Jimmy and— My thoughts ended there. I had no idea what she could do to make him give up his fascination with killing himself.

"No. I flew over the mountains. They weren't there, so I'm waiting at Sawyer's."

"Ditch that. He's with me."

"Sawyer? But how—"

"What has four legs and likes to howl at the moon?"

"Oh. Then why—"

Quickly I filled her in on what had happened since she'd flown off.

"Don't tell Jimmy he's here," I finished.

"You think I'm an idiot?"

"I'll assume you don't really want me to answer that."

I heard a soft laugh on the other end of the line and found myself smiling. Sometimes talking to Summer was almost like talking to Megan.

Son of a— I rubbed my forehead. I needed to call Megan.

"Head to Red Rock," I continued. "You know it?"

"A little place near Las Cruces. Jimmy's there?"

"Yes."

I didn't wait around for her to ask me how I knew where he was, just continued giving orders. It was my strong suit.

"He's planning to attend a traveling show on Friday." I paused, frowned. "What in hell day is it anyway?"

"Friday."

"Fuck."

"Relax. I can get to Red Rock pretty fast."

She *could* fly.

"What kind of traveling show?" she asked. "I can't see him attending the latest touring presentation of *The Lion King*."

"A circus. With Gypsies."

Silence came over the line, and I got an even worse feeling than I'd had before.

"What's so bad about Gypsies?" I asked.

"You don't know?"

I wasn't going to explain again how little I knew, how woefully inadequate I was to lead the forces against Armageddon, the Apocalypse, Doomsday, end of days. Whatever you called it, I so wasn't ready for it. Luckily Summer didn't make me explain; she did.

"Gypsies know all about dhampirs, including how to kill them."

"First off—there are still Gypsies?"

"There are still Italians, Navajo, Irish, and every other nationality you can think of. Gypsies are no different." She paused. "Well, they are different. Even though they spread all over the globe centuries ago and have wandered on every continent, they rarely interact with anyone else, except in cases of commerce. If a Gypsy intermarries with a *gaje,* a non-Gypsy, they're banished."

"Feudal much?"

"It's their way."

"Tell me why they know about dhampirs."

"Because they started them."

I glanced at Sawyer, who'd turned off the hunting channel and now stared at me avidly. I had no doubt that his superior hearing allowed him to catch both sides of the conversation.

"That makes no sense. Dhampirs are the offspring of a Nephilim and a human, same as any breed. Which means the Nephilim started them."

"Yes and no." She took a deep breath. "Gypsies are nomadic. They've traveled all over the world, and in doing so, they've seen things."

"Nephilim kind of things?"

"Yes. Many of them have the sight."

"Why haven't we recruited them?"

"They don't deal with the *gaje*," she repeated. "But they do pretty well killing Nephilim on their own. The word *dhampir* means 'son of vampire' in Romany, the language of the Rom, which is what the Gypsies call themselves."

"And how, exactly, did the Gypsies start the dhampirs?"

"I shouldn't have said started; they discovered their powers, gave them a name and began to use them to fight the Nephilim long ago."

"Are you saying Jimmy's mother was a Gypsy?"

"It's possible, though the term *dhampir* has come to mean any offspring of a vampire and a human. Dhampirs can recognize vampires; they're extremely good at killing them. Legend says that they have all the good attributes and none of the bad."

"Tell it to Jimmy," I muttered.

"Unless they share blood," she continued. "Then they become more vampire than human, and the Gypsies kill them. Unlike the majority of the world, the Rom believe in the supernatural."

"Which is why Jimmy is headed there. He'll bare his fangs, snarl a little, maybe bite someone—"

"And they'll put a stake through his heart," Summer agreed. "Twice."

Hell.

"Stop him," I ordered. "Stop them."

"I'm on it," she said, and was gone.

I glanced at Sawyer. "I'm sure you heard that."

He blinked once, which I took as a yes, then padded to the door and waited for me to open it. Once I had, he loped to the overgrown field behind the motel and disappeared into the tall, dry grass.

I glanced around. Not yet dawn, no one was in the parking lot, thank goodness. I didn't want to explain why I had a pet wolf.

Sure, I'd tell anyone who saw him that Sawyer was a dog, and maybe in this area—city, not country—people would believe me. But if I'd been in rural Wisconsin, Minnesota, Michigan, definitely Canada, not only would people laugh in my face, they'd probably shoot Sawyer before I even had the chance to lie.

Myself, I thought wolves were beautiful, or at least I had until I'd turned into one. Now I thought they were practical.

Wolves can run at speeds of up to forty miles an hour and can cover a hundred and twenty-five miles in a day. They've been known to follow prey at a run for five miles and then accelerate. They're good fighters, better killers, and in my new life, there were some situations where only a wolf would do.

However, folks in the northern reaches of civilization considered wolves varmints, and they shot them if they could get away with it. Sure, the species was endangered in some places, protected in others, but tell that to a farmer who'd lost several sheep or a calf. He'd blast the wolf into the next dimension, then bury the thing in the woods where no one would ever find it.

I remained at the open door in a towel, unwilling to take my eyes off the field where Sawyer had disappeared to do whatever wolves did in fields. What if a trucker with a rifle showed up?

Not that a bullet would have much effect on a skinwalker, or so I'd been led to believe. Though tales of Sawyer's indestructibility might have been greatly exaggerated just to keep me from blowing his brains out.

Still, that Jimmy hadn't ended him spoke volumes. I didn't need to be psychic to know that if Sanducci could have killed Sawyer, he would have and vice versa. Which was why Jimmy had gone looking for him in the first place. When he hadn't found him, Jimmy had moved on to Plan B.

While I waited for Sawyer, I retrieved my cell phone and hit speed dial for Megan. Anyone else, I'd be worried that I might wake her, but Megan was always up long before dawn. She said it was her only "alone time."

"You know, don't you?" Megan didn't bother with hello. Why waste words when you had caller ID?

I frowned. "Know what?"

"I was going to call you as soon as the sun came up."

Unlike Megan, I didn't need alone time, and getting up before the sun was considered cruel and unusual punishment. Or at least it had been before I'd gone on call twenty-four/seven for Nephilim disposal. Two months ago, if I didn't get out of bed, someone might have to wait for their beer; now people would die.

"Why were you going to call me?" I asked.

"There's been a murder."

"There are a lot of murders in Milwaukee."

The average person didn't know that Milwaukee was

one of the top ten big cities on the murder hit parade, often coming in above Los Angeles in the ratings. Considering that Milwaukee was actually on the small side of big and L.A. was on the big side of large, that was just embarrassing.

"Not in Milwaukee," Megan clarified, "in Friedenberg."

"Shit."

"At your place."

Was *double shit* a word?

"Who? How?"

"Do you know a woman named Jenny Voorhaven?"

The name sounded familiar, but I couldn't place her. In my line of work that happened a lot. People introduced themselves at the bar; we became great pals for a night while I listened to their incredible sob story—I'd heard some doozies—then I never saw them again.

"Maybe," I said.

"She was found on your doorstep, or at least what was left of her. They've asked for help from the FBI."

"Who?"

"The locals. There hasn't been a murder in Friedenberg in the past ten thousand years."

"You're exaggerating," I said. But not by much.

"Voorhaven was from Ohio, died in Wisconsin, and . . . well, they can't exactly figure out how she was killed."

"They're the FBI, and they can't figure it out?"

"It appears she was torn in two, and since everyone knows that's impossible . . ." Megan's voice said that she knew differently.

So did I. I'd seen Jimmy tear some*thing* in two not two days ago.

Jimmy. Ah, crap.

My breathing increased to hyperventilation rate.

Megan must have heard it because she said, "Liz?" and then she said it again, really loud. "Liz!"

"I'm here. Just let me think a minute."

And when I thought about it, I knew that Jimmy could not have traveled from the Ozarks to the Great Lakes, then back to Sawyer's, and on to southern New Mexico, stopping to tear apart someone on the way. He was damn quick, but he wasn't that damn quick.

On the heels of those thoughts came another, and I strode across the floor, yanked Jimmy's list from the pocket of my discarded jeans, and found Jenny's name smack-dab in the middle. No wonder it had sounded familiar.

Jenny had been a seer from Cleveland; she'd no doubt missed the e-mail and phone call warning her to stay away. I had a bad feeling there might be others right behind her.

Most seers weren't like me, capable of defending themselves against supernatural bad guys by virtue of their own supernatural strength and speed, which was why only Ruthie had known the seers' identities once upon a time. Even so, they didn't usually go far without a DK to protect them; all of Jenny's must be history.

I could see what had happened clearly. Jenny in hiding, cut off from anyone she knew. Confused, lonely, scared, she'd waited as long as she could stand, then she'd come to me for help.

She'd arrived on my doorstep, rung the bell, then heard the whisper that announced a demon. She'd called for me, screamed, maybe cried, while the woman of smoke had smiled and torn her into pieces.

Sometimes this leader of the light job really, really sucked.

"Did that nai— Ne— Neph." Megan broke off with a

growl of annoyance. "Did that freaky, disappearing bitch goddess do it?"

"Yeah." Either her or one of her minions. Didn't matter. Jenny was dead.

"Liz?" Megan murmured. "What's going on?"

"She was a seer, like me."

While I'd been thinking, I'd also been pulling out my laptop, waiting for it to boot up, then to connect with the Internet. I checked my e-mail. Three seers had replied, agreeing to stay put. They could guide their remaining DKs while in hiding, and according to them there was suddenly a lot to do. It appeared that the Nephilim had regrouped and were having a field day.

I sighed. Nothing to be done but keep trying to plug up the floodgates as best we could with what we had left.

I'd hoped for more responses—hell, I'd hoped for one hundred percent—but other than those three e-mails, all I'd gotten was spam.

"Megan," I said, "there might be more coming."

I wasn't sure how to stop them.

"Your building is wrapped in yellow crime-scene tape. A blind person could see it from the space shuttle. If I were a superpsychic seer hiding from the bad guys, I'd take one look and run like hell."

There was that. My mood lifted slightly, then plummeted.

"They might come to the bar. She probably has something watching the place."

I didn't think the Nephilim would bother with Megan, but then again, they did like to kill just for the hell of it.

"I don't want you hurt."

What I wanted was to send a DK to camp out on a barstool, but I didn't have any to spare.

"I'll be fine."

I didn't answer. Megan was tough, but she wasn't that tough.

"I'll get someone to help." Who, I had no idea.

"I said I'd be fine." Megan was getting testy. She hated it when anyone intimated that she couldn't take care of herself, her bar, her kids, or anything else she considered hers.

Like me.

"I'm sure you will be," I lied. "But if the Nephilim send a toady to watch the bar, I can send a DK to kill it and anyone else who comes along. It's just good business."

"Oh," Megan said slowly. "Well, that makes sense."

Now all I had to do was find one. It occurred to me that Summer should know a few DKs from her centuries of being one. Maybe she had a better way to contact them than I did. Who knew?

As soon as I hung up with Megan, I called Summer again. She didn't answer; I suspected that flying, even without a plane, took all of her attention, and she let any incoming calls go to voice mail.

Sawyer came into the room while I was leaving a message, his dark coat speckled with dry grass, pollen, and a few burrs. I should brush him before we got into the car.

I shook my head. I could not treat a wild animal like a pet. That was a good way to get bitten. Or worse.

"Summer," I said when her "leave a message" message ended. "Call me when you hear this. I—" I paused, not wanting to admit it, but unable to find another way to say what had to be said except, "I need your help."

Sawyer snorted. I glanced his way. He didn't know about Jenny, the dead seer, so I told him. It always felt bizarre, talking to a wolf, but I knew he could understand me. He just couldn't answer me. In words.

In actions, he got his point across fairly well. As soon as I was finished, he picked up my discarded jeans in his mouth, dragged them across the carpeting, and dropped them on my still bare feet. The message was clear.

Get dressed and move your ass.

I was oh so tempted to drive straight back to Milwaukee and protect Megan myself. But along with that temptation came the certainty that such a move would play right into the woman of smoke's hands.

I wasn't sure why she hadn't come after me again; it probably had something to do with Sawyer, or the turquoise, maybe both. If I allowed myself to be sidetracked, if I backtracked, disaster would follow.

Sawyer and I were on the road within half an hour. I stopped in at the desk, grabbed a complimentary Go-cup of coffee and a disgusting cellophane-sealed cheese Danish. I also took one for Sawyer, but he sneered at it, so I ate that one, too. I couldn't recall the last time I'd had any food.

I suspected Sawyer had made use of his time in the long grass to not only take care of business but chomp on a rabbit or a mouse. How a mouse could be more appetizing than a mushy Danish, I had no idea, but perhaps I'd feel differently if I had pointy ears and a tail.

"As soon as we send your mother to hell, we need to figure out a better way of contacting seers. Set up some kind of contingency plan for emergencies."

The one we had was pretty half-assed, but I'd discovered that a lot in this world was. Humans weren't perfect and neither were their plans.

Sawyer, who'd been hanging his head out the window, pulled it back in and waited for me to continue.

"I know, our whole life is one long emergency, but still, cell phones, even e-mail, probably aren't the best idea. I'm thinking the Nephilim, having lived longer than long, have bought some pretty impressive technology."

Cell phones could be traced. Monsters, with their abnormally good hearing, could listen in on conversations they had no business hearing. Hackers came in all shapes, sizes, and supernaturalities.

We rolled into Detroit before noon. Trulia Street was located in a somewhat seedy section, the house cozied up to all the others on the block with very little space in between. The gray bungalow was surrounded by a small patch of dried grass; the bright red shutters only served to emphasize the bars on the windows.

When we rang the bell, the snarl of a very large dog on the other side made Sawyer's hackles rise. He pushed himself between me and the door, crowding me backward until I nearly tumbled off the porch.

A sliding sound followed by a click revealed a tiny window at eye level. The inside of the house was so dark I couldn't get a good look at the eyes beyond a tiny sparkle as a murky cloud-covered sun traced across the glass.

Then the peephole slammed shut. I tensed, prepared to pound on the door and shout a while, but the locks were released, bolts were pulled back, the door swung open, and a voice murmured from the darkness, "*Ciao, bella*. Been waitin' for you."

CHAPTER 15

Though the door was wide open, I still couldn't see anyone in the long, dark tunnel of the front hall, but I could hear that dog growling. He sounded both monstrous and mean.

"Are you—" I paused. How was I supposed to ask if the woman who belonged to the haunting, melodious, somehow sexy voice was a witch? Was that considered polite? Or an open invitation for the dog to eat me?

Sawyer walked inside, legs stiff, hackles still raised. He lifted his head, sniffed the air, shook himself as if he were soaking wet, then glanced at me with an expression I could only label confused.

"Am I who, *bella*? Or perhaps you mean what?"

She laughed, the sound so rich and full of joy, I couldn't keep myself from smiling. I wanted to laugh with that much happiness, too, but I had a feeling I might never do so again.

"Since you mentioned it," I began.

"This is no place to have such a conversation. You on the porch, me in the dark, your poor wolf—"

"Dog," I blurted.

"Certainly," she answered without missing a beat. Her voice was not only beautiful, smooth and clear, like an aria soaring through a darkened opera house, but lightly accented. English was not her first language; however, she'd been speaking it for a very long time. "You must both come inside, then shut and lock that door behind you."

I hesitated. Locking myself inside with Lord knows what, and her dog, might be a very dumb move. I tried to avoid them.

"Elisabetta," she murmured, and I tensed, though my name wasn't a secret any longer, if it ever had been. "I am Carla Benandanti."

Well, that was convenient, although anyone could name themselves a good witch. Didn't mean that they were.

"You were sent to me by a woman who is both your friend and mine."

"Ruthie," I whispered.

"She told me you would come."

"You spoke to her?" I took an eager step forward. "Recently?"

"No. She's a bit dead, is she not?"

"Then when did she tell you—"

"Years ago."

"Years ago she knew that I'd come here?"

"Ruthie knew many things."

She had me there. Of course, Ruthie could be self-fulfilling her own prophecies. She'd been the one to send me to Detroit in the first place.

"Including," Carla continued, "that you would need a benandanti at some point in the future. Come along, *bella*, and your little dog, too."

Didn't *bella* mean "pretty" in Italian? Or maybe it

was "beautiful." I had a sudden flash of the Wicked Witch of the West. *I'll get you, my pretty, and your little dog, too.*

The wicked-witch thoughts made me even more nervous. I was supposed to be visiting a good witch, but one never knew anymore who was good and who was bad and who might turn evil if an evil wind blew.

As if in answer to my thoughts, a sudden breeze came up and nearly slammed the door in my face. I grabbed it just in time, glancing over my shoulder, scowling at the evidence of another swirling thunderstorm on the horizon.

What was up with all the storms lately? They seemed to be following me wherever I went. Since I had no control over the weather—yet—I returned my attention to Carla, who waited for me to decide. Was I coming in or was I running away?

I hated all this uncertainty. I had powers, so did Sawyer; together we should be able to keep a benandanti from killing us.

I stepped inside and locked the door behind me. A flash of movement at the far end of the hall had me heading in that direction. Sawyer had seen it, too, and his nails clicked against the scratched wooden floorboards as he led the way.

He slunk into the living room, gaze darting everywhere as he searched for the dog that still growled intermittently. The room was empty but for—

Wow, talk about the wicked witch. Except for the lack of a green complexion, Carla Benandanti could be Elphaba's twin: long, drawn, pasty face; hooked nose; a wart or two combined with bony fingers; and long, skinny feet covered in slippers the shade of rubies.

I glanced up and met the woman's laughing eyes. Bright blue, they seemed to sparkle—with life, with joy, with . . . magic. Every power this woman had was reflected there. I couldn't believe an evil witch could have eyes like that, but I also couldn't believe a good witch would choose the appearance of a hag.

"I can see what you're thinking," she said. "What's a witch like me"—Carla swept her age-spotted hand down a skeletal body clothed in a black sacklike robe—"doing in a place like this?"

She might as well set a pointy hat on her silver-threaded, long black hair and be done with it.

"I am who I am," she continued when I didn't comment. "I have no need for glamour."

"Do you have the talent?"

"I choose not to use it. Beauty is fleeting, only the soul lasts forever." Her smile was like her laugh and made some of the heaviness in my chest lighten. "I prefer not to draw attention to myself. It's safer."

"Safer how?"

"A beautiful woman is seen by everyone and remembered. An ugly one is easily forgotten."

Sawyer trotted past, breaking my concentration. He sniffed every corner, peered under the furniture and behind the curtains, but found nothing.

"Where's your dog?" I asked, and the benandanti's smile widened. "You have an invisible dog?"

"I have no dog at all."

"But—"

She waved a hand and vicious snarling filled the room. Sawyer, who'd had his head beneath a chair, jumped, thumped his head, and backpedaled, growling as he swung around to face his attacker. The expression on his muzzle when he encountered only us was priceless.

"I conjure the sound whenever the doorbell rings," Carla explained. "It scares most people away."

"And if it doesn't?"

She shrugged. "Then I conjure a dog."

"Why continue to live here if it's so dangerous?"

"Some places are magic, and this is one of them."

I'd felt such energy swirling through the air atop Sawyer's mountains as surely as I'd felt the chill brush of evil the first time I'd seen the strega's lair of glass and chrome pushing into the overcrowded skyline of Manhattan. Even though Jimmy and I had burned the place to a cinder, I doubted anything built there would ever put to rest the ghosts that remained.

This house had an aura, an essence, a waiting presence, but not of evil. Of anticipation, a sense that good might happen if you only knew where to look, who to ask, what to do. The longer I stood here, the more my skin tingled, and the louder the air seemed to hum.

"I came here as a child with my parents," Carla explained. "My father worked in the automobile factories. It was a good life. Much better than the one we left behind. We were happy. So much so that it seemed like magic. Later, I learned that it was."

"What were your parents?"

Every witch I'd encountered thus far had been something else, as well. Sawyer was also a shape-shifter, his mother an evil spirit, and the strega a vampire. That didn't mean there couldn't be a witch who was just a witch, but I wasn't betting money on it. Magic came from somewhere; magic was born in the blood.

"My father was human; my mother a walker."

"Ruthie said *benandanti* means 'good walker,' which, according to her, is a good witch with the power to end bewitchments."

"All true. I took my mother's place. I am both witch and walker."

I glanced at Sawyer, who was still sniffing everything. "Like him?"

"Not a skinwalker. No." I didn't ask how she knew what Sawyer was. I'm sure they had some kind of witch radar. "Benandanti can only shift by bathing in a moon-drenched lake. When I fight our fight, I will descend to the underworld through the water."

My confusion must have shown because she elaborated. "A benandanti is a werewolf who leaves behind its human form when she descends to the underworld to battle the wicked."

Sawyer trotted over and sat in front of Carla, staring into her face as if she were a long-lost friend. Considering what she'd just revealed, perhaps she was.

"I thought the wicked were on earth," I said. "The Nephilim."

"The Nephilim are the offspring of the greatest evil ever known, the Grigori. In the Bible, they're often referred to as the wicked. There have been times over the centuries when the Grigori have tried to break free."

"But a benandanti has always stopped them?"

"Thus far."

"What would happen if the Grigori succeeded?"

"It is written, *Within the kingdom of the beast will once again be a mingling of men and demons.*"

I got a shiver. There was so much I didn't know. I should probably take a course. At least buy a copy of *Doomsday for Dummies*.

"Where was this written?"

"The Book of Daniel."

A copy of *The Bible for Dummies* probably wouldn't be wasted, either.

"Kingdom of the beast means the Antichrist," I murmured. Whoever that was this week.

"During the great tribulation, that period of chaos and immense suffering, the gates of Tartarus, the pit of hell, will be opened, and the Grigori unleashed once again upon the world."

"*How* will they be opened?"

"If we knew that, we might know how to stop them."

"And that would never do," I muttered. "Heaven forbid that we're one step ahead of the bad guys instead of one step behind for a change."

"Everything will work out. Have faith." Her lips curved and she glanced at Sawyer. "I plan to."

Carla was right. Faith was a big part of our arsenal. If we didn't believe in the promise that we would eventually win this war, it was likely the federation wouldn't survive.

"What will the Grigori do when they're released?" I asked.

"A clear sign of the end times will be when the fallen angels once again mate with man and produce a legion of Nephilim."

Legion. Another word for *army.* Swell. We were already outnumbered. What in hell was I going to do when there was an army marching against me? I guess I'd just have to make sure that didn't happen.

"So you only become a werewolf when you descend to the underworld to fight the Grigori?" I asked, and Carla nodded. "That happen a lot?"

"In my lifetime, not at all." Her smiled faded. "But I can feel it coming."

"You can feel it?"

"Can't you? There's a storm waiting just over the horizon."

I glanced at the window, remembering the roiling clouds in the west and Ruthie's words. "Literally or figuratively?"

"Both. When the end of days approaches, the weather reflects the chaos that threatens the earth. In the past few years, the weather has been very unruly."

"Global warming," I murmured.

"Can't explain all of the strange occurrences. Certainly the thousands upon thousands of broken temperature records, the melting of the polar ice cap, the extensive flooding, can be rationalized that way. But what about the tornado in New York City, the cyclone in Iran, the snow in South Africa? And, of course, Katrina."

"Katrina? You're blaming that on the approach of Doomsday?"

"What else should I blame it on?"

"Don't you think building a city below sea level is kind of asking for it?"

"Except they've never gotten 'it' before. How many hurricanes have shifted at the last minute and missed them? How many times has New Orleans been threatened with extinction and gotten nothing but a gentle rain? It's always been theorized in my circles"—which I interpreted to mean witch circles—"that the magic there is what's kept the city safe."

"Magic," I repeated. "Voodoo?"

Carla nodded. "Voodoo is all about balance, and obviously the world's become extremely unbalanced. I don't think they were able to keep things stable."

"You're blaming Katrina on a lack of stability brought about by the failure of voodoo magic?"

"Do you have a better idea?"

I could quote statistics, if I knew them, but it wouldn't do any good. Carla believed the weird weather was a portent of Doomsday, and who was I to argue?

Doomsday would be back. All I could do was try and stay alive long enough for the federation to replenish their ranks so they'd be able to fight. That I'd be dead when all this happened didn't seem so bad anymore.

"Were you born with magic or is it something you . . ."—I spread my hands—"learned later?"

Carla's smile returned. "What you're really asking is if I took my magic?"

There was another way to become a witch—the way Sawyer's mother had become one—by killing someone you loved. When I'd called her an evil spirit bitch, I'd actually been practicing restraint.

"Did you?" I asked.

"Black magic is taken. White is given."

"Still not answering my question."

"My mother gave me her magic, through her love, by giving me life. Because life is magic, isn't it, Elizabeth?"

I laughed. I couldn't help it. That was just too much Susie sunshine for me, especially when the cheery point of view was coming from someone who looked like the latest advertisement for the Broadway production of *Wicked*.

Sawyer, who'd continued to sit at attention staring at Carla, growled without taking his eyes off her.

"Well, honestly," I said to him, "life's magic? That's not an answer."

"It's all the answer you'll get," Carla murmured. "I am a good witch and I am a werewolf."

"Like him," I said.

"No." Carla smoothed her ancient hand over his head in a gesture both tender and slightly erotic, though how it could be, I wasn't quite sure. "He is a skinwalker—more than a werewolf, and much, much more than a witch."

"Really?" I turned my gaze in Sawyer's direction, while Carla played with his ears. I couldn't believe he was allowing that.

"You'd like me to remove his curse?" Carla asked.

I jerked my eyes back to hers. "What?"

"He's cursed. I can see it in his aura." She waved a hand over his head in a circular motion. Sawyer watched the movement, his snout making tiny circles, too.

"You can remove curses?"

"What do you think a bewitchment is, Elisabetta?"

I'd been thinking in terms of jewelry—the amulet, my turquoise—not in terms of people. I started to get excited. Having Sawyer at full power—as a man and as all of his beasts—on the loose in the world, no longer confined to Navajo land, just might turn things around with the woman of smoke.

At the least, it would really piss her off.

CHAPTER 16

Ruthie had to have known that Carla could de-curse Sawyer, which was probably why she'd insisted I bring him along, but why hadn't she just told me the truth?

Because the rules on what she could tell me and what she couldn't were kind of wanked.

"What did you come here for, if not for him?" Carla asked.

"This." I removed the amulet from my pocket.

Her gaze sharpened, and she snatched it from my hand. "An amuletum. To protect from trouble. The inscription is Latin and reads, 'Hidden is the face of evil.'"

It certainly had been.

"Where did you get it?"

Quickly I told her about the *Naye'i,* who she was, what she'd done.

"Only a strega could have created this," she murmured.

The strega had bewitched the amulet. Hadn't seen that coming. But if he'd had the power to keep me from seeing what he was and what he was up to, then why hadn't he?

Because he'd wanted me to come to him; he'd meant to make me his concubine queen.

Once again, so glad he was dead.

"Why are you certain a strega created it?" I asked.

"For such a bewitchment, a very powerful witch is needed. To bind the magic requires bathing the amuletum in the blood of one who craves blood."

"A vampire."

"Certain spells, certain amulets and the like, are native to certain types of witches. Witch, plus vampire, plus Latin." She spread her hands. "Strega. Where is the witch now?"

My eyes met hers. "In hell, I assume."

"Excellent." She nodded once. "That saves me a trip."

My lips curved. I liked her.

"What about the *Naye'i*?" she asked.

"Could be anywhere."

Carla sighed. "They're like that."

"Can you remove the spell?"

"I'm the only one who can." I lifted my brows, and she continued. "Balance, Elisabetta. An evil Italian witch placed the curse—"

"So only a good Italian witch can remove it."

"Precisely."

And since the strega was no longer with us, the woman of smoke might have a tough time getting her tentacles on another.

One problem down, three or four hundred to go.

"You'll remove the spell now?" I asked.

"Now?" She glanced at Sawyer, who cocked his head. "But what about—"

"The amulet first, please."

Sawyer could remain a wolf for a little while longer, but the amulet was bugging me. With my luck, the woman of smoke would appear and not only take the copper medallion back but kill the benandanti, as well. If the amulet became just a necklace, there'd be no reason for any of that.

"All right," she said. "Come with me."

Carla headed toward the rear of the house, Sawyer following after. I had to hurry to keep up. She moved pretty well for an old hag.

At the farthest end of the hall, she opened a door beneath the stairs. I reached her just as she began to descend. Hesitating, I stared down the shadowed cement staircase, which disappeared into a chilly gloom.

It was never a good idea to go into the basement. Legions of teen scream queens learned this lesson every Halloween in Technicolor across the silver screens. However, what choice did I have? I could stay upstairs and wait, but then I'd never know for certain if she'd done what I'd asked.

Besides, I wanted to watch.

Sawyer had already trotted downward in her wake. He didn't seem at all spooked by the idea of serial-killing basement murderers. But Sawyer didn't own a television; he'd probably never entered a movie theater in his life.

Still, Sawyer knew about evil. He'd been born of it.

So either Carla was truly a good witch and the basement was just a basement or Sawyer planned to tear her into itty-bitty bloody pieces so that no one would ever find her.

The thought didn't even bother me. And that it didn't should really bother me. I'd come a long way from the cop I'd been, even farther from the bartender I'd become.

I went downstairs. The basement wasn't just a basement; it was a laboratory.

Beakers, bottles, Bunsen burners lay scattered across

several tables. Dusty books were stacked everywhere. Canning jars lined shelf after shelf, and they weren't full of applesauce.

"Are those eyes?" I blurted. As I did, I could have sworn one of them glanced at me.

I gave a squeak and stumbled backward, tripping over the last step and landing hard. Both Carla and Sawyer stared at me as if I were a foolish child who'd fallen in the mud.

"I don't like eyes," I murmured defensively. "Especially in jars." Really, who did?

"Those are pickled onions, Elisabetta." Carla flicked a hand at them dismissively.

Sure they were. When I glanced in that direction again, the "eyes" faced the wall, revealing only their onionlike white, round rears. All hints of humanoid awareness were gone, along with the pupils.

I narrowed *my* eyes on Carla, but she'd already moved to one of her workstations and laid the amulet on top. I left the jar of onion eyes behind to join her.

As I came closer, the air that brushed my cheeks became hotter and hotter. When I cleared the heavy table, I saw why. The entire inside wall of the basement consisted of a furnace. Maybe it was an oven. It definitely looked like something she'd stolen from Auschwitz.

I glanced at Carla as she hunched over the amulet. With the fire blazing merrily at her back, she'd make a good model for a poster of *Hansel and Gretel, the Return.*

"Do you bake down here?" I asked.

"You might say that. My kiln comes in handy for the disposal of just about anything. Or anyone."

"Sawyer," I murmured as I inched toward the stairs. I'd seen good guys go bad. Jimmy in particular. I didn't really want to see it again.

Sawyer ignored me. I was tempted to grab him, but that would be the hard way to lose a finger or two.

Carla's smile faded. Her brow creased. "Where are you going? I thought you wanted me to remove the bewitchment?"

"Go ahead." I remained near the stairs, ready to run up at the first sign of trouble, or at least try. I had no doubt she could wave her hand and freeze me in my tracks, maybe even send a lightning bolt to drop me dead. If a lightning bolt would kill me. I wasn't sure.

Carla picked up the amulet and, without another word, without a single deed, tossed it into the blazing furnace. Then she dusted off her hands and turned her attention to Sawyer. "You're next."

His mouth opened, and his tongue lolled out. If I didn't know better, I'd swear he was smiling.

"Hold on," I said, taking a step forward in spite of myself. "That's it?"

I indicated the kiln, where the flames leaped ever higher, as if they were feeding off the amulet. I couldn't see that a bit of copper would be all that combustible. Maybe the flames drew power from the magic.

The thought made me uneasy. Magic fire might be a serious problem.

"No spell?" I continued. "No eye of . . ."—I waved at the "onion" jars—"whatever? You just toss the thing into the fire? I could have done that."

Carla raised a brow. "Are you benandanti?"

I could be—if I had sex with one.

I looked Carla up and down. I didn't want to be benandanti that badly.

"Be grateful it's dust," she said.

I thought about it, then shrugged. "All right."

Carla turned to Sawyer, who still stared at her as if

she were the most fascinating being on the planet or perhaps as if he smelled Scooby snacks in the pocket of her black sack dress.

She began to chant. Italian? No, Latin. Always a good chanting language.

Energy zipped through the room. Sawyer looked as if he'd stuck a claw into a light socket. Every inch of his black fur lifted toward the ceiling. When I touched my own hair a spark of static electricity sizzled.

Carla's pale, bony fingers seemed to glow silver against the dancing orange flames of the open oven-kiln. She made a motion, as if she were throwing something at Sawyer.

I expected him to fall down, rise up, shape-shift. Instead, Carla jerked with a pained cry, as if the power she'd tossed his way had been tossed right back, and she stumbled, then crumpled to the ground.

By the time I reached her, she was already struggling to sit up. As I knelt at her side, the ends of her hair glowed with the remnants of whatever had knocked her down. A singed scent hovered in the room. Her gown began to smoke where cinders had sparked, and she patted them out with absent but shaking hands.

"What the hell was that?" I asked, glancing at Sawyer.

He sat on his haunches, gazing at both of us with a wary expression in his gray eyes.

"I didn't know," Carla murmured.

"Know what?"

"He isn't a breed."

"He isn't?" I asked, though I had been told that before. By Jimmy.

"He's other," Carla said.

"Other what?"

"Nephilim plus Nephilim creates something apart

from both humans and monsters. Something that can never truly be either one."

Sawyer continued to stare into my eyes.

"His father was a medicine man who wore the robe," I murmured. "An amateur. Not a Nephilim."

"No?" Carla gained her feet, brushing away my offer of help. "You think that turning into an animal, even by use of a robe, is something humans can do?"

I could, but I wasn't entirely sure how human I was.

"So he's other," I said. "So what?"

"They can't be trusted."

I let out a short, sharp bark of laughter. "I knew that even before I knew what he was."

Sawyer rolled his eyes. He didn't seem overly concerned about Carla's observations or my lack of trust. Sawyer never seemed overly concerned about much.

"Breeds have power, but they're more human than Nephilim," she continued. "Those that are other, by combining two forces of evil, can become stronger than either one of them."

"Which explains a few things," I murmured.

"If he were to go to his mother's side . . ." Carla left the rest of the sentence unspoken.

"We'd be fucked," I finished. "I know. So maybe you should remove the curse she placed on him. Might make him pledge everlasting devotion to our side, don't you think?"

She laughed, that sound of pure joy, which made me think of Christmas trees and sugar cookies. "You have a lot of strange ideas, Elisabetta."

"And you're stalling," I said. A thought occurred to me, one I didn't like much at all. "*Can* you fix him?"

"Fix? No."

I got a sudden pain in my chest. I'd have to continue to flail around alone, with Sawyer's satanic mommy trying to kill me, and Sawyer of no more help than an extremely fast, very strong, really mean wolf could be.

I would die. But, thanks to the *Naye'i,* dying was nothing I hadn't done before. I just wasn't certain I could keep coming back from it.

"What she's done to him," Carla continued, "is too strong. Because he is not a breed, he's drawn to that evil. It calls to him in a voice from his childhood. The only way to completely end this curse is to kill the one who cursed him."

"Got it on my list. Right below 'Find the bitch.' "

Sawyer sneezed. Carla cast me a disappointed glance, and I muttered, "Sorry."

"I believe she is trying to discover how to open Tartarus, or if she already knows, then she is preparing to open it."

I glanced at Sawyer. He blinked; so did I.

"Wait a second," I said. "Tartarus is opened during the time of the great tribulation. The chaos that follows Doomsday."

"Yes."

"But I stopped Doomsday when I killed the strega."

Carla's sharp blue eyes met mine. "Does it seem to you as if chaos were interrupted?"

Well, it had. Sure, the seers I'd been in contact with had their hands full, but we were short on soldiers and long on demons.

"You didn't know?" Carla asked.

"Know what?" I managed between clenched teeth.

"The strega was a minion, not the leader of the darkness. The leader of the darkness was—"

I cursed. "The woman of smoke."

CHAPTER 17

"But if she's already the leader of the darkness," I said, "she doesn't need to kill me to *become* the leader."

"That's correct."

"So why is she so obsessed with trying?"

"Ask him." Carla inclined her head in Sawyer's direction. He lifted his lip in a silent snarl.

"I don't think he's going to tell me." Even if he was capable of speech.

"The *Naye'i* is an evil spirit," Carla said. "She doesn't need a reason to kill you beyond the pleasure of doing so."

Sadly, that made sense.

"And it's common practice in battle to take out the opposition's leader. With no one to follow, armies disintegrate, some soldiers change sides, others desert."

"Mine won't." My voice sounded much more positive than I actually felt.

"Time will tell," Carla murmured.

"How could I not have known this? I lived"—if you called sexual slavery living—"in the strega's lair for weeks. I never caught a whiff of the woman of smoke."

Or heard a whisper. That damned amulet was proving more of a pain in my ass than I'd ever thought possible.

"She wasn't there," Carla said.

"Ever?"

"She didn't have to be." Carla swept her hand in an arc, from left shoulder, upward and over, as if she were drawing a rainbow in the air. A sparkling window of static appeared a few feet above our heads. "Watch."

The sound of that static swirled around the room. Sawyer woofed once and the silver, black, and white particles cleared.

Though the strega appeared to be in his thirties with olive-toned skin stretched tightly over fine bones, his onyx eyes were ancient. He brushed back his shoulder-length ebony hair with hands that ought to have been permanently bloodstained, but instead drew the eye with their long-fingered, supple grace.

His room had been decorated by Pashas 'R Us. Filmy curtains surrounded a low, round bed; a huge fountain poured water into a stone pool that had probably been stolen from a Roman bathhouse, back when they still had them. The walls were equipped with several pairs of cuffs and chains. The only illumination in the room came from the large white candles blazing from several candelabra.

Obviously we were viewing the past since the strega was not only dead, but his lair was toast.

He set a bowl on the end table. The flickering flames of the candles reflected in the shiny, maroon surface. I knew a bowl of blood when I saw one.

He chanted in Latin, dipped a finger into the blood, then traced it around the edges of the framed photograph of the woman of smoke—the one I'd stolen and fed to the garbage disposal.

"I always meant to ask you about that picture," I murmured.

Sawyer growled as the photograph began to talk.

"We have the information we need. Send the shapeshifters after Ruthie Kane."

"Yes, mistress," the strega said.

That certainly didn't sound like him.

Her eyes flared, and her lips pulled back from her too-white teeth. "Make it bloody."

The strega lifted his head and smiled. "What other way is there?"

My hands clenched. Ruthie had died badly. Not that there was a good way to die—unless it was at the age of a hundred and nine asleep in your bed after having just had sex with your seventy-year-old boy toy—but it hadn't had to be the way it had been. The leader of the light dies, setting in motion Doomsday. Pain and blood and fear weren't part of the equation. Those had been added just for the amusement of the Nephilim.

Well, two could play at that game. I made a note to myself: Make it bloody right back.

"Once your son is under your control," she continued, "unleash the vampires."

The strega bowed his head in an uncharacteristically submissive posture. He was either really scared of her or totally up to something.

"My identity will be kept a secret," she whispered. "It's better that way."

The photo of the woman of smoke became just a photo once more. The strega walked to the window and pulled back the curtains to gaze at the bright lights of the city against the ebony night. I could see his face reflected in the glass.

He was smiling.

"What's he so damn happy about?" I wondered.

"She's ordering him around like her stupid little brother, not to mention offering him up to me like a—a—a goat without horns."

"Which is exactly what he was," Carla said. "Her goat. The sacrifice."

"I guess he was a stupid little brother if he couldn't figure that out."

"Oh, he did figure it out," Carla said. "That's why he's smiling."

"You lost me."

"He planned everything. He needed her to gather all the Nephilim."

"He couldn't do it himself?"

"I don't know if you noticed, *bella,* but he was kind of a dick."

I choked. "Excuse me?"

"Is that the wrong word?" She turned to Sawyer. "Asshole, perhaps?"

Sawyer's mouth hung open as his tongue lolled out. He had to be laughing.

"The strega was definitely that," I agreed. "How did you know?"

"Stregas are all the same." Carla shrugged. "He would have had a difficult time getting the Nephilim to follow him."

"But they'd gladly follow the psycho hell bitch?"

"They like to back a winner."

I shivered. She couldn't win. I had to stop her.

"So what was the strega's secret plan?" I asked.

"You."

"Again I say, 'huh?' "

Carla wiped her hand from the right to the left, erasing our view of the past. The vampire, his lair, and everything in it, disappeared.

"Did he not try to seduce you to his side?"

"Doesn't everyone?" I muttered.

"Why do you think that is? You are powerful beyond anyone this world has ever known."

"But I'm not—"

"You can be, *bella*. You can be anything."

Silence settled over the room, broken only by the merry crackle of the fire in the oven. As much as I hated to admit it, Carla was right. I could be anything. If I'd given in to the strega, I could have been . . . well, a strega.

"He didn't know what I could do," I said. If he had he would have realized that once I'd slept with his son, I would have the power to kill him.

"No," Carla agreed. "But he sensed the depth of your strength. I'm sure he thought that the two of you could rule the world."

Together we'll rule this rock.

Yep. That's what he'd thought.

"Why didn't Ruthie know the woman of smoke was pulling all the strings?"

"The amulet."

I glanced at the fire. I hated that thing.

The sense of urgency I'd been feeling since I became the leader of the light increased so much I got dizzy. Once again, the Nephilim were ahead of us, and we were playing catch-up. I needed Sawyer to be Sawyer very badly.

"Do not despair," Carla said. "I can do a spell of my own, which will allow him to walk as a man under certain conditions."

I straightened, the weight on my chest lightening. "Seriously?"

"All I will need is some earth from the Glittering World."

The Glittering World was another name for the Dinetah. Navajo Land.

My chest went tight again. The Dinetah was back in New Mexico. By the time we fetched dirt from there we'd all be dead. Unless—

"I could have Summer—" I reached for my cell phone only to discover it had no signal in the depths of the basement. Figured.

"No need." Carla walked over to the shelves that held all her canning jars. As she passed the jar of eyes, she tapped it with her fingernail, and the single eye that had been watching me again faced the wall with a flick so quick I was left uncertain if I'd actually seen it at all.

She brought an empty container back to the table. A few more Latin words, a jab of her twig fingers, and between one blink and the next, empty became full.

Carla attempted to remove the top with a twist of her wrist, but couldn't, and after a glance at Sawyer, she handed the thing to me. I held it up. The clear glass container appeared to be stuffed to the brim with reddish-brown earth.

I screwed off the cap and took a pinch between my fingers. Felt like earth.

I lifted the particles to my nose. Smelled like earth.

I handed the jar back to her, along with the screw top. "How did you do that?"

She smiled. "Abra-kadabra?"

"That jar was empty."

"What's your point?"

"Then it was full."

"What is there about magic that you don't understand, Elisabetta?"

A helluva lot apparently.

"You conjured dirt from the Dinetah?"

"Isn't that what I said we needed?"

"And if you needed, say, a jar of money?"

Carla merely smiled.

"Now what?" I asked.

"Now I will do my spell. Run along."

"Excuse me?"

"Leave," she said.

"But—"

"What I will do is between him and me."

I frowned. "I don't think so."

Carla shrugged. "He's been cursed this long, I'm sure a few more centuries won't hurt him."

"I thought you were a good witch."

"I am." She made a disgusted sound. "I'm not going to hurt him, Elisabetta, I'm going to help him. You think he can't take care of himself?"

Sawyer dipped his chin and threw his head up, then repeated the movement, as if saying both *Yes* and *Get lost*.

I was still uneasy. If she wasn't up to something, why did they need to be alone? Then again, what could they possibly be up to?

Sawyer crossed the floor and shoved me with his nose toward the basement stairs. "All right, all right. I get the hint. I'll be in the car."

"Go to a hotel," Carla ordered. "This will take a while, and it isn't safe to loiter in my neighborhood."

"I'll be fine."

"You think he can't find you?" Carla made a shooing motion. "Go!"

I could stand here and argue but Sawyer wasn't getting any more human, so I went upstairs. As I reached the hallway, Carla murmured, "Payment must be made."

Payment? When dealing with magic, payment was usually in blood, guts, your soul—things you really couldn't afford to lose.

I took a step back toward the door, and it slammed in my face. No amounting of tugging could get it open again.

I pounded. I shouted. I went quiet and I listened. It was as if I were alone in the house. Whatever they were doing in the basement, they were doing very quietly. For all I knew, they weren't even down there any longer.

I hung around, tried the door again, got nowhere. Considering the superior strength I'd attained from Jimmy, I should have been able to yank the door from its hinges. That I couldn't made me think the portal had been fortified in some way, most likely by magic. Which meant I wasn't getting through unless I went out and found myself another witch. I wasn't in the mood.

By the laws of my gift of empathy, I would possess Sawyer's magic if he'd been born with it. That I didn't meant he'd either learned his witchery, or taken it the same as his mother had. He'd never been quite clear on which.

I wandered through the house, which was dark and dusty—an old lady's house—where a lot of cats might live, though I didn't see evidence of a single one. Maybe they were invisible. Like the dog.

The only bizarre thing I found was a nursery. For a baby, not plants.

The place didn't appear to ever have been used. Had Carla lost a child? Or perhaps she was expecting a grandchild. I hoped she didn't frighten the kid to death.

As time passed, I began to feel vulnerable. In the Impala lay all my weapons of warfare. Besides—I glanced at my phone—I still couldn't get any service. What if Summer had called while I was loitering in this dead zone?

I couldn't hang around any longer. I needed to let her in on the news that while we'd been moving forward with the assumption that Doomsday was on hiatus, it was, in fact, here.

The sun was setting as I stepped onto the porch. As

soon as the latch clicked shut behind me, I was sorry, but it was too late to go back. The front door was as impenetrable as the basement door had been.

I stood in the fading light, and the permanent bull's-eye on my back began to burn. I scanned the swirling shadows but saw no one, heard nothing.

If another Nephilim had been dispatched to kill me, if the woman of smoke had returned, I'd have some warning. The amulet was, if not ashes, definitely a lump of molten metal.

Of course, in this neighborhood, someone could very well be watching me with no more designs than to rob me, perhaps rape or kill me—maybe all three. Sadly, that scenario would be preferable to the first, if only because I could handle human monsters with ease. The problem would be getting rid of the bodies so I didn't have to explain how I'd done it.

Wasn't that always the rub?

Carla had said I should not wait in the car but head to a hotel. I could only hope that Sawyer would survive whatever she might do to him and find me as promised.

I checked my cell phone, which now had plenty of service and no indication of any missed calls.

"Damn." Summer hadn't gotten back to me. What was she playing at? She'd gone after Jimmy this morning. She had to know I'd be waiting to hear what had happened. Unless—

I broke off the thought. I didn't want to consider what might be keeping Summer from getting back to me. Anything that could take out a fairy and a dhampir was something I didn't want to meet but no doubt would. Soon.

There were bound to be hotels near the airport, so I followed the signs, picked one, checked in, called Summer. She didn't answer. Again.

I was too nervous to sleep, too nervous to eat, too nervous to read or watch TV, which was full of stories about the increasing chaos in the world. All I could do was pace.

I had to know so I picked up the phone again, then remembered my other connection.

"Touch something he did," I whispered.

I sank onto the bed, lay back, brushed my hand over my stomach, my breasts, my lips.

Nothing.

The last time I'd tried this, I'd been aroused, on edge, lust had been thrumming in my blood. Now I was too upset to feel anything but scared.

I took a deep breath, let it out. Forced myself to relax, and as I did my mind spun backward.

As kids, Jimmy and I had fought. There'd been jealousy over Ruthie's attention, a wrangling to be the leader of all the little children. We'd poked at each other, played tricks. After he'd put a snake in my bed, I'd bloodied his nose and loosened a few of his teeth. But he'd never laid a hand on me in violence, and for Jimmy that was downright saintly. Then had come a time when we'd realized there was something more than rivalry between us.

The heat of a summer day, the breathless excitement at the touch of his hand, his mouth, the knowledge that what we were doing was big trouble, but we were going to do it anyway.

Hiding in closets to steal a kiss. We'd sneak outside in the depths of the night. The moon spilled over us as we lay in the grass. He was so beautiful—skin smooth and dark, his hair shaggy and soft, his face full of everything he felt.

He'd worshipped me. I was quite certain he'd killed for me.

For an instant I heard another voice, saw my tears,

the bruises, Jimmy's face, and I forced those thoughts away.

"Jimmy," I murmured. "Where are you now?"

I needed a memory of love. It wasn't as if I didn't have quite a few. Even if he'd never loved me, as I'd come to believe, I had loved him enough back then for both of us.

Once we'd bumped into each other in the upstairs hall; he'd been heading down to help Ruthie bring in groceries from the huge van that was our only vehicle. I'd been heading to my room to grab my shoes and do the same thing. All the kids had been outside. We could hear them through the window.

It was early autumn. School had just started, and the air was still muggy and hot. I had on shorts and a tiny white top.

We'd looked both ways and crossed the hall, our mouths crushing together, my back meeting the wall, even as his fingers brushed my thighs, sliding upward, beneath the material, to caress the barely hidden curves.

As always the instant he touched me my heart beat so fast my skin flushed, becoming supersensitive, so that every stroke seemed to echo everywhere.

He lifted me; I crossed my ankles behind his hips and he pressed his erection between my legs. All that lay between us were some flimsy nylon shorts and underwear. I could feel the heat of him, the pulse. I took a breath to cry out and he drank in the sound with his mouth, as together we shuddered. Then he laid his forehead against mine, the dark drift of his hair across my cheek making my heart tumble into love as the scent of his skin was forever imprinted upon me.

"Lizzy," he'd whispered. "I—"

Then Ruthie had shouted for us and we'd fallen apart, straightened up, hurried down, whatever he'd been about to say as lost as we were soon after.

But I would remember until the day that I died how I'd felt right then when he held me, when he'd said my name in a voice so full of longing my eyes had burned, and my chest had ached. I'd believed that for the rest of my life, the only man I'd ever truly love was him.

Now, in a rented bed in a rented room in Detroit, I touched my chest, where my heart lay, where Jimmy had touched me that day merely by saying my name, and I tumbled out of myself and into the vision.

New Mexico. Different terrain from Sawyer's place on the reservation. The rock was still red, mountains still loomed, but the grass, the scrub, the cacti were slightly off. Still I recognized it instantly.

I assumed the white tents set up in an open area outside a small town were for the Gypsy traveling show. Especially since I could just make out the sign WELCOME TO RED ROCK on the dusty road beyond.

Though the place blazed with spotlights, it appeared deserted. From the litter here and there across the ground and the wispy scent of popcorn and cotton candy still in the air, the show had gone on.

The lights went out with a tinny thunk, one by one, and darkness crept over the desert like a thief. In the distance coyotes howled, and the hair on my arms tingled.

I inched closer, my gaze searching for movement. Where was Jimmy? Where was Summer? Hell, where was anyone?

A light came on in one of the tents. Figures moved beyond the canvas. I was drawn forward, through the air, across the earth and into the tent.

Jimmy was tied to a chair with golden chains. The Gypsies definitely knew what they were doing. Silver does nothing to a dhampir, but gold is something else. It wouldn't kill him, but it would certainly sting. Already his wrists and ankles had red, raw ridges. They'd heal, but much slower than wounds made by anything else.

I'd wondered if his vampire nature would overcome the sensitivity to gold. The metal certainly hadn't bothered the strega. But considering Jimmy's reaction to the chains, gold still remained his Kryptonite.

The tent was full of what I assumed were Gypsies. Dark skin and hair, rough hands, they wore jeans, white shirts, a few had hoops in their ears, but other than that, they could be anyone.

"You dare to come here, to touch our women?" one of the men shouted, then backhanded Jimmy across the mouth.

His lip split, blood ran down his chin, his tongue flicked out to taste, and his fangs flashed. He hissed at them—oh, he was playing this to the hilt—and his eyes blazed red at the center. He lunged, struggling against his bonds, the pressure of the golden chains against his skin causing smoke to rise.

The man who'd shouted held out his hand and one of the others slapped a gun into it.

"Bullets?" he asked.

"Gold."

The man smiled. "This will hurt," he said, and shot Jimmy in the chest.

I screamed. No one heard me. I wasn't really there. I could do nothing but watch. I'd never felt so helpless in all my life.

This was the end. I'd never see him again, never touch him, never work through all the issues I had with him. But even worse than that, he'd be removed from my arsenal of Doomsday weaponry. I'd lost DKs right and left, but losing Jimmy would be fatal for our cause.

All of this went through my head in a millisecond.

The bullet plowed into Jimmy's heart; his head lolled; he died with a smile on his face.

The Gypsy's finger tightened on the trigger again and just as suddenly released before firing that second fatal shot. Something was happening. Every guy in the place had stilled as sparkly dust rained down.

Summer walked in, took the gun from the man's hand and tossed it into a nearby bucket of water. There were several in the corner; I'm not sure why. Perhaps one of the Gypsies had planned to water the show animals after they ended the dhampir. All in a day's work.

"About time," I murmured. Where had she been?

Although now that I thought about it, today was still Friday. So much had happened, I figured we'd moved on to Saturday or Sunday a few days ago. Summer still should have gotten there more quickly, but maybe she'd had to buck a headwind.

With her head.

The fairy went directly to Jimmy, patted his face, smoothed back his hair in a gesture that made my stomach dance with an emotion I didn't want to examine too closely. She was there; she would save him, and I needed to be grateful.

The golden chains were locked. I expected her to demand the key, or have one of the Gypsies release him. Instead, she hit them with fairy dust, and they fell to the dirt floor with a hollow thud. I was liking that dust more and more as time went on.

Jimmy was still unconscious. His split lip had healed, but his black T-shirt was slick with blood.

Summer patted his face. "Jimmy?"

He didn't react. She slapped him, hard. "Right now, dammit!"

Her voice shook. She was pissed.

When he still didn't wake up, she snatched one of the buckets and poured water over his head. He inhaled a bit and woke up choking.

One hand went to his chest, which must have hurt like a bitch. He stared at his bloodied palm, then glanced up at Summer. His mouth tightened, and he came out of the chair with a roar of fury, fangs flashing. She flicked him a handful of fairy dust, and he went as still as the Gypsies.

How could she do that? Her magic shouldn't work on us.

She took his hand and led him toward the tent flap. Jimmy went with her like a child. They reached the exit and she turned back, giving the Gypsies a second coat, before she looked up and straight into my eyes.

No one had ever seen me watching them before, but Summer wasn't like anyone else.

She said a few words that I thought were Gaelic and together they walked from the tent.

I hurried after, but once outside the desert darkness closed in. No moon, just stars, the only light from the tent and the distant town of Red Rock. No movement anywhere that I could see.

Jimmy and Summer had disappeared.

CHAPTER 18

The buzzing of my cell phone tumbled me out of the vision. I reached for it with my free hand, the other still over my chest. I needed to return to New Mexico. I had to figure out where they'd gone.

"Hello?"

"Don't come after us."

"Summer?"

"He needs to be alone. I can help him."

"If *you're* going to help him then he won't be alone," I pointed out.

"I've blocked you."

I sat up. "And how can you do that? For that matter, how did you know I was there?"

"I'm a fairy," she said, as if that explained everything.

"Big fucking hairy deal." I was so articulate when I was furious. "How did you zap Jimmy? What happened to your magic not working on DKs and seers?"

"It isn't that my magic doesn't work on you, it doesn't work on those on errands of mercy."

"So?"

"I doubt Jimmy recalls what *mercy* means at the moment."

She was right, but I still didn't like it.

"The reason I sent you was because I knew—" I stopped, not wanting to say it, but Summer had no problem.

"You knew I'd think of him first. That I'd protect him, even from you."

"Things have changed," I said. "The woman of smoke is the leader of the darkness."

"She can't be. You're still alive and annoying."

I almost laughed. If I hadn't been so panicked about the situation, I might have. Quickly I told her what Carla had told me.

"It doesn't matter," she said. "Nothing's changed."

"Everything's changed. She's trying to open the gates of hell and release the Grigori."

"That's her job."

"And it's my job to kill her before she does it." If I actually killed the leader of the darkness rather than one of her minions, everything should go back to normal. Or as normal as it got.

"I thought we'd have more time to replenish the federation," I continued. "More time for Jimmy to get his shit together, but we don't. Bring Jimmy and meet me at Sawyer's; we'll figure this out."

"No," she said. "Jimmy isn't ready. He has to find himself again before he can give himself to the cause."

"There won't be a cause if he doesn't come back!"

"You told me to do anything," she murmured.

"Now I'm telling you to bring him in."

"I won't," Summer said. "I can't."

"I'm going to kill you," I muttered.

"You're going to try." She didn't sound worried. She didn't need to be. To kill her, first I'd have to find her.

"I'll do what I can as quickly as I can," she continued, and I knew that I'd lost. I think I'd known I was
going to lose from the beginning.

"Wait," I said desperately, before she hung up. "You
know a few DKs, so does Jimmy."

"Yes," she agreed warily.

"Get in touch with them. I need one to watch Megan
Murphy in Milwaukee." I told her about the seer's death
on my doorstep, and how I feared that others might
come and experience the same fate.

"I'll send someone," Summer agreed. "He can take
out any lurking Nephilim and inform any seers who
show up that they should disappear again."

"Great. If you get in touch with anyone else, have
them tell everyone they know and so on."

"A supernatural phone chain," Summer said.

"Right. Maybe I can get things figured out and settled
down and we could all have a . . . a conference call or
something."

Summer snorted. "Sure. That'll happen."

"You think Jimmy might be better in a week or so?"

I heard a vicious snarl from her end of the phone, and
Summer sighed. "I wouldn't count on it."

I tried again to find them, but I got nowhere, saw nothing. Then I tried to contact Ruthie, but the connection
was pretty one-sided.

She came to me when the Nephilim did, or when she
had something to say. Obviously the situation with
Jimmy didn't warrant a visit. Or maybe she didn't know
about it. Maybe Summer had blocked her, too.

I glanced at the clock. I'd been messing around with
Summer and Jimmy and my vision for close to two
hours. Where in hell was Sawyer?

I'd taken a room at the back of the hotel so he could

slip in without notice if he were still on four feet instead of two. Carla had seemed pretty certain whatever she planned to do would work, but I'd learned long ago never to count my chickens. Especially around a wolf.

I heard voices outside. Considering the time, I figured I'd better investigate. Considering the anger I heard in them, I'd better investigate fast.

I opened the door. Sawyer and his mother stood in the parking lot.

He wore athletic shorts and nothing else. I doubted Carla had had much on hand to lend him. His skin glistened beneath the harsh overhead lights.

If the situation had been less dire, I might have paused to admire the view. No matter how I felt about Sawyer, he was a beautiful man. It seemed a crime to have marked that body with so many tattoos. But beneath the ink, the skin was supple, and the muscles rippled and danced.

Beyond the spray of electric lights clouds roiled; the wind kicked up and tossed trash across the parking lot. Sawyer's long, black hair twisted in the breeze, as did his mother's.

"Who did this?" Her voice deceptively quiet, her face was far too still. Behind her, lightning crashed into the ground; the earth shook and the dry grass began to burn.

"Stop that," Sawyer ordered, his voice equally calm. A flick of his wrist and rain tumbled down, putting out the fire. As soon as the flames died, the rain did, too.

"You don't command me, boy. I command you."

"Not for a very long time."

I stood frozen in the doorway. Fascination and fear held me captive. I wanted to hear what they said to each other, but I didn't want them to know that I was listening. I especially didn't want her to look over Sawyer's shoulder and see me. I wore the turquoise, I should be safe, but there were hundreds of people in this hotel, and she'd love to kill every one of them.

The woman of smoke stepped closer to her son. Sawyer tensed, but he didn't move back. When dealing with vicious animals, any show of weakness was an open invitation to get your throat torn out.

"You think you're so powerful?"

She drew a fingernail down his face. I half expected a gash to open and blood to pour out. Sawyer didn't flinch. God, he was good.

"You think you can *take* me?" she whispered.

He didn't answer. She continued to slide her fingernail down his neck, across his chest. I frowned. The way she was staring at him made my skin crawl, as if she wanted to—

The *Naye'i* leaned forward and licked Sawyer's collarbone, then pressed her face to his neck and breathed in as she ran her palms down his back, her fingers drifting beneath the hem of his shorts to caress the tight curve of his ass. Yuck!

"Join with me." She raised her head, took his lip in her teeth and tugged, then kissed him full on the mouth. It seemed like there was a lot of tongue. I fought not to gag.

When she removed her lips from his, she stayed so close their noses were only a wisp away. "I'll give you her," she whispered.

I stiffened as a dizzying sense of déjà vu washed over me. The strega had promised me to Jimmy, although in the end he'd planned to have me for himself. Actually they'd planned to have me together.

"Who said I want her?" Sawyer asked.

Yeah, I thought. *Who said?*

The woman of smoke laughed, and the wind answered.

I eyed the burgeoning storm warily. The way she was whipping up the elements, we were due for a tornado any second.

"You know the darkness calls to you." The *Naye'i* trailed her mouth along his jaw as she whispered temptation. "You want to go there. With me."

His shoulders tensed; his hands clenched. Should I go to him now? Or would that only make things worse?

"The light is swallowed by the dark," she whispered. "Only pain and death wait for you there."

"That's not what the prophecies say."

"Their prophecies. Not ours."

Theirs? Ours? What was she talking about?

"We're good together." Her hand slid around to the front of his shorts.

I took a step forward. Sawyer made a staying motion, palm out, in my direction. Hell, he'd known I was here the whole time. Did she?

"You know that you want it," she murmured.

What did she mean by "it"? The world? The power? Me?

Or her?

The way she was touching him, murmuring, rubbing, made me sick. The way Sawyer just stood there and let her wasn't helping.

No wonder he was so screwed up. No wonder sex for him was a job, a weapon, a blip on the radar of his life.

Oh, he was good at it, but when it was over he stood up and walked away as if nothing had ever happened. For Sawyer, sex was a means to an end. He used it to unblock someone's powers, to get what he wanted or what the federation paid him to get. And now I understood why.

"I know what I don't want," he said in that too calm voice.

The sky swirled with wind and rain. The *Naye'i*'s

face was as white as the lights shining above, her eyes black pools, her mouth a slash of blood-red lips.

"You think I went through childbirth for nothing?" she shouted.

Lightning sizzled, striking the pavement all around her. Her hair stood straight up, making her appear not only crazed but electrocuted.

"I did it for you," she roared, her voice a bestial growl.

"Thank you," Sawyer said mildly.

She screamed and the earth shook. I half expected a crevice to open and swallow them both. But that would be too easy. And did I really want to lose Sawyer, even if it meant losing her, too?

I just didn't know.

"I will kill her slowly. I'll eat her intestines while you watch. I'll make her beg to die. I'll make her hate you."

"She already does."

"Then why do you protect her? Why did you mark her as yours?"

I leaned forward, straining my ears, but he didn't answer.

Without warning, the *Naye'i* threw out her arm, pointing in my direction. Fire shot from her fingertips. I had no time to duck, not that ducking would have done one damn bit of good.

However, the flames stopped several feet from me, roaring and dancing, flaring upward, then rolling back down as if turned away by an invisible firewall.

I lifted my hand to the turquoise; the stone was hot to the touch. As my fingers curled around it, the *Naye'i* shrieked again and disappeared in a column of smoke. The instant she did, the flames died, along with the storm.

CHAPTER 19

Sawyer walked across the parking lot, his skin golden even beneath the silver flare of the lights, his gait as smooth as a panther's. We were really going to have to find him some clothes; he'd stop traffic like this.

I couldn't help it, my gaze dropped to his crotch to see if he was aroused.

He wasn't. Thank God.

I knew nothing about incest. The very word made me wince. The thought made me nauseous. But I had to think that the perversion had a permanent effect on the psyche of the victim. Even if the victim, and the victor, weren't entirely human.

Sawyer seemed no worse for the encounter. The same couldn't be said of me. I was shaking.

He herded me inside, shut and locked the door, then threw out his arms, threw back his head, and sang a Navajo chant to the ceiling. Watching him in the half-light, nearly naked, tattoos dancing, his long, dark hair cascading past his shoulders, I wanted him, too. And that I did disgusted me. He'd been preyed on enough.

Seeing Sawyer as a victim disturbed me. He'd always been the bane of my life. I'd feared him. I'd hated him, as he'd said. But there'd been something between us from the first moment we'd met. I hadn't understood at fifteen what that something was; I'd only known that it, that he, was dangerous.

He stopped chanting, lowered his arms, and then his head, though he didn't look at me, continued to face away from me. "That should keep her out for a while," he murmured.

I glanced at the door. "She's coming back?"

"What do you think?" Sawyer took a breath, then released it.

I found myself fascinated by the play of muscles beneath his skin, the inked images of the shark on his shoulder and the hawk at the small of his back. The crocodile on his forearm—

The image made me pause. It was new, except I'd seen it before.

In his dreams.

I wondered momentarily why he'd gotten it, then remembered what I'd felt as my fingers brushed the image—strength in my jaws, the furious urge to chase and to kill, the power over all that swam in the waters. Every being etched into Sawyer's skin was a beast of prey. Really, what good would it do to shape-shift into a lamb?

But I also had to wonder if his tattoos were begun as a defense against the indefensible. His mother had preyed on him; he'd had to become an überpredator in order to survive—both physically and mentally. Not that Sawyer had ever seemed to have a lot of psychological problems.

Considering what I'd just witnessed, Sawyer's not having psychological problems was a problem.

"What did you do?" I asked.

He glanced over his shoulder; for an instant his face

was stark, haunted, and I caught my breath. Was he going to tell me about his past? Could I handle it if he did? Then the unguarded expression was gone, replaced by his usual indifference.

"I cast a spell of protection. It'll keep her out for a few hours, maybe even the rest of the night."

"Why don't you cast that spell over and over and over again? Keep her away forever."

"She's too strong. Once she breaks this spell, it doesn't work anymore. And there aren't very many that work against her at all."

"You need to save them."

He nodded.

I opened my mouth to ask why tonight, then shut it again. Why not tonight? I could certainly use a rest from her popping in and trying to kill me.

Sawyer turned away from the door, and my gaze was captured by the tiny bottle hanging from a strip of rawhide looped around his neck.

I reached out and captured it between my forefinger and thumb. Inside was a bit of red-brown dirt.

Sawyer had gone still; he barely seemed to breathe. I lifted my eyes to his. "What did Carla do?"

He looked away, then back again, shrugged. "A spell. As long as I wear this talisman, I can walk as a man anywhere that I wish."

"And if you don't wear it?"

"Woof."

"Very funny."

"I thought so."

Yet he wasn't smiling. He so rarely did. After today, I could understand why.

"Talisman," I murmured. "Not an amulet?"

"An amulet is for protection, a talisman brings good fortune."

"Your mother—"

"Don't call her that." He didn't raise his voice; nevertheless I flinched at the fury in the words.

"All right," I agreed, though what was, was, and the *Naye'i* was his mother. "The woman of smoke had an amulet."

"To protect her from her enemies by hiding her from their seeking eyes."

"And this?" I lifted the bottle a little higher.

"A talisman to bring me . . ." He spread his clever hands. "Me."

I nodded, laying the talisman against his chest. My fingertips brushed his skin and he shuddered, then took a step back.

"You okay?" He'd never reacted that way before; it was almost as though he couldn't stand to be near me.

"Fine," he said, and brushed past. "Without my fur, the air's too cold."

It was summer, nearly eighty degrees out there, but I didn't bother to point that out. He wasn't cold and we both knew it.

"I'll take a shower." He disappeared into the bathroom.

"I guess we're sharing a room," I murmured to the closed door.

I hadn't had much choice when he was furry, but now . . . I wasn't so certain staying in the same room with Sawyer was the best idea. Not that his being furry had done anything to stop the sex—at least in our minds.

I wandered around the room, uncertain what to do with myself. I picked up the TV remote, hit the on button, then just as quickly hit the off. I wanted silence. I needed to think.

I sat on the bed, but every time I tried to mull over

our situation, I saw again the woman of smoke trailing her fingertip over Sawyer's chest. Was I ever going to get that out of my brain? How did he?

Bam!

A dull cracking thud reverberated through the room. I glanced at the door, but it was still on the hinges, then up at the ceiling, but nothing huge and scaly was peeling back the roof and preparing to climb inside.

Bam!

The sound came again. From the bathroom.

I crossed the short distance, then turned the knob and walked right in.

The water was still running, the room full of steam. The red athletic shorts lay in a heap on the floor.

Sawyer leaned against the sink, shoulders hunched, head bowed. His hair was wet, he smelled of hotel soap, though even that couldn't erase the scent of fire, the mountains, distant lightning.

My gaze swept the room. Two huge holes gaped in the tile wall, and Sawyer's knuckles were bleeding.

"That isn't going to heal unless you shift," I said.

"It'll heal, just not right away."

"Was that really necessary?"

"Yes," he said simply.

I wanted to touch him, but I wasn't sure how, wasn't sure if touching him was the right thing, or the worst thing, I could do, so I stayed near the door and I waited.

He shivered and gooseflesh sprang up across his skin. He really was cold, or maybe in shock. Seeing him like this scared me. Sawyer was afraid of nothing and no one. Or so I'd believed.

"The door," he murmured. "It's chilly out there."

I shoved it a little too hard, and the resulting bang made him jump. "Sorry," I said.

He didn't answer, didn't move, just kept leaning against the sink as the mirror fogged and his knuckles bled red rivulets across the white porcelain.

I couldn't just stand there, so I strode forward, twisted the water on, and shoved his hand beneath the stream. That he let me caused the already nervous fluttering of my stomach to flutter some more.

"Why did you let her touch you like that?" I asked.

"You think I could have stopped her?"

I lifted my hand, tilted his face toward mine. "You're not a child anymore. You could have stopped her."

He yanked his chin from my grip. "Fighting only excites her."

I fought the gagging reflex at the image his words conjured. I was going to find out how to kill that bitch, and I was going to do it, no matter the cost. If there was justice on earth, and most of the time I had my doubts, the killing of a *Naye'i* would be a slow, drawn-out, and extremely painful process.

"Did you know she was the leader of the darkness?" I asked.

He shook his head. "I'm a witch, not a mind reader."

I narrowed my eyes. Sometimes I wondered.

"I haven't seen her in a long time. She hasn't answered my call." Sawyer pulled his hand out of the water, turned it off with a flick of his wrist, then stared into the sink as if all the answers had just swirled down the drain. "I should have known she was up to something."

Yeah, he should have. But after witnessing how she behaved with him, I could understand why he'd just been glad she was gone.

"She offered me to you."

His gray eyes met mine. "Yes."

"I didn't know you wanted me."

"Liar," he murmured.

Suddenly the room was too small, and despite the steamy heat, my skin tingled as if I'd just stepped into a snowstorm.

"I wanted you the first time I saw you, Phoenix."

"I was fifteen."

"Age means nothing to me," he said. "What matters is what's beneath. The soul is eternal."

I wasn't sure what he was getting at. "Obviously age meant something. You never touched me when I was at your place."

"I didn't?"

My face heated at the memory of what had happened at his place last month. "I meant the first time."

"So did I." He came closer. Even if I'd had room to move back, I couldn't. Backing up was considered backing down. That was a good way to get my throat ripped out. Figuratively. At least for now.

"Did you dream of me, Phoenix? All those years between when you left and when you came . . ." He leaned over me, nuzzled my neck, his breath tickling the fine hairs and making me shiver. All the connotations of *came* ran through my head, just as he'd wanted them to. "Back?" he finished, as he kissed my throat, nibbled my collarbone, then suckled the skin where my pulse throbbed.

I couldn't quite recall what we'd been talking about. The steam was so thick, I could barely see the room around us. We seemed lost in the swirling fog, only the two of us left in this world.

I grasped desperately at sanity, caught it by the coattails just before it fled, and managed to lift my head, to speak. "Dreams aren't real."

"They are if they're memories."

He was trying to make me believe that he'd had sex

with me as a teenager, that he'd somehow seduced me and made me forget it had ever happened, except in my dreams. But I knew that wasn't true. The first time I'd ever had sex had been with Jimmy. Blood doesn't lie.

Sawyer was trying to push me away. He didn't like that I'd seen her touch him, that I knew what she'd done to him. He didn't want my sympathy. But he did want me. I felt that as surely as I felt his heat, despite his protestations of cold.

The urge to show him some tenderness, to teach him that sex could be about something other than nothing, overwhelmed me. I couldn't have stopped what was happening between us any more than it seemed I could stop Doomsday.

I stared into his eyes. "You're trying to push me away."

He stared right back. "Is it working?"

"No," I said, and kissed him.

CHAPTER 20

I figured he'd push me away literally, that I'd have a battle on my hands. But Sawyer surprised me by kissing me back.

His mouth was desperate, his hands were, too. In the past he'd always taken his time; there'd never been any rush. One thing about Sawyer, even when he was doing you for the good of the world, he always made being fucked worthwhile.

He tasted both sweet and spicy. I licked his teeth; his fingers tightened on my arms, one squeeze and then he released me. I grabbed at him, afraid he'd fly away, and when my left palm met his right bicep, everything flickered.

"Open your eyes," he whispered.

I did and saw his had gone wolf. A growl rumbled, and it took me a second to realize the sound was coming from me. If I could see my face in the mirror past the steam, I had no doubt my eyes would reflect my wolf, too.

I yanked my hand away. When we had sex and I touched his tattoos, the essence of his beasts swirled through me. I didn't become them, but I felt them, smelled them, knew them as intimately as I knew him.

"Do you want to change?" he whispered.

I stiffened. He'd said one day I'd mate with him as a wolf. I wasn't ready for that, didn't think I'd ever be. Becoming a wolf wasn't part of who I was, the way it was a part of what he was.

His expression as he watched me, wolf eyes sharp, man's mouth amused, made me realize he was trying to get me to run again.

"No chance," I answered, and his lips thinned.

"Phoenix," he growled.

I wrapped my hand around his penis, and the deadly call of a rattlesnake filled the air. I concentrated on him, on this, on us, and the urge to flick my tongue at him passed, although the urge to flick my tongue around him was irresistible.

I sank to my knees, took him in my mouth. He wouldn't be able to resist, either.

The rattle increased, drowning out the sound of the water. I touched his thigh, ran my fingers across the head of the tiger depicted there, and felt the long, dry grass brush my fur-covered body.

I used my teeth, not too hard, just enough, and was rewarded with a soft curse. I glanced up. The fluorescent lights were dim; the steam swirled around us like fog at sunset. I should probably shut off the water, but I liked the mist. It sparkled in Sawyer's hair like diamonds in a midnight sky.

His head was thrown back, his face tight, his hands clenched at his sides as if he were afraid to touch me. We couldn't have that.

"Hey," I murmured, and his chin slowly dipped toward the sleek, slick pane of his chest until his half-open eyes met mine. The wolf had receded, though it lurked, waiting to pounce.

I rolled my tongue lazily around his tip and his cool

gray gaze flared. Then I took him into my mouth, as far as he would go, and I sucked.

His back arched as he pumped and withdrew, but still he didn't touch me.

I wore all my clothes; he wore none. I licked him one last, long time, then drew my tank top over my head, flicked the front snap on my bra, was reaching for the button on my jeans, when he hauled me to my feet by my elbows.

"That's enough," he said.

I leaned forward, brushing my breasts across his chest. With Sawyer nothing was ever enough.

"There's no reason for this, Phoenix."

"There has to be a reason?"

He appeared confused. "Yes."

Poor man.

"Fine," I said. "How about this?" I took his clenched hand, pulled on his fingers until he released the fist, then I placed his palm against my chest, where my heart thrummed fast and sure.

"I don't understand."

"The reason is desire. My body and yours together because we have a connection."

"We do?"

He might be ancient, yet he was a child in so many ways. Had he ever been touched in love? Had he ever had sex simply because he wanted to?

He thought I hated him, and I couldn't claim differently because sometimes, hell, most times, I did. But there *was* a connection between us. Had been even before I'd become like him.

"I'll show you," I murmured.

I began with kisses, soft and sweet, lips only, just a wisp as our breath blended together. He sighed, relaxed, closed his eyes when I trailed my fingertips across his lids. Leaning against the sink at my urging, he let me touch him and kiss him everywhere.

His skin was slick with steam; so was mine. He tasted of the sea. My fingers raced along his ribs, given speed by the moisture that beaded like dew.

His hands clenched in my hair. I didn't have much. Not like him. He held me closer, traced his thumbs across my brow, my cheeks, as if memorizing the bones beneath.

I leaned in to press my mouth to his neck, to inhale that fire-and-wind scent of him, and he wrapped his arms around me in the first hug from him I'd ever known. Together, we stilled. I wasn't sure, but I thought his lips brushed the crown of my head. For just an instant, my eyes burned, and my chest felt as if it would burst. This just might be the dumbest thing I'd ever done.

I didn't have time to dwell on it. Sawyer's patience was gone. Or perhaps he'd felt something, too, and it scared him as much as it had scared me. At any rate, he tugged at my zipper and I took the hint, losing the jeans, underwear, shoes, and socks.

The water had gone cold at last. I reached in and shut it off. Sawyer watched me, arms braced against the sink, biceps bulging, erection jutting forward. I started for the door; quick as a snake, he reached out and drew me back.

"What—" I began.

"No time for that," he said, swinging me around, lifting me onto the countertop, and stepping between my legs in one smooth movement.

All thoughts left my head as he filled me completely. My legs hung awkwardly, so he put his hands beneath my knees and hitched them up and over his hips. The change in angle made him slide ever deeper.

I opened my eyes, just as he slapped his hand to the

switch and the room went dark, the only light a slim band creeping beneath the door.

The steam that had moistened our skin now chilled, but I didn't feel cold. I didn't feel anything but Sawyer inside of me. Harder and faster he pumped. I cradled his head as he took a nipple in his mouth, his hair spilling over my wrists, the ends tickling my belly.

Each press of his lips and tongue brought an answering tug between my legs. He suckled as if he'd draw something from me—my heart, my soul, sustenance. Then he used his teeth, biting down just short of pain, before kissing his way to my face, brushing his lips across my eyelids, my mouth. His palm cupped my cheek; his breath stirred my hair, and I stilled, something flitting through my mind like a prophecy.

But his thumb stroked the seam of my lips, the pressure insistent, as he continued to flex his hips, filling me, emptying me, filling me again. I forgot thoughts and feelings and prophecies of doom or glory as I caught his thumb between my teeth. I suckled him as he'd suckled me, bit him just a little, then let him go. He reached between us with that thumb, using the moisture from my own mouth to rub my throbbing center until I came.

As I did, he grasped my hips, buried his face in my neck, and did the same. Smoothing my palm down his damp back, I pressed my cheek to the top of his head.

We stayed that way, I'm not sure how long, until he kissed me. Just once on the lips, in the dark, and then he turned away. "I'll order food," he said.

Airport hotels, which catered to the business traveler, usually had room service, and this one was no exception. One of the reasons I'd chosen it.

"Great." My voice was too cheerful. I hopped off the counter, restarted the shower, hoping like hell the water heater recycled at the speed of sound, then I cleared my throat and tried again. "Whatever you want is fine with me."

There, that sounded better, as if what had just happened had meant nothing.

Even though we both knew that it had.

The shower was just warm enough to endure, just cold enough to be unpleasant. When I drew back the curtain, my duffel sat on the toilet seat. I glanced at the closed door. Nice of him.

I was running out of clean clothes. Tomorrow we'd have to hit Wal-Mart. Not surprisingly, I'd seen one just across the street. The superstores seemed to be multiplying like bunnies. I kind of liked it. Wherever you went, there they were. It was comforting.

Sawyer had put the athletic shorts back on. He didn't have much choice. He'd also draped a dry towel around his shoulders.

"Still cold?" I asked as I came into the room.

He shrugged, not looking at me, and one end of the towel slid down his back.

"You okay?"

"Why wouldn't I be?"

I shouldn't mention the woman of smoke. I didn't want to upset him again. Except I had to.

"Your mother—" He glanced up sharply. "Sorry. The psycho bitch from hell said they have their own prophecies."

"So I've heard."

"What are they? Where are they?"

"There have always been whispers of a book, composed by a Nephilim that wrote down the prophecies it received in visions from Apollyon."

"Revelation in reverse."

"Balance," Sawyer murmured, echoing Carla.

It made sense in a weird sort of way. Christ versus

Antichrist. Angel versus Devil. God versus Satan. Bible versus—

"What's their book called?"

"I don't know."

"Who's got it?"

He spread his hands.

I had so many questions. I paused a minute to get my thoughts in order. "Who in hell is Apollyon and where is he now?"

"Confined in Tartarus."

"A Grigori."

"*The* Grigori," he corrected. "Apollyon means 'Abaddon' in Hebrew."

"I'm a little rusty," I said.

"The Destroyer. The one who will rule when the Grigori are released again on earth."

"The Antichrist." I frowned. "But your mother's jockeying for that job."

For once, he didn't correct my use of the term. "Your point?"

"How can she be trying to become the Antichrist by opening Tartarus when the Antichrist is already locked up there?"

"The prophecy of the Antichrist has always been that he—"

"Or she."

He inclined his head. "—will not just appear on earth, but will have lived here and become a great leader, who is eventually possessed by Satan."

Understanding dawned. "When Tartarus is opened and the Grigori are released, Apollyon—Satan—will possess the one who released him."

"Yes."

"I wouldn't think the woman of smoke would take kindly to that."

"To rule she'd do anything."

And who knows, maybe she had another plan up her sleeve. Though what it could be, I had no idea, which was typical lately. I never knew what was going on.

"I'd really like to get my hands on that book," I murmured.

"You and everyone else on heaven and earth." At my curious glance he continued. "One of the prophecies in the book states the army that carries it is invincible."

"Son of a—" I broke off. "Like the Arc of the Covenant?"

"Balance," he reminded me. "If the forces of light have an icon that promises invincibility . . ."

"Then the forces of darkness get one, too. How in hell are we supposed to win this war again?"

"Who says that we will?"

"The proph—" I choked as I realized what he meant. For every prophecy existed a counterprophesy. They canceled each other out.

I'd been working under the assumption, the belief, the faith, that in the end our side would triumph. But that was because the good guys said so.

The bad guys said so, too.

Sawyer's eyes met mine. "Faith means nothing if the outcome is preordained."

"What?" He was reading my mind again, and I was too shook to think straight.

"Faith is belief in the unbelievable. Rock-solid conviction that the unseen is real. Support of a truth that could very well be untrue."

"A prophecy."

"Exactly. To win, Phoenix, you have to believe that you will."

CHAPTER 21

In order to win, I had to believe that I would.

Easy for him to say.

We slept in separate beds, which seemed stupid after what we'd shared, but it wasn't my idea. I wouldn't have said a word if Sawyer had climbed in beside me. I wouldn't have said a word if he'd wanted to *be* inside me.

But he'd pulled back emotionally, and he seemed to be following up by pulling back physically. I figured he didn't know how to handle feelings. How could he?

And right now I didn't have time to psychoanalyze, even if I were capable of it. I had enough issues of my own.

I had a hard time sleeping, and not just because of the new info on prophecies—good, bad, and potentially worthless. Every time I started to drift off, the wind howled like a furious woman, rattling the window so loudly there were times I thought it might shatter. Since I thought there *was* a furious woman out there trying to break the protective spell Sawyer had cast over us, I had my doubts that what I heard was the wind.

And then there were my unvoiced fears. Would we win? Could we win? Who would die and how many?

I finally fell into an exhausted and fitful rest. I should have known that Ruthie would come.

I opened the white gate, walked up the pristine sidewalk, caught the scent of summer wind and burgeoning flowers. In Ruthie's heaven, the sun always shone, and the rains never came. It was heaven, after all.

She was in the backyard with the kids, at least a dozen. Had they all come from Lake Vista? Did it even matter? I hated when Ruthie had a full house. It was like a big guilt party thrown just for me.

I sat next to her on a bench near the wall, where the overhang cast a bit of shade. Our arms brushed. She was solid; so was I. Everything here was just the same as it was on earth, even when it was different.

For instance, Ruthie looked the same, but she was dead. The house looked different from the place she'd died, yet it was still her house. These visions were like dreams—a combination of the familiar and the bizarre. Yet, somehow, I understood they were also real.

"Do you know anything about a book of Satanic prophesies?"

"Mmm-hmm," Ruthie murmured, eyes closed, head resting against the white aluminum siding.

"This wasn't something you thought I should be clued in to?"

"What for?" Ruthie opened one eye. "No one's ever found the thing."

"How do you know?"

"You think if they had it, we'd still be breathin'?"

"You're not breathing," I pointed out.

"Not because of the Book of Samyaza."

"I suppose Samyaza is just another name for Satan."

"Yes." Ruthie opened both eyes and sat up, casting a quick glance at the children.

They'd begun playing king of the mountain on a

grass-covered hill that hadn't been there five minutes ago. When I'd arrived they'd been playing softball on a diamond that had now disappeared. Talk about a heavenly playground.

"Samyaza was the leader of the earthly angels," Ruthie continued. "His name means 'adversary' in Hebrew."

"Adversary, destructor. What's Hebrew for 'asshole'?"

Ruthie turned her head. She wasn't above smacking me in the mouth if the occasion warranted it. I could tell by her expression, I was skating perilously close to such an occasion.

"Why all the different names?" I asked in a respectful and contrite voice.

Ruthie's attention returned to the children. They all played together—toddlers and tweens. Whenever we'd tried to start a game of king of the mountain, on the mammoth snowpiles left behind by the city plows, Ruthie had always put the kibosh on it as too dangerous.

Someone's gonna get hurt and then there'll be trouble.

Social services took a dim view of broken arms in foster care. Sadly, they were rarely an accident.

I doubted arms could be broken here no matter what these kids did. So a game of king of the mountain, even with someone three times your age and five times your weight, wasn't going to be dangerous at all. I'd envy them, except they were dead.

"The true name of the Devil is known only to God," Ruthie answered, "who stripped Satan of all identity when he rebelled."

"Then where did the word 'Satan' come from?"

"Hebrew term for the Devil was *Ha Satan*. Lucifer is the name given to him by the Babylonians. He said he was the angel of light, the morning star."

"When, exactly, did he claim this?"

" 'How you have fallen from heaven, O star of morning, son of the dawn!' " Ruthie quoted. "Isaiah—chapter fourteen, verse twelve."

"I don't remember that one."

Ruthie's eyes narrowed. "Mebe you should have paid better attention in church."

"I knew I was going to regret that." Perhaps not then, but I sure did now. Wasn't that always the way? Church never seemed like a good idea until it was too late.

"The evil one was called different things by different prophets." Ruthie paused, tilting her head until the sun sparked a halo around her graying Afro. "I believe John used the term '*evil one*.' Matthew, Mark, and Luke called him 'Beelzebub,' Prince of Demons. In second Corinthians, Paul calls him 'Belial,' or worthless."

Despite Ruthie's admonition, I had a hard time believing I'd zoned out during a sermon on the multiple names of Satan. I doubted the info would be of much use to a layman.

"I still don't understand what purpose is served by confusing everyone with all these names."

"Having too many names is worse than having no name at all. Who are you? No one knows. No one cares."

"People care." Way too much.

Sometimes I thought the modern world was more interested in Satan, in all his incarnations, than they were in God. Which was probably why we were in the fix we were in. Despite my stupidity about all things Doomsday, I did seem to recall the end times following a period of disintegrating moral values.

"Naming Satan based on a characteristic separates him into pieces," Ruthie said. "He's parts, not a whole. With no true name, no true identity, he is defeatable."

"You believe that?"

She met my eyes, and in hers I saw utter conviction. "I do."

I took a deep breath and leaned back against the house. I wished I had Ruthie's faith. But I couldn't tell her so. She might knock my block off, and I liked my block right where it was.

Ruthie had always had many colorful ways to threaten us. Along with the aforementioned knocking off of the block, there had been "slap you silly," "slap you stupid," "knock your head to a peak and then knock the peak off," "knock you into next week," "kick your butt so hard you'll be wearing it for a hat," and my particular favorite, "pull your lip over your head until your inside is your outside."

In truth, she rarely touched us except with love. The warning was all that was needed. Usually.

"Why you smilin'?" Ruthie asked.

Remembering Ruthie's threatened retaliations for misbehavior had only made me think of how very much I wanted to save the world. The world was worth saving. Ruthie had been worth saving. Too bad I hadn't known she'd *need* saving until she was dead.

"No reason," I said, and she lifted a brow. Of all her children, I'd probably been the least inclined to smile for no reason. Didn't mean I couldn't change. Not that I had.

"If Satan's confined in Tartarus," I continued, "and has been since the angels fell"—whenever that was—"then how is it that the apostles and prophets were chatting about his deeds long after his imprisonment?"

"Just 'cause he's locked up don't mean he can't cause trouble. That's what the Nephilim are here for. And make no mistake, he's been pullin' their strings all along."

"What about possession?" I sat up again. "Exorcist-type stuff? Does that happen?"

"Of course."

"So not only do I have to worry about actual demons on earth—"

"Half demons," she corrected. "Least until one of them opens Tartarus."

"Fine." I rubbed my forehead. "Right now I'll worry about half demons and people possessed by demons."

"I wouldn't worry too much about the possessed."

"Why not?" I'd seen *The Exorcist*. I wasn't sure I'd ever be able to stop worrying about that.

"These days when people start gibberin' in other languages, throwing up pea soup, and discussing the demons whisperin' in their heads, what do you think happens?"

"They're given antibiotics and a free vacation at Camp Psycho."

"Got that right," Ruthie agreed.

Which meant that the possessed were incarcerated. Though I was certain not all of them were.

"Have you ever tried to find the Book of Samyaza?" I asked.

"No."

"Why not?"

"No one's ever seen it. We have no idea what that book looks like, or if it truly exists."

I had a feeling it existed. A really, really bad feeling.

"Wouldn't it be better to have it in our hands, to destroy it?"

"Better it stays hidden. Find the book and there's a good chance the thing could be stolen or used by the one who found it to—"

"You think one of us would try and rule the world?"

"Lizbeth," Ruthie said quietly, "even Christ was tempted."

Silence fell between us. When she was right, she was right.

"Never mind," she said at last. "Huntin' for the thing ain't practical. No one knows where the Book of Samyaza is. No legends, no rumors, not a hint."

That we knew of. I couldn't believe that if the Nephilim had a weapon like that, they didn't have some inkling where it was. I couldn't believe they weren't searching for it.

"The benandanti has more information to help you," Ruthie said.

The thud of a basketball against pavement had me glancing at the kids. A cement court complete with two baskets had replaced the grassy knoll.

"She couldn't tell me yesterday?"

"You didn't ask." Ruthie stood and moved into the sunlight.

"Ask what?"

"How to kill the woman of smoke."

I blinked. "Seriously?" Ruthie nodded. "Why don't you tell me?"

"I don't know."

"Why didn't you tell me to ask her that when you told me to go and see her?"

"There are rules." Ruthie's lips compressed. She didn't appear too happy about those rules at the moment. "There are things you must do. A path you must take. A path others must follow. Everything happens in its time."

We'd had this discussion before. Since hundreds of people had just died by werewolf, and I hadn't been able to stop it, I wasn't too thrilled with the rules then, either.

Ruthie turned and laid a hand on each of my shoulders. Her bony fingers felt like bird talons against my skin. "You're gonna have to be brave, Lizbeth."

I lifted my eyebrows. "Have I been particularly cowardly so far?"

"Listen," she snapped, and her grip tightened. "You'll have to do things you don't wanna do; you'll have to hurt people you don't wanna hurt."

She turned away as quickly as she'd turned to me, dropping her hands to her sides and clenching them tightly.

The house, the kids, Ruthie began to fade. Before it disappeared completely, I could have sworn I heard her whisper, "I did."

I awoke in the hotel room. The sun spilled around the edges of the closed curtains and traced patterns across the floor. Sawyer was gone.

That got me out of bed in a hurry. I pulled back the shades. The Impala sat exactly where I'd left it; there wasn't a sign of Sawyer anywhere.

Cursing, I hopped around trying to shove my legs into my jeans, catching one foot in the trailing material and nearly falling on my face. I'd just zipped them when the doorknob rattled. I had my gun in my hand before Sawyer came inside. His calm gray gaze lifted from the barrel, pointed at his chest, to my face.

"What did you expect?" I muttered.

He wore one of my dirty T-shirts, a pastel purple I'd never been wild about. The material strained around his pecs and biceps. I was surprised he hadn't burst through it like the Incredible Hulk.

Combined with the red shorts and my tennis shoes—which seemed too big—he looked like a street person. The bags he juggled only added to the ensemble.

"You went shopping?" I was incredulous.

"I have been known to."

I'd figured he lived on his land near the mountains and rarely, if ever, ventured into a nearby town. Though he had to sometimes if only to buy coffee and eggs.

Sure, Sawyer had been confined to the Dinetah for who knows how long, but Navajo land was the size of West Virginia, so they probably had plenty of malls—definitely a Wal-Mart or ten, which, according to the emblem on the bags, was where he'd been.

I upended several. Clothes poured out. Underwear, shoes, socks, also toiletries. His bags held food. Tiny chocolate doughnuts and bananas, granola—I don't think so—juice and a pack of cigarettes.

I picked them up. "Seriously?"

He lifted a brow. Stupid question. He was probably half mad for a cigarette after loping about without any for however long he'd been loping.

I didn't bother to preach about the dangers. I was a bartender, after all. Those who smoked, smoked. Those who quit would still be smoking if it weren't for that killer of joy everywhere: lung cancer. Since Sawyer didn't have such a worry, I tossed him the pack.

"Any sign of her?" I asked.

Sawyer shook his head.

"You were taking a chance going off on your own."

His lips curved. "You think you could protect me?"

Probably not, but—

"She could have killed you. Then she'd have come for me." I fingered the turquoise. "Will this thing work if you're dead?"

He shrugged. I had a feeling that was Sawyer code for no.

I ate a doughnut, slugged some juice, wished for coffee and started the tiny pot in the bathroom.

"Why hasn't she killed you?" I didn't think the woman of smoke would be bothered by a little kidicide, or whatever the term was for murdering one's own child. In my opinion she'd done worse—the thought of which put me off my doughnuts.

Sawyer glanced up from his handful of grass and pinecones—I mean granola. "I told you, she wants my power."

And the only way for her to get it was to seduce him to her side or kill him and remove it from ours. "Still not seeing why she hasn't hit you with a lightning bolt or something."

"She's not ready to give up on bringing me to her point of view."

I went into the bathroom and poured coffee into two Styrofoam cups. His words made me uneasy. I didn't see the woman of smoke as the eternal-optimist type, which only meant there was a better than average chance that Sawyer would turn traitor.

Hell, *I* should probably kill him. But I still didn't know how.

I returned to the main room and handed Sawyer his coffee.

"I'm not going to help her," he said softly.

Sawyer insisted that he didn't read minds, he read faces, and mine was easy, but sometimes I wondered.

"You think after what she did to me that I could?" he continued.

I held his gaze, saw nothing there but honesty, which I didn't trust because I didn't think he knew what honesty was. And while I really couldn't blame him for not knowing—evil spirit bitches were notorious liars— I needed more of an answer than just another question.

"Jimmy said you aren't a member of the federation, that you only train DKs and seers for money."

"So?"

"The 'If you aren't with us you're against us' adage works for you, too."

"Where am I now if not with you?"

"Question with a question," I muttered. He ignored me.

"You say you won't join the woman of smoke, but what about other leaders who've come and gone, did you join them? Would you join a promising up-and-comer in the future?"

He took a sip of his coffee. "Hard to say."

I resisted the urge to stomp my foot and throw something. He could be so damned annoying.

The man who'd touched my face, kissed my hair, who'd held me last night was gone, and that was probably for the best.

I'd wanted to show him that sex could mean something, and maybe I had. Maybe that was why he was behaving the way he was. Neither one of us could afford to get attached. Most likely we were both going to die.

War was hell; in the case of Armageddon, the cliché was going to be literal.

"Let's get out of here before your mo—" His eyes narrowed. "Before *she* comes knocking."

I took the bag that held what I assumed were my new clothes, considering the tank top with the flowers and the white denim shorts, then went into the bathroom where I'd left my duffel. Ten minutes later I returned, dressed, brushed, and packed.

Sawyer sat on the bed, also in shorts, though his were khaki, and a white wife-beater T-shirt. On his feet he wore brown huaraches sandals that matched the white ones on my own feet. If not for the tattoos he might look like a tourist.

I snorted. Sawyer could never, under any known circumstances, resemble a tourist. Instead, he resembled a member of the New Mexico branch of the Hell's Angels who'd lost his knapsack and been forced to shop at Wal-Mart. Which was damn close to the truth if you took *Hell's Angel* in the literal sense.

We each brought another cup of coffee along for the ride, tossed our bags in the backseat, and I slid behind the wheel. Sawyer never asked where we were going—until I turned off the freeway and then down Carla's street.

"Wait—" He put his hand up, palm facing the windshield, as if he could make the road in front of us disappear.

I cast an uneasy glance at the pavement, but it was still there.

"Ruthie said I should talk to Carla again. Ask her how to kill your— Woman of smoke."

"She isn't mine," he muttered as I pulled up to the curb.

I had a strange thought. What if Sawyer had been wigged last night by whatever Carla had done instead of by his mother's attempted seduction? Anything that could overshadow that was something I didn't want to hear about but probably should.

"Sawyer," I began, but he got out of the car and strode up the walk.

I hurried after. He didn't knock, just tried the door and, when it wouldn't open, put his palm up again like before and—

Bam!

Open it went, flying back so hard it smacked against the wall with a crunch. He hadn't punched it; I don't think he'd even touched it.

"Hey!" I called, but he disappeared inside.

Sawyer was quick, but I was quicker, thanks to Jimmy. I arrived right on his heels, surprised when a dark-haired young woman appeared in the hall.

I glanced at Sawyer's face. Funny. He wasn't surprised.

The girl was tiny and slim, with olive skin and long black hair. She wasn't pretty; her nose was unfortunate, her eyes too small and too light against the sallow skin of her face, but she gave off a lively energy that reminded me of someone I couldn't quite place.

"Back so soon?" she asked.

I knew that voice.

CHAPTER 22

I spun toward Sawyer, who met my gaze with his usual infuriating calm.

"What did you do?" I demanded.

The benandanti—turned young overnight, or perhaps turned young last night—laughed her joyous laugh. "Payment must be made, Elisabetta, or the spell would not work."

"You—you said you could practice glamour but you chose not to. Beauty is fleeting."

"You call this beauty?" she asked. "I call it youth. Two very different things. Youth is worth having. Aches and pains, my memory was fading, my magic would go next, along with several other very important talents. I couldn't have that."

"So you—" I paused. I had no idea what she might have done. But I had a pretty good idea what Sawyer had.

Whenever things changed—people became more magical, more powerful, more anything—and Sawyer was around, sex was involved.

Carla had said, *Payment must be made*. And since Sawyer had left home a little short on pockets and long on paws, he'd depended on me for cash.

But he hadn't used cash this time. I doubted he used cash very much at all.

I turned away. Last night had obviously been one more in a long line of meaningless nights to him. I shouldn't be surprised, couldn't afford to be angry or hurt. For Sawyer, sex was business. I doubted he was capable of understanding it as anything else.

I returned my attention to Carla. "You bypassed the curse and in turn he made you young?"

"I bypassed the curse," she agreed. "He paid me as I asked; the result was that my dream came true."

She was talking gibberish. But magic so often was. I let it go. I really didn't want a play-by-play.

"How do you kill a *Naye'i*?" I demanded.

"I don't know."

My heart took a slow, painful tumble toward my squeaky Mexican sandals. "But—"

"There is someone who might."

My heart now leaped toward my throat. I was getting nauseous.

She smiled beatifically. Were her teeth whiter? "His name is Xander Whitelaw."

"Xander? As in Alexander?"

Carla's forehead wrinkled. "I never considered that, but you are probably right. You kids are so clever with your nicknames these days."

Obviously Carla hadn't been watching *Buffy* reruns, unlike me. I doubted I'd be watching them again if I ever got near a television for more than a minute. They just wouldn't be fun anymore.

Since Carla now appeared about ten years younger than me, the term *you kids* nearly made me laugh. Would have if I didn't want to put my fist through her brand-new face.

"He is a professor at Brownport Bible College," she

said. "In southern Indiana. He teaches a course on prophesy."

"Ours or theirs?" I muttered.

"Oh, ours, I'd say. The layman knows nothing about the Book of Samyaza."

"What do you know about it?" I asked.

"No more than you, I'm sure. I've never seen it or known anyone who did."

"No rumors of a location? No tingles about its truth or falsehood?"

"I'm sure it's true."

I shouldn't have bothered to ask. Carla was the one who'd told me about the whole balance-in-the-universe theory in the first place. Of course she'd believe in the validity of the Satanic verses.

"I've never heard a whisper about where the thing might be hidden," she continued.

She could be lying, but why? I put aside the issue of the Book of Samyaza for the moment. "Getting back to Xander Whitelaw," I said.

"He's written several books on Revelatory prophecy."

"Good for him. I know the prophecies." Kind of. "What I need is to discover how to kill an unkillable evil spirit."

"Xander did not begin as a prophecy professor. That came after his original interest in obscure supernatural legends gave rise to some interesting questions."

My ears perked up. "He's one of us?"

Carla shook her head, and her long, gleaming, pure black hair swung. "He has no special powers—not a breed, not psychic, just curious."

"I'd think he would be helpful to have on board if he's been researching obscure supernatural legends."

"That is up to you," she said. "Ruthie had me keeping

an eye on him, monitoring his research, his papers and his lectures."

"In case something interesting turned up."

Carla smiled. "If you think, after meeting him, that he should be told of the federation, asked to join us in our work, it is your choice. You are the boss now."

I didn't feel like the boss, probably because no one ever listened to my orders. Sure, Summer had gone after Jimmy. Then she'd nabbed him and disappeared, *against* my express orders. I should probably do something about that once I caught up to her, but how did one punish a fairy?

I glanced at Sawyer, who leaned against the wall near the front door, staring outside as if waiting for an attack. I doubted he'd ever taken orders from anyone, or ever would, especially not from me.

And since every other member of my elite team was hiding, missing, or dead, and I couldn't give them orders even if I had orders to give, my position as "the boss" wasn't as impressive as it should be.

I returned my attention to the benandanti. "You've been watching Professor Whitelaw," I began, then paused. "Exactly how have you been watching him when you were too decrepit to leave your house?"

Her eyes widened like bluebonnets beneath the sun. "Why would I need to leave the house to watch him?"

"Minions?" I asked.

"Magic."

Duh.

"He has information on the woman of smoke?"

"Not her in particular but the *Naye'i* in general. His doctoral thesis was on Navajo witchcraft."

Sawyer's head jerked up. I glanced that way, one hand on the hilt of my knife, the other reaching for the gun at the small of my back. Despite their uselessness with most things I'd met, I still liked having them nearby whenever possible.

However, Sawyer wasn't looking out the door; he was looking at Carla.

"No one talks about witchcraft," he murmured. "No one."

"How'd you manage that?" I asked.

His lips tightened and he didn't answer.

"The Navajo believe that anyone who discusses witchcraft knows too much and might therefore be a witch," Carla explained. "They also believe that if a person discusses it, the witch might come after them."

"Would you?" I asked Sawyer.

He stared at me stoically. We both knew that he would.

Which probably accounted for the many attempts his people had made on his life. They wanted to get him before he got them. Always a good plan when dealing with supernatural creatures.

"Dr. Whitelaw recently began to write an article on the *Naye'i*," Carla continued. "Because it's taboo for the Navajo to speak of such things, legends are rarely shared. However, Dr. Whitelaw managed to piece together a good bit of information from several different sources. If there's a way to kill a *Naye'i,* Whitelaw knows it."

"Then why don't you?" I asked.

"He's just begun to piece together his research."

"I'm going to have to go to him," I said. "Pick his brain."

"Yes."

"Fine." I strode past Sawyer and out of the house, shutting the door behind me. I was halfway down the steps when it banged open. I kept walking.

At the car I turned. "You don't have to come with me. You can stay here."

Confusion washed over Sawyer's face. "Why would I stay here?"

"I don't know. Why?" I glanced at Carla's place, figuring she'd be standing in the doorway watching us. But the door was closed, not a curtain moved at the windows.

"Sometimes, Phoenix, you make no sense at all," Sawyer said.

"That makes two of us."

He reached for the door, and I put a hand on his arm. For an instant the desert wind stirred the sand beneath all eight of my black legs, and the sun beat hot upon my back as I scurried along searching for prey.

I snatched my palm away from the inked image of the tarantula. In theory, I needed to open myself to the change. In fact, sometimes when I wasn't thinking hard enough about *not* shifting, the shifting sneaked up on me.

Sawyer turned his head, his gray eyes startling in his bronze face. He searched my gaze as if trying to see into my brain. I stared back, wishing I could see into his, but he'd always been able to block me.

"What's wrong with you?" he asked.

He was behaving as if he hadn't slept with Carla, then come immediately to me and done the same thing. To him, the two incidents were probably no more momentous than having first juice then coffee with his breakfast this morning. Both pleasant, but hardly necessary, or meaningful, or even memorable.

Sawyer wasn't like regular people. Perhaps that was because he wasn't people. He was other. No one seemed to know what that meant. But I was starting to.

He'd never be quite right; he'd never be quite human. And most of all, he could never, ever be trusted.

"Nothing's wrong," I lied. "I just want you to know that you don't have to come with me."

"You think I'd leave you alone for her to kill?"

"I have this." I lifted the turquoise.

"As long as you don't take it off, leave it somewhere, and then forget to put it back on."

Yeah, that had been dumb, but—

"I learned my lesson."

He straightened, letting his hand fall away from the car. "Obviously you've learned nothing if you think I'm going to let you go anywhere without me."

"Why do you care?" I asked. "You have no allegiance. You only train DKs and seers for the money."

"If it was only about the money, don't you think that the Nephilim would have me on their side by now? They've had eons to pad their bank accounts."

True. "Then why *are* you helping us?"

"You think I want her in charge? I've turned her down a thousand times. She didn't take it well. If she rules the world—"

"You'll die."

"I'll definitely want to long before she lets me."

I shivered despite the heat of the summer sun.

"Fine," I said. "Get in."

His lips curved. That was what he'd planned all along; I'd never had a prayer of stopping him.

I got behind the wheel. "Do you know how to drive?" The road to southern Indiana was a long one. I figured it would take us eight hours not including stops.

Sawyer shook his head. "Never learned. Didn't need to."

Since he could get anywhere in the blink of an eye as one of his beasts, and he couldn't leave the Dinetah as a man until he'd banged a benandanti, I could understand his lack of the skill. But it certainly would have come in handy right now.

"Carla said this professor interviewed the Navajo and discovered legends about the *Naye'i*."

"I was there," he said dryly. "I heard."

"How is it that a stranger has more information than you do?"

"My people don't talk to me."

They were scared shitless of him.

Smart people.

"You're telling me that in all the time you've been on earth you've never once heard a whisper of how to kill the woman of smoke."

"I heard things; I tried them. They didn't work." He stared out the windshield, his face a chilly mask. "Nothing does."

"So you think talking to Xander Whitelaw is a wild-goose chase?"

"No. I definitely think I need to discuss a few things with the professor."

"Oh, no, you don't," I said. "You are not going to kill Xander Whitelaw."

"Who said anything about kill?"

He didn't need to say it. His eyes screamed it. But then they usually did.

"You will not touch him," I said, then remembered Sawyer's hand going up and Carla's door slamming open. He didn't need to touch anyone. "You will not harm him in any way."

He didn't answer.

"I mean it, Sawyer. We need to hear what this guy has to say."

"And we will."

"And then we'll leave. With him in exactly the same

number of pieces as he was when we got there. He could be useful in the future. Who knows what he knows."

"Who knows," he agreed.

"You won't hurt him?" I pressed.

"No."

I was surprised he'd agreed, until I remembered that Sawyer lied. A lot.

I considered dumping him out of the car, but he'd only shape-shift and lope alongside me the rest of the way. Better to have him with me so I could keep an eye on him.

He lit a cigarette before we'd gone a mile. I was tempted to tell him that Summer wouldn't like the smell of smoke in her car, but if Summer could magic away memories, she could do the same with the scent of smoke. Besides, Summer was as scared of Sawyer as anyone else with a brain in their head.

I stopped at the nearest gas station and bought a map of Indiana. I was getting quite a collection. While I was inside, I tried Summer. She didn't answer. I wasn't surprised.

I'd had no more panicked phone calls from Megan, so I had to assume my paranormal phone chain had worked. Unless a Nephilim had gotten to her and ended any chance she had of ever phoning me again. My hands shook as I hit speed dial.

"This had better be so good, I'm going to have an orgasm from the joy of it," Megan growled. In the background, I could hear water running.

I glanced at my watch and winced. Eight A.M. She was in the shower.

"Sorry," I said. "You're alive. Gotta go."

"Hang up and die slowly," she snapped.

Megan would make a great DK—if only she was half demon and not a mommy.

"Sorry," I repeated. "Just checking in."

"You think I wouldn't have called if there was something to say?"

"Unless you couldn't."

"Ah, hence the comment 'You're alive.'"

"Bingo."

"Nothing going on here out of the ordinary." Something squeaked and the sound of water faded. "Except the new first-shift bartender is a total moron. I swear, if I didn't know better, I'd say he was trying to screw up."

I hadn't realized how much I missed her. Now that I realized, I missed her even more.

"Sorry," I said again.

"Say *sorry* one more time and I'll—" She broke off.

"You'll what?"

"No clue. Anything I threaten you with is going to be tame compared to what's threatening you now. You kill the bitch goddess yet?"

"Still working on it."

"Work harder."

"Gee, why didn't I think of that?"

Megan snickered. "Seriously, how's it going?"

"I think we have a lead."

"Who's we?" Megan asked casually.

"Just the general *we*," I lied, watching Sawyer through the station window.

He stood next to the Impala with the hot wind blowing through his long hair. The shorts, tank top, and sandals looked foolish, like putting a silly hat on a pit bull. No outer trappings could disguise the inner ferocity. Even when Sawyer was in this form, anyone with eyes could see that he was dangerous. I didn't want Megan anywhere near him. I didn't want her to even know his name.

"The royal plural?" she asked.

"Yeah, that's it."

"Don't let all this leader-of-the-light stuff go to your head."

"Believe me, I won't." That would be a good way to get my head torn off. "Have you noticed anyone hanging around?"

"You mean the bodyguard you sent?"

I frowned. If he was any kind of bodyguard, she shouldn't have been able to spot him.

"No," Megan continued. "I haven't."

Sawyer saw me watching him and spread his hands impatiently. I guess I had been in here a while. I held up one finger. "I'm going to have to go."

"Don't worry about me," she said.

"Yeah, like that'll happen."

"Same goes, Liz. Same goes."

CHAPTER 23

I drove. Sawyer sat. Neither of us talked. He'd never been one for chitchat. I didn't know what to say to him that wouldn't end in an argument, or worse, with him staring at me with that confused expression that told me he had no idea what he'd done to make me angry.

At least I had no worries about disgusting STDs. Anything that Sawyer might have contracted we'd both be able to heal, and I had no doubt that Carla could do the same, or at least devise a potion.

Pregnancy was another issue. Obviously Nephilim could procreate, hence the existence of Sawyer, Jimmy, Carla, and every other breed I knew and didn't. However, I'd been on the pill since long before Jimmy. I might have loved him, but I'd also seen enough girls in my situation ruin their lives all over again by believing that love would make everything all right and a baby would tie someone to them. What it did was make that someone run away all the faster.

I hadn't even needed a baby to make Jimmy run like hell.

I frowned at the Indiana countryside. We'd bypassed Indianapolis an hour ago—a much larger city than I'd

expected, with a good number of skyscrapers and the
traffic patterns to match.

The terrain I drove through now was a welcome contrast. Rolling hills, fields bursting with crops, grassy
knolls; we'd even seen several vineyards. I'd always
thought Indiana was as flat as Illinois. I was wrong.

But there were also areas of obvious poverty. Trailers
and trash and trailer trash. I'd be driving along admiring
the scenery and suddenly there'd be a broken-down house,
a graying aluminum single-wide, or a sad, pathetic excuse for a town.

As we drove slowly through the latter, at a reasonable
speed to avoid a ticket-happy smoky just waiting for an
out-of-state license plate to harass, Sawyer suddenly sat
bolt upright, then stuck his head out the car window, letting the breeze smack him in the face. If he weren't human, he'd look just like a dog. As it was, he looked just
like a dog.

"What is it?" I asked, but he couldn't hear me with
his head out the window.

I reached for his left shoulder, steeling myself against
the brush of cool ocean water and the distant scent of
blood that would signal the shift to shark. I had to wonder how often Sawyer became a shark, living in the desert as he did.

Before my skin touched his, he fell back into the seat.
"We have to stop."

"When you gotta go, you gotta go," I said.

"What?" His eyes were intent, but not on me. On
something he'd seen, heard, smelled, perhaps felt. Out
there.

"That way." He pointed, voice urgent, desperate—
two things Sawyer rarely was—so I followed that finger
down an overgrown gravel road that led away from the
town.

"What is it?" I asked.

He ignored me, staring out the windshield, practically vibrating with suppressed excitement, like a hound dog that had picked up a trail.

The trees were thick at this time of year; the branches hung low, swiping the sides of the Impala. The scent of summer—shimmering heat, fresh leaves, dandelions—raced in through the open windows. The tires crunched across the stones strewn in our path, seeming to accentuate our isolation.

It was in places like this that people died badly. Serial killers, perverts, rapists, men with hooks for arms—they all lived down overgrown roads in isolated small towns with inbred law enforcement agents who weren't bright enough to write a parking ticket let alone deal with a psychopath.

I shook my head. My imagination was far too vivid sometimes. Unfortunately my life was often even more so. There was something down here that had Sawyer quivering, which only made me want to run away and never, ever come back.

"Stop," Sawyer ordered, and I did. "Turn off the engine."

I flicked the key. Silence settled over us like a misty blue fog.

Sawyer got out of the car, closing his door carefully so that it didn't make a sound. He cast me a quick glance, and I did the same.

He jerked his head to the right, beckoned me once, then took off through the overgrowth, crouching low to avoid both tree branches and easy detection. I had little choice but to follow.

Well, I had a choice; I could stay with the car. Except that would only allow whatever was out there to catch me alone.

Wasn't going to happen.

In seconds I clung to Sawyer's heels as, head down, he made a beeline for whatever or whomever he'd found.

Ahead, the brush thinned, and I caught a glimpse of a ramshackle cabin surrounded by a scrabbly bit of yard. Sawyer stopped so fast that if I'd been only human, I would have plowed right into him. As it was, my barely clad breasts brushed his scantily clothed back. He didn't seem to notice.

I opened my mouth to ask where, when, who, how— something—and he held up a hand. Into the continued silence tumbled voices.

"You're gonna be sorry you ever came here, boy."

"Yeah, sorry."

"Don't know who you think you are just settin' your-self up in this house 'tain't yours."

Though the words were childish, the voices were those of men. Teenagers, I thought, even before Sawyer and I inched closer, then a bit to the left, to bring the posse into view.

Big, farm-bred white boys. No shock there. I doubt they had many minorities this far south of Detroit. I counted four in a semicircle around a fifth.

That fifth proved my all-white theory wrong. He was most definitely part something else, like me. Tall and skinny with it; his hands were big and his feet were big-ger. His hair was long and kinky, a mixture of browns and golds reflecting every shade of the earth and sun. He hadn't yet grown into his body or his face. When he did, he was gonna be dangerous.

Right now his nose was too prominent, as were his eyebrows, and his eyes glinted startlingly light in his darker than suntanned face. From this distance I couldn't tell if they were gray, green, or blue, and it didn't matter.

Those eyes made him different in one world while his skin made him different in another.

The kid didn't speak. He held himself ready, weight forward, hands loosely clenched. His gaze remained on the biggest, loudest boy. I figured that would be the one to throw the first punch. They usually are.

I was wrong again. Or maybe not so much. The big boy sneered the N-word—a more painful strike than fists could ever be—and the skinny kid popped him in the face.

Blood spurted. "You broke my nose."

The breeze kicked up, stirring my hair but not the trees.

Marbas, Ruthie whispered.

Was she referring to the black kid, the white, or both? Hard to say. Beyond the certainty that it was a breed, I didn't know what in hell a Marbas was.

"Kick his ass," the leader of the pack snarled, and the three huge beastie boys moved forward like hulking monsters from a Dark Horse comic book.

I took a step forward, too, and Sawyer put a hand on my arm. "Wait," he breathed. "Watch."

I nearly ignored him. I couldn't just stand here and let the kid get pummeled. He might be as tall as the others but he wasn't as solid. They'd been eating steadily and well for most of their lives. He had not. Besides, it just annoyed the hell out of me when someone got picked on because they were different.

It *did* go back to my childhood. Sue me.

However, in the short time it took for Sawyer to speak and me to hesitate, the boy took care of himself.

One came at him from the right, another from the left, and a third from behind. He snatched the hands of the two on each side as they tried to punch him, and swung them toward each other. They slammed chests, then foreheads, and went down like bricks.

The boy did a front flip over their prone bodies, and the guy who'd been about to bear-hug him fell on his face. The bleeding mammoth lumbered upward, and the boy kicked him in the chest with a tattered tennis shoe. His attacker not only landed on his rump, but the momentum made him crash onto his back and his head thunked against the dirt and dry grass.

The one who'd meant to squeeze the kid to death sat up, rubbing his forehead. The boy was leaning over the kid whose nose he'd broken; he wasn't paying attention. I opened my mouth to shout a warning as the guy lumbered toward him like an out-of-control locomotive on a downhill track, and Sawyer clapped a hand over my lips.

At the last possible instant, the boy ducked, twisted, and kicked out with his left leg. The attacker flew off his feet and back several yards. He was slow getting up, as were the other three. They shook their heads, dazed, but they came right back.

A low rumbling growl swirled around the clearing, increasing to a roar—a lion's roar—so loud and forceful I could have sworn the trees shook, and the earth trembled. If that wasn't scary enough, the kid's eyes blazed amber and his mane of tangled golden-brown hair stuck out from his head like Medusa's snakes.

"Marbas," I said.

"Some kind of lion-shifter," Sawyer murmured.

"What kind?" I asked.

Sawyer shrugged. He knew some things, but not everything.

The bullies ran, crashing through the underbrush like wounded water buffalo. The Marbas clenched and unclenched his hands, bouncing on his toes, his light eyes intent on their retreating forms.

His need to chase them vibrated in the air like an approaching electrical storm. When prey ran, predators pursued. It was what we did.

Even when I'd been a cop, the principle applied. Only the guilty ran. Not to chase them had been as against my nature then as it must be against this kid's nature to let the vanquished escape. But he did.

I contemplated him and wondered why we had come here. To stop him from killing those kids? He hadn't, and he could have, which made me think he wasn't evil, but you never could tell.

I pulled my knife from its sheath. Silver worked on most shifters and was always worth a try.

"You can come out now," the kid murmured, still staring after the departed boys.

I didn't realize he was talking to us until Sawyer skirted the trees and strode into the clearing.

The Marbas looked him up and down. "I guess you aren't from social services," he said.

Sawyer didn't answer.

"What about her?" He jerked his head toward the trees.

He was good. I slipped out, and as soon as I did, the boy's lips curved. "I don't think you're a social worker, either."

I supposed the knife gave me away.

"So who are you and how did you find me?"

Sawyer had found him. Which, come to think of it, was weird. He wasn't a seer, that was my gig, but I hadn't had a tingle until I'd gotten close. To figure out once and for all why we were here, I needed to get a little closer.

"I'm Elizabeth Phoenix." I put away the knife, then

held out my hand for a shake. A risk, true, but Sawyer could take a lion. I hoped.

The kid hesitated, as if he weren't used to people shaking his hand, then he stuck his out. "Luther Vincent."

The instant his huge paw enveloped my much smaller appendage, I saw where he'd been. Foster home after foster home. No one had had the courage to keep him. Strange things happened around Luther that no one could explain. Bloody things. Deadly things.

His parents had been—

The kid tugged on his hand. I didn't let go. I closed my eyes and opened my mind.

Killed by lions. In a suburb in—

My fingers tightened. *Cleveland.*

I wondered how those in charge had managed to explain that.

When he tugged again, I let him go, and the instant before our hands separated, I caught a word: *Barbas.*

I needed a quick session at Starbucks with my laptop. Then, hopefully, the great and wonderful World Wide Web would make all things clear.

"You okay, lady?"

I opened my eyes. *Lady?* I was twenty-five.

"How old are you?" I asked.

Luther glanced away. "Eighteen."

Sawyer snorted, and the kid's cheeks darkened. "I am!"

He wasn't. But we didn't need to go there right now.

"Who are you?" Luther glared at Sawyer. Was he just being a kid, problems with authority and all that, or was his inner lion sensing Sawyer's inner . . . menagerie?

"Sawyer."

"Sawyer what? Or is it what Sawyer?"

"Just Sawyer."

"Like Beyoncé?" Luther sneered.

Sawyer glanced at me. "Nephilim?"

I shook my head. "Singer."

His forehead creased. "Siren?"

"Is this guy for real?" Luther asked. "Been caught in a time warp, man?"

"In a way," I murmured, but the kid wasn't listening. He had other, better questions.

"Who sent you?"

I'd like to hear the answer to that myself.

"Who do *you* think sent us?" Sawyer murmured.

Oh, brother. Question with a question. That oughta get the kid talking.

"Is there someone chasing you?" Sawyer continued. "Do you have something to hide?"

Luther's eyes, which appeared more hazel now than amber, flickered. "This is my place. You can both just get the hell off."

"Is it your place? If I ask around, what will I find?" Sawyer moved closer to Luther. And Luther moved closer to me.

"Sawyer," I murmured. "I don't think he wants you to be so close."

"I don't care what he wants," Sawyer began.

The kid grabbed my knife. From the way he'd been retreating toward me, as if he needed my protection, as if he were backing down, I hadn't expected the move, and I stood there gaping like an idiot.

The kid was quick as a cat—wonder why?—and would have buried my knife in Sawyer's stomach. Except Sawyer was quick as . . . a lot of things.

He snatched Luther's wrist before the boy could even start a downward arc and squeezed. The knife dropped to the ground; the pointy end stuck in the dirt the way Luther had wanted it to stick into Sawyer.

"You're somethin'." Luther's voice lowered; the lion purred just below the surface. "Somethin' different."

I tensed. How did he know that? Sure, Sawyer didn't look like a regular person, but he didn't look like an unperson either. I suddenly understood why Sawyer had brought us here.

"Seer?" I murmured.

Sawyer shook his head.

DK.

Which brought back the original question.

"Why do you think he's different?" I asked.

The two tussled, the kid trying to break loose, Sawyer expending a minimum of effort not to let him. Luther showed me his teeth and said nothing.

Sawyer twisted the boy's arm behind his back and said, "Answer her."

"Hey!" I protested. "No need to get rough."

"He could get out of this if he tried." The kid's head went up; his face reflected his confusion.

I was starting to get the feeling that Luther had no idea what he was. How frightening would that be?

"Why did you think that I was different?" Sawyer repeated.

"I can feel it, okay?" Luther's voice was strained. The more he tried to break free, the tighter Sawyer's grip became on his arm. "I've been feeling it my whole life."

"What, exactly, do you feel?"

Sawyer must have loosened his hold a little because when Luther spoke again, his voice had returned almost to normal. Oh, the fury still rumbled, but the pain was gone.

"I walk by someone, and there's a hum, like bees or flies, but there ain't none. Sometimes they stare at me and their eyes . . ." He shuddered. "It's like there's a demon in there."

Silence fell over us all. Luther sighed. "I know I'm crazy." His shoulders slumped. "Just like they always told me."

Sawyer let him go. "They were always wrong."

Poor kid. I saw Ruthie's hand in this. I understood why I'd had to take this trip—to Detroit, to Indiana—and why I'd had to bring Sawyer.

"You're coming with us," Sawyer said.

"You think I'm stupid." The kid sneered.

Like the beast he was, Luther went for Sawyer's throat. Like the beast *he* was, Sawyer sensed the movement and jerked back. Luther's fingers tangled in the rawhide strip that held Sawyer's earth-filled talisman and broke it in two.

I had to close my eyes against a sudden bright light, and when I opened them again, Sawyer was a wolf.

CHAPTER 24

Luther stared at Sawyer; Sawyer stared at Luther, then Sawyer lifted his lip in a silent snarl.

"Dude," Luther said. "Cool."

Sawyer's lip lowered back over his sharp, pointy teeth.

"What is he?" Luther asked.

"Skinwalker."

"Werewolf?"

"Not exactly."

Quickly I explained that Sawyer was more than a werewolf, much, much more than a witch.

"What are you?" he asked.

"Psychic." I kept the sex-empath, ghost-channeling, psychometric part to myself. "What we call a seer. I can see—hear—what they are."

"What *are* they? Demons?"

"Half demon, half human."

The kid got a faraway expression in his eyes. "They don't seem human."

He was right about that.

I reached out and took the talisman from Luther's

hand. He blinked as if he hadn't realized he'd been hold-ing it. "Sorry," he said.

I tied the thing around Sawyer's neck and then stood back to watch the transformation. Sawyer's shifting of shape was different from any I'd ever witnessed.

His dark fur twinkled, as if dusted with diamonds, then his outline re-formed, growing larger, taller, push-ing against a circle of light until he burst free a man.

A very naked man. His clothes and shoes lay in tat-ters on the ground. Luckily, he'd bought a few sets.

He straightened, unashamed of his nakedness. Lu-ther looked away, then quickly back, then away again.

"You said you can see what they are," Luther began. "Can you see what I am?"

"Marbas."

He choked. At first I thought he was coughing, then I realized he was trying to hold back a sob. "I *am* a demon. I'm evil. I did those things I dreamed about."

"What things?"

He closed his eyes. "Terrible things."

I brushed my palm over his shoulder, as if I were of-fering comfort and *bam*—I nearly sobbed myself.

For the most part foster care is given by caring indi-viduals who truly want to help. And then there are those who prey on the weak. Perhaps Nephilim, perhaps not.

Luther had been molested. They'd found his foster father in pieces all over the backyard.

Good for Luther.

But the kid didn't remember doing it? That was . . . strange.

I tried again, touching him lightly on the hand. He'd only changed at night, when deep dreams had allowed him to open to the magic. He had no control over the shift. Yet.

"You aren't evil," I said. "You didn't kill those bullies, and you could have. Killed them, buried them, and moved on. No one would have ever known. That's what evil would have done."

"Really?" The kid's voice was hopeful.

"Really." I glanced at Sawyer, who dipped his chin, answering the question I hadn't even asked. "Sawyer can help you understand what you are and how to use it."

"Sawyer?" Luther's voice trembled. "Not you?"

After what I'd just seen, I understood his reluctance to work with a man. If it were that big of an issue, maybe I could get Summer to help him. Once I found her.

"That's not my job," I said. "He's training and I'm—"

Luther lifted his head. His eyes were shiny, but no tears had fallen. Crying was a weakness kids like Luther, kids like me, couldn't afford. "You're what?"

I opened my mouth to explain and Sawyer jumped in. "We'll talk in the car."

I glanced at Luther, afraid we'd have another fight on our hands, and if he got really upset, we might have a lion on our hands. How in hell would we get *that* in the car?

But he rubbed his eyes and nodded. "Okay."

He disappeared into the ridiculous excuse for a building, and I turned to Sawyer. "How did you know he was here?"

"That's what I do, or at least what I did before my mother confined me to the Dinetah."

"That's right. Ruthie told me you were good at recruiting new federation members."

"There's no need for recruitment. We are what we are; we're born for a reason. I bring out special talents, refine and train them."

I remembered how he'd brought my talent out. "You can't—"

His nostrils flared, fury sparked in his eyes. "The child is a Marbas. He has shifted; he has killed. He doesn't need to be opened to the magic, he just needs to be taught to control it. To bring it out when he wishes to and not when his anger or fear releases the beast against his will."

"But—"

"You think I'd touch him?"

"You touched me."

"You'll never forgive me for that, will you?"

"You want to be forgiven?" I asked.

He thought a minute, then shook his head. "I did what needed to be done." He glanced at the sunny sky. "As you will. We're more alike than you know."

"We're nothing alike."

He didn't answer, which was answer enough. Sawyer believed what he believed. He didn't care if I agreed with him or not. Which, come to think of it, *was* a lot like me.

"How did you know he was here?" I repeated.

Sawyer tapped his temple.

"Voices?"

He shook his head.

"Then what?"

"As the boy said, it's a buzz. Bees, flies. You feel the power along your skin."

"You feel DKs?"

"And seers."

"But he felt Nephilim." I frowned. "How can that be?"

"All DKs have the ability to a certain extent. They know evil; they can sense it, feel it, some smell it. But they don't know what it is without their seer. That sixth sense means less mistakes."

"They see evil people," I murmured.

Sawyer's face creased. "What?"

Why I bothered to make pop culture references around him, I had no idea.

I supposed things could get confusing. Demons in a crowd, which one is "the one." You think you know, but then again maybe you don't. But if you can feel, sense, smell it, then you can kill it without a qualm. Worked for me.

"In theory"—I bent to pick up my knife and return it to the sheath at my waist—"a DK could just stick a Nephilim with silver, see if they burn."

"And if they don't, the DK is dead. Better to wait for the information from your seer and kill them right the first time. The federation was set up the way it was because their method works and has for a very long time."

"If it worked, they'd all be dead."

"They will be," he said.

"You really think so?"

"No."

Why did I try to talk to Sawyer at all?

Luther reemerged with a backpack as battered as his shoes. I remembered very clearly showing up at Ruthie's with everything I owned in a similarly sized package.

I didn't even consider what legal issues might exist in transporting a ward of the state—and probably not even this state, but who knew? Someone might be searching for Luther, and then again no one might be. Sadly, when troublesome kids went missing, they were often written off as lost.

In my mind, Luther was already part of the federation, which made him my responsibility. I'd deal with the legalities if we managed to save the world from the prophesied invasion of the demon horde. If we didn't, I doubted there'd be anyone left to care about Luther, which probably wasn't too far removed from the present situation.

"Is there someone who might miss you?" I asked, just to be on the safe side.

Luther rolled his eyes.

"How is it," Sawyer asked as he led the way back to the Impala, "that you came to be here, in this town, this road, this house?"

"I just drifted, you know?"

Jimmy and I had both drifted when we were much younger than Luther. There was something in this kid's eyes that reminded me a lot of Sanducci the first time I'd seen him. The big mouth that masked the fear, the need peeking out from behind the bravado.

"When I got here, this seemed like a good place to wait."

"For what?" Sawyer asked.

Luther shrugged, his shoulder bones shifting beneath his threadbare shirt, reminding me of the shoulder bones of a lion, sliding beneath loose skin as he moved across the savannah.

More and more I was getting the sensation that everything happened for a reason, in its own time, or whatever other cliché applied. Life was fate, if you weren't of the opinion that God had a plan.

Right now I knew with rock-solid certainty that Luther had been waiting for us.

Ahead, the powder-blue Impala shimmered between the low-hanging, leaf-heavy limbs of the trees. A few scratches marred the once perfect paint. Summer and I were going to have words, but then that had been a given from the beginning.

We got back on the road to Brownport, and after pulling on some clothes, Sawyer explained things to Luther. I don't think I'd ever heard him string together that many words at one time. He laid it all down—past, present, and future prophecy. What the kid was, what he would become. He took it pretty well.

"Sweet," Luther said, and then he went to sleep.

I stopped at the first Starbucks I found, grabbed my laptop and went inside. Luther didn't stir. We opened the windows and let him sleep.

I ordered two iced lattes, handed them both to Sawyer, and set up shop where we could keep an eye on the kid. Then I accessed the federation Web site with the code Summer had given me and typed *Marbas* into the search column.

"Descendant of the demon Barbas." I glanced at Sawyer, who handed me my latte.

"Makes sense."

He took a sip of his, looked as if he might spit the iced coffee on the ground, then swallowed thickly and set his cup down with a disgusted click and a very dirty glance in my direction. I guess he'd never had one before. And wouldn't be having one again.

"A breed is the son or daughter of a demon," he finished.

"Half demon," I said.

"The Nephilim might be part human but they don't act like it," Sawyer said, echoing Luther's earlier comment. "When the legends refer to a demon, they're talking about the Nephilim."

"So what kind of demon is a Barbas?"

Sawyer shrugged and motioned at the computer. I typed some more.

"'A great lion that, at a conjurer's request, changes into a human. From the Latin *barba,* a type of plant used to invoke demons.'" I sat back. "So a Barbas is a lion that turns into a person, but a Marbas—"

"Would appear to be a person," Sawyer said, "who turns into a lion."

"Okay," I agreed. "His parents were killed by lions."

Sawyer's gaze sharpened. "How interesting."

"Why?"

"One of his parents was a lion and from the description you read, I'd say the other was a conjurer whose magic allowed his or her spouse to remain human."

"Why would lions—Barbas or Marbas—kill their own kind?"

"In nature, there's only one alpha male per pride. Battles are fought, and when a male is vanquished, his cubs are killed, too."

My gaze went to the Impala. Luther slept on, the descending sun shining on his hair, picking up the gold in the brown and making it sparkle. "That's horrible."

"Law of the jungle," Sawyer said.

"The jungle sucks." My voice was too loud and several people glanced my way, then went back to their books, their kids, their laptops. I lowered the volume. "This isn't the jungle."

"It is to them."

My gaze was once again drawn through the front window and back to the tangled, golden-hued hair of the man-child in my backseat.

"Then why did they leave this cub alive?"

CHAPTER 25

"Who knows?" Sawyer reached for his iced coffee, seemed to remember that he'd hated it, and let his hand fall back to his knee.

"Maybe the kid does." I tossed my cup, packed up the computer, and headed outside. People inside glanced furtively at Sawyer as we passed.

The second set of tourist clothes weren't any better at disguising Sawyer's otherness than the first had been. His biceps bulged, the white tank only made his skin appear sultrier, and his tattoos, the ones that were visible, seemed to shimmer and dance beneath the electric lights. His hair billowed around his shoulders like an ebony river.

As we climbed into the Impala, Luther sat up, rubbing his eyes like a child. "Where are we?"

"Not a clue." I turned, extending a bag of muffins and several cartons of milk over the seat.

Luther's face lit up. His teeth were white but crooked. My tongue skimmed over my own not quite right teeth—typical in foster care. The government wasn't going to pay for a million and one sets of braces.

As he reached for the food and the drinks, I asked,

"What do you know about your parents?" then brushed his hand with my own.

Lions. A lot of them. Stalking through the suburban house. Blood everywhere.

Mommy, her eyes like mine, yellow-green and angry. She screams for Daddy to let her change, but Daddy is with me. Daddy touches me and then—

"I wasn't there," Luther said.

He was telling the truth, or what he thought was the truth. His dad had touched him, and Luther had no longer been there. Because his father—the conjurer—had sent him somewhere else.

Sawyer was looking at me. I shook my head. I didn't think Luther knew anything useful, and I didn't think the lions—be they Marbas or Barbas—knew he existed. Or if they did, they had no idea where he'd gone. If they had, they would have followed, and Luther had been in no position then to stop them from killing him.

Luther downed the muffins and milk like the hungry lion he could easily become, then fell asleep again. He was such an odd, yet endearing, mixture of little boy and almost man. I found myself drawn to him. I wanted to protect him, even though he could no doubt protect himself much better than I ever could.

Once I was certain the kid was out cold, I murmured to Sawyer, "I saw something strange."

That I could use the word *strange* in a conversation about lion-shifters and conjurers was in itself strange.

"Luther loved his parents; they loved him and each other."

"Why is that strange?"

"They're demons, or at least the mother was."

"You think love is only for humans?"

"What about your—" I paused, but he knew who I meant.

"Just as there are humans who are much less than human, there are Nephilim who are much less than half human."

"So she was an exception?"

"Unfortunately she was more of the rule and what you saw in the boy's past an exception. It may be that the conjurer was not only able to control the shifting of the Barbas but also her evil tendencies."

It was something to think about—all the way to Brownport.

The town was small—mostly college—but it didn't have the usual college-town feel. Or perhaps it didn't have the usual Wisconsin college-town feel.

For instance, there wasn't a bar on every other corner. There wasn't a bar anywhere at all. Brownport just might be dry, which was understandable considering the college was Bible.

Instead, the businesses all reflected service to the people who lived and worked there and to the entity they served. There was one church, and it was huge.

Brownport Bible College spread out at the south end of town. Backed by a ripe and swaying cornfield, it consisted of ten buildings with two dorms—one male, one female.

Both the school and the town seemed empty. According to the Web site, which I'd also accessed at Starbucks, most of the students went on mission trips at this time of year. But I'd been assured by Carla that Dr. Whitelaw was in residence—he lived here—and that I could find him in his office in the late afternoon, right before his evening summer school course.

Finding him wasn't difficult. Instead of having their offices in the buildings where they taught, each professor had one on the third floor of the administration building.

The structure was ancient—no elevator that I could see. The tile had yellowed. The walls showed water damage. On the third floor, only one door was open and through it spilled light.

Inside a man sat at a desk all alone. Books were piled on every surface not covered by papers. The bookcases overflowed; bound term papers had been stacked along two walls. On top of the highest stack sat a hat that made something tickle in my head. I recognized that hat, but I didn't know why.

The guy didn't hear us. No big surprise considering I was with a shape-shifting Indian and a lion in human form. They tended to move quietly, and I was no slouch in that department myself. However, the man's ears were plugged with white ear buds and cords trailed down each side of his neck, making a V that disappeared into the pocket of his light blue, short-sleeved button-down shirt.

He wore a tie and khaki trousers, loafers with socks, all of which had to be hell in this heat. The administration building either wasn't air-conditioned, or the powers that be didn't see the point of turning it on in the summer. The place was probably cold as hell in the winter, too.

A book lay open in front of him, and a yellow legal pad covered with illegible scribbles lay next to that. He tapped a pen on the desk to a beat I could easily distinguish since I had superior hearing, and he was blasting it. Of course Guns N' Roses sounded best at top volume.

Sawyer stepped forward, and I lifted my hand. I wanted to get a good look at the guy first, get a feel for him. Xander Whitelaw could be our salvation. Or, if what he knew turned out to be bogus, the seal of our doom.

His blond hair curled over the edge of his collar too long for an interview, but probably acceptable for the summer semester. I'd figured his skin would be sallow,

even sickly—did prophecy professors get out much?—
but instead his arms sported a golden tan. His shoulders
were narrow, but sculpted. From what I could tell, he
looked like a long-distance runner.

Suddenly the man shifted to the right, bringing his
pen up to his mouth like a microphone as he sang the
last line of "Paradise City" at top volume.

Axl really had nothing to worry about.

His jazzy side move must have brought us into his
peripheral vision, because the man froze and turned his
head. He was younger than I'd expected, around my age.
Perhaps this wasn't Xander Whitelaw at all but a grad
student.

His face was long, chin square with a tiny scar just
beneath his lip; his blond hair sifted over dark brown
eyes, framed by rimless glasses. He was cute if you
were into book people—teachers, writers, librarians.

I expected him to be flustered that we'd heard his
solo, perhaps blush. Instead he grinned, the expression
making him appear even younger if possible and quite
a bit more interesting than he'd been without it. If it had
been another time, another place, make that another
world, and I'd been another person, I might have smiled
back, given him my number, or taken him home.

As it was, I didn't return the expression, just stepped
closer and motioned for him to remove his ear buds.

"Oh." He did, then hit a button, cutting Axl off mid-
wail. "Sorry."

"I'm looking for Dr. Whitelaw."

"You found him."

His voice had a soft Southern lilt that made you want
to lean forward in expectation of his next words.

"You must be one of the youngest Ph.D.s in recorded
history," I muttered.

Whitelaw laughed. "Not really. You'd be surprised at

the rate of genius in the hallowed halls of education, Miss . . ."

"Phoenix." I led with my hand. "Elizabeth."

Our fingers touched. I didn't get much. He was excited about his new book, enjoyed his summer class, thought I was exotically attractive—I nearly yawned at *that* observation. How many men had told me the same in my lifetime?

"And you are?" He glanced past me, gaze avid.

If I hadn't gotten that flash of interest in me, I'd think he was gone on Sawyer. As his hand slipped from mine I understood why. Sawyer was Navajo. Whitelaw couldn't wait to get him alone and interview him about his life, his family, his past. That would make for an amusing conversation. Too bad it would never happen.

Sawyer and Luther introduced themselves politely enough, though they both refused to shake hands by folding their arms across their chests, then staring Whitelaw down. I half expected them to start snarling.

Whitelaw didn't seem insulted. The Navajo weren't very touchy-feely, so he'd probably had his handshakes ignored before.

He turned to me. "How can I help you?"

"We—uh—" I stopped. How was I going to explain what we wanted and why we thought he had it?

Silence fell over the room. Sawyer and Luther were no help at all. They seemed to have taken an instant dislike to the professor, and I wasn't sure why.

As I floundered, trying to figure out how to bring up the subject, my gaze fell on the book Whitelaw had been studying, which had flipped closed when he stood.

The Benandanti.

That was too much of a coincidence to be a coincidence.

"You're interested in ancient Italian legends?" I nodded toward the desk.

"Among others. I've studied the benandanti before, but lately——" He spread his hands, smudged with ink. I got the impression that when he studied, he did so with the same blissful abandon that a child would finger-paint in kindergarten.

"Lately?" I prompted.

"I've felt oddly compelled to learn more about them."

Oddly compelled. Hmm.

One person's odd compulsion was another's super-natural push. Was the good doctor just a bit psychic? Had he felt Carla watching him? Had he sensed what she was?

"What have you found out?"

"Fascinating stuff. You've heard of them?"

"I know the basics."

"Excellent." His slow Southern drawl was at odds with the precisely clipped commentary. Colin Firth channeling Atticus Finch. "The power was passed from mother to daughter. Only daughters did a benandanti bear, and if she were killed in the underworld before she gave birth, her magic would be lost forever."

A familiar story. Ruthie had passed her power on to me before I was ready for the very same reason. Better to fry my brain circuits and send me into a short but freaky coma than to allow all that power to disappear.

"A benandanti was haglike," Whitelaw continued. "Which made it a bit difficult to procreate, unless——"

"Enough," Sawyer interrupted, his deep voice cutting the professor off mid-explanation.

Confused, I glanced behind me, prepared to tell Sawyer to zip his lip, let the man finish.

Sawyer stood deceptively still, his face reflecting

nothing but the fluorescent lights, but I sensed his urgency and understood it.

Certainly I was interested in what Whitelaw knew about the legend of the benandanti, but I didn't *need* to know that information. We'd come here for other, much more important clues and we didn't have time to chat.

Who knew when the woman of smoke might show up. Knowing her, she'd arrive just as Whitelaw began to tell us what we needed to know and she'd rip his tongue out of his head before he finished.

"Excuse me," Whitelaw apologized. "I get carried away sometimes. You're Navajo, Mr. Sawyer, is that correct?"

Sawyer inclined his head. His gaze flicked to me then back to the doctor. His muscles flexed, the cords in his forearms tightening. If he got any more territorial, the two of them might begin a pissing contest.

However, Whitelaw seemed oblivious to the undercurrents. "I did my dissertation on the Navajo."

"So I hear," Sawyer murmured, and I sensed the rumble of his beasts just below the surface.

"Your people are fascinating," Whitelaw continued. "I've researched the Witchery Way." His words tumbled out more quickly as he warmed to his topic. "Most of my subjects equate the word *wolf* with the word *witch*. Would you agree?"

Sawyer just smiled, then struck a match against his thumb and lit a cigarette that had appeared out of nowhere.

"You—uh—can't smoke in a public—" Whitelaw began.

Sawyer lifted his brow and blew a stream in Whitelaw's direction. The professor coughed and gave up.

"I see you have a wolf on your . . ." Whitelaw flicked a finger at Sawyer's bicep, which rippled and twitched as if the wolf wanted very badly to get out. "Are you a—" He stopped as if suddenly realizing that asking a witch if he was a witch might be a very good way to get dead. He swallowed, his throat clicking loudly in the sudden, waiting silence of the room.

I jumped in before things got too uncomfortable. "I'd love to hear more about your research into the Navajo," I said. "That's why we came."

"Really?" Whitelaw's face lit up again.

"Yes—" I began.

"Tell us what you know," Sawyer ordered, and words spilled from Whitelaw's mouth like a fountain. I cast Sawyer a suspicious glance. I hadn't seen him do anything to make Whitelaw talk, but that didn't mean he hadn't.

"Navajo witches are shape-shifters. Skinwalkers." Whitelaw's gaze flicked to Sawyer's tattoos again, and he licked his lips nervously. "They have sex with the dead, practice cannibalism, and possess the ability to kill from afar with the use of ritual."

"Go on," Sawyer murmured. He didn't seem shocked by the professor's words, but I was.

"Dogs will bite a witch when the witch is in human form."

"And?" Sawyer said.

Next he'd be asking Whitelaw where he'd gotten his information, and then deciding just who needed to die—those who'd told secrets or the one who'd listened to them. There were times when he was very much his mother's son.

"Witches are most dreaded when the wind blows. They travel on the storm; they take their power from lightning. They say the rain is a woman."

I doubted Whitelaw would have needed much encouragement to give us a history lesson, but the way he couldn't seem to shut his mouth was too suspicious.

"Witches are associated with death and the dead, also incest."

I jerked so hard I nearly put my neck out of whack. Sawyer's hair lifted. Just a little, as if a fan had stirred the air nearby. But there wasn't a fan anywhere that I could see. Sawyer took another drag of his cigarette, then fixed his eyes, which were the same shade as the smoke coming out of his nose, on Whitelaw as he continued.

"To take a witch's power you must repeat their true name four times."

"True name?" I asked.

"At birth the Navajo are given a secret war name. This name is that person's personal property, never used by anyone, even his or her family."

"How are people distinguished if no one knows their name?"

"Most have nicknames," Whitelaw answered. "Something for the white people to call them. It's still considered bad manners by many of the old ones to call someone by their name in their presence."

I glanced at Sawyer. He'd lost his cigarette and was staring at Whitelaw with murder in his eyes.

"What do you know about the *Naye'i*?" I blurted.

"Dreadful Ones. The most evil spirits the Navajo have."

"Ever hear how to kill one?"

"Kill?" Whitelaw's face creased. "An evil spirit? I don't think that's possible."

Carla had said we might have to help him piece things together. But how would I do that if I didn't know the pieces in the first place?

"Spirits are good and evil," Whitelaw mused. "Both light and dark. There was something once . . ." His voice trailed off; he stared out the window.

I glanced at Sawyer, whose stoic gaze remained on Whitelaw. Luther still hung by the door; he'd be the first one out if getting out were a good idea. I had a feeling he'd be hanging out by the open doors for several years to come. Poor kid.

Suddenly Whitelaw spun and headed for his desk. He flipped through a pile of books, tossed several papers aside. "It's not written anywhere; I heard it. Someone told me." He rubbed his forehead for several seconds, then "Something," he murmured, "something about killing the darkness."

It was only because Sawyer's eyes had made me uneasy before that I bothered to glance at him now. He was lifting his hand, still staring at Whitelaw. I didn't think; I stepped between them.

Behind me, Luther's snarl rumbled. I didn't dare glance back and see what was happening. I didn't dare move at all.

Whitelaw's eyes had gone wide, the dark brown irises looking like demonic egg yolks in the middle of a sea of white. He saw that Sawyer meant murder; I could smell it. That scalding scent of ozone in the air, the very same scent that signaled fury in Mommy Dearest.

"Go on," I ordered, and when Whitelaw hesitated, I snapped, "Hurry."

Whitelaw wasn't stupid. He knew he was in trouble, that he'd better spit out the information because once he did there'd be no more reason to kill him. Once the method to kill the darkness was shared, it could no longer die with him.

The question was, why did Sawyer want it to?

CHAPTER 26

"Stop that!" I ordered the room at large.

Luther's snarls faded, which was as good an indication as any that Sawyer had lowered his hand. Didn't mean he wouldn't raise it again. Didn't mean he couldn't kill Whitelaw in some other way. Although I had to think that if Sawyer could have, he would have.

"What are they?" Whitelaw whispered, eyes still too wide and too white.

"You wouldn't believe me."

"I think I might."

I thought he might, too, but—

"Not now," I said, and he nodded, understanding the urgency was still there.

"To kill the darkness," he murmured, "one must embrace it."

"Embrace?" My lip curled. That was *so* not going to happen.

"Embrace or become. I remember asking and he said—"

"Who said? A Navajo?"

It seemed impossible that the Navajo would know that their evilest evil spirit would be the future leader of

Hell's army. Hell being a Christian concept as well as its leader.

However, I was finding out that Christianity didn't mean so much in terms of end-time prophecy. Sure, the Christians were the authors of it, but maybe that was only because they'd been the first to write it down.

Whitelaw shook his head. "The Navajo believe in evil, which is why they don't like to talk about it. Sometimes talking about it"—he lowered his voice, pointedly keeping his gaze from straying to Sawyer—"brings it forth."

"Let's hope not," I murmured, and Whitelaw shuddered, making me wonder if his yapping about supernatural entities, his writing down of those legends, had brought forth things that had no business being brought forth.

"When I was doing research for my book on Revelation," he continued, "I spoke with a rabbi who had an interesting theory about the end of the world. He said that the final battle would be between good and evil."

"What's so interesting about that?"

"He didn't use those terms. He used *darkness* and *light*. Said the only way to defeat the darkness was with the light. That the light would have to . . ." Whitelaw squinted, closed his eyes, then blurted the rest. "Embrace the darkness and in doing so would become it. Only then could evil be defeated."

"Become," I repeated, glancing at Sawyer. He shrugged, but he wasn't looking at me, he was still looking at Whitelaw as if he wanted to do something very unpleasant to the man.

Luther stood between us, back to me, his gaze on Sawyer. I'd been wrong. The kid hadn't gone out the door at the first sign of trouble, he'd stepped forward to face it. I was so impressed.

"I had no idea what he meant," Whitelaw mused. "Those old languages are difficult to figure out and sometimes the translations are wrong and sometimes they mix dialects."

He was gibbering. The longer I was here, the more I thought Whitelaw just might be a little psychic himself. He was certainly feeling the "gonna kill you" vibes that were washing off Sawyer like bad BO.

"This rabbi," I said. "Where can I find him?"

Whitelaw winced. "He was killed. Very strange case. Wild dogs."

"Wasn't me," Sawyer murmured.

Whitelaw opened his mouth, then shut it again. Smart man.

"Did the rabbi say how he'd discovered this information?"

"In a grimoire."

"Huh?"

"A textbook of magic. Most are instructions for invoking angels or demons."

"Are?" I straightened. "They still exist today?"

"Parts of them. In translation. Which is why the rabbi wasn't certain of the exact wording." The professor frowned. "I don't know why he told me any of this in the first place, but he seemed determined that I know it."

I was getting more and more certain that this rabbi had been one of us, had known somehow that I, or someone like me, would eventually come to Whitelaw and need this info. So he'd told the doctor and then he'd died. From the sound of it, by shape-shifters. Werewolves, coyotes, possessed puppies—didn't matter. He was dead.

"Do you have a copy of the grimoire he used?"

Whitelaw shook his head. "He said he'd gotten the information from the *Key of Solomon,* which is a book attributed to King Solomon. There are translations and parts of it all over the place. But this particular section"— Whitelaw bit his lip—"he swore it was from the original book."

"And where is that?"

"It doesn't exist. Or rather, no one's ever found it."

Sheesh, could someone please play a new tune?

"The translations date from the Middle Ages," Whitelaw continued.

"But no one's seen it since?"

"Except Rabbi Turnblat. He insisted he'd read the recipe for killing the darkness in the original *Key of Solomon*."

"Do you think that was true?"

"If it was, the book disappeared; it wasn't in his effects when he died."

Probably because whatever had killed him had taken it. I didn't think that was going to prove a plus for our side.

"What else was in this book?"

"Spells to become invisible, gain favor and love, find stolen items, constrain and release demons."

Ah, hell. I had a pretty good idea who had the damn thing.

"We need to go," I said.

"Wait!" Whitelaw started forward, freezing when both Sawyer and Luther growled.

I cast them a look and they subsided, though they both appeared as if they might jump out of their skin, or perhaps into another, furrier one.

"I want to help," Whitelaw said.

"Help what?"

"I've been studying Revelation; I see the signs. I also had a pretty good idea that a lot of those supernatural legends I'd read about were real." He stared pointedly at

Sawyer and Luther. "Even before they showed up. I think you could use someone with my knowledge on your side."

I thought we could, too, so I filled Whitelaw in. It didn't take long; he was pretty up on the lingo. Since Sawyer didn't pop a blood vessel, I figured spilling the beans was okay with him. Not that I needed his approval, but it didn't hurt.

"You have any ideas on how one might become the darkness?" I asked.

Slowly Whitelaw shook his head. "According to you the Grigori made the Nephilim by interbreeding with humans. Despite the stories, you can't become one by sharing blood or being bitten or cursed—"

"Become one," I murmured, and suddenly I knew what I had to do. But first things first. "See if you can find any information on something called the Book of Samyaza," I ordered. "Ever heard of it?"

Whitelaw shook his head. "Grimoire?"

"Kind of a satanic how-to. Revelatory prophecies for the other side."

Whitelaw wasn't slow. Understanding spread across his face. "If we have that, we'll know what they're up to."

"Can't hurt," I said. "And see if you can get a lead on the *Key of Solomon*. I have a really bad feeling it's in hands it shouldn't be."

Whitelaw paled, but he nodded, said good-bye, and when I glanced back as we left the room, he already had his nose so deep in a dusty book, the echo of his sneezes followed us down the staircase.

Outside, night had fallen. I turned to Sawyer and shoved him in the chest. It was like shoving a building. "You knew," I said.

"Knew what?"

"Don't bullshit me, Sawyer. You were going to zap Whitelaw into the next world before he told me."

"I was?"

"Aaah!" I smacked both hands into his chest. Sawyer grabbed me by the wrists before I could do it again. Luther snarled.

"Back off, kid," I ordered. "This is between him and me. Wait in the car."

Amazingly, he did.

I tugged at my wrists, but Sawyer wouldn't let go. "Why were you going to kill the professor?"

"He knows too much."

"Like how to end your mother?"

Sawyer's jaw worked. He hated it when I called her that, but tough.

"Sometimes I wonder whose side you're on," I murmured.

"Not hers."

"No? Then why didn't *you* tell me how to kill her? You lied when you said you didn't know. Some people might think you were a spy. Some people might think it would be a good idea to kill you right now."

Too bad some people didn't know how.

"Who told you?" I asked.

"No one." He let me go with a tiny shove. "Everyone. It's an ancient legend, a prophecy that made no sense. Until you came along."

"Does she know?" I blew out a sharp, quick breath. "Of course she does." Another very good reason for her to try and kill me.

"There has to be another way," Sawyer said quietly.

"There's usually only one method of killing these things. Why would you think there's two just because you didn't like the first?"

"Whitelaw knew how to kill the darkness. But there also has to be a method of killing a *Naye'i*."

"According to Whitelaw, can't be done."

"He doesn't know everything."

"He appeared to know quite a lot."

"It's too dangerous," Sawyer said. "You'll be one of them, Phoenix. And then—"

He broke off, turned away.

"Then what?"

"Then I'll have to kill you."

I took a deep breath. "I'm counting on it."

Silence settled between us.

"It'll be all right," I said.

Sawyer had been the one to warn me that I should never sleep with a Nephilim; I might absorb their evil along with their strength. I'd figured then that there might come a day that the risk would be worth it. I just hadn't figured that day would arrive so soon.

"I'm the only one who can actually turn into a Nephilim," I said. "I'm the light that will become the dark."

"Because the darkness will swallow you. You'll be gone, Elizabeth."

I frowned. He never called me that. That he had scared me. But being scared had never stopped me before. Usually, being scared just got me started.

"I need to find a Nephilim," I began. "Shouldn't be hard. They're all over the damn place."

I glanced around. The campus looked empty. The entire town had rolled up the sidewalks when the sun went down. Where was a demon when you needed one? When you didn't need one, they were everywhere.

Stong, bare, brown arms came around me from behind. "I won't let you do it," Sawyer said.

"You can't stop me." I struggled but, as usual, he was

stronger. "I'll just bang the next Nephilim I see. One will show up. It's only a matter of time."

"It'll kill you."

"I doubt that."

The thought of sleeping with an evil thing made me slightly ill, but I'd do whatever I had to. Because if I didn't, the Grigori would once again walk this earth. They'd mate with humans; repopulate the world with demons. The chaos creeping over the planet now would be nothing compared to what would sweep over it then.

Sawyer sighed, his chest rubbing against my back, his arms sliding along mine. "There's another way."

I stilled. "What other way?"

"Sanducci."

"Sanducci? What—"

I paused as I heard again what Whitelaw had said—

You can't become one by sharing blood or being bitten or cursed—

Except that I could.

I'd gained dhampir powers from Jimmy. But I hadn't become a vampire—a Nephilim—because to do so I had to—

"Share blood," I murmured.

"Yes," Sawyer said, and let me go.

Sanducci hadn't been evil until he'd exchanged blood with his vampire father. He'd drunk from me in the strega's lair, but I'd managed to end his possession, obsession—whatever—by killing Daddy before Jimmy forced me to drink from him. Jimmy had begged me to remember that I must never share blood with a vampire, or I'd become one.

"Jimmy isn't a Nephilim," I pointed out, "he's a breed."

"When Sanducci is a vampire, he's a vampire. If you take his blood—"

"I'll become a vampire, too."

"Yes."

"He won't go for it."

"You'll have to make him."

That should be fun.

"I think I'd rather pick an evil demon, any evil demon."

"No. With Sanducci, there's a chance you might be able to put the demon back when you're finished with it."

"Put it back where? In him?"

"Inside of you. Trap it. Block it, perhaps."

"So it would always be there?" I fought an involuntary shudder. "Waiting?"

"That's better than the other option. You become the demon. Always."

"At least until you kill me," I muttered.

Sawyer didn't answer.

"Jimmy wasn't having much luck putting the demon back in the box. Can it be done?"

"Theoretically."

I guess theoretical was better than "not a snowball's chance."

I remembered Jimmy's anguish in the cave, the reason he'd taken off and gone there in the first place. Having that thing inside of him was killing him piece by piece. Enticing Jimmy to make me that way, too—

"I don't want to hurt him," I blurted.

Sawyer's face hardened. "He didn't have the same concern for you."

"He was possessed by the strega. That doesn't count."

"Did it count when he and Summer—" Sawyer made an obscene hand gesture. "He knew you'd see, that he'd break your heart. He didn't care."

True enough. Still, two wrongs didn't make a right. Or perhaps, in this case, it did.

"How am I going to find him?" I murmured.

Sawyer stared at me for several ticks of the clock, but he'd decided before I had that the only choice was Jimmy.

"I don't know," he said at last. "Summer could hide them forever if she wanted to."

Or at least until Jimmy was better. I needed to get to him before that happened. And I knew exactly how.

Desperate times called for desperate measures, or at least the answer to my most desperate question. A plan formulated in my mind, unfolding with all its twists and turns, paths and possibilities.

"Don't do it," Sawyer murmured.

I glanced up. Reading my mind again, or perhaps just my face?

"I have to find him."

"Dream walking requires you to walk the line between life and death. What if you cross that line?"

"What if I do?"

"I won't do it, Phoenix. I won't kill you just so you can walk through Sanducci's dreams and find out where the fairy has hidden him."

"I don't need you to," I said, and shot myself in the head.

CHAPTER 27

Everything went neon white. In the distance rhythmic thunder, maybe guns, or horses, then a final burst that sounded like a word I couldn't quite make out.

Home? Come? Some? Done?

Whatever.

Had I made a mistake? Had I actually killed myself for real?

No. A kill shot would only work on me if it were done twice. So unless Sawyer had picked up the gun and finished the job, I was safe enough.

My eyes felt as if they'd been scalded with boiling oil. When I opened them, Jimmy was with me. Or rather I was with him. He was in a bedroom—stark and sterile. White sheets, single bed, a battered dresser with a mirror on the wall. Night shrouded the windows, but I could still see the bars.

He lay on the bed, naked, the moon shining through the glass, turning his olive skin the shade of alabaster. His body was long and lean, finely muscled, damn near perfect.

His eyes were open. He seemed dead, until he turned his head and saw me.

"Lizzy," he murmured. He sounded drugged, looked it, too.

"What has she done to you?" I asked.

"She's trying to help." He sat up, muscles rippling across his stomach and arms as he rubbed a palm over his face. "I think it's working."

Dread clogged my throat. If he was better, I was doomed. Nevertheless, beneath the dread, a tiny ray of joy fluttered. I wanted him to be better. I wanted him whole again. I didn't want to have to betray him the way I planned to.

"What do you need?" he asked.

"Need?"

"I know you're not really here. You must be pretty desperate to dream walk."

"Desperate." I laughed, thinking of the gun I'd put to my head. "You might say that."

Jimmy held out his hand. "Ask me."

I glanced at the windows, but the moon must have gone behind a cloud and it was too dark to see where we were. I reached for him, my mouth opening, my mind forming the words *Where are you?*, but the instant our fingers touched, I was thrown backward at a sickening speed. Jimmy was gone, so was the room. Instead I flew through a long, dark corridor with a whole lot of doors.

I'd been here before. Well, not here, here. But in someone's mind, so I recognized the décor. Memories lived behind those doors.

The wind took me, around one corner, then another, sometimes flinging me so fast I bumped an edge, hissed with pain, but the wind kept on.

Papers scattered, some hit me in the face, the hand; one stuck to my chest, and I snatched up the stub of Jimmy's first magazine paycheck. He'd sold some of the photos he'd taken at a dairy farm the summer I'd gone to

Sawyer and he'd stayed in Wisconsin to milk cows. Jimmy'd made the most of it, as Jimmy always did. Those photos had gotten him a scholarship to Western Kentucky. Not that he'd used it.

Littered across the floor were old baseballs, a few knives with suspicious stains, negatives, and in one corner the shirt I'd been wearing the day I'd lost my virginity. Amazing what strata haunt the corridors of the mind.

The wind suddenly died, depositing me in front of a pristine white door. Harmless enough, especially when compared to some of the others in this hall. Faded gray wooden slats to my right, so warped I could see light shining through them from the room on the other side. The rusted heavy enclosure from an old meat locker hung to my left. Behind me loomed something that appeared to have been hijacked from Bram Stoker's nightmares—a large, dark, curved entryway with a huge black bat for a door knocker. My hand itched to give that a rap, but Jimmy would probably end up with a brain tumor, or at the least a helluva headache.

Farther down the hall, one door keened outward, hanging from a single brass hinge. Wonder what had been behind there?

Curious, I took a step in that direction. Or tried to. My sandals felt glued to the floor. If there was a floor. When I glanced down, all I saw were my feet, my shoes, and a whole lot of nothing beneath.

"Okay," I murmured. "Guess the answer to my most desperate question is behind door number one."

I reached out and turned the knob. It didn't budge. I rattled it. Knocked on it. Slammed my palms against it.

"Hey!" I shouted, and tried to walk away again. I nearly twisted my feet off my ankles, but I didn't get anywhere. Then I saw the peephole.

Obviously, Jimmy didn't want me to know what was behind this door, but dream walking was a powerful thing. That he was able to keep the door locked against me was impressive. However, a desperate question, the blood I'd spilled to have it answered, took precedence. Hence the hole in the door.

I leaned forward. Instead of the reverse, blurry image commonly projected through peepholes if you peered into them from the outside, I was able to see quite clearly.

Jimmy and Ruthie, at the house in Milwaukee. Years ago from the looks of them.

Though Ruthie had never appeared to age, this view of her showed me that she had. Her hair was less gray, her hands less bony, her eyes somehow more tired rather than less. How odd.

Jimmy was maybe seventeen. Tall and still just a little gangly, but with the promise of the man he'd become, his hair shining blue-black in the sun, his eyes sparking fury. What else was new? Jimmy had always been angry back then. It was his thing.

"Are you crazy?" he asked, the anger and something else making his voice crack.

Ruthie's face tightened. I waited for the eruption. Disrespect wasn't tolerated in any form. When she didn't speak, or smack him upside the head, I shifted uneasily, realized my feet could now move; however, I no longer wanted to be anywhere but here. What my most desperate question was, I didn't know, but I was certain it would be answered very soon.

"I can't," he continued. "She'll—"

"That's the idea," Ruthie said, and her voice was the coldest I'd ever heard. So cold, I wrapped my arms around myself, shivering alone in the halls of Jimmy's mind.

"But—" He scrubbed his fingers through his hair, a gesture I knew came from uncertainty, indecision, fear.

"Did you think I wouldn't find out?"

Jimmy dropped his hand. "I didn't know—"

"That I could see?" She smiled but the expression wasn't the one I was used to. The one that made every child smile back, that made lost boys and girls know they'd come home.

No, this smile was something else entirely. This smile was calculating. It was almost, but not quite, the smile of the woman of smoke. The smile of a being that would do anything, pay any price, sacrifice anyone, to get what she wanted.

"Would you have kept it in your pants if you'd known?" Ruthie murmured.

Jimmy glanced away and didn't answer.

"Well, you won't have to keep it in your pants now. Do what I told you. It's the only way."

"It'll kill her."

"She's stronger than that," Ruthie said. "What will kill her is loving you. She can't have a weakness. She has to be able to think of the world."

I rubbed my hands over my stingingly cold arms, shivering so badly my back ached from it.

"You can't have a weakness, either. They'll know," she continued. "And you have to be able to do what you do best."

"Kill." His voice had lost the fury. He sounded almost broken. I wanted to go to him, but he wasn't really there.

"It's what you were born to do," Ruthie said.

Born to kill? Ruthie was telling Jimmy he'd been born to kill? I wasn't a psychiatrist, but even I knew that wasn't a good thing to tell a kid. Sure, we all understood Jimmy wasn't killing *people,* but still—

He had.

I wanted to smack somebody, and I knew exactly who. Too bad Ruthie wasn't any more there than Jimmy was.

"There's no other way?" Jimmy asked.

"You think she'll believe you just left her behind? You think she'll stop loving you now that you've gone and been her first? I told you not to touch her." Ruthie's voice rose. "Didn't I tell you never to touch her?"

"I couldn't—" He stopped, and I leaned forward, smacking my nose against the door. He couldn't what?

But Ruthie didn't let him finish. "If you just leave, she'll search for you forever. She'll never get over you, and she has to. It's time for you to take your place. But she ain't ready. If she follows—"

"She could die." Ruthie nodded, and after several seconds Jimmy sighed. "Okay. I'll do it." He gave a short, sharp, unamused laugh. "I mean I'll do her. What was her name?"

"Summer," Ruthie said. "Summer Bartholomew."

I gasped, and both Ruthie and Jimmy glanced toward the door, but I was gone, being dragged out of Jimmy's head so fast my stomach roiled. Or maybe it was just the disgust over what I'd heard bubbling in my gut like acid.

Ruthie had ordered Jimmy to sleep with Summer, knowing full well that I'd see, that it would break my heart, that I'd wind up hating him. Ruthie, who knew everything about me, including how much I desperately needed to be loved, how much the betrayal would hurt, had coolly calculated the best way to turn me against someone who'd needed me as badly as I'd needed him. And he'd agreed.

But, hey, anything for the world, right?

CHAPTER 28

I slammed into my dream body with a thunk that sent me to the floor on my hands and knees. Jimmy sat on the bed in the same position as when I'd "left."

"Did you see what you needed to?" he asked.

His voice was merely curious. He didn't realize what I'd found out. I decided to keep it that way.

My most desperate question had been why he'd left me when we were eighteen. How pathetic. Almost as pathetic as his leaving because he'd been ordered to.

I tamped down on that anger. He'd been eighteen, same as me. Thrust into the federation long before I had been. He'd been adrift. Alone and floundering. I would have been no help to him at all. I would have gotten us both killed.

That Ruthie had been right in her assumption did not make me feel any more warm and fuzzy toward her right now.

But one thing at a time. I really needed to know where Summer had taken Jimmy. That I hadn't fallen out of his dreams and back into my cold, half-dead body in Indiana meant I could still discover the answer to My Most Desperate Question, Part Deux.

"Lizzy?"

I lifted my head, and my nose brushed his knee. The scent of him—cinnamon, soap and water—washed over me and my eyes watered. So much given, taken, lost. I climbed to my feet just as he stood.

We were only inches apart; the heat of his naked skin washed over me. I laid my palm against his chest, felt his heart beating, realized mine wasn't.

Uh-oh.

I should probably do what I'd come here to do and get back. I wasn't exactly certain how everything worked, but I had a feeling that once my body had healed, I'd be yanked out of here faster than I'd been dropped in.

Jimmy covered my hand with his. He was so warm I wanted to burrow into him and let that warmth, his scent, wash over me. Now that I knew what was behind the secret locked door, a lot of other doors were being unlocked. Like the ones I'd slammed closed the day I'd first seen him with her.

Damn.

I'd been swaying forward, face lifted, lips puckered. Now I stiffened, stepped back, and he let me go.

"What did you see?" Jimmy asked.

"Not much in there." I tapped on his head with my knuckles.

"Ha-ha."

My attempt at humor relaxed him. Obviously, if I'd seen what he hadn't wanted me to, I wouldn't be able to joke about anything.

Jimmy didn't really know me very well at all anymore. Did anyone?

I moved to the window. The bars were gold; they had to be. Jimmy could yank out anything else, though I had a feeling he'd have a hard time slipping through this small of a hole. He wasn't a shape-shifter, like me.

The moon that had shone in earlier had disappeared. The sun wasn't yet up and darkness ruled. All I had to do was ask Jimmy where he was, and he'd tell me. I was in his head; he didn't have much choice. Yet, I hesitated. Once I asked, once I knew, I'd come here, and I'd hurt him.

He moved behind me, silently, but I knew he was there. I always knew. We were connected in a way nothing and no one could ever break.

Unless it was me.

He put his hands on my hips. I felt his lips in my hair, his breath on my ear. I leaned against him, just for a minute. "You seem better," I whispered.

"I'm not."

Was I happy about that or sad?

"Summer cast a spell."

I fought not to stiffen at her name. None of this had been Summer's fault. Although her falling in love with him was just annoying. It made me feel sorry for her, and I didn't want to. I wanted to keep hating her. I did it so well.

"What kind of spell?" I asked.

"Subvert the demon."

"How?"

He didn't answer. Instead he stilled. Something had changed. It took me a few seconds to figure out what, and when I did, I stilled, too.

His skin seemed so hot; his hands on my hips had become almost bruising. Slowly I turned and for a minute, in the dark, I thought I'd imagined things. He smelled the same; his outline was so familiar; I'd seen it rise above me in the night so many times. The cadence of his breath, the fall of his hair, the curve of his neck into his shoulder were all Jimmy.

Then, behind me, the sun burst free of the night and

splashed merrily across his face. The center of his eyes flared red; his fangs had lengthened.

"It's coming." His gaze lowered from my eyes to my neck.

My pulse pounded in my temples. I guess something had jump-started my heart. Most likely the sight of his hellfire-lit eyes.

"I can't hold it back all the time." Jimmy stared at what must be my throbbing carotid artery and licked his lips. "Sometimes it gets free."

I backed up, smacked into the wall, threw a glance over my shoulder, and froze at the sight framed in the window.

I knew exactly where he was.

The next instant I lay on the pavement in the parking lot in the dark. I had a bad fucking headache.

The lopsided moon flaring brightly against a navy blue night confused me, as I'd just watched the sun come up in dream-walk world. Two heads appeared above me, haloed by that moon.

"Better?" Sawyer murmured, sounding completely calm, not at all freaked out by what had to have been a pretty freaky situation. There were a few good things about Sawyer, and that was one of them.

"What *are* you?" Luther sounded freaked out enough for both of them.

I sat up, touched my head, which still throbbed but appeared to be all there, though sticky with things I didn't want to think about. Then I glanced around. We were amazingly alone.

"No one heard?" I asked.

I'd been in too big of a hurry to worry about the noise and I should have been. This wasn't L.A. A gunshot should have brought the whole town running—at the least Whitelaw should have looked out a window.

"He did some fancy hoodoo shit," Luther said. "People came, but they couldn't see us."

That was another good thing about Sawyer. Magic. Centuries of it.

"I need a shower," I murmured.

"You need more than that," Luther said. "You healed a bullet in the brain."

"In that case, it sounds like I don't need anything." I stood up, swayed a little. The headache was fading but not fast enough.

"Why did you do it?" Luther's voice wavered.

"Sorry." I put a hand on his arm. "I should have warned you. That wasn't fair."

He bit his lip. Shrugged. I'd scared him. Pretty badly from the way he was shaking. Poor kid. He had the heart of a lion, literally, but he was still just a cub.

I rounded on Sawyer. "You couldn't tell him I wasn't in any danger?"

"I was a little busy keeping the invisibility bubble around us."

I stared at him a minute, trying to figure out if he was joking, but I didn't think he knew how. I shouldn't blame him for my own hasty behavior. I'd gotten the knowledge I needed, but at what cost to those around me? I hoped I hadn't scarred the kid more than he already was.

We'd told Luther the basics of the federation, about the Grigori, Nephilim, the leaders of the light and the dark, but there was so much that had happened, so many things we could do, I guess I'd left out the empathy part of my program.

"You absorb powers through sex," he repeated when I'd finished explaining. Then shook his head. "That makes no sense."

I'd never tried to make sense of it. What was, was. What happened, happened. It wasn't as if I had any choice. But now that Luther was questioning things, I had to wonder "What the hell?" myself.

"There's a reason for everything," Sawyer murmured. He didn't seem like the "reason for everything" type. More in the "life is chaos" category if you asked me.

"And the reason for me being the way I am?" I asked.

"Sex requires opening yourself."

I rolled my eyes. We'd gone round and round about that in the past. I wasn't exactly an "open" kind of gal. It had taken me a long time and a lot of hassle to be able to open myself the way that I needed to.

"For a woman, sex is the ultimate commitment," Sawyer murmured. "Giving yourself to someone isn't easy."

That just might be the understatement of the year.

"You give of yourself, but you also take," he continued. "The level of dedication required to do that assures that you won't be absorbing powers willy-nilly."

I choked. Had Sawyer actually said *willy-nilly*? If I didn't know the end of the world was on the way, I'd think it was already here.

"Powers are not to be acquired foolishly, just as sex isn't to be engaged in lightly."

Except for him. He engaged in sex pretty willy-nilly, which made his explanation of my empathy bizarre to say the least.

Even more bizarre was that it made complete sense within the boundaries of this clandestine world we inhabited.

Luther was nodding. It made sense to him, too. At least I wasn't completely delusional.

"Where's Sanducci?" Sawyer asked.

"You're so certain I found out?"

"Because dream walking requires great risk, it works."

That was comforting. I'd hate to have blown my brains out for nothing.

"New Mexico," I said, then paused. "I think."

"What makes you doubt?"

I'd been so certain when I'd seen the sun splash over the landscape, but as I thought back—

"The mountains were wrong. When I first saw their outline, I recognized them. They were yours, but from a different angle. Maybe the other side. But now . . ." I waggled my hand, wincing at the blood speckled across it. "I think of them, and I see green rolling hills, instead of pink, red, and orange. The flowers are different— more lush and . . . floaty. There's mist everywhere."

"It's the fairy. She does that."

"Does what?"

The three of us began to stroll toward the Impala, which stood a few hundred feet away, passenger door still hanging open, revealing that Luther had gotten out in one helluva big hurry.

"She makes my mountains look like the hills of Ireland," Sawyer said.

"Ireland? Why?"

"A lot of the fairies went there after the fall, which is how all the Fey stories began. It must look just like heaven to them."

"But Summer's . . . a rodeo fairy."

Sawyer's eyes widened, and I thought he might laugh. Luther glanced back and forth between us, absorbing everything, questioning nothing. He learned fast.

"She's different, true," Sawyer agreed. "But she was in Ireland for a very long time."

"No accent," I said.

"Glamour. She can be anything she desires."

Could she be anything anyone desired? For instance, was Summer a blond, busty, "come on and ride me" fairy because that was what Jimmy wanted? And if she was, had she become that way on Ruthie's orders?

I gritted my teeth. I couldn't worry about that now. I had to get to New Mexico and do what needed to be done before the woman of smoke figured out what I was up to and stopped me.

CHAPTER 29

"Plane or paws?" I asked.

We definitely needed to get to New Mexico faster than the Impala could take us.

Skinwalkers can move quicker than the eye can track, which is what gave rise to the legend that a skinwalker could disappear in one place and appear in another. I wasn't certain how fast a Marbas could run, but I was betting pretty damn fast.

"Plane," Sawyer said.

"Really?"

I was not only shocked at his choice but shocked that he wasn't going to argue with me. I'd been formulating a plan—what would I do if he tried to keep me here?—that involved yanking off Sawyer's talisman, then leaving him behind while Luther and I hopped a plane to Albuquerque.

The problem with that plan was that Sawyer as a wolf would probably beat us there. At the least he wouldn't be very late, which threw a wrench into the whole getting-away-from-him idea. But his being so agreeable, that was another kind of wrench.

"What's up with you?" I asked.

"Me?" He put a bloody palm to his now bloody white shirt, which made me think he hadn't been as calm as he'd appeared when I'd come out of it. He'd been trying to save me, even though I hadn't needed saving. "What did I do?"

"You refused to help me."

"I refused to kill you." He dropped his hand and sniffed. "So shoot me. Or did you use all your bullets on your own head?"

He was pissed. That was new. Guess I'd really scared him. Though I couldn't quite figure out how.

Luther stood off to the side, watching us closely. My gun had disappeared. From the way his saggy pants sagged more on his right side, I had a pretty good idea where it had gone.

"We should wait a while," Sawyer murmured. "We might find another way to end her."

"Have you found a way in all the decades?" He lifted a brow. "Fine. Centuries that you've been trying?"

"No."

"Then I doubt another method will drop into our lap any time soon."

"Miracles happen."

"Not to me."

"You've come back from the dead twice in the last week. That's not a miracle?"

I frowned. There was something about that statement that gave me the creeps, but I couldn't figure out what.

"I don't understand you," I said. "I'm the only one who can do this, yet you try to talk me out of it."

"I know what she's capable of." He took a deep breath as he stared at the dark shadows that composed Brownport College. "You'll sell your soul, and she'll still win."

"Gee, thanks." He shrugged. "So you want me to give up? To hide in a hole and let everyone die?"

Sawyer returned his gaze to mine. "I want you to, but I know you won't. So . . ." He spread his hands. "We'll go to New Mexico."

"On a plane," I clarified.

"We could go on four paws, all of us." Sawyer contemplated Luther. "I could help him change, but I don't think he'd be in control of his beast well enough to travel cross-country yet."

"I don't think I would be, either," Luther muttered.

"And a lion's going to stick out in Indiana, Illinois, Missouri, hell, everywhere, like a—" I searched for an appropriate simile and floundered.

"Lion in a haystack?" Sawyer offered.

Was that a mixed metaphor? Maybe. But basically . . .

"Yeah," I said. "You have ID?"

Sawyer nodded, so did Luther. I nearly asked how that was possible, then decided it didn't matter, as long as we got where we needed to go and fast.

By the time dawn lightened the Louisville skyline, we were pulling into long-term parking, then heading for the terminal. I'd showered and changed in the locker room of the Brownport Bible College field house while Sawyer and Luther kept watch.

Since it was well after midnight, the place was empty. But I'd needed to wash away all traces of my ticket to dream walking before we went anywhere. Traveling—in a car or a plane—looking as if I'd been on the losing end of a very bloody fight was not a good idea. Sure, we could get out of jams using brute force or magic, but that took time. And time was one thing in short supply.

I don't know how I knew that but I did. Ever since I'd woken up with the moon shining down and a good portion of my brains on the outside instead of the inside, I'd felt as if a dragon were breathing fire on my neck. In other words, I needed to move forward and fast.

Inside the Louisville International Airport, I paused in front of a news kiosk and read a few headlines.

EARTHQUAKE SHAKES ANTARCTICA

TORNADO HITS INDIA

BLIZZARD SWEEPS ACROSS KENYA

And the television was even worse. Riots. Murders. Fires. I'd say it was a day just like any other day, but the anchors couldn't seem to keep up with the reports. One bad thing tumbled into the next and into the next.

"Chaos," I whispered.

"Doomsday," Sawyer said.

The urgency I'd felt earlier increased. If they hadn't called our flight right then, I might have slipped into a bathroom as a woman and come out something else.

Time turned back as we headed west. When we landed in Albuquerque, we'd gained several hours, yet several hours had passed, and so much more chaos had ensued.

As we walked through the Albuquerque International Sunport, headed for the rental car booth, I caught snatches of conversations.

"Something blew up in Israel."

Nothing new.

"London, Paris, Rome, and Madrid, too."

I cursed and glanced at the televisions. Smoke poured from several well-known buildings. Military personnel and law enforcement scurried around like ants.

"So far, nothing's happened here," someone murmured.

So far, I thought.

"The world's gone crazy."

"Did you expect anything less?" Sawyer asked.

Not really.

"Why did they back off for a while?"

"I'm not sure that they did. You were blocked by the amulet, and I have a feeling a lot of others were, too."

"Just because we weren't seeing the chaos in our visions doesn't mean it wasn't happening."

"The world's screwed up. Until things really got out of hand," he lifted his chin toward the television, "it was just another day at Fox News."

Maybe he was right. Or maybe humans had started to feed off the evil of the Nephilim. Or the Nephilim had gone hog wild. And why not? Their time was coming; soon their creators would roam the earth, and the soulless would outnumber the souls.

Unless I managed to become the darkness as well as the light. I'd drop the dreadful bitch into the pit with all her friends, seal up any cracks in the door, then throw away the key. How was that for a plan?

"Compact, mid-size, full, or luxury?" the rental car clerk asked.

"What do they call those brand-new vehicles that resemble a tank on truck wheels?" Sawyer asked.

"Hummers?"

Sawyer's eyebrows lifted. "I always thought a hummer was something else entirely."

Considering this was Sawyer, I knew exactly what he was talking about.

So did the rental clerk. She looked Sawyer up and down—even in his stupid discount tourist outfit, he was hotter than hot—and licked her lips. "You'd like a hummer, sir? I think I can take care of that."

I just bet she could. Honestly, there was chaos all over the news, we were trying to save the world here, and I had to deal with slutty rental agents and Sawyer's innuendos.

"Any old car will do," I said.

"No." Sawyer quit having eye sex with the clerk and became all business. "Summer's place isn't easy to get to. We need that Hummer."

"Maybe you do," I muttered. Jimmy drove a Hummer. Last time I'd seen it had been when he'd dumped me at Sawyer's and run off to become evil. Things had gone downhill from there.

However, I could understand why such a car would be helpful where we were headed, so I nodded at the woman, signed the papers, took the key.

Fifteen minutes later I stared at the military assault vehicle I'd just rented. "Who thought putting these on the road was a good idea?"

"Bigger is always better." Sawyer climbed into the passenger seat as Luther clambered into the back. "It's the American way."

I'd put my foot down at renting a taxicab-yellow tank, so ours was a sparkly shade of beige, which should blend into the desert, but wouldn't. Anything this big was going to stand out like a—

"Lion in a haystack," I muttered. That phrase was really growing on me.

I pulled out of the parking lot and headed west.

The Navajo reservation spread across Utah, Arizona, and New Mexico, with the largest portion in Arizona. Sawyer lived near Mount Taylor, one of the four sacred mountains that marked the boundaries of the Dinetah. According to my walk through Jimmy's head, Summer's place should be near Mount Taylor, too, but on the far side.

I didn't know when Summer had moved to the reservation, but I did know why. She'd been sent to spy on Sawyer.

"You know where Summer lives?" I asked.

Sawyer's eyes were closed; his head lay back against the headrest. Luther, stretched out on the rear seat, was already fast asleep.

In this huge car, they both seemed so small. I felt like I was in a sci-fi movie—*The Incredible Shrinking Leader of the Light*. I had to reach up to get my hands around the steering wheel, tilt the rearview mirror way down. The only people who might be at home in this beast were Yao Ming or maybe Peyton Manning.

"You don't know?" Sawyer murmured.

"I got the gist," I said. "But what if she glamours everything up again?"

Sawyer opened one eye. "She will."

"Then maybe you should open both eyes and tell me where to turn."

He shut them instead. "Stay on this road. Wake me in an hour."

Silence settled over us; the steady, even cadence of both Sawyer's and Luther's breathing soothed me. I considered turning on the radio, but I was afraid there'd be no music, only news, and I'd heard enough.

What I needed to do was spend some quiet time preparing for what was to come. It was all well and good to say I was going to do whatever I had to, but when push came to shove, would I be able to go through with it? Would I be able to let Jimmy make me like him? Would I be able to battle with the woman of smoke and win?

The answer to every single one of those questions was: I had to.

We left Albuquerque baking beneath the summer sun and headed across flat, arid plains the shade of salmon and copper. Eventually mountain foothills appeared, dotted with towering ponderosa pines. In the distance, canyons surrounded by high, spiked sand-colored rock warred with red mesas, a landscape immortalized in the western movie classics of several previous generations.

An hour later, I reached for Sawyer's shoulder to shake him awake, but before my fingers even touched his skin, he opened his eyes and drew away from me.

Tiny houses dotted the horizon; the mountain rose behind them like a long, looming pyramid. Between 3.3 and 1.5 million years ago Mount Taylor had been an active volcano. Sometimes I still expected it to rumble.

The Navajo refer to it as their *sacred mountain of the south* or *the turquoise mountain*. Legends say it is fastened from the sky to the earth by a flint knife studded with turquoise.

I touched the stone still looped around my neck along with Ruthie's crucifix. "Did you find this on Mount Taylor?" I asked.

"Yes."

I thought that might be a very good thing. There was something magic about that mountain, always had been.

"Don't take it off," Sawyer said.

The turquoise had kept the woman of smoke from touching me. If I could capture Jimmy's evil essence, gain the strength that would allow me to fight her, and she couldn't fight back, then I'd win. This sounded like a slam dunk.

Which made me really, really nervous. I wasn't very old, might not get much older the way things were headed, but I'd learned long ago that when something looked like a slam dunk, it just meant you'd better get ready to eat the ball.

"You should probably remove the crucifix," Sawyer said.

I frowned. The crucifix had been Ruthie's. It was all

I had left of her, except for her voice in my head, her presence in my dreams, and her power in my soul. Still, if this worked, if I became the darkness by becoming a vampire, the crucifix was going to burn one helluva hole in me. I'd heal, but I'd still like to avoid that.

I pulled over to the side of the road and slipped the silver icon from the chain, then handed it to Sawyer, before replacing the turquoise around my neck and easing back onto the highway.

A few minutes later, Sawyer murmured, "Turn at the next road."

I wheeled the Hummer off the paved highway and onto a dirt track. The subsequent dips and bumps woke Luther.

"We there yet?" he asked, rubbing his eyes.

I smiled at him in the rearview mirror. "Soon. I think you should stay in the car."

He dropped his hand, his head jerked up, and his kinky blond-brown hair waved. "Like hell!"

"It might be," I murmured.

"I can help," he said. "I'm a lion."

"Cub," Sawyer corrected.

"Bite me," the kid muttered.

"I'd be happy to."

"Hey," I interrupted. "We're on the same side."

All I needed was for the lion and the tiger—or wolf, cougar, eagle, *whatever*—to start fighting. Someone would get hurt, and I knew who that someone would be. We needed Luther, and about two million more like him.

"You'll stay in the car," I told the boy. I didn't want him to see what I might become.

He subsided, grumbling beneath his breath, sounding very much like a full-grown lion rather than the cub, but I thought he'd listen. I thought he'd stay.

"There." Sawyer pointed.

· I slammed on the brakes. "Where?" I saw nothing.

"This is the fairy's house."

"What is?" Luther asked. At least he didn't see it, either.

Sawyer got out of the car and strode across the dry grass. He stopped, reached into his pocket, then, lifting his hands to the blazing sun, he chanted.

I got out, too, and followed, throwing one final "stay" glance over my shoulder at the kid. Sawyer finished whatever he'd been saying, then lowered his arms.

"I still don't see anything," I said.

He threw out his hands and something dry and powdery swirled in a sudden wind. The particles seemed to absorb then reflect all the colors around us—first yellow, then tan, deep brown, and cayenne.

The powder paused and hovered, lingering as if thinking, perhaps listening. Then the wind died, the particles fell away, and where they'd once been now stood a house.

"What did you throw?" I asked.

Sawyer merely smiled.

The building looked strange sitting in front of the mountain revered by the Navajo. It looked even stranger when compared to the other houses speckled here and there across the land. Hogans, the traditional Navajo dwelling, abounded.

The round structures, made of logs and dirt, contained no windows and only one door, which faced east toward the sun. Next to most of the hogans were living quarters of a more modern nature—trailers, ranch houses, a few shacks. But nowhere was there an Irish cottage made of stone.

"Is that real?" I murmured. "Or is it like the green hills and mists of Ireland?" Neither of which were in evidence today.

"Real enough," Sawyer answered, and at my exasperated hiss elaborated. "The dwelling changes, depending on her mood. I've come here and found a hacienda, a ranch complete with horses, a seaside villa, and a cabin deep in a dark forest of trees that would never grow in a place like this."

"Don't people in the area get a little wigged out?" I started up the cobblestone walkway, and Sawyer followed.

"I don't think people in the area are aware of her being here at all. If they were, they'd be forced to take action."

"Because they'd think she was a witch," I said.

Sawyer didn't answer. He didn't need to.

"What would they do?"

"Common practice is to tie a witch down, no food or water until they confess."

"And if they don't confess?"

"Hot coals to the bottom of the feet on the fourth day."

"And then?"

Sawyer slowly drew his finger across his throat.

"What if they do confess?"

Sawyer made the same gesture in the opposite direction.

"That hardly seems fair."

"Since when has life or death or justice, for that matter, ever been fair?"

What a bright and cheery outlook on life. Sadly, Sawyer was right.

"I guess the Navajo method is no better or worse than the Inquisition's test for witches," I said. "If you survive drowning, you're a witch and you burn. If you drown, whoops. Sorry. My bad."

Sawyer stopped and glanced at me with a deadpan expression. "I highly doubt any members of the Inquisition said *my bad.*"

"And I doubt they said *sorry.*" Or *whoops,* either.

For an instant I nearly forgot where we were, what we—make that I—was about to do, and smiled at him. Then, out of the corner of my eye, something shifted, shimmered, and changed shape.

I whipped my head in that direction to discover that the sweet, stone cottage had morphed into a gray stone prison, complete with an eight-foot concrete wall topped by barbed wire.

"She knows we're here," I said.

Turrets graced the corners of the walls, manned by—

I squinted at the great, hulking figures. Some had bodies like men, heads like animals. Others were part bull, part lion, part falcon perhaps, with large wings sweeping from their shoulders.

"Are those gargoyles?" Sawyer nodded. "I thought they were statues on buildings."

"Most gargoyles can turn to stone to avoid detection, then turn back into a chimera at will."

"What's a chimera?"

"Two animals as one."

"So all the gargoyles on all the buildings all over the world can come to life?"

Sawyer spread his hands. Who knew?

"Are they Nephilim?" He shook his head. "Breeds?"

"No. The gargoyles were animals that aided the fairies when they first fell to the earth. The fairies were lost. They had no idea how to survive here. They were suddenly humanoid. They needed to eat, sleep, protect themselves from the elements, and they didn't know how."

"The Grigori had their human lovers to help them," I reasoned.

"The Grigori were cast into Tartarus so fast they didn't have time to panic."

"I'll take your word for it," I said. "So certain animals helped the fairies, and in return . . . ?"

"They were given humanity."

"That's human?" I muttered. The heavenly rewards around here were kind of iffy.

"They have the intelligence of humans, with the assets of their beast, combined with the gifts of flight and shape-shifting. They're more than human," Sawyer said. "Once the fairies settled in, once they could manage on their own, the gargoyles were charged with protecting the weak and unwary from demon attack. The more humans they save, the more human they become."

I glanced up at the turrets. I guess that explained the human and animal combos.

"What are they doing here?" I asked.

Sawyer contemplated the towers as the gargoyles, standing as still as stone, contemplated us. The only thing that made them seem real were the colors of their flesh, their hair, their fur or wings, and the slight rise and fall of their chests. Their flat black eyes reminded me of the statues they could become and made me wonder if they were capable of showing any mercy at all.

"Summer must have enlisted them for protection," Sawyer said. "The gargoyles and the fairies are still very close."

We'd stopped halfway down the cobblestone walk, which was now just cement, as gray and hard as the walls of the prison. As we began to move forward, the air filled with the slow, methodic beat of giant wings.

My gaze flicked upward. The gargoyles had taken to the air.

I cursed. Sawyer kept walking.

"Hey." I scurried after. "They're going to protect this place from demon attack."

He lifted a hand, making his "stopping traffic, crossing guard" gesture, and the prison wall imploded.

"I'm not a demon," Sawyer said, and walked inside.

CHAPTER 30

Sawyer had put a pretty huge hole in the gray stone wall. Summer was going to be pissed.

I glanced at the gargoyles. They continued to hover in the sky above as if waiting for an order. Attack or retreat?

Maybe they couldn't attack if we weren't demons. Maybe they couldn't decide what we were. Hell, I still had doubts of my own.

I stepped through the jagged hole, my shoes crunching on busted concrete. Dust sparkled in the glare of sunlight through the un-door. I frowned at that sunshine. The angle was off.

Quickly I glanced back. The stone walkway seemed to stretch for miles. The Hummer sitting at the curb looked the size of a Pekingese. The sun had fallen a lot farther than it should have for the amount of time I thought we'd been gone.

"How long have we been walking?" I asked.

Sawyer, who'd been staring up a stone staircase that disappeared into a dark and shadowy second floor, turned, then shrugged. "Does it matter?"

I felt adrift, confused, and out of my element, which was probably what Summer was after. "Is she messing with time and space?"

"What do you think?" He gestured at the stairway that should not exist in a tiny, one-room Irish cottage.

"Why?"

"Because she can, but she should save her magic for someone who cares. It isn't going to make us run screaming."

"You'll never find him." As Summer's voice echoed through the shadowy darkness of the second floor, the prison seemed to swell, becoming taller and wider. "I won't let you."

There were now at least four floors above us; half a dozen halls led away from the gaping entry. Doors upon doors, hundreds, perhaps thousands, appeared.

"I won't leave," I said quietly, knowing she could hear me. "You can't make me."

Summer appeared on the fourth-floor landing. "Watch me," she said, and jumped.

I flinched before I remembered that she could fly. She floated gently downward, landing in front of me. Wearing her usual tight jeans, boots, and halter top, she'd left her cowboy hat upstairs. Her golden hair sparkled angel-like though her eyes sparked with near-demonic fury.

"Summer, listen—" I began.

She hit me in the face with a fistful of fairy dust. I choked.

"Go away," she said. "Never come here again."

I turned and headed for the door.

"Phoenix," Sawyer murmured, but I didn't care. I had to leave. Now. I would never return. Why had I ever come here in the first place?

"Where's Sanducci?" Sawyer demanded.

"Who's Sanducci?" I muttered.

Summer laughed as I stepped out of the gaping hole in the wall and into the orange light of the setting sun. The gargoyles circled, bizarre silhouettes in the sky. The Hummer no longer appeared the size of a Pekingese. It wasn't very far away at all. I'd be there in seconds. Luther and I would go home. I really, really wanted to go home.

However, I'd only taken a few steps when she cried out, and the compulsion to leave drained from me as quickly as a hard rain down a steep gully.

I went inside. Summer and Sawyer faced each other. From her outcry, I figured he'd done something violent, but there wasn't a scratch on her, just a four-leaf clover stuck in her hair.

"Why does your magic suddenly work on me?" I asked.

Summer gave me an evil glare. "You are *not* on an errand of mercy."

My eyes widened. "Saving the world isn't merciful?"

"You'll hurt him," she said. "Permanently."

"How do you know what I'm up to?" I hadn't talked to her since before we'd found Xander Whitelaw.

She tapped her head. Shorthand for *psychic flash.*

"Summer, I don't have any choice."

"Go screw a demon. Leave Jimmy alone."

"It's too dangerous," Sawyer said. "As much as I hate to admit it, Sanducci is the best course for her."

"He's in agony over what he is. Forcing him to make her that way, too—" Her eyes met mine. "It'll destroy him."

She was probably right.

"Quit punishing him for something that wasn't his fault."

"This isn't about punishing—" I began, then stopped. "What isn't his fault?"

"Him and me." She looked at her feet. "That was Ruthie."

"I know." Her chin jerked up, and I tapped my own head. "I saw."

"Then how can you—"

"I have to!" I shouted. "Jimmy will understand."

"You wish," Summer said at the same time Sawyer murmured, "I doubt that."

I opened my mouth, then shut it again. Regardless of whether he understood or he didn't, I was still going to do this.

"Where is he?" I asked.

Summer stuck out her tongue.

"Oh, that's mature."

She gave me the finger. Even better.

I glanced at Sawyer. "Can you do something?"

"I've exhausted the magical options," he said. "Saint-John's-wort allowed us to see this place." He held up a hand before I could speak. "And I used all I had to get that far."

So he couldn't make the cavernous gray prison revert to whatever it really was.

"What's up with that?" I lifted my chin to indicate the tiny green plant still stuck in Summer's hair.

"A four-leaf clover blocks her influence."

"She can't sway anyone with her 'make me' dust while she's wearing that?"

"Exactly."

"She can't just yank it out?"

Sawyer gave me a withering glare. "Please," he murmured.

As if to illustrate, Summer swiped at the clover, then

hissed in pain as if the thing were embedded in her skull along with her hair.

"I have to remove it," Sawyer said. He lifted a brow at Summer. "So you'd better be nice."

She gave him the finger, too. She'd really been hanging out with me way too much.

"If you're blocking her influence, why is this place such a maze?" I lifted my gaze. The prison had continued to grow—hall upon hall, stairway beyond stairway.

"We're talking two different things—innate magic and spells. Clover, for one—" He swept his hand out, empty palm up.

"Saint-John's-wort, which you're out of, for the other." Sawyer nodded. "Why are you carrying these things in the first place?"

"There are a lot of fairies, Phoenix, and I'm rarely merciful."

I glanced at Summer, who was too busy trying to pick the clover out of her hair to comment. She was going to snatch herself bald if she didn't knock it off.

"Where do you stock up on antifairy meds?"

"Wal-Mart," he said simply.

"I can understand the Saint-John's-wort"—it was an herb used for a lot of ailments—"but the four-leaf clover? I doubt they carry them."

"The benandanti did," he said simply.

That made Summer pause. "The benandanti is dead."

"What was that?" Sawyer's voice betrayed no emotion beyond mild curiosity.

"She went to the underworld to fight the Grigori. And she lost."

"So they're free?" I asked.

"Not yet. I assume there are more steps involved."

I glanced at Sawyer.

"I don't know what they are," he said.

That hadn't been why I was looking at him. I thought maybe he'd be upset, at least a little, that a woman he'd recently slept with was dead. The way Sawyer was behaving, you'd never even know they'd met.

I thought of Carla as I'd seen her last—young and strong again thanks to Sawyer. Nevertheless she'd lost the fight and we'd moved one step closer to Armageddon's Apocalypse.

"I need to see Jimmy," I blurted.

"Good luck with that." Summer indicated the still-multiplying cool gray corridors and the ever-increasing stairway to heaven.

I grabbed her by the arms, planning to shake her until the truth rattled out along with her teeth, but as soon as I touched her, I saw the path that led to the single cell-like room that housed Jimmy.

Touch something he did. Worked nearly every time.

I ran down the nearest hall. Summer followed, keeping up admirably well considering my dhampir speed. But then she could fly, and did, hovering above me, chattering like a damned squirrel as she continued to try and convince me that I shouldn't do this.

"He's better," she said. "He won't do what you want."

I didn't point out that if that were true, he wouldn't be locked up, and she wouldn't be working so hard to keep me from finding him.

I reached the golden door—how obvious was that?—and Summer's feet touched the floor just as Sawyer caught up.

No doorknob, no latch, no way to open the thing that I could see. I glanced at Summer, who lifted a brow and crossed her arms over her chest. She wasn't going to open it, and I couldn't make her.

I studied what appeared to be a solid-gold structure,

as thick as any bank vault. Obviously she'd bespelled the thing somehow. I placed my palm on Summer's head, hoping for a clue, but she was ready for me this time, and all I got was a blast of her and Jimmy rolling in the sheets.

I snatched my hand back as she smirked. I was pretty certain that had been recent.

"Those who peek into heads uninvited deserve whatever they see," she said. "You told me to do anything."

I hadn't told her to do him, but—I shrugged. Whatever worked. I couldn't throw stones at that glass house.

I returned my attention to the door, knocked and called, "Jimmy?"

My answer was a snarl that wasn't even close to human, then something slammed into the other side so hard the entire building shuddered.

I lifted my gaze to Summer's. "You call that better?"

"I did a spell," she admitted. "It subverts the vampire."

I tilted my head, remembering the term from my dream walk. "Subverts how?"

"Channels the demon." Summer lifted her hands, pressing them together as if making a snowball. "He fights and fights—"

"Which means the demon gets stronger and stronger because he won't let it free," Sawyer said. "It's like damming up a creek. The water's got to go somewhere."

"So it overflows the banks," I murmured, "or bursts past the dam."

"When's he set to explode?" Sawyer asked.

In answer, Jimmy snarled again, and this time, when he hit the door, the outline of a fist expanded outward.

"I'd say right about now," I murmured.

Sawyer frowned. "Maybe you should wait before going inside."

"Not."

"Tomorrow *would* be better," Summer agreed.

If she wanted me to wait, I knew I *had* to get in there. "What happens tomorrow?"

Sawyer stared at Summer, his expression considering. *"Plenus luna malum,"* he murmured, and her eyes narrowed as her fingers clenched. She really wanted to zap him and couldn't.

"Something Latin about the moon," I guessed.

"Translates to 'full moon evil,'" Sawyer explained. "She channeled his vampire tendencies into the night of the full moon. Every other night, he's normal. Or as normal as Sanducci gets. But when the moon is whole, he goes—"

Jimmy slammed into the door again.

"Batshit," I muttered. "I take it the full moon's tonight."

"You think?" Sawyer asked.

I hated it when he repeated my sarcasm back at me, but as Ruthie always said, you get what you pay for, and I'd definitely paid for that.

There were times when nothing went right, one incident right after the other making me think I was cursed. And then there were times, like now, when serendipity made me believe that everything did happen for a reason, and in the end the forces of good would win.

Could it be a coincidence that Jimmy was only a vampire under the full moon, and we'd just happened to show up on that particular night?

Perhaps. But I didn't think so.

I contemplated the door again, biting my lip, trying to figure out a way to get in.

"He'll tear you apart," Summer said.

I wasn't certain tearing me apart would actually kill me, though I wasn't wild about finding out. "I'm fast and I'm strong."

"Not like he is when he's—" Summer drew back her lips from her teeth, hooked her fingers into claws, and hissed to illustrate.

"I'll be all right."

"He'll drain you."

I shrugged. I'd been drained before. I hadn't died; all I'd done was dream walk.

"Once he finds out what I want," I said, "he'll be game. The thought of making me, the leader of the light, into a dark force . . . When he's in vamp mode, he won't be able to resist."

"And when he comes back to himself," Summer whispered, "he'll be in agony."

"If I've spoiled Doomsday, he'll be thrilled."

"Even if you win, you'll still be a vampire. That isn't going to go away."

I paused, imagining what I would become. Could I do it?

I remembered the woman of smoke, what she'd done to Sawyer, his father, and so many others. I thought of all I'd seen in the short month I'd been aware that there was another world that existed parallel to our own—an evil world full of evil things—and I knew the truth.

"It doesn't matter what happens to me." I looked into Sawyer's eyes, and he nodded. He'd do what had to be done when all of this was through.

"Any ideas?" I flicked a finger at the golden prison door.

Summer started forward. Sawyer lifted his hand and flung her back. His eerie gray eyes shone on her like the full silver light of the moon. "If you continue," he murmured, "I will bind you with rowan."

"Rowan kills a fairy," I said.

"Eventually." Sawyer didn't sound concerned.

"I don't think that's necessary." In the past, I'd wished

Summer dead on several occasions, but now . . . not so much.

"Don't do me any favors, Phoenix," Summer said. "I've sold my soul to protect him—"

"You what?" I said softly.

"Figure of speech," she muttered. "If I'd gone to the dark side, don't you think you'd have heard about it by now?"

Hard to say. Ruthie'd been suspiciously silent. Was I unconsciously blocking her voice now that I'd learned of her betrayal? I didn't think so. I wasn't even certain I could.

"Don't kill her," I ordered Sawyer.

"If you do this," Summer murmured, "you'll devastate him. You think I'll care if I'm dead once that happens?"

Guilt beckoned, but I pushed it aside. Guilt was a weakness I couldn't afford.

"How do I get in?"

Sawyer still held one arm up to keep Summer back. He held the other out to me, the index finger of that hand pointing toward a thin gap between the floor and the bottom of the door.

At first I didn't understand, then my gaze caught on the tarantula creeping across his forearm.

"Be careful," he murmured.

Summer shrieked and tried to get off the floor. He smacked her back with a twitch of his thumb.

"No matter what you hear, no matter what I say, don't open the door."

"Phoenix," Sawyer said, his voice exasperated, "if I *could* open the door, there'd be no reason for this." He lifted his arm encouragingly. "And we both know that you'd cut out your own tongue before you'd admit you shouldn't have gone in there."

"Don't follow me," I said.

"Wouldn't dream of it."

"I mean it."

"So do I."

I leaned forward and pressed a quick, hard kiss to his mouth. I might never again be the me I was right now, and I needed him to know something. "Thanks," I said.

I lost the clothes. After removing the turquoise from my neck, I shoved it under the door, then covered the tarantula with my palm, and reached with my mind for the essence of the black eight-legged creature.

Bright, icy light consumed me, followed by a sudden heat. I dropped so fast my head spun; the thin stream of light beckoned from the other side of the door, and I scurried in that direction.

Behind me another furious scream erupted, then a whirlwind of air pushed me forward an instant before a heavy thud shook the ground.

Danger loomed. A shadow in the shape of a shoe coming right for me.

Another thud, like a body hitting the wall, then all went still; the whirlwind died, and I scuttled safely beneath the prison door.

CHAPTER 31

As soon as I was on the other side, I imagined myself as myself, and the heat became again a sudden chill. My view of the world, since I now had eight eyes, was epic; as I changed it narrowed. My fangs retracted; my legs and arms decreased by half.

I was three inches tall, then three feet, and then five-ten. I didn't take time to glance at the room. I'd been here before. I understood now why the place was so plain and empty. Prisons were like that.

Jimmy stood at the window, as naked as I was, staring at the coming night. On the floor next to the bed lay one of his never-ending supply of T-shirts. This one declared TOM PETTY—WORLD TOUR.

It was a status symbol among those whose images graced tabloids and CD cases to have the great Sanducci wear a T-shirt bearing their name or likeness. If Sanducci wore your shirt, he'd taken your picture and you had arrived. I doubted Tom Petty cared, but I was certain his "people" did.

I'd heard that dozens of T-shirts a month crowded Sanducci's mailbox. He donated those sent by people he'd never photographed to a homeless shelter and packed the ones that were true into his suitcase. He liked to wear them with jeans and a jacket—neither of which were in evidence on the floor of the prison cell.

I snatched up the turquoise and Tom's tee and put them on. The material smelled like Jimmy, and I resisted the urge to rub my face in it, to just inhale a while.

Some movement or small sound on my part made Jimmy glance toward the door. He sighed and hung his head. "Are you really here?"

He looked worse than he had in the dream—paler if possible, exhausted, emaciated, sad, and very defeated.

I crossed the room and laid a hand on his shoulder. He flinched. "Hey," I murmured. "It's me."

He didn't ask how I'd gotten in. He knew what I could do.

"Change back and get out."

Or maybe he didn't.

"I can't shift on my own."

Jimmy cursed, and in a movement so swift I couldn't get away, even if I'd wanted to, he grabbed my arms and shook me. "Get out!" he roared.

"Oh, that'll help." I kept my voice calm. No use for both of us losing our minds.

"You don't understand." His fingers still dug into my flesh, causing bruises that would disappear almost as fast as they appeared. "You can't be here. The moon is coming. I can . . ." He swallowed, closed his eyes, shuddered. "Smell it."

"You can smell it," I repeated.

"Hear it, feel it. Like the tide it pulls."

I put my palm against his forehead. He jerked away. "I'm not sick."

" 'Like the tide it pulls'? You're spouting poetry and that isn't you." In the past, Jimmy's idea of poetry had been "Do me, baby, one more time."

He pulled at his hair. "It's whispering."

"The moon," I clarified.

"Yesssss."

The way he hissed the word caused gooseflesh to ripple across my bare arms and legs.

"It tells me to—" He paused and his dark gaze slid over my neck, my breasts, the juncture of my thighs, barely covered by his complimentary T-shirt. "Do terrible things." He licked his lips, and I caught a hint of fang.

Once the moon finished whispering, once he became the beast his father had made him into, he would want to hurt me in the most vicious way possible. Because when Jimmy was a vampire, he was as Nephilim as the rest of them.

I couldn't tell him why I was here, that I wanted him to drink from me, that I needed to drink from him. Because even though he became something other than himself when he became a vamp, he remembered everything, and if he knew why I aspired to become like him, he'd make certain that I didn't.

Tact was necessary, never my strong suit.

"Everything will be all right," I murmured, and brushed his sweat-dampened hair away from his face.

He cast me a quick, suspicious glance—I'd never been the nurturing type, probably because I'd never been nurtured—and put his palm to my forehead.

"*You* sick?" he asked, and I had to smile at his attempt to joke. He was still Jimmy, at least until the moon came up.

I tangled our fingers together, and when he tugged to be released I didn't let go. I had an idea.

Since he was still Jimmy, for now, the best way to get him to do what I wanted was to give him what he wanted.

Me.

I could tell by the way his gaze kept straying to my legs, my breasts, and my neck that he did still want me. He always had. No matter how long we'd been apart, how we'd fought, what he'd done, what I had, that one thing never changed.

He'd fight making me like him; he might even win. That he'd been able to push the dark side of himself back as far as he had, that he hadn't killed anyone in the month he'd been free, revealed how strong he was.

To do this, I'd have to slip beneath his defenses and seduce him—mind, body, and what was left of his soul.

I slid in close, brushing my unbound breasts against his bare chest, just a little, as if "oops!" it were an accident, and Jimmy tightened his lips, closed his eyes, his face going as taut as his body.

For a vampire, sex and violence, blood and lust, were all rolled together. Get him to lose control in one way, he'd be powerless to exert control in another. In the throes of passion, in the midst of an orgasm, he'd bite me. He'd done it before.

Guilt flickered, and again I shoved it away.

"I've been so worried." My free hand trailed up his forearm; I leaned in and let my breath trickle over his collarbone. Gooseflesh rose across his shoulder, and I licked him, then grazed him with my teeth.

"Lizzy, stop." He grabbed my shoulders and held me away, but he couldn't keep his gaze from drifting lower, catching on where my nipples must be thrusting at the thin, overwashed material of the shirt. Begging to be touched, calling out for one man to do the touching.

"Please," he whispered. "Don't make me."

Then, as if he were hypnotized, his hands slid down

my arms, scooped inward and cupped me, lifting, kneading, thumbs rolling over the turgid peaks.

My head fell back as I offered my neck, my blood, myself. He buried his face in the soft mounds, his lips closing over me, taking cotton and flesh within. The heat, the pressure was both pleasure and pain. My hands tangled in his hair, holding him closer, urging him on.

I needed to feel his skin against mine, so I snatched the hem of the shirt, tugging it upward. The material got caught on his face; he released me as I whipped the shirt away.

But that tiny instant was my mistake. As soon as his mouth left me, sanity returned, and he stepped back.

"No," he muttered. "We can't."

"Since when?" I followed him. "This has always been the one thing we *could* do. Very well."

"I'll lose control—"

I snatched his hand and brought it to my lips, pressing a kiss to his palm, flicking my tongue across the center, then grazing the wrist with my teeth as I pressed my bare belly to his erection. "I like it when you do."

He tore away and crossed to the other side of the room, staring at the door as if he were trying to figure out how to break free. "What are you doing, Lizzy?"

He was too smart by half and far too strong-willed. But I couldn't give up now.

"I'll make you feel better."

"I'll make you feel dead," he muttered.

"You can't hurt me, Jimmy. Come on." I lowered my voice. "You know you want to."

"I've done nothing but hurt you," he said, eyes wide, voice desperate. "I—I slept with Summer on purpose. I knew you'd see."

"And I know you were ordered to do it."

He went very still. "Who told you that?"

He wouldn't remember I'd walked through his dreams. Dream walking was like that. The victim might think they'd dreamed of you, but they wouldn't remember when or what or why.

However, Jimmy was a dream walker, too, and he understood what those wisps of memory meant. Comprehension bloomed across his face, and he cursed. "You saw it in my head. Along with where I was."

I shrugged. What could I say?

"You walked on the brink of death just to find me?"

"You needed me," I lied. What was one more in a long, unholy line of them?

"Oh, baby, no," he whispered, and I nearly caved and ran away.

But I had nowhere to go, no way to leave, so I stayed and I lied a little more.

"I'll be with you all night. I'm the only one who can." That was true enough. "If you fight the bloodlust under the full moon and you win, maybe it'll be gone forever."

He tilted his head. "Is that possible?"

Doubtful, I thought.

"Anything's possible," I said.

God, I was such a Judas.

Jimmy sighed. "You forgive me for Summer?"

"There's nothing to forgive." Considering what I was about to do, the betrayal with Summer had been child's play. Literally. "You did it for me, Jimmy. That only makes you more of a hero in my eyes."

"Shit," he muttered. "And Manhattan? When I made you my slave? When I kept you prisoner and drank from you until you nearly died? Was I a hero then?"

"You were as much a victim as I was. The strega was at fault, not you."

Although it had been Jimmy hurting me night after night, or at least something that looked just like him. I still woke up sometimes and thought I saw him rising above me, eyes flame-red, fangs flaring, as he raped me mind, body, and soul.

"You stay here, and I'll do the same thing to you to-night that I did to you then. Probably worse."

I was counting on it.

"I'm not a hero and you know it," he continued.

I knew nothing of the sort. We'd both been played by forces more powerful than us. We'd been moved around like chess pieces in this fight to save the world, and in doing so we'd been hurt. Hell, we'd died—not that dying was a permanent condition for either one of us.

"I killed for you," he murmured.

I cast him a quick glance. I'd never been certain what had happened that night.

"If you want to cast me as a hero," Jimmy continued, "you need to know everything I've done."

"It doesn't matter," I said.

"It did to Mr. Nix."

The name caused my mind to roll back over ten years. I'd stayed after school to sign up for the gymnastics club. I was so excited to be part of something, anything. I was humming as I shut my locker and turned to go home.

My heart leaped, nearly choking me, when a shadow loomed up and blocked my way. Though the neighborhood was fairly safe, the schools downright decent, we were still close to a large city with a high crime rate, and face it—

Shit happened. I'd just hoped it had finally stopped happening to me.

My gaze had slid right, left, searching for a way to escape; then the light splashed across the man's face, and I nearly fainted with relief.

"Mr. Nix. You scared me."

"Elizabeth," he murmured, his German accent giving my plain English name a lilt. "Why here so late"—he smiled—"and so alone?"

The skin at the back of my neck prickled as my well-developed self-preservation instinct whispered, *Why is a male math teacher in the girls' locker room?*

I didn't want to turn, to take my eyes off the man. When he grabbed me, and he would grab me, I didn't need to be psychic to understand that, I wanted to be facing him. The idea of having those thick, hard hands clutch at me from behind made me sick.

I shouldn't have been so scared. I'd been hassled before, many times. I'd been groped by new "brothers," "fathers," and even on one occasion a "big sister." All it ever took was my reciting a secret I'd plucked from their head, and they'd not only let me go in a big hurry, they'd made certain I didn't live with them any longer.

But Mr. Nix was a teacher, and even though he'd made me nervous on occasion, staring at me too often and too long, I'd just figured he was curious about my background. A lot of people were. I'd never figured on something like this.

For a large man—at least six-four, two-sixty—he moved fast, and when he grabbed me I didn't have time to think about running, let alone do it.

As soon as his skin met mine, I heard music. Loud, strange, foreign. Not a polka—I'd lived in Milwaukee more than a minute—a polka I knew, but similar. Same instruments, different beat.

Following close on the heels of the sound came the images—ponds, lakes, streams, and rivers. Girls upon girls, floating dead in those waters, and the flashes of what he'd done to them before he'd tossed them away.

He tore my shirt in half with one big, meaty hand. I

was a well-developed thirteen, and my breasts nearly burst from the bra that had fit just fine only a month ago.

"I can play a while," he murmured, his milky blue gaze crawling over my dusky skin. "Play, play, play."

He drew two pale index fingers over the swells, down to the nipples, which he gave a vicious tweak. I thrust my knee up so hard his cock got very friendly with his larynx.

Instead of going down, he flared his nose like a bull's, then he swept his arms toward me in a bear hug. I ducked, and his face kissed locker.

Considering how fast he'd grabbed me in the first place, I didn't expect to get away. But it wasn't in my nature to just stand there and take it. The instant he fell, I ran.

"Who you think you are?" he shouted, voice guttural, accent even more pronounced with pain. "Nothing yet. No one ever. I will kill you first, fuck you after. It is better that way."

I burst out of the locker room and ran straight into Jimmy.

I screamed, and he slapped his hand over my mouth. From the expression on his face, he'd at least heard the last part. He was furious, and for an instant I thought he might charge into the locker room and—

I'm not sure what. At thirteen Jimmy hadn't grown into his hands or his feet. He'd never grow into a body as large as that of Mr. Nix.

If he confronted the bigger man, Sanducci would get hurt, maybe die, because of me, and while I'd told him on several occasions, just that morning in fact, to "drop dead"—or had it been the more colorful "eat shit and die?"—I didn't want him to actually do it.

"Come on," he said, and took my hand. The anger in

his eyes smoldering, he dragged me out the nearest door and into the night.

I shivered, and not just because my shirt hung in shreds, or even because my math teacher had just molested me. But also because it was spring in Milwaukee and snow was still piled at the edges of the driveways, the yards, the corners of the roads. Here and there daffodils pushed through the half-frozen mud, their bright yellow petals brighter because of the remaining splotches of white.

The slick slide of the switchblade registered seconds after the pure silver weapon appeared in Sanducci's hand. I lifted my gaze from the knife, sparkling merrily in the glow from a distant streetlight, to Jimmy's face. What I saw there made me shiver even more.

We kept to the alleys and backyards, to the shadows. I didn't hear sounds of pursuit—the guy couldn't be that stupid, could he? Of course he didn't know about Jimmy and his pet knife.

A few dogs barked, a few lights went on as we skittered through yards, but half an hour later we entered Ruthie's empty kitchen. I'd hoped to creep upstairs, take a scalding hot shower or ten, burn my clothes, and pretend nothing had happened. But as soon as the door shut, Jimmy shouted, "Ruthie!"

"Are you nuts?"

He let his eyes drop to where I clutched my shredded shirt over my breasts. "Are you?"

Ruthie came in, took one look at my torn clothes, at the livid red scratches that marred my skin, then folded me into her arms, and hustled me upstairs. Right before I left the room, I turned back, but Jimmy was already gone.

I begged Ruthie not to call the police. My word

against his. I knew how things worked. So did Ruthie. She nodded slowly, and then she put me to bed.

The next day Mr. Nix wasn't at school. Or the day after that or ever again.

CHAPTER 32

"You killed him," I said. "Mr. Nix."

Jimmy shrugged, and his muscles rippled seductively beneath his bare, smooth skin. "He touched you."

"Jesus, Jimmy," I muttered. "There are a lot of guys you'd have to kill if that were the criteria."

"And I have," he murmured. "Killed a lot of guys."

My eyes narrowed on his too still face. "How many were actually guys?"

"A few."

"And Mr. Nix? What was he?"

"A Nix is a German shape-shifter. Horse, snake, fish, or mermaid."

"Merman," I corrected absently.

"Whatever. Legends say they have sex with their victims then drag them into the nearest body of water to drown."

I guess that explained what I'd seen when I'd touched him. Lots of dead girls in the water. And if it weren't for Jimmy, I'd have joined them.

I heard again the swish of his silver blade. "You killed him," I said, "and he was ashes."

"Would explain how he disappeared."

"You didn't see?"

"I stuck him and ran. I wasn't stupid. The guy was huge."

I frowned. "You didn't know?"

"That he was a shifter? Not then."

Which meant Jimmy had thought he was killing a man. A molester, true, but human.

Jimmy saw the understanding cross my face. "He hurt you; he died. End of story."

I wasn't sure what to say about that. Nix had been a demon; that Jimmy hadn't known it when he killed him hadn't changed what Nix was, what he'd done to more girls than me, and what he would have done to countless others if not for Sanducci.

"Why didn't you know? Why didn't Ruthie?"

"Seers can't see every demon. You'd go loony."

I wasn't certain we weren't.

"There are just too many of them," Jimmy said. "We do the best that we can."

Silence fell between us. But it didn't last long.

"Do you hate me now?" Jimmy asked.

I'd hated him for years, but not for that.

"Nix was a demon," I said.

"I didn't know that."

I moved closer, wrapping my arms around his waist, capturing him when he would have tried to escape, though there was nowhere for him to go, then laying my cheek against his chest and listening to the familiar beat of his heart. "I've known for years that you killed him, Jimmy, and I thought he was human, too."

That shut him up.

"I touched you; I loved you; I gave you myself; and I knew all along what you did."

"Mr. Nix disappeared. You didn't know jack."

"I knew."

He leaned back, and I lifted my head to meet his curious eyes. "You saw?"

"No." Amazingly, I *hadn't* seen what had happened to Mr. Nix any of the times I'd touched Jimmy, which meant that the killing of the man hadn't bothered Sanducci all that much. He hadn't thought about it, dreamed of it, or agonized over it. Neither had I. The guy had deserved to die. Some just did.

"Then how—" Jimmy asked.

"I can add," I said. "Knife, you, Nix. Deadsville."

I didn't tell him that there'd been other times when I'd touched him that I'd gotten wisps of his past, seen faces of others, known things that he'd done. It didn't matter.

Of course the police had come eventually. A taxpaying citizen—and Nix was that, too, as well as a demon—couldn't disappear without questions being asked. So they'd quizzed everyone, especially those of us who lived at Ruthie's place, especially Jimmy Sanducci.

Jimmy had spent time in jail once—juvie, sure, but jail nevertheless. Something about a knife. No shock there. But the incident, whatever it was—and I'd never been able to get him to tell me with words or memories—had been enough to make the cops suspicious.

There'd been other incidents, both before Jimmy had come to Ruthie's and afterward. Things that Ruthie had somehow managed to make go away. Which explained the wisps I saw sometimes when I touched him.

At the time I'd thought Nix was a run-of-the-mill serial killer. Since he'd disappeared, and I had a pretty good idea how, I kept my mouth shut. I'd learned young not to talk about the things I "saw." I was happy to "keep it in the family," as Ruthie advised.

Now that I knew what Nix had been, I had some

questions of my own. "Was he after me because of who I'd become?"

Jimmy frowned, considering, then shook his head. "None of the Nephilim knew about Ruthie's until—" He broke off.

Until Jimmy had been infiltrated. I shouldn't have brought that up.

"Seems too much of a coincidence that a demon would try to kill me less than a year after I got there," I mused.

"Even if Nix knew somehow, the knowledge died with him. Otherwise there'd have been a line of Nephilim on the lawn waiting to kill you."

"How . . . comforting," I said. "Still, don't you think it was weird?"

"Unfortunately, no. The majority of the evil pricks in the world are Nephilim. Serial killers, child molesters, terrorists."

"Televangelists," I muttered.

"Very funny," he said, but he wasn't laughing. Instead he stared toward the window, and he looked scared. "You have to go now."

"How do you suggest I do that?" I motioned at the door, which didn't have a knob on this side, either.

Jimmy banged his fists against it again, putting two more dents in an already dented structure. "Summer," he shouted. "Get her the hell out!"

"Summer's a little tied up," I murmured.

Jimmy spun to face me. "You brought Sawyer?"

"Did you think I wouldn't?"

He leaned against the door, defeated again. "Lizzy, you don't know what you're doing."

But I did know. I was doing what had to be done.

I took him by the arm, led him to the bed, then sat beside him. A fine sheen of sweat had broken out all over his skin. The moon was coming, and he was fighting the change.

I leaned in, letting my breasts brush his arm as I rubbed his back, pretending at comfort. "We'll fight this together. You and me. Just like when we were kids."

"You and me against the world," he murmured.

"You and me *for* the world," I corrected, but he didn't seem to hear me. "Jimmy?"

He lifted his head, and his eyes held a single pinprick of red at the center. He was losing the battle. I lowered my soothing hand from his shoulders to the small of his back, continuing to rub, letting my fingertips trail across the swell of his ass. He shuddered.

"What if I make you like me?" He licked his lips, his gaze locked on the curve of my neck.

"I can take care of myself."

"Not when I'm like that." He grabbed me by the arms again, hauled me against him. "It's damnation, Lizzy. For both of us."

Perhaps. But sacrifices must be made. Damnation for us, salvation for everyone else. I was willing to take that chance.

"This darkness is a fate worse than death," he said.

"I won't leave you."

"You should kill me."

"Been there, done that, didn't take."

He let me go. "I didn't give you up then to turn you evil now."

"Why did you give me up?"

"For your own good."

Which was why I was doing this now. His good. Mine. The world's.

Jimmy closed his eyes and whispered, "You're going to break me."

I put my hand on his arm. I'm not sure what I meant to say, maybe nothing, perhaps everything, but silver trickled through the windows, across his face, across mine, and his eyes snapped open.

Fire flared at their center. The moon was up; Jimmy was gone.

I had to make him believe that I was too preoccupied with doing him to realize I was supposed to be helping him fight the fight. He'd drink from me; I'd drink from him and then—

I didn't want to think about that. For now, I'd just enjoy the press of his mouth, the brush of his hands. Jimmy'd always been a sexual savant. When he touched me, I melted. Couldn't help myself.

Sure, Sawyer was the best sex I'd ever had, but Sawyer *was* sex. Jimmy was love, childhood—all that was good and right before everything went badly wrong.

Even in the strega's lair, when Jimmy had said and done terrible things, if he shut the hell up, turned off the lights, and touched me, it was as if we were seventeen again.

Talk about breaking someone. In Manhattan, he'd been very, very close to breaking me.

Now he was rough, hungry, that was fine. The faster he took me, the faster he'd lose control and do what I wanted him to.

I opened my mouth, welcomed his tongue, suckling it. He growled and yanked me closer, crushing my breasts to his chest, then shimmying back and forth, creating pressure and friction.

My body was twisted at an odd angle, so I swung my leg over his lap, straddling him. He was hard, no surprise, and I rode that hardness against my belly just enough to make him crazy.

He tore his lips from mine, kissing his way across my jaw, down my neck, then teasing the tips of my breasts with his tongue.

"Harder," I muttered. "More." And he grazed me with his teeth.

I yanked on his hair, and he bucked beneath me, the pressure against my now slick and swollen center both exquisite and excruciating.

The moon spilled across us; the chill silver light seemed to scald my naked skin. My fingers skated over him, my nails raking his back, his chest.

His eyes were completely red now; his fangs had lengthened. I'd accomplished what I'd set out to do, seduced him into forgetting the fight.

He flexed his hips, pressing against me, sliding just a little within. I lifted myself and let him plunge. My head fell back, and I clutched at his shoulders as I tightened around him.

"Your blood is like wine," he whispered against my breasts. "I can smell the power pulsing under your skin. What could I do with you beside me? What could we, together, become?"

What was it with the evil throng? Give them an inch, they take the world, or at least covet it.

He arched, pressing into me even as he pulled my hips down. I couldn't think anymore, could only feel, the pressure, the pain, the possibilities.

What *could* we do, together?

I shook my head hard enough to hurt. *Focus!* Jimmy needed to drink from me, I needed to drink from him, and then . . .

Shazaam, I'd be a vampire. Or close enough.

I had to move this along, and I knew just how.

"Maybe this isn't the best idea," I murmured. "I should probably—"

I flew to the side as he tossed me onto the bed, following me there, slipping inside again even as he captured my hands and drew them above my head.

"Too late now," he said, eyes burning into mine as he began to move. In and out, slick, hard heat.

"But—"

"Quiet, Elizabeth."

Jimmy never called me that. But the demon did.

He held me captive with his hands, his legs, the weight of his body. I struggled a little to make it look good, and he laughed the laugh of his father. I'd always hated that laugh.

"I've taken blood from you in so many ways. What *was* my favorite? Here?" He licked my neck. "There?" He grazed my shoulder. "Perhaps this?" He shifted, and his thumbnail coursed along the inside of my thigh.

I jerked, the movement making my breasts jiggle, and he smiled, lowering his head, nuzzling me.

"So pretty. So round and soft." He lazily licked a nipple, then blew on the moisture left behind, becoming fascinated when the bud peaked.

In perfect syncopation with his thrusts, he suckled. I matched each of his movements with my own, forgetting what I was about, only caring what was to come.

Suddenly, he tensed and spurted, full and hot. I wrapped my legs around his waist, pulling him closer, reaching for my own release but unable to find it.

Until his fangs pierced my breast. The pain made my body bow, pressing me into him and making me come with such ferocity I would have shrieked if I could have breathed.

His rhythmic sucking seemed to pull first at my belly and then ever lower. My head went dizzy with blood loss. Despite his orgasm, he stayed hard inside of me, kept pumping against me. Then he lifted his head; a quick flick of his tongue traced away the last drop of blood from his lips, and I wasn't disgusted. I was intrigued.

Blood was both life and death. What did mine taste like? What did his?

Jimmy leaned closer, pressing me deeper into the mattress as he whispered my own enticement back to me. "Do it. You know that you want to."

At first, I thought he meant come again; boy, did I want to. And when he seemed to grow even larger, swelling inside of me, stretching the already sensitive flesh, I did come. And then I did it. I bit him. Because he was right.

I wanted to.

He tasted like wine, just as he'd said, deep and rich. I became drunk with it; I couldn't stop. Didn't have to. Because Jimmy wouldn't die any more than I would.

The heady combination of sex and blood flowed through me, strengthened me. Together we finished what we'd started—shuddering through a shared orgasm and completing my transformation into the darkness.

As I think back on things now, it scares me. I blundered ahead, doing what needed to be done. What choice did I have? But if I'd thought more about it I would have wondered: Once I was possessed by evil, why in hell would I want to fight the *Naye'i* and stop the coming Apocalypse?

Except I did. The instant I became a vampire, I was consumed by the need to kill her. As I'd thought just moments before, why did every evil thing want to rule the world? And as soon as I was an evil thing, I knew.

Because I could.

I was better than all the others. I'd chosen this. The choosing gave me strength and ambition.

The whole world seemed different. With dhampir powers I could see farther, run faster, hear more. But as a vampire everything became magnified. Colors flared, agonizingly bright and surreal. Sounds reached me long before they should, altering my sense of time and place.

I unwound myself from Jimmy's embrace, the slide of our skin so intense I could literally hear the hair on his legs swish; the blood coursing through his veins hummed like a song.

When he spoke, I flinched at the volume. "Do you like it?"

"Mmm," I purred.

He took my hand and led me to the mirror above his dresser. That bit about vampires having no reflection? Total BS. I could see both of us—along with our flaming eyes and sparkly fangs. It was a good look for me.

I fingered Sawyer's turquoise. I was now as strong as the woman of smoke, and while I wore this, she couldn't touch me.

The bitch was toast.

I laughed, the sound deep, throaty, and utterly demonic. I liked it so much, I laughed again.

A heated breeze blew in through the window. The breath of evil, it smelled like brimstone, and I drew it in like ambrosia.

The wind called me closer; I peered through the bars and up to the top of the mountain. The full moon shone across a gathering mist. Rain tumbled from the sky, but only on the peak, and the dormant volcano rumbled.

The rain is a woman, Whitelaw had said.

Old Navajo legends that hinted of the truth.

"The woman of smoke," I murmured.

She was here, and she was waiting for me.

CHAPTER 33

"How are we going to get out?" Jimmy asked.

I turned reluctantly away from the mountain, which had begun to rumble my name.

Phoenix, it said. *Come to me.*

Jimmy stood by the golden door, dressed in black jeans and a tee that read HANNAH MONTANA. In my old life that would have been hysterical. In this one, all I could think of was how sweet the blood of a child.

I didn't even consider clothes for myself. Such trivialities meant nothing to me anymore.

"They aren't going to open it," I said as I joined Jimmy. "Sawyer can't."

"And Summer won't."

This close to the exit, the heat of the metal made every inch of my skin throb like a bad sunburn. The thought of touching it made my fingers sting.

"How *did* you plan to get out?" he asked.

I hadn't planned, I'd just moved forward. I really needed to stop doing that.

My skin is my robe.

Sawyer's voice came to me out of the past. I turned away from the pulsing heat of the golden door and strolled back to the window—the only way out. Beyond it lay the mountain, where she awaited me. If I were a bird—

I tilted my head, suddenly understanding what Sawyer had meant.

I faced Jimmy. "Do you have a knife?"

Jimmy pulled his switchblade out of his pocket.

Stupid question.

I took the weapon and carved a bat into my forearm. The image resembled the icon for Batman—a stick bat at best, I'd never been much of an artist—but I was pretty certain it would do the trick.

It began to heal almost immediately. I never thought I'd wish my preternatural healing abilities away, but right then I did.

"What the hell?" Jimmy growled as the blood dripped from my arm and onto the floor. He inched closer, tongue flicking across his lips, still-glowing eyes fastened on the rolling river of red.

"It's the only way." Reaching up, I removed the turquoise from around my neck and set it on the window-sill.

"How am I going to get out?" he asked.

"You aren't." I pressed my palm to the steadily heal-ing bat carved into my arm.

Seconds later I took the chain into my mouth, flap-ping my black wings harder to offset the downward pull of the turquoise as I headed upward toward the full sil-ver moon that hung above Mount Taylor.

Jimmy shouted something, but I wasn't listening. I wanted no one at my side when I met the woman of smoke. I'd always known it would come down to her or me.

Instead, the sonar that accompanied my shift—the ability of bats to "see" by sound—took over. The term *blind as a bat* had come about because bats use their incredible sense of hearing rather than sight to fly in the dark.

Now that I was a bat, I realized that it wasn't exactly sound but feeling. A buzzing awareness all around me that there flew a mosquito, ahead loomed a tree, and soon, very soon, I'd reach the mountain and my destiny.

The moon's glow made the whirling mist atop Mount Taylor luminescent. The rain had stopped, and I circled, unable to see the ground beneath, but somewhere in that fog I felt her.

I dropped through the shroud, making use of my bat supersenses to avoid trees, rocks, and one evil Navajo witch. A few feet from the earth, I reached for, then became, myself, landing in a crouch that allowed me to scoop up the turquoise and flip the chain around my neck. Just in time, too.

Naked as I, the woman of smoke stepped from the fog. "A bat," she murmured. "How . . . cliché."

"An evil spirit bitch," I returned. "Right back atcha."

"This will be a fight to the death," she said.

"Qué será, será."

The *Naye'i* appeared confused. I guess she didn't listen to much Doris Day.

From the first moment I'd seen her—as a spirit of smoke in the desert and as flesh in Murphy's bar—I'd known she was dangerous. The more I learned about her, the more I hated her. But I'd hated as a human. A paltry, pathetic hatred, unworthy of the word.

As a spirit of darkness, I understood hate; I welcomed the desire to wreak havoc, to maim and kill just for the joy of it, and I saw why I'd needed to become like her to win.

The *Naye'i* had no humanity, no compassion, no restraint. And now neither did I.

We circled each other like all-star wrestlers waiting for an opening. I wasn't worried. I could still taste Jimmy's blood; the strength we'd shared pulsed through me; supernatural power lay at my fingertips; and the turquoise would prevent her from laying a hand on me.

The word *cakewalk* strolled through my head, and the *Naye'i* smiled. That smile made me pause. It was the smile of someone with a secret.

The woman of smoke's hand snaked out and closed around my throat. I blinked, shocked. "Wha—" I managed before she lifted me from my feet, squeezing off all the air.

Wherever her fingers touched, pain erupted, but not the icy burn that had occurred the last time her skin had met mine. Something had changed.

My legs flailed, my arms, too. I reached for the turquoise, but she was there before me.

"You thought this would protect you." She broke the chain with a single jerk and tossed the stone away. "Not anymore."

I couldn't breathe, which made thinking damn difficult. Even when she dropped me to the ground, I lay gasping like a fish on the shore.

"The turquoise marked you as his, but you chose another," she whispered, her brimstone breath washing over my face, making my skin flame. "And when you chose him, the stone became just a stone."

Shit. This was going to be a lot more difficult than I thought. But I guess if she were easy to kill, everyone would do it.

I sat up, and the *Naye'i* backhanded me so hard I skidded across the ground, stray rocks gouging my bare ass. One of my fangs pierced my lip and blood flowed.

Her laughter echoed in the mountain's rumble. "You

thought it would be simple. Become the darkness and swallow me whole. But *I* am the darkness." She lifted her hands to the silver-tinged night, and lightning rained down. "And you will be the one to die."

If I didn't move, I *would* die. I scrambled to my feet; her smirk said she'd let me. The fury came back, both icy and hot. I would bathe in her blood; I would use her bones for chopsticks. When she was dead I would dance a jig on her corpse.

There, that was more like the new me.

I tried to sweep her legs from beneath her. But she jumped my sweep, then hovered above me.

I leaped upward, very Matrix-like, and tried a round-house kick. She leaned back and my foot missed. My momentum swung me downward so fast I nearly ate dirt before I managed to get my hands in front of me.

"How to kill a vampire," she mused.

My back exposed, I flipped over just as she snapped her fingers. A wooden stake appeared in her hand, and as she threw the thing, I rolled. The stake stuck in the ground where my heart had just been.

Fire billowed all around me. Beyond the flames, the *Naye'i* seemed to dance.

"I'll kill you every way there is to kill a vampire. Little by little you'll die; then I'll do it again. And when you're nothing more than a pile of blood and empty skin—no Sawyer, no robe, no way to shift and heal— then the gates of hell will fly open, and I will rule every demon on this earth."

"Killing me will open Tartarus?" I asked.

She shrugged. "Can't hurt."

"Do you *know* how?"

I leaped through the fire; the places it burned healed almost instantly.

The *Naye'i* looked as if she'd sucked on a lemon. "You think I'd tell you?"

"Can't hurt."

"This might," she said, and opening her arms, fingers spread wide, she swept her hands toward me.

Rocks flew, hundreds of them in all shapes and sizes, raining down on me, crushing me into the earth, piling up until I was buried.

When things stopped pinging against the cairn, I shoved upward and they all fell away. "What the hell was that?" I asked.

"Cover a vampire's grave with stones and she will never rise."

"I'm not *dead,*" I said.

"Good point." She flicked her wrist and something small and sharp and shiny flew, sticking in my temple before I could catch it.

"Ouch!" I yanked out a three-inch nail, and the *Naye'i* shrieked her fury to the stars.

"Why don't you die?"

"Why don't you?" I countered.

She was trying to kill me nature by nature—a common cure. I'd tried it myself with Jimmy, hadn't managed it yet. But killing a vampire/dhampir/skinwalker was going to be a very neat trick. Not that she couldn't do it if I kept letting her try. Sooner or later the woman of smoke was going to hit on something that did kill a vampire, and then she'd ease on down the road to the next nature. I had to take away her magic, and thanks to Whitelaw I knew how.

"I hate to keep calling you psycho hell bitch," I said. "Though it does fit."

She flicked her wrist and a gun appeared. Before she could point it in my direction, I smacked the weapon out of her hand, and it slid across the dirt with a metallic ping-ping-ping. When she predictably went for my throat, I snatched those hands in mine and murmured, "What is your name?"

It was an old trick but a good one. She didn't have time to block me, to think of something else, to even figure out what I was doing. I touched her just as she thought, *Lilith.*

"Lilith?" I let her momentum carry her past me, and when I released her she sprawled in the dirt. "Not *the* Lilith?"

The woman of smoke flipped onto her back.

"You can't be that Lilith."

Her eyes widened as she realized what I meant to do. Her arm began to rise, no doubt to throw some other deadly magic my way, but I finished the spell with a final, "Lilith."

She screamed, but instead of sound a cloud of black sparkly dust rose from her mouth, swirling away on the wind and disappearing into the night.

"Aw. I think that was your magic. Bummer," I said, and decked her.

I had vampire strength; she flew about ten feet, scrambled to get up, and I hit her again.

She'd had the advantage as an evil witch, but without the witch, she was just evil.

That made two of us.

She landed on the far side of the gun, which lay about halfway between us. With my vampire speed I snatched the thing before she could slither in its direction, then pressed the muzzle to her temple.

The woman of smoke froze; her burning black eyes rolled up to mine, and she sneered. "Go ahead."

My finger twitched. The idea of blowing her brains to kingdom come was so damn appealing, but something stopped me. Probably the smirk lurking beneath her sneer.

"You'll just heal," I murmured, and tossed the gun far, far away.

The smirk bloomed. "I can heal anything."

"Heal this," I said, and pulled a Jimmy—tore her apart like the wishbone on a chicken.

I could never have done it if I'd remained human. Not only the lack of strength but the yuck factor. However, in my present state, I found the spray of blood exquisite.

The temptation to let it wash over me, feel the heat and the life and the energy against my skin, was nearly overwhelming. I probably would have done it, except the body stood up and reached for me.

"Oh, come *on!*" I stumbled back, and what was left of the woman of smoke followed.

"Give me my head."

I glanced down. I still held the skull in one hand, and it was talking. My life was a Tim Burton movie.

The body kept coming; the hands weren't reaching for me but for the severed head. Once retrieved, would they then set it back on the gushing neck, and would the wound heal?

"How do I end her?" I muttered, my mind grasping for every detail I'd heard, everything that I'd learned.

She no longer possessed any magic; all she had left was the spirit of evil. There'd been something, somewhere about evil.

The truth hit me like a spotlight. The memory of what I'd seen in Sawyer's dream when I'd walked there—words the shade of fresh blood splayed across the pristine white ceiling.

"Toss evil to the four winds," I whispered.

"No!" shrieked the woman of smoke.

Which made tossing seem like a helluva good idea.

I threw the still screaming head to the north with all of my strength, then finished the job by sending the arms to the east, the legs to the west, and the rest down south.

Welcome silence settled over the mountain, but it didn't last. At first I thought she was coming back, because the shrieking that had faded to nothing as the woman of smoke was carried away on the four winds got louder and louder until it surrounded me. An ocean of sound blaring in my too sensitive ears, driving me to the ground with my hands pressed to my head.

Even though my eyes were closed, I felt the light-dark, light-dark flickers across my face and forced myself to look at the moon.

Ghostly shadows pranced across the surface too quickly for me to determine what they were.

"That can't be good," I murmured, even as something inside of me rejoiced and whispered: *They are free.*

CHAPTER 34

The sun shining across my face woke me. Or maybe it was the sensation of being watched. Because I opened my eyes to discover myself surrounded.

I snarled and did a backflip, landing in a crouch. A growl rumbled low in my throat. All that goodness made my head ache.

In the bright light of morning, the colors of the world seemed epic. The jewels on the collar in Sawyer's hand nearly blinded me.

"What's wrong with her?"

The kid—Luther, I remembered—appeared horrified. I lifted my top lip and gave him a good view of my fangs, then found myself distracted by the throbbing vein in his neck. I could hear every one of their hearts beating; the swish of blood through their veins was a seductive whisper. I took a step forward and Jimmy blocked my way.

"She's gone vamp," he said, his voice so full of pain I breathed in. I could almost taste his tears.

"You said we could fix her," Luther whispered.

Mmm. The tremble in his voice, the fear on the wind.

"Not fix," Sawyer murmured. "At least not yet."

"Put the collar on her," Summer ordered. "Otherwise she's going to do to us what she did to the woman of smoke."

I remembered the geyser of blood. I wanted to see that again. My gaze crept over the four of them.

"Eenie, meenie, minee, mo," I whispered, and lunged at the fairy.

Sawyer's hand flicked out and sent me flying backward so hard my head thunked against the ground.

"Oh, God," Jimmy murmured.

"Quit whining," Sawyer ordered. "What's done is done. We have to move forward. Give me a hand."

My legs were pinned, so were my arms. I shrieked my fury to the sky, and in the distance, something answered. Sawyer cursed softly.

I could have taken every one of them separately. But together they were stronger, which only made me snarl and slaver and buck against the restraints.

I snapped at Sawyer's hands as he slid the collar around my neck. He smacked me in the nose like a bad dog, and my eyes watered. As soon as the latch clicked shut, I stilled.

Sawyer's eyes met mine. "Better?"

I nodded, and they released me, then backed up so fast I winced. Both at their reactions and at the memory of what I'd said and done and been.

I needed a shower, a scrub brush, and about a pound of soap. The woman of smoke's blood was speckled all over me; my hands and forearms appeared painted sienna, and the crust under my nails was so thick it felt as if I'd been digging in a garden for days.

A pile of clothes lay at my feet. I donned them quickly, no longer comfortable with my nakedness, even though fifty percent of the people here had seen it all before.

The shirt—BLACK SABBATH REUNION TOUR, ha-ha— was obviously Sanducci's, but someone had gone through my bag and found my last pair of clean under- wear and shorts.

I glanced at Jimmy, but he wouldn't meet my eyes. Luther tensed as if he expected me to attack him at any second. Summer wanted to slug me. We still had that in common. Only Sawyer appeared the same as when I'd last seen him.

My fingers brushed the collar. "What's this?"

"Bespelled," Sawyer answered. "While you wear it, you're you."

I lifted my hand, touched my teeth. The fangs were gone, along with the desire to tear out everyone's throat. But I didn't think I was me. Deep down inside, the de- mon still howled.

"Whose spell?" I asked, and Summer raised her hand. "You had to bespell a dog collar? Wouldn't the magic work just fine on a nice silver chain?"

Her lips curved. "Where would be the fun in that?"

I almost smiled back, and then I remembered the shrieking in the night, the strange flickers across the face of the moon, the roar in the distance in answer to my call.

"What happened?" Sawyer asked.

"I kicked her ass, then tossed her in pieces to the four winds."

Sawyer frowned. "That's an old Navajo saying."

"Which I got from an old Navajo."

His brow lifted and I shrugged. "Dream-walk world."

"Interesting," he murmured. "I always thought it was a proverb. Merely a short pithy way to tell the Diné how to live a good life." He flicked his hand toward the sky. "Figuratively, we must toss evil away."

"Worked pretty well literally, too."

"Fascinating," Sawyer said. "You found that old proverb in my head, and you didn't even know you would need it."

"Yeah, worked out great." I really didn't want to talk about it anymore. While I'd enjoyed the blood flow last night, this morning it was making me kind of ill.

"Once you tossed her," Summer interjected, "then what happened?"

They are free.

"Something got out."

Sawyer, Summer, and Jimmy exchanged glances. Luther had wandered off to peer at the dark patch of earth where I'd spilled the blood of the *Naye'i*. That probably wasn't healthy.

"Kid," I muttered. "Come back here."

Luther seemed like he wanted to tell me to kiss off. Instead he shrugged and strolled to Summer's side, where she took his hand. I frowned at the gesture, but it seemed more about comfort than anything else so I let it pass.

"What's free?" I asked.

"The Grigori," Sawyer said.

I opened my mouth to drop the F-bomb, caught a glimpse of Luther's face, and bit my lip instead. "That's impossible."

"Not according to Ruthie."

"Ruthie?" I racked my brain; I couldn't recall talking to her lately. But since the entire night between the death of the *Naye'i* and waking up this morning was a blank, who knew?

"Did I—"

"No," Sawyer answered. "You probably won't be hearing from her for a while."

"Because?"

"She's in heaven. No demons allowed."

Now I did drop the F-bomb. Couldn't help it. "Get this thing out of me."

"Baby—" Jimmy began, and I flicked him an evil glare, which he didn't see because he still couldn't look at me. "There's no getting rid of it."

"Confine it, refine it. Whatever Summer did to you, she can do to me."

The fairy choked.

I glanced at her and knew why. "It's a sex spell."

She shrugged. "You told me to do anything."

I was *so* sick of hearing that.

"Fine. Sawyer can do it."

"No," he said.

"No? You never had a problem before."

He sighed. "Ruthie doesn't want that."

"You seem to be pretty up on what Ruthie wants. She been talkin' to you?"

Sawyer shook his head, so did Summer, even Jimmy twitched—left, right—without ever meeting my eyes. Luther nodded.

My brows lifted. An interesting development. "What did she say?"

Luther opened his mouth, and Ruthie's voice came out. "Gates of hell done flew open, girl. Trouble ain't comin'; trouble's here."

"That's just creepy," I murmured.

Not only did the boy sound like Ruthie, but he now moved like her, too. Hand gestures, head tilts, even his eyes had darkened from gold to brown, or perhaps that was just the shadow of the sun across the mountain. Though I didn't think so.

"He's the most accomplished channeler I've ever seen," Sawyer said.

Channeling, a way to talk to the dead. Some people, like me, went to them. Others, like Luther apparently, allowed the dead to speak through them.

"Could he do that before yesterday?" I asked.

Sawyer spread his hands.

"Lizbeth!" Ruthie-Luther snapped. "The demons are free, and these are worse than anything that's been on this earth since the fall."

"How'd they get free?" I asked. "I killed the darkness. Everything should go back to normal."

"Normal." Ruthie snorted. "What's that? You're gonna have to find the book."

"Key of Solomon?"

Ruthie-Luther shook her-his head. "The key says, kill the darkness, all is well. But it ain't. We're gonna have to get a peek at the other side."

"Terrific," I muttered.

"And you're gonna have to stay evil."

"Excuse me?" I tugged at the collar, which was driving me nuts.

"The only way to fight the Grigori is with a darkness as complete as they are. You and Jimmy are our only hope."

"Jimmy's got his demon all pushed beneath the moon. Is he supposed to let it back out?"

"No," Jimmy said, at the same time Ruthie murmured, "Yes."

Crap.

"It has to be done," Ruthie-Luther said. "And you know it."

I glanced uneasily at Jimmy, who continued to stare at the desert below us.

"He's already broken," Summer muttered. "What's one more slap when you're down?"

They were both right. It had to be done, and he was already broken.

I sighed and turned my attention back to Ruthie-Luther. "When we're—" I made my fingers into claws and hissed. "We aren't exactly on the side of justice."

"But you are on the hunt. Summer and Sawyer will use their magic to unleash your power in the right direction."

"Unleash," I repeated. "Like a damn dog."

"Hence the collar," Summer murmured.

"I think I'm the kind of dog who turns on its master."

"Lucky I'm not going to be holding your leash."

Sawyer would.

I turned to him. "Did you know your mo—" I broke off. "The *Naye'i*'s name was Lilith?"

He shook his head.

"I don't think she was *the* Lilith," I murmured.

"No," Ruthie-Luther said, "She was just *a* Lilith. Storm demon. She ruled the night and the wind; she rode the rain. There's a Lilith demon in every culture."

"There are more like her out there?"

"Of course."

"Double bleeding hell," I muttered.

"I'm hungry." Luther's voice was once again his own.

"Let's head back to Summer's place," Sawyer said.

We began to walk in that direction, except for Jimmy. He continued to face away from us as if he didn't even know we were there.

I paused. "We'll be down soon."

"I don't—" Summer began, but Sawyer silenced her with a glare. She stomped off, her cowboy boots raising angry puffs of dust around her feet. With a shrug, Luther followed.

Sawyer hung back. "Will you be all right?"

"As long as I wear this." I fingered the collar.

His gaze flicked to Jimmy, then to me. "Don't let him make you feel guilty. It was the only way."

My eyebrows lifted. "This from the man who tried to convince me to let everyone rot."

"I knew you wouldn't."

Sometimes I thought Sawyer knew me better than I knew myself.

Sawyer followed the others, and I turned to Jimmy. Was he ever going to forgive me? Hopefully quicker than I'd forgiven him.

I crossed the pebbled ground, ignoring the pain in my bare feet, and stood right behind him. Below us, Summer's place was once again an Irish cottage. Her spring-green lawn was peppered with stone statues of gargoyles. I suspected they'd stay that way until the demons were no longer in residence.

"I—" I stopped, uncertain what to say. Not sorry. Because I wasn't.

"I asked you not to, Lizzy. I begged you."

I'd been there. I knew what had happened.

"You let me turn you evil for nothing."

My head came up. "Not for nothing."

He turned, his face furious, and his eyes so damn sad. "The Grigori are loose. What good did it do?"

"The woman of smoke is dead."

"You heard Ruthie. There are more just like her."

I'd heard Ruthie, but I still didn't think there was anything quite like Lilith around. "She needed to die."

And I was the only one who could kill her.

"You betrayed my trust, Lizzy."

"Then we're even."

"Baby," he murmured, "even is something we can never be."

I guessed he was going to be as forgiving about my betrayal as I'd been about his. That hurt, but I deserved it.

"You don't understand what you've done," he said. "There'll be consequences."

"There always are."

"Not like this."

He looked so haggard, so beaten down and sad, I wasn't sure what to do, except what I did best. Move on.

"Are you going to come back with me?" I asked.

Or will I have to make you? I thought.

His gaze was drawn in the direction of that strange howling that had earlier answered my furious call. There was something out there. A whole lot of somethings.

"Yeah," Jimmy said. "I'm coming."

The job was what mattered; Jimmy had known that long before I had.

"But I'm starting to think that—"

His voice faded; what I saw in his face scared me. I stepped forward and put a hand on his shoulder. What he hadn't said whispered through my mind and came straight out of my mouth.

"No matter what we do," I murmured. "Apocalypse happens."

They are free.

Those words had whispered through my head only a few weeks ago. Taken out of context, the phrase should be uplifting.

Freedom's good. Right?

Unless you're talking about demons.

The earth is full of them. They're called Nephilim—the offspring of the fallen angels, or Grigori, and the daughters of men.

Yes, the angels really fell. Hard. Their story is a perfect illustration of why everyone should toe the proverbial line. Piss off God, wind up in Tartarus—a fiery pit in the lowest level of hell.

Word is God sent the Grigori to keep an eye on the humans. In the end, the angels were the ones who needed watching.

So God banished them from the earth—bam, you're legend—but He left their offspring behind to test us. Eden was a memory. We'd proved we didn't deserve it. But I don't think we deserved the Nephilim either.

Fast forward a million millennia. The prophecies of Revelation are bearing down on us like runaway horses.

Perhaps four of them? No matter what the forces of good do to prevent the end of the world, nothing's working.

And that's where I come in.

Elizabeth Phoenix, Liz to my friends. They call me "the leader of the light." I got dropped into the middle of this whole Doomsday mess, and I'm having a helluva time getting back out.

For reasons beyond mine or anyone else's comprehension, Tartarus opened; the Grigori flew free; and now all hell has broken loose. Literally.

"Dammit, Lizzy! Duck!"

I ducked. Razor-sharp claws swooshed through the air right where my head had been. Not only did I duck, but I rolled. Good thing, too, since seconds later something sliced into the ground right next to my head.

I'd come to Los Angeles with Jimmy Sanducci, head demon-killer and my second-in-command, to ferret out a nest of varcolacs. Eclipse demons. Kind of rare considering they hail from Romania, but I'd seen stranger things.

Sure, the smog in L.A. could be blamed for the dark splotches that kept appearing over the moon and the sun, which was what everyone around here believed. But I knew better.

The varcolac tugged on its arm, trying to free the needle-like appendages it used for fingers from the desert dust. Part human, part dragon, varcolacs are rumored to eat the sun and the moon, thus causing said eclipses. And if they ever succeed in actually devouring those celestial bodies, the end of the world is nigh. Since I've been trying to prevent that, Jimmy and I came to L.A. and started hunting.

Before the varcolac could use its other arm to kill me, Sanducci sliced through its neck. When dealing with Nephilim, head slicing usually worked. At the least, being without a head slowed down even the most determined demon.

Jimmy's dark gaze met mine. "Get up," he ordered, before turning away to dispatch more bad guys.

I tried not to let the chill in his eyes bother me. Sanducci would never allow anything to hurt me; he'd loved me once. Right now, however, love was no longer on the table, and I had no one to blame for that but myself.

I did a kip, from my back to my feet in one quick movement—a state champion medal in high school gymnastics had been coming in very handy lately—then retrieved my own sword and went back to hacking.

Once in L.A., it hadn't taken Jimmy and me long to find the varcolacs in the desert. Most days they appeared human. They lived their lives, they blended in, only going dragon beneath an eclipse.

Which came first, the chicken or the egg? The dragon eating the moon, or the moon going dark and bringing out the dragon? Hard to say.

What I did know was that as soon as the Grigori flew free, all the Nephilim stopped hiding. Their time had come. And things, for me and my kind, had become a bit dicey.

Previously, each demon killer had worked with a seer—someone who possessed a psychic gift to see past the Nephilim's human disguise to the demon that lay within.

I'd been a seer once myself, but things had changed.

Oh, I was still psychic—always had been. Since I was old enough to talk, maybe before, I could touch animate and inanimate objects and I'd know things— what people had done, where they'd gone, what they thought.

But later, when I'd become the leader of the light, I'd inherited the ability of the woman who'd raised me. As

Ruthie Kane died in my arms, all her power had transferred to me. I'd wound up not only psychometric, but suddenly I could channel, too. Ruthie might be dead, but that didn't mean I couldn't hear her, talk to her, sometimes even see her. She became my conduit. Whenever a Nephilim was near, I heard about it in Ruthie's whisper on the wind, and when they were up to something major—they always were—I received a vision to tell me all about it. At least until recently.

"Too many," Jimmy muttered.

We were covered in varcolac blood. We'd hacked up a dozen, but a dozen more had appeared. We needed help, but there wasn't any to spare.

The federation—that group of demon killers, or DKs, and seers who'd been charged with fighting this supernatural war—had been seriously depleted after Ruthie's death, and we couldn't just pick up a few new demon killers at the demon-killer superstore. They had to be trained. New seers had to be discovered. I hadn't had time to do much recruiting, even before the whole Tartarus-opening, Grigori-escaping incident. And now . . .

Now I wasn't going to have time to do much but ride the runaway train to Armageddon. Basically, we were fucked. But that didn't mean we were going to quit. Besides, I had a secret weapon. What I liked to call a vampire in a box.

I lifted my arm, traced my fingers along the magic jeweled dog collar that circled my neck. As long as I wore the thing, I was me. But if I took it off—

"No, Lizzy."

I glanced at Jimmy. He'd seen me fingering the necklace. Even if he didn't know me better than just about anyone, it didn't take a genius to figure out what I'd been contemplating.

One of the varcolacs charged, dragon wings flapping,

talons outstretched. Jimmy hacked off its head with only a token glance in that direction. He was good. I still needed to put a bit more effort into killing things.

I let go of the collar, faced the next varcolac with both hands around my sword, and did what needed to be done. I lost track of Jimmy for a while. The damn demons seemed to be multiplying. For every one we killed, two more came out of the darkness. Their wings flickered against the silvery light of the gibbous moon, reminding me of the night the Grigori had flown free, their spirits darkening what had then been a perfectly round orb.

Jimmy cried out, the sound making my heart jolt, my head turn. One of the varcolacs had speared him through the shoulder with a talon, lifting him clear off the ground. Blood dripped into the sand, turning the moon-pale grains black. Jimmy's sword lay at his feet.

There appeared to be an army of dragon men behind them. Their scaly wings flapped in syncopation, filling the sky with a morbid tick-tock. Dragon heads and arms, human legs and torsos that sprouted dragon's wings.

"Surrender, seer." The varcolac snorted fire from his nose. Jimmy hissed when the flames started his pants on fire.

"No." I lopped off the nearest varcolac head, which hit the ground with a dull thud, rolled a few feet, and disintegrated into ashes along with the still-upright body. If you killed a Nephilim correctly, cleanups weren't any problem at all.

"You can't win," he said. "We are legion."

He was probably right, but giving up . . .

Just wasn't my style.